Praise for J. Lincoln Fenn and *Poe*

"A delightful, bravura piece of gothic pop . . . fans of Neil Gaiman and . . . *Buffy* will be immediately taken, but there's a literate edge to the pyrotechnics that makes for an unlikely and welcome marriage between the spook story and literature of altogether less ectoplasmic substance."

—*Publishers Weekly*

"Hitting the high notes of multiple genres, [Fenn's] talent is wicked raw and proudly untamed. [We] can't wait to see what comes next."

—Bloody-Disgusting.com

"J. Lincoln Fenn's *Poe* is a shining display of humorous morbid entertainment. With a thrilling mystery, Fenn takes dark themes and gives us a witty novel with ties to history and magic. Suspense and intrigue are the name of the game."

—Literary Escapism

"Bowled over by *Poe* . . . The novel jumps into my own top five of my best novels of [the year] and is nipping at the heels of number one. I highly recommend this to anyone who likes great well-paced fiction."

—The Novel Pursuit

ALSO BY J. LINCOLN FENN

Poe

DEAD SOULS

a novel

J. LINCOLN FENN

GALLERY BOOKS

New York   London   Toronto   Sydney   New Delhi

G

Gallery Books
An Imprint of Simon & Schuster, Inc.
1230 Avenue of the Americas
New York, NY 10020

First Gallery Books trade paperback edition September 2016

GALLERY BOOKS and colophon are registered trademarks of Simon & Schuster, Inc.

For information about special discounts for bulk purchases, please contact Simon & Schuster Special Sales at 1-866-506-1949 or business@simonandschuster.com.

The Simon & Schuster Speakers Bureau can bring authors to your live event. For more information or to book an event contact the Simon & Schuster Speakers Bureau at 1-866-248-3049 or visit our website at www.simonspeakers.com.

Interior design by Davina Mock-Maniscalco

Manufactured in the United States of America

10 9 8 7 6 5 4 3 2 1

Library of Congress Cataloging-in-Publication Data is available.

ISBN 978-1-5011-1093-1
ISBN 978-1-5011-1094-8 (ebook)

For my husband

The true horror for me is that overnight suddenly all the people you've known and loved can become monsters, and that people underneath the veneer of civilization or love or any kind of affiliation are kind of monstrous creatures.

—Colson Whitehead

Hell is empty and all the devils are here.

—William Shakespeare, *The Tempest*

PROLOGUE

WE NEVER TALK ABOUT him at first, and we never say his name. But after an hour or more, after a few drinks or more, when the light in the bar becomes golden and woozy, talk usually drifts to a safe circumference, the sphere around him. We speculate about the news. Which crimes might be a favor he called in. Things like school shootings, downed planes, drone strikes that hit a wedding instead of the terrorists are always likely suspects, our shared paranoia. As for the other, more macabre stories—the mother who drowned her children in the bathtub, the grandmother clubbed by her grandson and then left to rot while he spent out her pension, the man who sliced off the face of his wife before he ate it—we hope—no, we *pray*—that these are just the random acts of random people in a depraved society. It's the TV; no it's the video games; no it's the patriarchal structure and the glorification of violence to sell deodorant and car insurance.

Because the other explanation is far, far worse.

The other explanation is that it will be us one day.

CHAPTER ONE

SCRATCH. He said his name was Scratch.

But no, it starts before that, over a year ago on a dark Friday night in Oakland, California, rain pouring down like it's the next biblical flood and I've just seen the thing I've been afraid I'd see. Justin opening the door of a taxi for a woman with effortless blond hair that almost reaches, but stops short of, her shoulders. She wears a pink coat. I've always despised pink. He holds a newspaper over her head protectively as she gets in, and the taxi driver pops open the trunk for their suitcases.

He said he had a business trip. *Seattle.*

Justin looks gaunt in that way I always found Byronesque: pale shadows under his eyes, a military-ish buzz cut that makes his cheekbones starker. I miss his hair, the feel of it in my hand. Did he cut it for her? There hadn't been much of an explanation—something about a new barber who got carried away.

He doesn't see me standing in the shadow of the apartment building across the street, but then that's always been our inside joke—*the invisible girl,* he calls me. I'm constantly startling the shit out of him. He swears he doesn't hear me when I walk into a room, and has actually shouted more than once after finding me just behind him, opening a cabinet door when he thought I was asleep. It's a skill that anyone with abusive parents learns, and learns early. How to slip into the kitchen and get a soda and a candy bar for dinner without causing a blip on the radar.

But still, I wish he'd look over this way for once. I long for it, I *will* it—I send a psychic message that if he doesn't look over this way it means he doesn't love me, that he stopped loving me months ago.

He gets into the taxi, closes the door. The cab pulls into the street, causing an arc of water to splash in the gutter. Gone.

It's cold. I should have put on a jacket, but there had been that note in his voice when he said he was going to Seattle, a tinny drop that caused a shudder near the base of my spine, an emotional 5.0 tremor. He'd been strange for months. Distant. I don't remember walking out the door of my apartment. I do remember when I stepped outside and realized it was cold, and I was barefoot. But my car was right there. I'd gotten lucky with a spot right in front of the apartment, no circling the neighborhood for fifteen minutes trying to land within three blocks.

Then I realized I'd left my keys in the apartment. Locked out.

The next steps—finding someone to buzz me back in, let me use their phone to call the super, making up some cheery explanation: *Oh, it's been such a stressful week at work, amazing I remember my head*—was a calculation that seemed unfathomable.

So I started to walk. Not impossible—I'd done it before, although never at night. I pushed aside all the reasons this was a bad idea. Tried not to look at any of the souls folded in alleyways, huddled under trash bags and newspapers. Ignored the occasional catcall.

The rain hit about ten minutes in, and in fifteen I was completely drenched and my feet were numb, but it felt good somehow. Like I was present, a high-definition version of myself. I began to imagine scenes: Justin opening the door—looking perplexed in that way that always made him seem about ten—our having a good laugh at my neurosis again. Me taking a warm shower. Justin joining me. A smaller part of me tugged at the thought that I would seem pathetic, that his furrowed brow would really be a sign of his rising discontent, a precursor of the end. There was, or would soon be, someone else. When that thought hit I'd raise my hands to the rain, let it slide through my fingers. Wash it away.

This is how I got through the next twenty minutes, and by the time I reached his street I had convinced myself of the first version, which left me utterly unprepared for the pink coat. Just the sight of it made me dart into the entry of the apartment across from Justin's. Left me breathless.

And then they were in the taxi, and then they were gone. Vanished. The night, and the rain, closing over them like a cloak.

THE FIRST RULE of marketing is desire. And it's not about making people want a thing; it's making them want a different version of themselves, someone better-looking, more in control of their lives, unique. Everyone wants to think they're living a version of carpe diem when really they're lemmings on a treadmill. I know this because I'm a professional treadmill designer.

People think I'm joking when I say that the third circle of hell is reserved for marketers, but I'm not. It's a truly twisted area of expertise. My specialty is backpacks, specifically backpacks for those who sit behind a desk 365 days a year but like to imagine they're only a travel agent away from scaling Mount Everest. The soccer moms who buy sports utility vehicles so they don't feel like Mrs. Brady. We sell them backpacks that cost us four dollars but will cost them a hundred and fifty because we don't tell them these are nylon sacks with zippers made in Chinese sweatshops. No, we give these backpacks names that are evocative of adventure, of pristine wilderness, of empowerment. For women, SkyTrail in colors like Sonoma grape (purple), poplar (green), and truffle (brown). Octane for the executives who amuse themselves in board meetings by imagining the crushed scent of pine beneath their feet. Things that sound vaguely Swedish are always popular. Stores can't keep the Utrecht 1000 stocked even though you can't fit much more than a map and a sandwich inside it. We estimate that about 90 percent of these backpacks make it to a closet where they will remain, gathering dust, until the eventual yard sale.

To make it in marketing you have to have a good sense of your own fragile, easily manipulable mind. You can't have any illusions. You know that when you're in the grocery store and they're playing music, it's been chosen to fit your demographic. The colors on the cereal boxes make you hungry. The milk is at the back to increase the odds of impulse buys along the way. You know you're a rat in a maze, and even knowing you're a rat in a maze is no protection.

Justin was the one place where I felt I was outside of the maze. Where I was tangibly human.

A thought probably implanted by the marketers who sell dating services.

SCRATCH. He said his name was Scratch.

I couldn't believe it at first, was sure I heard it wrong, thought maybe he had mistaken me for a bar wench and was trying to order a Scotch. Not that I looked like I worked there, drenched, barefoot, shivering. I was sipping at my second mojito royale in Make Westing that I'd snuck on someone else's tab, having forgotten that my wallet was also in my locked apartment. But it was packed at the bar, and warm, and if my piracy was discovered I could pretend I was heading for the bathroom and make a break for the door instead. I was even thinking about ordering baked Brie and some artisanal pita chips.

Somehow he'd inserted himself next to me, causing the hipster guy on the next stool over to lean uncomfortably left, his sense of space obviously violated.

"Is that any good?" asks the inserter.

Cocky bastard, I think to myself. I try ignoring him, take a long sip.

He raises a finger to catch the attention of the bartender, who has to lean in to hear him it's so loud. Music pounds from a band in the back with Pearl Jam aspirations.

"I'll take one of whatever she's having," says the inserter with an accent that sounds English, or Irish—something. "And her tab's on me."

He knows, but he's not outing me. What's he want? Still, free is free so I order the foie gras sandwich instead and another mojito. The cold has made me hungry. The hipster takes his garden gimlet and pushes his way to the bocce ball lane, then the inserter settles himself down on the vacated stool and I take a look at what I've indentured myself to, at least for the next few hours.

This is where things get hard to explain. I get the impression he's not bad-looking, although his nose seems like it might have been broken and not reset correctly. I feel like he has longer hair, and is olive-skinned like he's Italian, or Arabic. But there's something wavering about these impressions too, like the shimmer of heat over hot asphalt, and not then, nor now, would I ever be able to say exactly what he looked like. No one who's ever seen him can either.

A part of me realizes that my wet shirt is inappropriately clingy, that I might be giving off the wrong signal. I fold my arms over my chest protectively.

The bartender drops off my sandwich and the two mojitos. I've never seen a sandwich look so good in my life.

"I'll take one of those too," says the inserter, pointing to it. The bartender sighs, as if his life would be simpler if we had just ordered all at once.

I pick up the sandwich and take a bite. Heaven.

"You know how they make foie gras?" he says.

"Not really," I say with a mouthful. Although a part of me knows it's bad. Veal kind of bad.

He rubs a finger along the bar top. "They stick a gavage, which is a kind of tube, down a duck's or goose's throat and then force-feed it so the liver becomes fatty. Enforced gluttony." There's a cheerful lilt to his voice as he says this. "Personally I think it's the suffering that gives it flavor. But what you're eating, that's probably not the real thing. They passed a law against it a few years back. No, that must be humanely fattened goose liver. I don't know if the goose appreciated the difference though in the end."

I look at my foie gras benefactor and get the impression of twinkling eyes. What color, I couldn't say.

"Do you mind if I just enjoy my sandwich?"

The bartender slides a plate with the inserter's sandwich to him. He picks up a half. "Not at all. Bon appétit."

AN HOUR LATER and each clunk of the bocce ball with the accompanying cheers or groans makes the bar feel festive, like we're all on vacation, like we're not the working drones we are, released for forty-eight hours before we're back in the cubes, voluntary prisoners for cash and health benefits. I'm nursing my third (fourth?) mojito, he's switched to Guinness; crumbs from the sandwich soak up the water rings on the wood counter. The bread was really good.

"What kind of a name is Scratch?" I say.

He's leaning on the bar now, half turned to me, half turned to the crowd, fingers keeping time with the music. His black denim jacket fits him like a second skin. That level of tailoring is expensive.

"Just a nickname," he says. "My real name is hard for Americans to pronounce."

"So say it." I tuck a strand of clumped wet hair behind my ear.

He does, a tumble of syllables that rise and fall in odd ways. The lights dim briefly. Huh.

"Is that Gaelic?"

"Not exactly," he says. "But you still haven't told me *your* name yet."

"Ah, that." I lick the rim of my glass. "Some call me the invisible girl."

There's a pang as I say this, a soft betrayal. Justin's inside joke trotted out for a stranger to see.

"Some?"

"My boyfriend."

"Maybe you need a new boyfriend."

This isn't really funny but it strikes me so, and I cover a laugh with the back of my hand. The mojitos at work. Still, I feel lighter. Freer. Like a balloon cut loose.

"Wouldn't it be cool though, to really be invisible?" My finger reaches for the water ring and starts to doodle with it. X's and O's, the way Justin always ends his texts.

"I don't know," says Scratch. "You'd have to wrap yourself in bandages for anyone to know you existed, right?"

A problem I hadn't considered. "On demand then," I say. "But you could go anywhere. You could find out what people are really up to."

"On-demand invisibility. Hmm. That'd be a right challenge. Corporeal or non-corporeal?"

"What do you mean?"

He sits back, takes a long sip of his Guinness. "Well . . . would you want to be invisible with a body, able to move shit, or invisible without a body, like a ghost?"

This invisibility stuff is more complicated than I thought. "Yes."

He laughs. It's a nice laugh. "Such an American answer."

I have a vision then of myself, a ghost-twin standing in Justin's living room, where he sits on the couch with Pink-Coat Girl. She unbuttons the top of it, slowly, seductively. *Asshole.* There's a pleasant throb of self-righteous indignation that more than makes up for my disclosure.

Scratch reaches for a nearby bowl of popcorn and his wrist brushes mine. "But do you need to know what people are really up to?"

"What *he's* up to."

"Oh. I see."

Now I feel exposed, revealed, so I take another sip of mojito to bolster myself. But there's scarcely any left.

Scratch raises a hand, orders another.

THE BAND IS PACKING UP and the boisterous crowd has dwindled down to a small cluster of alcoholics. The bartender wipes down the bar with a blue, micro-absorbent towel. I have a friend who worked on the product design at REI.

"What color is that?" I ask the bartender.

He arches an eyebrow, but we've run up a decent bill and Scratch has been a generous tipper.

"Uh, blue," he says.

I lean over like I'm revealing a secret. "No," I whisper. "That color's called *Puget Sound.*"

With that, I start into a peal of laughter that nearly causes me to tip over, but Scratch catches me by the elbow and keeps me upright. Thick man-hands. I imagine them in other places. It takes more moments than it should for the guilt to kick in.

"How many drinks have I had?" The overhead lights glow like headlights in fog.

"I lost count," Scratch says.

"Me too." I know he's kept up with me, mojito for mojito, with a few shots in between *and* the Guinness, but he's as sober as if he's been drinking coffee all night. Outside, the rain still falls in sheets, a lonely sound. I don't want to go back to my apartment. I don't want to think about the pink coat.

Scratch doesn't seem to be in any hurry to leave either. He doesn't even check his watch, which must be a knockoff of a Vacheron Constantin Tour de l'Ile unless he's actually wearing $1.25 million on his wrist.

"So they call blue Puget Sound now? I had no idea."

I nod. My head feels twice as heavy as it should, like I've entered a different gravitational field. "According to our research, if you rebrand the color you can charge double. So beige isn't beige anymore. It's not taupe either, that's too eighties. It's timber wolf."

The lead singer clicks off the microphone and there's a momentary loud squeal.

"Clever," says Scratch.

A couple of guys stand, one putting the arm of the other over his shoulders. They head out the door. I pick up whatever number mojito is in front of me and give the glass a swirl. It catches the lingering light nicely.

"Yup. Marketing is so very, very clever. All started with a very, very clever man. Do you know who coined the term *public relations*?"

"I have a feeling you're going to tell me."

"That I am," I say, tipping my drink and it sloshes over unexpectedly, spilling on my thumb. "Edward Bernays. Freud's nephew. Used his uncle's research to create marketing that operated on subconscious desires."

"What does that have to do with public relations?"

"He coined the term. After World War II, 'propaganda' got a bad name, so he just did the same shit but—poof—called it public relations."

"Seems a little deceptive."

Now I lean in to Scratch, or not lean so much as try to adjust for the fact that the bar seems to be listing, like a ship in high seas.

"Oh, he was just getting warmed up. What's *really* sneaky is how he used PR for crowd marketing. In 1929 Lucky Strike wanted to open up the market to women, but a woman caught smoking in public could get arrested. Not good for business."

"I'd imagine not."

"So. Bernays pays off models to light up during the Easter Parade in New York. Calls Lucky Strike 'torches of freedom.' What's brilliant is it plays off women's desire for equality and the subconsciously sexual act of women wrapping their lips around a phallic symbol. Makes such a big stir that the papers can't avoid covering it like real news, and then suddenly a woman smoking is acceptable in public. Or not suddenly . . . it takes a few years to change perception. But it starts with that tap. If you really want to manipulate an individual, you start with a group. Seems counterintuitive, but it works."

"Interesting," says Scratch. He pushes his glass of Guinness toward me. "How would you market this?"

"Beer?" I say. "Oh please, give me something hard."

"Not just beer," he says, a hint of something defensive.

"*Guinness*. I don't know why you Americans still drink crap like Pabst."

"Our culture is founded on crap."

He nudges the glass another inch toward me. This is fourth-grade marketing stuff.

"Okay," I say. "First you have to imagine me blond and two cup sizes bigger."

"Done."

"You don't have to sound so eager." With clumsy hands, I unbutton the top button of my shirt, give it a think, then unbutton one more. I cock my head at him, offer a grand smile, reach for the Guinness without looking at it.

"Now I say something insipid, like . . . *there's only one reason to go for a guy with a Guinness.*" I angle the glass slightly so I can reach in with my index finger, dip into a nice amount of foam. "*Taste.*"

I take my finger out of the glass, touch my sternum with the foam, and then trace my finger up my chest, neck, and face until I reach my lips. I give a campy wink, open my mouth, and lick my finger. Hold a moment before bowing.

Scratch leans back on the bar. "And people pay for that?"

"Very well. Sex sells anything. Make it self-aware-slash-ironic, and you can catch all the people who think they're immune to messaging, too."

"Doesn't seem very viral."

"Internet's a baser channel. For that you just throw in a debutante with a well-oiled ass and launch a meme generator."

"But you haven't even tried the product. How can you sell something you don't know anything about?"

"Because you're never selling product. You're selling desire.

You're tapping misery, or creating it so your product can then fix that misery."

Persistent, he pushes the glass of Guinness another couple of inches toward me.

"Truth is, I don't even like beer," I say. My nose wrinkles. No, I actually abhor it. Growing up, the rank stink of piss and beer was forever in the carpet.

"I think you might like the bitter stuff. Unless, you know, it's too masculine for you."

"Too *masculine*. That didn't sound sexist at all."

"You just don't strike me as a mojito kind of person."

"No?"

"No."

There *was* something tasty about the foam, more like an exotic dessert than a beer. *Oh, what the hell.*

My hand isn't as steady as I'd like it to be, but I manage to lift the heavy glass, take a sip. Dark, and rich, and yes, bitter. Nothing girly about this draught.

I *do* like it, and take another, longer sip. Warmth tingles through my esophagus, lands nicely in my stomach. I place the glass back on the counter, concentrating hard so I don't drop it, like I'm playing Jenga. *There.*

Scratch takes one of the bar napkins, scrunches the end of it, reaches toward me, and gently starts to wipe the foam from my upper lip. A strangely comforting, paternal act.

"So you know what I do," I say. "What do you do?"

Scratch smiles, or I think he does. "I'm actually in a similar line of work. Maybe I should hire you." He takes a moment to inspect my upper lip for any leftover traces of foam, then, apparently satisfied, tucks the napkin in his back pocket.

"Are you in sales?"

"No," says Scratch. "I'm the devil."

Well, I think. *Not only has he gotten me wasted but he's fucking with me too.* "Wow. What's that like?"

"Fun," he says. "Depending on your idea of fun."

"There money in being the devil?"

"There is," he says, and when he says *there* it sounds like *ter*. That foreign lilt. "But that's not the fun part."

"What's the fun part?"

"The trade."

Ah. An investment banker with a hand in the subprime crisis feeling a little angst.

"Fortunately for you," I say, leaning into the bar. "I'm an atheist."

He leans in too, and I catch a faint hint of something smoky, and damp. "Most are, until they meet me."

The conversation has gotten complicated in some strange way, off track. Either that or I'm just out of touch with flirting—it's been a few years—or he's going to try to sell me something. I sit a bit more upright, reach for my mojito for something to do. A queasy feeling builds in my stomach. Maybe the foie gras was a bad idea. Maybe this all was.

"It doesn't have to be like this," he says. "*You* don't have to be like this."

An insult. Even though I recognize the manipulation, my damned ego bristles.

"I don't have to be like what?"

"Powerless. Helpless. Defeated."

Each word falls like a hammer. *Yes*, and *yes*, and *yes*. "Is that what you think?"

"No," says Scratch. "It's what *you* think."

I drop my mojito glass on the bar. It rolls and then falls onto the tile floor, shattering into pieces. All eyes turn to me. The drunk barefoot girl.

"Oh fuck," I mutter. There are so many, many pieces.

But Scratch doesn't seem to notice, or care. "So, Fiona, what can we do to change that?"

I told him my real name? Shit. I don't remember that. A vein throbs near my temple—the precursor to the mother of all hangovers. I want to push myself up, say something about the ladies' room, splash some water on my face and have a cogent moment, but I'm barefoot and surrounded by broken glass. I look hopefully in the direction of the bartender, but he must be in the back.

"What do you want?" Scratch asks softly.

What *do* I want? I want parents who don't shoot up and call me for bail, I want to stop being so desperately afraid of life, I want to take that pink coat and tear it apart by the seams.

But most of all, I want that ghost-twin, so I can know. Beyond a shadow of a doubt and all that.

"Maybe I want to be the invisible girl . . . sometimes," I whisper.

In the distance, there's the wail of a siren.

"What would you give up in exchange?" Scratch asks.

"I don't know."

"Would you give up your soul? How about it?"

I shrug. Giving up something you don't believe in doesn't cost a thing.

Or so one thinks in the moment.

CHAPTER TWO

THE SHEET IS COOL against my cheek, but my body feels hot, disturbed, feverish. Sound of traffic outside, the soft patter of rain, a floorboard heater that rattles and clinks. *God, how many drinks did I have?* Remnants of a nightmare linger—there was a dark shadow of a man with arms that grew, twisting down the block, wrapping around light poles and electric wires, fingers constantly searching, probing, until all the colors of the world bled to gray.

My head throbs. My throat itches. My arm automatically reaches over to the left for Justin, but all it finds is a pillow. Right. Seattle. And then it comes back to me, at least some of it—Make Westing, mojitos, a guy called Scratch. A name that isn't a name, not really.

And I'm naked.

Holy shit.

Panic hits—*what the hell happened last night?* A flutter of a memory: the sensation of a man's hands at the small of my back . . . no, I didn't, I *couldn't*. I risk opening my eyes and instantly regret it. The morning light feels like an attack, the room spins, and a rush of nausea overtakes me, but I see that at least I'm home, in my own apartment, not in a stranger's bed. A small but tangible comfort.

I'm in my apartment?

Impossible—I was locked out. Unless I did call the super, or Scratch was able to find someone still awake and willing to buzz us in, or he had superior lock-picking skills.

How *did* I get home from Make Westing? And more important, what did I *do*? There was broken glass around my feet, I remember that much, and the sense of being lifted from the barstool, but beyond that—nothing. A complete blackout. It takes me back to my early twenties, when I confused drunken promiscuity with worldly sophistication, when I smoked clove cigarettes and tried to be French. I listen carefully for the sound of someone else in the apartment—creak of floorboards, a toilet flush, a cabinet door opening or closing.

Nothing. I breathe a nearly inaudible sigh of relief.

But then my stomach heaves and I'm quickly reaching down by the side of my bed for the small, modern trash can—Italian, ninety dollars retail, twenty-five on eBay—and everything I ingested the night before returns in a much different form. I'm grateful for the can's weighted polycarbonate white lid, which automatically closes, and sink back into my bed.

An assessment is obviously required. Sleeping naked is something I avoid. It's a first-date, one-night-stand kind of thing—the single days when you still shave the places that don't like to be shaved, when you still think about what you last ate before a kiss.

If I'd stumbled in drunk and alone, I'd have just passed out on the covers—not a good sign—but even if, theoretically, I'm in the worst-case scenario, ADULTERY DEFCON 1, I shouldn't feel this dark, settling guilt, should I? *Justin* started it; Justin is the betrayer, him and the pink coat. That hair of his is ridiculous, *ludicrous*, trying to look like some kind of military recruit, and she's probably the kind of whore who's into that sort of thing, the rounded nape of her collar looked decidedly Republican.

Of course, beneath that is the familiar, worrying thrum.

Have I become boring? Staid? Dull? It's true I've started to shelve personal grooming on the weekends, and now that I think about it, I can't remember the last time we went on a real date instead of ordering Thai from the restaurant around the corner and watching something on Netflix. But the work has been insane lately, or not lately so much as always. There's always a meeting that could have gone better, or the Web traffic is down, or I'm over budget, or under budget, or the vice president wants to know why sales aren't meeting projections (although does the analyst ever consult me, *ever*, before forecasting?), and then there was the whole fracas from the casting call for our new ad campaign that specified *white* in the audition demographic. Had to outsource to a specialized PR agency to handle the Facebook comments alone. And Justin, his company might launch as an IPO, so he's been putting in extra hours; I can't even get a hold of him during the day.

But isn't this the life we're supposed to lead? Two busy professionals taking their careers seriously? Separate apartments, separate IRAs, separate stock options; we each do our own laundry. Non-wedded bliss.

Christ, maybe I should have taken those women's magazine admonitions seriously. They were always good for a laugh, those headlines, and Justin and I would actually kill time standing in the Safeway checkout line and point out the best and worst ones to each other: "10 Things Guys Crave in Bed"; "The Jeans That Instantly Make You Look Slimmer"; "Hausfrau Fashion Finds." But maybe secretly he longed for a partner with flawless skin and thigh gaps, or maybe all relationships are doomed to get comfortable, atrophy, and die.

It's strange how knowing you're being fatalistic is no protection.

Suddenly there's a series of knocks at my front door, followed by two more, sharp, brisk, and cheery.

BARELY ENOUGH TIME to pull on yoga pants from the floor, where I keep most clothes, and a ratty T-shirt that reads BUSH LIED—*would it kill me to buy something new, form-fitting, with color?*—two more staccato knocks, oddly persistent, especially because no one knocks on my door, ever. I maintain a strict regimen of urban solitude, avoiding eye contact and small pleasantries, and if someone says hello or even holds open the door, I pretend they don't exist, check e-mail on my phone instead. East Coast habits die hard.

Knock, knock—pause—*knock.*

Hell. My apartment, like all the others in this circa 1920s building, is small, vintage, quaint. In other words, no room for storage and an absolute ban on stickpins or nails in the plaster walls, so floor space serves many purposes. As I reach for the knob of the front door, I'm keenly aware of the paper stacks that loom like miniature skyscrapers, made up of outdoor magazines, research about the spending habits of millennials and boomers, competitive analyses of other companies. My free-standing IKEA IVAR shelves can hold only so much.

And then an unsettling thought hits—*what if it's Scratch?* There's no peephole in my solid, wood front door.

Knock, knock, knock. An imperative.

Nothing for it—I unlock the dead bolt, turn the doorknob, open the door just a crack, hope the chain holds.

A middle-aged woman in a neatly pressed suit, an actual Gucci bag—she didn't get the memo that toting such items can get you mugged these days—stands in the hallway. Her dark brown hair is coiffed and sprayed into something that looks as hard as a bird's nest, small droplets of rain clinging to it like dew, and in her free arm she cradles a grocery bag.

"Oh, you're *home*," she says as if we know each other, which we don't. "Hi, I'm Gloria, your neighbor?"

I say nothing. She does look vaguely familiar—I think I've passed her in the hall, giving little more than a nod of acknowledgment. Her accent is a touch Southern, which is inherently suspicious.

"You *are* Fiona . . . ?" Not so sure now. She peeks behind me, as if she's hoping that a more friendly Fiona will appear.

"Yes."

She's a boomer, part of the healthiest, wealthiest, and most-active generation of women in history, due for a double-inheritance windfall when both her parents and her husband die. Expected to travel widely, so we're working on a new pack, the Istanbul, lightweight with a slim, detachable waist belt to hold a passport, cell phone, cash, and credit cards. I make a mental note to add a small pocket for lipstick and a compact.

She offers the paper bag. "I believe these are yours."

Curious now, I unlatch the chain, open the door a little wider, and take it. The bottom is wet, and soggy. I unroll the top of the bag and inside I find my damp clothes from the night before, neatly folded.

"They were outside on the front stoop," says Gloria. "Just lying there in a pile. I folded them for you. I hope you don't mind."

My heart goes cold. The clothes I was wearing were left outside? So I walked, or was carried into my apartment, *naked*?

"And I found *this* in the skirt pocket, so I thought . . . well you're the only Fiona here, I'm pretty sure."

So helpful, and so proud of being helpful, she hands me a business-size card. It's nice, good, thick stock that feels soft to the touch. Expensive.

At the top, the words BILL OF SALE in ominous black print, followed by DATE, next to which is handwritten *Friday, October 12*. Only when I look more closely at the handwritten part, I see it's not ink . . . more like the writing has been burned into the card, like a brand. Pyrography. Something my middle school art therapist thought would help direct my destructive tendencies, burning images of horses into square bits of leather.

SOUL: *Fiona Dunn*
TIME: *4:05 a.m.*
FAVOR:

Nothing written here, a blank space that looms large, dark and oppressive. Is it just my imagination, or does the card carry a waft of sulfur?

"Are you okay?" Gloria asks, and for good reason—I can imagine how pale my face has gone. "I thought maybe it was some kind of an invitation. And it had your name. That's your name, right? I got it right?"

"Yes," I manage, tucking the bag under my arm, crumpling the card in my fist. "No. I mean . . . I'm fine. I must have left my laundry on the stoop when I buzzed in. Thank you."

With that I rudely close the door, lean against it. There's a hesitant pause on the other side, as if Gloria's about to knock again, but then she must think better of it, because I hear the *click-click* of heels against the hardwood floor, followed by the chime of the elevator.

I slide onto the floor.

Impossible. *Impossible.*

I FRANTICALLY TRY TO ASSEMBLE the fragments of memories I'm left with, but they blur, they resist. *Scratch.* What the hell kind of name is Scratch? We'd been joking, flirting—*oh God, flirting*—and every time I looked at my mojito, it seemed to be full. I definitely had two before he even sat down, I remember him ordering two more, but after that . . . What did he say he did? Sales? But really, why would he tell the truth, why would anyone in a bar tell the truth unless, like me, they were wasted.

I focus my mind to the moment I *do* remember, when the glass broke—the floor littered with sparkling pieces, the bartender in the back, patter of rain outside. I visualize myself there. Smell of beer, damp clothes, and cold popcorn. Slowly the memory develops, like a photo in a film tray. *He said he was the devil. He asked if I'd be willing to give up my soul.*

I said yes.

Christ, *Christ*, now the sick fucker knows where I live. All the news stories over the past decade about a woman meeting a man for a drink at a bar who then was found raped and/or decapitated play through my head. How could I be so *stupid*? Even *my* parents warned me not to talk to strangers.

I open my fist for another look.

Slowly, ever so slowly, the card unfolds like a flower opening to the sun. It then relaxes and flattens into a pristine state, like it'd just been cut from the press, like it wasn't just balled up in my sweaty palm moments before.

For a moment, me and reality have a serious issue. There's a drip of a leaky faucet in the kitchen, a rhythmic second hand, marking time. *This can't be. This can't be real.* I'm hallucinating. I remember the days when I shooed the nonexistent spiders off my parents' limp bodies, applied Band-Aids to patches of smooth skin they swore were melting off, checked that the walls weren't breathing.

I had too much to drink. Way too much to drink. I make a solemn promise—no, a vow—to never get that drunk again. I can't afford to end up like my parents. I couldn't live with myself if I did.

So next I try to tear up the card, rip it to pieces, the evidence. It bends, it twists, but it won't tear.

SOUL: *Fiona Dunn*
SOUL: *Fiona Dunn*
SOUL: *Fiona Dunn*

Why do I feel like this card is mocking me? I jump to my feet, head for the kitchen, with its cracked 1920s porcelain sink, cabinets that have been painted so many times the doors stick shut. *The lighter, where's the lighter?* I pull out the junk drawer, dig through the detritus of three years—coffee loyalty cards, rusty screwdriver, unidentifiable keys, coupons long expired, emergency votive candles, paper menu for the Chinese restaurant down the street that changed owners and is now a patisserie—*there it is*, brass cigarette lighter, the one I'd stolen from my father in one of my middle school attempts at hiding my parents' drug paraphernalia. It's silver, with a red stripe advertising Filter Tipped Winston Cigarettes.

It takes a couple of clicks to ignite the flame, then I hold it to the tip of the card over the sink.

The card doesn't catch fire.

I've heard of indestructible business cards, made from synthetic recycled materials—*it's probably a mix of used baby diapers and plastic shopping bags*. This isn't a sign that I'm losing it. *Get a grip, Fiona*. The world can get fucked up, really fucked up, but it's always fucked up in some identifiable way, a quantifiable series of interdependent causalities. If you have the time, and the patience, you can track down the reason for anything. At least that's what my therapist used to say.

An idea strikes. An aging carrot has been sitting in a small bowl on my countertop for days, so I use it to shove the card down the garbage disposal, turn on the faucet, flip the switch. The disposal whines a complaint, but eventually the carrot spins and disappears. I let it run for another minute for good measure, then turn off the disposal. Then the faucet.

I got drunk in a bar called Make Westing.

I look at the drain.

I met a guy, a creepy guy. Creepy guys in bars are a constant. Like e in $e=mc^2$.

Take a moment.

Of course he locked onto the alone girl, the sad girl, the bare-foot girl. Not surprising.

Reach my hand in. My wrist cringes at the slimy rubber part that I never think about cleaning. I feel the dull disposal teeth with my fingers, and then I find the card, still there. Intact.

He plied her with drinks, got under her skin. A cliché if ever there was one.

I pull out the card. It's in one piece. Not a scratch, not a tear, not even a wrinkle.

SOUL: *Fiona Dunn*

"And then what?" My voice out loud surprises me. *And then what happened?*

A dull, throbbing ache starts at the base of my spine, a familiar sensation, long forgotten. When my parents shot up, it was like the walls of our apartment melted away and I could feel all the people around us, trapped in their own boxes of low-income housing, stacked one upon the other, a storeroom of the poor, an ever-expanding radius of faceless strangers, none of whom gave a shit about the girl with the ponytail in the purple room pressing her headphones against her ears. The quietly desperate sense of being surrounded by people, utterly alone.

Think. One thing at a time. *Breathe.*

I was sitting on a barstool in Make Westing.

I focus on the stool. It was a hard stool, with a low wooden back, modern, dark green. A green that almost perfectly matched my skirt. *My clothes.* The woman found the card in my clothes.

I quickly walk back to the living room, grab the grocery bag, still damp, from the floor, and pull out each piece carefully, checking to see what secrets they have to tell me. My shirt—plain white, right front pocket—empty. My green pencil skirt—soggy receipt in the left pocket for lunch that day, the hot bar at Whole Foods plus an Italian soda. Next out comes my bra, and, disturbingly, my underwear, black, a little bit lacy and equally itchy, a concession to Justin because he'd been so . . . distant. The fact that the neighbor touched them—*what was her name again? Gloria? Lydia?*—causes an unpleasant shiver. But there's nothing else from that night: no bar bill, no phone number scratched onto the back of a matchbook, no folded paper napkin.

I lay the clothes out on my second-hand sofa, head to toe. It looks like a snake's shed skin, like I was lying there and simply evaporated. The sleeve of my white shirt droops over the side, touching the floor, acquiescing to the inevitable. I sit down on the coffee table, tapping my jittery knee with the card.

Think.

The band was packing up. I remember a man in a black T-shirt rolling up cable around his elbow, and there was glass on the floor, and I was barefoot. *Barefoot*. Immediately I hold up one foot, then the other, examining for cuts, or slivers.

They're perfectly fine. Unscathed.

So someone *did* lift me off the stool . . . and then what? Carried me home, or worse yet, drove me home? And then maybe stopped off somewhere in between, removing my clothes? I shudder.

What if Scratch put something in my drink?

A much more logical, but equally frightening explanation presents itself. It would explain the gaps in my memory, the state I was left in, hallucinations.

I glance at my underwear.

My stomach heaves again and I race to the bathroom, barely making it in time.

I KNEEL IN FRONT of the toilet bowl, vomit everything that's left, and then five heaves that yield nothing. Afterward I feel empty, eviscerated, cold.

Should I call the police?

This is the point where people call their family or friends for moral support and advice, but I have no one except for Justin. Acquaintances, plenty of those, work people good for a chat in the break room or a quick lunch. They get the edited-for-television version of my life, minor dramas that end well—parking tickets, hijacked Wi-Fi, near-miss accidents on the freeway. But no one to really call in an emergency, not a real friend; it'd be pushing it to even ask one of them for a ride, let alone get involved in what could be a trip to the hospital for a vaginal examination. Parents? A joke. Assuming the phone hasn't been turned off, assuming they aren't doing time, the call would only end in some guilt-trip attempt to get me to wire a couple hundred dollars.

Plus I was drunk. Everyone would say I was drunk and there'd be plenty of witnesses . . . not that drunk equals consent, but it sure doesn't help a case where memory is spotty already. But if Scratch did slip me a roofie, there'd still be traces, right? I pull off some toilet paper, wipe my mouth, and decide to ask Dr. Google.

It's still raining outside, and my small bedroom looks somber, pensive, claustrophobic. More of a junior bedroom, barely enough space for a full-size bed and a small end table that also serves as a desk, although the ceiling is tall, which helps somewhat. I flip open my laptop, type in my search. "Roofie side effects" include: hallucination, decreased blood pressure, memory impairment, drowsiness, visual disturbances, dizziness, confusion, and gastrointestinal disturbances. Check. *Traces remain in the bloodstream for twenty-four hours, can be detected in urine for seventy-two hours.*

Christ. I'm horrified but also relieved in a strange way, because at least this is the fucked-up world I'm familiar with. There is a logical, although vile, explanation. What will Justin think? *Hey, honey, I was in a bar drinking with a strange guy last night.* I glance at my purse on the floor, the one I left behind. Pull out my cell phone.

No missed calls. I don't think I've ever longed so much for a person in my entire life.

I'm about to swallow my pride, call his number, when I get a flash—the pink coat folded over the back of some anonymous hotel chair, or no, it's on the floor, they pulled each other's clothes off as soon as they got through the door, hungry. I remember those kinds of days with Justin. The early ones. I see the back of her head, blond hair disheveled and floating above her now-naked shoulders. She orders room service, probably something rich and decadent, like eggs Benedict or cinnamon bread French toast, with coffee and a fruit plate to share and then wheat toast, no butter, for Justin. He's taken to an austere diet over the past couple of months—nothing nonorganic, lots of raw vegetables, a drastic reduction in anything with milk. Lost about ten pounds, making his features even more chiseled, dramatic. I should have guessed there was a woman's hand behind it. *I should have known.*

Rain *tap, tap, taps* on the fire escape outside. No, I'm in this alone.

The fire escape. I look at it through the window. The rain has turned it from gunmetal gray to a slick black.

Maybe that's how Scratch got me back in? A sick feeling gathers. I've always had a hard time with that window, nearly impossible to get it open or shut, so it doesn't even cross my mind to lock it anymore, but that Scratch had an athletic build, and the way he held me upright, kept me from tipping over—yes, he was strong. I can almost picture it, him pulling me up the rungs, forcing the window open. And then. *And then.* And afterward—what? Went down the elevator? Why would he leave my clothes out by the entry?

To screw with the evidence, obviously. Blur the trail. But leaving the card as a parting favor, to instill a sense of dread, make that dread personal, intimate.

Christ, why did I ever go to that damn bar? Get drunk with a stranger?

You think you're better than me, but you're not, my father would say, often. *You think you're a good person, but you're not. Apple never falls far from the tree. Never does.*

I jump to my feet, take the two or three steps needed to reach the windowsill, find the latch unlocked. A possibility. But when I try to push it open, it doesn't budge, like it hasn't been opened in months, which it hasn't, not since the super shoved it closed over the summer and told me to leave it alone.

I touch my forehead to the cool glass. God, I wish I could just disappear, melt away into some other version of a life, one where things would make some kind of sense.

My cell rings. *Justin?*

Pulse racing, I scramble to get it before voice mail kicks in. Click *Accept* without even looking at the number.

"Justin!" I'm just about to blurt out my woes, pink-coat woman be damned, but it's another voice that answers.

"No, it's me, Tracy."

Tracy, my assistant Tracy. My heart plummets. Still, I manage to pull myself into the mannequin I usually present as myself. Competent, terse, juggling too many things.

"Hey, it's a Saturday, and I don't remember signing off on your overtime."

"Focus group?"

Right, *shit*, right. Weeks spent organizing a group of extreme urban nomads to evaluate the Istanbul prototype, people who live out of a pack for years at a time and never stay in a country longer than three months. Early enthusiasts who set a trend and then abandon a product once it takes off and becomes commercial. It took almost six months to get five in a room at the same time.

I look at the clock. I'm already a half hour late. I can feel the gears of my life making the decision for me, and I'm grateful to be back in the mundane. I can always call the police later. *Maybe I'll remember more by then too.*

I don't know if I quite believe myself.

"I'm really sorry. I had some issues here. Tell them I'm running late," I say. "Get them all whatever they want from Whole Foods, and let them know that after the focus group, we'll let them choose three packs from our stash in addition to the seventy-five-dollar stipend."

I search the floor for jeans and shoes.

Tracy is pointedly silent for a good second or two. "Those are for the editors coming Wednesday. I don't know if the warehouse could even get me another set by Wednesday."

The one thing I can always count on Tracy for is a passive-aggressive critique of my lack of organization.

"Could be worse," I say, and hang up.

How it could be though, I have no idea.

CHAPTER THREE

THE OFFICES FOR SUMPTER, INC. are located on the fifth floor of an art deco building that used to be a department store, its copper-plated siding burnished into a graceful green patina. The building is the lone holdout from the 1930s on a block of otherwise squat, concrete offices designed by a sixties East Berlin defector. No problem finding street parking on a rainy Saturday—the area is inhabited only by worker bees Monday through Friday, with the population trickling down to the homeless on weekends.

I get out of my car, a Honda too old to be interesting enough to steal, make a mad dash for the portico since of course I left my umbrella at home, and then dig around in my purse for the magnetic card that will unlock the front door of the building. Try not to think, for the millionth time, that Justin hasn't called me yet, even to check in.

Sumpter has always been a problematic name, recalling deep Southern forts and lost Civil War ambitions, but the company started in Georgia in the late nineteenth century, making packs, sleeping bags, and gear for hunters, so now we call attention to its founding date to evoke durability and to massage perception away from its antebellum origins. *Sumpter—Est. 1855. An American Original.* There was a professor of African-American studies in Oklahoma who wrote a pretty accurate and detailed journal article, "We Don't Need No More American Originals," about our company's founder, Mr. James A. Sumpter, petty-thief-turned-slave-catcher, who single-handedly tracked, kidnapped, and returned 145 poor souls to their owners. He then used the profits to buy a cotton plantation and a couple of mills in New England. It was not unusual for Sumpter to check those New England hires, if black, to see if there was a bounty out for them, in which case he would either return them and collect the reward or, if it was a case of mistaken identity, simply install them on his own plantation. We outsourced a PR firm to handle any negative publicity just in case, but the same week that the article was published coincided with the arrival of a major hurricane, and other than a few comments from fellow academics, it died a natural death.

Before I reach the door, I take a folded five-dollar bill out of my purse and let it drop to the sidewalk. I have no doubt that even in this weather it'll be gone by the time I head out. There're always two or three homeless people tucked out of sight, watching. It's a habit I picked up after I first started making money of my own, part good-luck charm, an offering to the deities—if they exist—because I remember the days when a found dollar bill was the difference between eating or not, part proof to myself that I am a good person, that my father was wrong about me.

I open the door, step into the entry of the building, quiet as church. Dark gray marble floors that match the marble walls, a ceiling of brass plates imprinted with bold, Frank Lloyd

Wright–style patterns and not a column in sight, the entire three-story space held up by magical engineering and the backs of goddesses or angels that bear more than a passing resemblance to Ayn Rand.

The middle-aged guy behind the security desk looks up from his computer screen and raises an eyebrow—short gray hair, thick glasses, a name I should remember but don't.

"Hey, you made it," he says, that annoying touch of both familiarity and reproof. "Tracy's been frantic."

I put on a smile, search for the least interesting explanation possible. "Power went out and my clock reset." Not that I have to report to him, but security guards, receptionists, and interns are career-deadly fonts of gossip.

"You need to get a clock that takes batteries too," he says, sticking to his point. "I've been using the same alarm clock since ninety-eight. Haven't been late to work in years."

I feel my smile stiffen. "Good advice. I better head up now."

He nods and returns to his computer while I head for the elevator, press the brass elevator button, burning. *If I had a penis and my voice was two octaves lower, he would've never said that to me.*

The elevator chimes, then the doors open. I step inside. For some unknown reason, the building's owners saw fit to nail cheap mirrors over the otherwise beautiful mahogany paneling, a nod to modernity, or vanity, or the seventies.

I don't look right. Something about my reflection is slightly off, or not so much off as *with*, like one of those hidden pictures puzzles where you're supposed to find the image in the negative, not positive, space.

I turn around, press the button for the fifth floor, try to shake the feeling off. The doors close, slowly, and there's the familiar rattle as the gears shift before the car starts to rise.

I take a sideways glance at myself in the mirror. Long dark hair scooped into a ponytail and pulled back from my high forehead—bangs, always an issue—a minimal amount of Saturday makeup, my nose leaning slightly to the left from where my father broke it when I was fourteen. I'd tried to wake him from a drug-induced stupor for lunch money; he thought I was trying to steal his coke, so he "accidentally" pushed me down the stairs. Too stoned to drive, one of his nameless friends took me to the emergency room, dropped me off at the curb with a twenty and a piece of advice: *It'll all work out in the end. It'll all come out in the wash. You'll see.* I didn't bother going inside the hospital, just washed the blood off in a bathroom at the 7-Eleven across the street and spent the money on a weekend matinee and popcorn.

Did I take my Xanax today? I don't think I did.

Still, I turn my head, step in for a closer look. No, it's the cast of my skin and the color in my eyes—they're wrong, dialed down, as if one of my graphic designers has taken the bar for brightness and moved it twenty points negative. Is it the lighting? It has to be the lighting. Unless it's another hallucinatory side effect from whatever that asshole Scratch slipped me. I shouldn't have come; I should have told Tracy I was sick. *Christ*, if only I had some time, time to think . . .

I close my eyes and ferociously wish I were back home, in bed. For a moment, I can almost hear the clink of the floorboard heater, and something softens inside me, a gentle lull like a wave receding—

The elevator chimes, and as the doors open, I register a whoosh of cold, air-conditioned air. *Time to get my game face on.* I open my eyes, about to step into the hallway, when I feel something strange beneath my feet.

The cool marble of the elevator floor.

I look down. I'm barefoot.

Not possible. So not possible. But when I turn around to see where my shoes could possibly have gone to, I find my Keds and white ankle-high socks just a step behind me, askew. Like they dropped from the ceiling, fell from the sky. Like I wasn't wearing them just moments ago.

TRACY HAS THAT LOOK, the one that starts when I tell her a package has to be overnighted to an editor and yes, I know it's only a half hour before FedEx closes. She sticks out an arm—impeccable shirt, crisp, robin's-egg blue—and holds the glass office door open for me, helpful and condescending in equal measure.

How the hell did I take off my shoes and not even know it? Am I having blackouts too?

"Good morning," says Tracy, in a tone that means just the opposite. She's short, with a blunt cut that would look stupid on someone else without the right bone structure. She also has the organizational skills of a general with the polish of a news anchor, and very much wants my job.

I pretend that I don't notice the look, the tone, and try to settle my mind in the reality that presents itself. "How's the group?"

"Pissy, obviously," she says. "Not a great introduction for early adopters, and . . ."

What if Scratch didn't slip me a roofie but something else instead? LSD? PCP? PCP comes with amnesia, I know that much. Tripping on PCP, my father killed my pet kitten—a stray I stubbornly tried to keep hidden in my bedroom—and afterward, when I presented her small, limp, furry body, he became furious that I would even accuse him of such a thing. Even though I saw him throw her from my bedroom window, pitching her like a baseball.

". . . would have started. Did you get my text?"

Tracy's been talking this whole time, but I have no idea what she's said. I ignore the fact that my laces are still mostly untied and flop with every step. "Did you get them food?"

"Yes. I just said that." She holds a manila file to her chest possessively, a brief on all the participants that she directly gave to my boss to review—trying to impress, didn't show me first—but I handpicked them and know their names, e-mail addresses, and short bios by heart.

Douglas Close and his partner, Ed Rigby—travel-slash-food writers who live nowhere in particular in Asia; Melissa Wright—a photographer specializing in documenting the displaced tribes living in South American slums; Liza Willoughby and her boyfriend, Sam Reed—planned to summer in England three years ago and haven't spent more than a month in one city since; Alex Fujita—another photographer and a professional urban nomad, his free-living blog on making it in metropolises like Chicago for under twenty dollars a day getting a hundred thousand weekly visitors; and finally an aging hippie, Raven Light, writer for various adventure and outdoor magazines and advocate of turning abandoned city lots into community gardens.

Vegetarians, every goddamned one of them.

I bet if I asked my parents, explained my symptoms, they'd be able to tell me exactly what drug he used. For once, they could prove useful.

"Surveys ready?" I ask, and Tracy nods, because of course they are. We head toward the conference room. She walks just slightly ahead of me.

Of late, at work I've noticed a slightly poisonous vibe pointed at me. Assistants are a tricky thing. You need their help making the sausage, but you have to keep the spice recipe a secret, you have to perpetuate the illusion that the distance created by your title and pay discrepancy is an insurmountable moat, that you always know more, see more. But I have a strong feeling she's waking up, planting seeds in the break room about how she'd improve everything that I've built for this company. And, quite frankly, she's hungrier for it than I am. Middle management isn't all that it's cracked up to be. Not anymore. You're the working poor until you get to CEO golden-parachute status, and I really don't know how many people you have to kill to get there.

"Got pencils this time?" I say.

I watch Tracy's shoulders stiffen. When she was still new, the first time she helped with a focus group, she forgot the pencils. She had to go hunting through desks to find them—not a big deal, but a good dig I save for special occasions.

"Of course."

The truth is, I'm shaky and can't afford to be, not for a moment around this girl.

Even though it's still raining, a good amount of light streams in through the tall, narrow windows. I try to center myself on this, where I am. The office is a wide-open space, not much different really from its department store days when it sold wallpaper, bedroom linens, and children's clothing. Desks have been placed here and there, with Aeron chairs of course, all the electric and cables tucked under a subfloor tiled with cork, the ceiling left exposed to showcase ductwork and rough, wooden beams. The absence of walls and privacy is supposed to facilitate communication and workflow, but instead even the smallest sound echoes loudly, which makes people feel paranoid about who's listening to phone calls and directs them to gossip in the bathrooms.

I hear a muffled snort of laughter.

Our subjects are in "the fishbowl"—the sole conference room, set up in the center of the space, glass walls on all sides. Wrappers and recycled food containers are littered across a conference table repurposed from barn doors, and Tracy's right—from their hostile sideways glances, it's easy to tell they've coalesced into a peevish group. Nothing unites people so quickly as something to complain about. On the plus side, the ice has effectively been broken and they'll be more likely to identify problems, which is a better win at the end of the day for product development.

I feel the pinpricks of their eyes on me.

I'm actually in a similar line of work.

The way Scratch leaned on the bar, relaxed in an almost feline way, like he was the apex predator in the savanna.

I push away the memory—compartmentalizing inconvenient truths is something I'm adept at—and open the glass door, smile.

"Oh my God," I start. "Hey, guys, I'm so sorry you've been

waiting for so long." All of them are leaning back in their chairs, quietly resentful. "But I got a last-minute call from Oprah's people—her magazine is considering the Istanbul for their must-have travel gear list. But I got here as soon as I could."

Dropping a celebrity name in general always gets the attention of a focus group, and Oprah in particular is a panacea for almost all problems, even here, among hard-core travel enthusiasts. They now relax a little in their chairs, suddenly interested in seeing these packs dusted with *O, The Oprah Magazine* interest.

"You've all met Tracy, and I'm Fiona Dunn, director of marketing for Sumpter, Inc."

I nod to Tracy, and she pulls out a box of Istanbul packs from under the conference table. The box is fresh from the factory, still sealed. Crap, one of us should have opened it to check—if the warehouse got the order wrong, we're screwed. No, sorry, *she* should have opened it to check. Now I'm almost hoping it's wrong, just so I have a new dig to keep her in line.

"We are so grateful you came today, and we wanted to keep it to a few, select industry experts," I say, opening my gambit with flattery. "This is a pack for the real urban nomad. What we're looking for here is your one hundred percent honest opinion on everything. Today, *you're* the CEO of Sumpter, Inc. Whatever you say, goes."

I can tell by the way I'm holding their attention that they're now slightly mollified. Everyone loves the concept of holding unconditional power, even if it's only for a few hours.

As Tracy slices through the tape, Liza Willoughby gets up, unasked, to collect the trash on the table. She's the youngest in the group, the daughter of an Exxon executive, daddy issues—in college she chained herself to a fracking rig along with her Planet for the People student organization. After the fallout, she quit school to live in sin with Sam, the son of a plumber, whose main skill set is drumming on buckets for spare change. Her feedback is probably the most important since we're thinking of launching the Istanbul as our introduction into a low-key luxury line, i.e. luxury that only someone who's in the know will be able to identify—a way the 1 percent can show off without suffering the accompanying evil looks from the other 99. But no matter how much Liza wants to be bohemian, she'll never be able to quite scrub the taste for one-thousand-count linens and two-hundred-dollar earbuds. The vintage Tiffany bracelet on her wrist tells the story. Twenty-five grand, easy.

I help Tracy lay the packs out on the table—thankfully, they're the right ones—which are accompanied by the waft of fresh plastic and Styrofoam, and now the energy in the room finally starts to shift from interest into something approaching excitement. The design is based on Parisian bicycle messenger packs, Euro-mod, not terribly practical but good if you're carrying everything you own and need to squeeze into public transportation. The small pack can be zipped onto a larger pack, the Ankara, that still legally fits in an airplane's overhead compartment bin. Colors range from the bright like framboise, vermillion, and tropical cover to neutrals like samovar, tatami, and chinchilla.

"Remember, there are no right or wrong answers." I say. "But we're very excited about some of the innovative technology we're launching for the first time. Like the back panel with sleeves for a tablet or a fifteen-inch laptop that unzips to lie flat for security screening."

Tracy demonstrates this with a thin laptop.

"And the shoulder straps and side handle that transform the pack into a horizontal briefcase-style bag."

With the efficiency of a game show hostess, Tracy unclips the shoulder straps and refastens them to turn it into a briefcase.

Maybe I want to be the invisible girl . . . sometimes.

I suddenly feel disassociated from the room, from the people in it, like I'm standing outside of myself, a ghost-twin observing the slight tremor in my hand, dimly registering the pause as Tracy waits for the next line in my spiel. Like I'm an actor in a play, but watching from the audience too.

"The large fleece-lined front pocket . . . it . . . it . . ."

Would you give up your soul? How about it?

Would I?

Did I?

Everyone feels the off note, and Tracy gives me another look now, but this time it's one of real concern. Four seconds. Four seconds of an awkward pause is all it takes to start breaking group dynamics, to begin the buildup of negative emotions, and let's face it, this room wasn't too positive in the first place. There's no way in hell we're going to get an accurate read from them. Goddamn, I've blown it.

"Oh shoot . . ." I say, stumbling for words, another excuse. I feel my back pocket for my cell phone, pull it out, pretend to look at something important on the screen. "Sorry, guys. Gotta take this. Oprah's people again. Tracy, you can manage from here, right?"

My stomach gives an alarming heave as I race from the room, and I can feel the burn of my lie falling flat. I quicken my pace.

I don't want this, I don't want this, I don't want this.

Whatever *it* happens to be.

THE FIFTH-FLOOR BATHROOM is really beautiful as far as bathrooms go, with white, scalloped pedestal sinks and light pink marble floors, hailing from a different era for women. There's a long vanity counter just after you enter, with worn, dark pink velvet stools from the days when ladies sat to apply powder to their already porcelain skin, but now are used by nursing mothers. An opaque window lets in some natural light, giving the wan, overhead antique fixtures a needed boost. My pulse is racing—I can actually hear the blood in my veins throbbing near my temple.

Breathe. Breathe, Fiona, breathe.

I approach one of the pedestal sinks, turn the right faucet for cold water. Splash a little into my hands, then onto my face. It feels good, so I do it again.

Then I stand, looking at my reflection in the mirror.

That odd, dark cast to my skin again. Not the light in the elevator then.

I lean in closer. Another side effect? For the first time, a real fear lands, that I'm in true, immediate, physical danger. I seem to remember a grayish cast to my father's skin, but God only knows which drug caused it, or if it was all of them together. What's strange is that if I look very carefully, the slight shadow extends about an inch from me, as if the surrounding air is contaminated too. I raise a hand in front of the mirror, wave it fast, and there's the faintest dark shimmer, like heat rising off asphalt. And my eyes—normally a warmish brown, the irises have gone a shade darker, pupils wide and dilated. Even the whites seem to have a slight gray tinge.

Cheap-shit mirrors. The only possible explanation. We think all mirrors are the same, but they're not. Clothing store mirrors are warped enough to make their clientele appear thinner, driving sales. I bet these made for brisk business in the makeup department.

There's a part of me that knows I've seen my reflection in these mirrors a thousand times and never noticed this kind of effect. But already that notion is being bricked into a new compartment in my mind, until the lack of attention causes it to atrophy and die slowly. I have a whole mausoleum of things I prefer to never think about again. A cemetery of dead memories.

I splash more cold water onto my face.

Are you in sales?

No, I'm the devil.

My stomach suddenly heaves again, riotous, and I stumble for one of the stalls, the only nod to modernity with thick, floor-to-ceiling walnut panels featuring a horizontal grain. I kneel in front of the toilet, my forehead starting to feel clammy again. Nothing happens for a minute, then another. False alarm.

It's quiet here in the bathroom, just the soft hush of traffic filtering in through the window. A hum from the overhead light fixture. I don't have to go back to the focus group—Tracy's more than capable of damage control. I should have just told her to handle it when she called me at home, but I was . . . *in* so many pieces.

I take another look at my cell phone—no missed calls from Justin—but even that doesn't seem to bother me very much, because the marble is cool, and there's nothing to do, at least not right now.

I lean back against the wall. Take a moment. The air is shadowy, in a soothing kind of way. *Finally*, a chance to think, even if it is in a stall and I'll have to soak my hands in Purell later.

Growing up, the world often didn't make sense, not the kind it should have according to the glimpses I saw in other kids' homes. So I'd make probability lists, narrow things down to what was most likely my reality. Take the fridge. At a friend's house, a tray of Jell-O would be an after-school treat, something to snack on while watching a sitcom, but in mine, a tray of Jell-O wrapped in cellophane presented a broader array of possibilities. I'd have to consider who was in the house, whether some of it was already gone, and if my parents and their friends—frighteningly anemic, thin creatures with bags under their eyes and nervy twitches—were giggling in the living room, the volume of the TV turned full blast. Probability the Jell-O was safe to eat—low. Probability it was laced with ecstasy—high. Ninety percent of my adult life has been trying to exorcise that past, fly within the boundaries of normal, where things are safer, life is safer . . . or so I've been told.

So why the hell did I go to a bar last night?

Because swimming just underneath my veneer of normalcy is the other me, the twisted me. The me that dabbles in *self-destructive behaviors to cope with trauma*, my therapist had said. Better than running the scissors over my thigh again I guess.

But now's not the time for introspection—I can think about all that later. Or not. Instead, I pull the indestructible business card from my jeans, the only constant.

Time to think this through logically.

Possibility number one. I have actually sold my soul to the devil. For real. And that has to be a load of bullshit. I mean, for starters, there's no such thing. With all the bad stuff I've seen happen to innocent people, I can't even entertain the idea of a just and loving God . . . a paranormal Big Brother monitoring system watching all, doing nothing, with accounts paid only after death. Finding a dead toddler in a car on a hot summer day with the windows rolled up because the junkie parents were shooting up with mine will do that to a girl.

But even if God and his evil nemesis *did* exist, with seven billion people around, I can't see why the devil would bother trolling bars in Oakland, California—surely there'd be easier, and bigger fish to catch, like drug-running despots and military generals with their fingers on the trigger of nuclear weapons. Or if he was collecting low-hanging fruit—like oh, say, desperate women shafted by their cheating boyfriends—the probability of running into him would be extremely low. I'd have a better chance of getting struck by lightning, winning the lottery, or contracting Ebola.

Unless he was targeting me specifically.

But again, if there's anything I know for sure, it's that there's nothing so remarkable about the soul of Fiona Dunn. I firmly represent Generation X's postfeminist, post-seventies

lack of optimism; we're generally pessimistic about our financial futures, we've seen, up close and personal, the popped balloon of the American dream, and suffer from an overall sense of
malaise shaded by cynicism. I share shopping habits and music
preferences with about forty-one million others of my ilk who
came of age between 1988 and 1994, which is why they play
the Cure in Banana Republic and the Smiths in Whole Foods.
There would be no reasonable answer to the question: *Why me?*

It's just a card.

Whoever this Scratch really was, he went through a lot of
trouble inscribing my name with a wood-burning pen. But the
probability that I've sold my nonexistent soul to the devil? Low.
Again, bullshit.

So. I'm left with two other more likely possibilities, neither
of them good.

Possibility number two. Scratch slipped me a roofie. The
easiest course of action is to do nothing, pretend that it never
happened. I'm very good at that. Stoically enduring catastro-
phes is a strong suit. I don't have to go to a hospital—I hate
them. *Hate* them. I could build a new mausoleum in my mind
for last night, seal off the door, and eventually forget about it.
Or if maybe not forget entirely, just make sure I never take a
path that comes near it. I would need to get checked out, blood
tests, that kind of thing. And it would have to be a secret between me and Justin, but he's the one who started keeping secrets, *so there*.

Possibility number three. I'm just hungover. I was blackout
drunk. The kind of slip that I'm supposed to alert my therapist
about. But then I'd have to start seeing him again, and I have
him under the lovely illusion that I've made good progress,

mainly by telling him things like *I've been finding alternative things to do with my anxiety*, or *if I feel angry, I sit down and meditate to get in touch with my feelings*, and *I'm going to a support group and I'm really enjoying the people*. He loves that one. Again, what's done is done, and even if something happened without my consent, I have no name, no face even to describe. In fact, other than some purely circumstantial conjectures, I have no proof that anything untoward happened. I mean, nothing's sore. No bruises, no clothes torn, no skin under my fingernails. Of course, I woke up naked under the sheet. But for all I know, I was so blitzed that I took off my clothes myself.

I might have done other things too. Like that one time in Vegas, at the branding conference. Afterward, I promised myself, *never again*.

No, doing nothing has a definite appeal.

But then the ghosts of doing nothing whisper: *AIDS . . . STDs . . . He knows where you live . . . What if he breaks in? What if he comes back?*

Goddamnit. Motherfucker.

I listen to the rain outside, a soothing patter. Once, Justin talked about us moving to Seattle where he has family, but I said I couldn't take all that rain; it'd be too depressing. *Depressing* is my safe word—I try not to use it too much, but it does fold any possible disagreement quickly, and generally in my favor.

Christ. I hate this, hate it, *hate it*, but I simply just can't do nothing.

I mentally begin to prepare myself to go to the hospital. Forms in triplicate, hard plastic chairs in the waiting room, examination rooms filled with the strange antiseptic smell tinged with urine, which nothing can quite get out. My favorite place. If the doctors find something, they'll call the police, even though the probability is slim to none of anything other than a statement being taken. Tracy's car was stolen right out of her driveway, and even when she tracked it down—the idiots got her phone number from a piece of mail stuck in the visor, left her prank messages, and she was able to *69 them—the police just shrugged. They had real cases. Drive-by shootings, international child-sex trafficking, the Mexican Mafia dissolving the bodies of their victims in acid, sometimes without the grace of killing them first. You know, things like that.

My heart aches with the complete and utter loneliness of this moment, marooned in a city of people who don't give a shit.

I pull my cell phone out of my purse.

No missed calls.

Idly, like I'm just playing with it, like there's no intention, my fingers tap the screen—*Contacts, Justin, Call.* A small green icon is all that stands between me and his voice, even if it's just to listen to his voice mail message, *Hey, you know the drill, beeeeep.* My finger hovers over his number, just millimeters above the reflective glass surface.

Justin is perfect in emergencies, large and small—he always knows exactly what to say, what to do. When I dropped my iPhone in the toilet, he talked the store manager into covering the replacement under the warranty, plus free tech support to get my contacts transferred. When a kitchen grease fire broke out in the apartment next door, he quickly directed me to the exit stairs and then helped put it out. People think I'm with him because of his looks, his job at a tech company with good dividends, but really I just need that guy on the *Titanic* who knows how to get two spaces on the lifeboat, because I'm never entirely sure how bad my life will get.

I tap the number, then hurriedly tap to hang up. He'll see it on his missed calls though.

Five minutes. *I'll stay here five more minutes and if he doesn't call back, then I'll take the elevator down.*

I lean my head back. I like the grain of the wood in the stall; the colors are a nice contrast. We could do a version of the Istanbul in leather, dark autumn colors with light trim. I wonder what the group would think of that option. Something deep inside of me relaxes. I feel the tug of something else, an invisible current.

And just like that, I'm back in the fishbowl.

IT'S LIKE ONE OF THOSE STRANGE, waking dreams where you're in it but somehow separate too, dreams that always seem to follow that third glass of wine or an Ambien. I'm standing right behind Tracy in the fishbowl—she isn't at the head of the table, good girl, but is seated at one of the more democratic sides. This close, I can see the tiniest flecks of dandruff on her right shoulder, marring ever so slightly the effect of her lilac J.Jill collared jacket.

All the colors seem brighter somehow, the hue intense, almost luminous. I can hear her laptop hum.

"I just don't know about the zipper." Ed gives the Istanbul's main zipper a good tug. He's thin, yet perfectly chiseled, like Michelangelo just finished with him.

"Yes, we're in and out of our bags three times a day," adds

Douglas. Sixteen years older and obviously still infatuated. His hand rests closely next to Ed's. I see a faint, soft glow extending from his fingertips, the inverse of the dark aura I saw around myself in the mirror. The glow drapes over Ed's wrist, curling around it like the vine of a phosphorous plant.

Curious.

Ed says, "That's why we buy the—"

"Warranties," finishes Doug. "I'm surprised the North Face even lets us buy their gear anymore, especially after—"

"—that time in Taipei."

"Disaster. All my stuff fell out—"

"—And I'd already gotten off the railway car."

"My passport landed on the tracks. Wallet. Gone. Money. Gone. So I called them—"

"*I* called them."

"*We* called them. Paid for the shipping, but they were terrific and replaced it for free."

"Or was that Chiang Mai?"

Tracy is busy scribbling notes, too busy to observe the subtext—if the design was better, they wouldn't be giving a damn about the zipper; people line up for iPhones even though there always seem to be questions about the battery life. But if this is a dream, the details are strangely consistent, a little too true, accurate. Even the pencil in Tracy's hand is right, a number two cracked open from a new pack I'd bought the day before; I prepped them myself after a lengthy building-wide search for a pencil sharpener. People are more comfortable writing what they really think if it's easy to erase. The possibility for revision allows people to speak the truth.

Is this actually happening?

No, impossible. How many times have I used that word today? I look to the glass wall where my reflection should be, and don't see it. When I look down, yes, my body's there, although I am strangely, and completely, naked.

Okay. That's . . . that's not good. A lucid dream?

"This pocket, what's it for?" asks Liza. Even though I'm standing right next to Tracy, naked, she doesn't seem to see me. I try a wave, and she doesn't even blink.

Tracy looks up from her note-taking. "That's actually a pocket that you can completely unzip out of the pack and use as a waist belt."

She goes back to scribbling. She should be selling it more—it's a focus group but also free PR. I get a small amount of satisfaction that she's not better than me at everything. Yet.

Assuming this is all real. I pinch my right arm—strange, I can feel the pain. Maybe try reading something, looking away, then reading it again—if the words change, definitely a dream. Over Tracy's shoulder, I see her note: *Should have gone with zipper upgrade.* An obvious stab in my direction—my idea, I was trying to decrease the cost of goods—but that's not the most important issue at hand. I look away, then read her note again—still there. Not a lucid dream then.

Cool air brushes across my nipples, causing them to pucker. Okay, a hallucination. Obviously this is a hallucination.

"A waist belt could work." Liza rubs the fabric between her fingers. It's a new polyester blend, durable, dries fast, and has a soft, silky feel. "I had my purse stolen in Marseille."

The conversation is so dull though, so typically inane, that I can't shake the feeling this is actually happening.

"Not my fault," says Sam.

"I didn't say it was." Liza drops the waist belt, looking hurt. "Whatever."

I think of where my body must be right now, slumped in the bathroom stall. I hope I didn't hit my head on the toilet, or that I'm convulsing, choking on vomit, an ignominious rock star death that will eventually be the punch line to a series of dark jokes in the break room—after a respectful passage of time, of course; three months, maybe four. Whatever it is that I'm experiencing, I need to wake up, right now. Something loud, and noisy, might do it.

There's a stray pencil resting on the corner of the conference room table. I try moving it with my mind, because that's actually supposed to work in hallucinations. But staring at it does nothing. So I let my finger hover over it, just like I did with the cell phone moments before. One centimeter . . . half a centimeter more . . . and then my finger touches the pencil, registering waxy paint.

I flick it. The pencil flies off the table, ricochets off the glass wall before tumbling to the floor.

Everyone in the room jumps, startled, like a gun just went off.

"What was—"

"I . . . did you see—"

"How—"

Alex Fujita half gets out of his chair, maybe to bolt—I'd imagine living in Chicago for under twenty dollars a day would give you hair-trigger reflexes. But Tracy takes control.

"Sorry, errant pencil." She leans over, scoops the pencil up from the floor. "Must have knocked it off with my elbow."

No one can see me. I marvel at how resilient this hallucination is. Like it's actively fighting me.

There's a settling, nervous titter, accompanied by a nice bonding energy. It's always a mystery to me how this happens, the osmosis where strangers let their boundaries fall to form a group, how quickly hierarchies are formed, pecking order established. And then it all dissolves again afterward, so that a year from now, or two, they won't be able to remember one another's names, what they said. All that will be left is the flotsam and jetsam of memories that will themselves be further warped by the future, because we don't really remember what happens; our brains just roll back to the last time we thought about that memory. A copy of a copy of a copy.

"Room for a bladder?" Raven Light is methodically going through her Istanbul, jotting down notes.

Internally, we detest that word; *reservoir* is preferred, or even *hydration system*. But among the plebeians, bladder is the one that seems to stick.

"We're thinking it's more for urban settings," says Tracy. "Is there any reason why you'd want a hydration system?"

"Oh, definitely," says Melissa, with a hint of a Spanish accent even though she grew up in Tennessee. "I always boil tap water the night before if I have to, then fill up my water bottles. A hydration system would be much easier."

"Plus you can fill it with beer and no one knows you're drinking," adds Sam.

Everyone politely ignores him, except for Liza, who folds her arms over her chest, ashamed.

So. What to do next? Can I open a door? Maybe if I was

able to make my way back to my body lying in the bathroom, I could splash some hallucinatory water on it and wake up. But that would likely blow the focus group—if the pencil incident was any indication, a door to the fishbowl opening all by itself would incite panic. Scratch the surface and everyone reverts to the superstitions of their birth religion.

Only this isn't real.

I wish something else trippy would happen, like a giant cat peering in through the window, the chairs melting into the floor. Just one more thing to confirm where I'm standing in the overall spectrum of reality.

Then I catch something out of the corner of my eye—Sam pretends to pick up another Istanbul but actually slides the waist belt that Liza had been holding off the table onto his lap, as dexterous as a street hustler swapping peas in a shell game. *Bastard!* He quickly crumples it and stuffs it in his back pocket, poker-faced. No one notices.

Some kind of corporate espionage, or is this how Sam contributes to the relationship: the poor bad boy in need of saving by the good rich girl? Even though this entire experience might be the result of something Scratch slipped in my drink, I hope the imaginary Tracy got the imaginary focus group to sign our very real nondisclosure agreement. I'd hate to see the waist belt show up on eBay, and then the North Face gets it into production before we do.

Tracy turns back to Liza, who she's obviously most comfortable with, her age equal. "So would you consider wearing a waist belt?"

A good question, but shit, she should *hello, look and see where it went.*

"I use one now, but it's too small to hold anything but money and one credit card," says Liza.

"What if it was bigger?"

"Well," says Liza, "then it'd be like a fanny pack, right?"

Fanny pack. *Good God, Tracy, jump on that. If people start referring to the waist belt as a fanny pack, we're already dead in the water.*

Meanwhile, Raven inspects the shoulder straps of another pack. Alex and Melissa lean over to see what interests her, all of which is lost on Tracy, who is too busy bonding with Liza.

"Doesn't seem very comfortable," says Raven quietly.

"No compression straps either," adds Alex. "Hey, wasn't there a piece about you recently in the *New York Times?*"

Raven nods, looking like she couldn't care less when I can see that she does, very much. "Mm-hmm." *No, no, no,* they're getting completely off track, we didn't spend all this time and money, to give them the opportunity to professionally network.

But Tracy is *still* absorbed with Liza. "Do you remember how much your waist belt cost?"

The impulse to take over is strong, but given no one can see me, not exactly possible. I've always known I was fiercely competitive but never realized how entrenched it was—even in a hallucination, it clings to me like a second skin. If I were leading the group, I'd be touching base with each of them, digging deeper but also heading off the formation of mini-groups, off-topic conversations.

Although.

Although.

There *is* something enjoyable about being the proverbial fly on the wall—I can see all the twitches and behaviors people usually mask when they think you're looking, let alone Sam's sticky fingers. Meanwhile, he's now completely checked out of the conversation and is busy tapping his thighs with two pencils, drumming, bored. Melissa pulls her chair a little closer to Alex and plays with the top button of her V-neck shirt, subconsciously unbuttoning it. She doesn't know that Alex is at the forefront of an asexual movement, having been famously burned after a well-known affair with a married celebrity. Alex quietly leans back, vacating the personal space Melissa has invaded, and pulls out his cell phone to check something, the international call sign for *not interested*.

Maybe, hypothetically, there's something to that conversation Scratch and I had about the invisibility thing. Access to closed-door meetings with the exec team, listening in on bathroom gossip, looking over people's shoulders as they type in passwords and then accessing their files later. I could potentially know everything about everyone. That *would* be interesting. Interesting enough to sell one's soul for, though? Even if I believed in souls, I'd need more convincing.

Sam yawns, stretches, hands almost bumping right into me. "Where's the bathroom?"

He pushes his chair back and just like that I'm—

—BACK IN THE BATHROOM STALL. Only now I'm naked, sitting on a pile of my clothes and shivering with cold, like I've just stepped out of a walk-in freezer, or the temperature has dropped twenty degrees. All is quiet; the same church-like hush.

I don't remember taking off my clothes. That's not good. *God, I'm losing it.* Unless this is a hallucination within a hallucination? How deep does this rabbit hole go?

And then a more disturbing thought tickles my brain.

What if this *is* real?

Through the walls, I hear the gurgle of water rushing through pipes—Sam. In my hallucination, Sam was going to the bathroom—he must have just flushed the toilet in the men's room next door. So there were a few minutes there before I came to.

He put the waist belt in his pocket.

In my hallucination. Anyone could be in the bathroom. Anyone.

A significant part of me doesn't want to know the truth, is afraid. Not knowing can sometimes be preferable to knowing—you can sketch in whatever version of the truth suits you.

But I'm naked, cold and shivering. *Fuck it.* Quickly I throw my clothes back on—shirt's backward, screw it, panties inside out, screw it—grab my cell, my coat, the damn card, shove my socks into my purse and then my feet into my Keds, squashing the backs of the sneakers, no time to lace. I unlock the stall door, race past the sinks, ignoring my reflection in five mirrors, and open the heavy oak women's room door, then step into the darkened hallway, which seems to stretch, lengthen, pull away from me in both directions like someone is pulling taffy.

I feel sweat bead my upper lip—why is it so hot all of a sudden? Another gurgle from inside the men's room: the faucet.

He's washing his hands. I should've washed my own, I'll probably get hep A on top of everything else the way my luck's going. *Christ, it's taking so long.* Tick, tick, tick, tick. I feel like a small, nuclear weapon has been detonated in my chest: *What if? What if? What if?* Finally I can't stand another minute, another second, and open the men's room door. Charge inside.

The security guard is the one washing his hands, while Sam stands in front of a urinal, holding the turtlehead of his penis, mid shake-off. His head snaps in my direction, startled. "What the hell?"

The security guard—*his name, why don't I know his name?*—smirks, takes in my disheveled appearance, head to toe, making mental notes. Something to chat up Tracy about, I'm sure.

I swallow but hold my ground, even though the men's room is inherently intimidating, ten urinals total with those, whatever the hell they are, bars of something at the drain. Pedestal sinks and cracked mirrors that look like they haven't been cleaned since Kennedy was president, puce tiles the color of split peas that line the floor and creep up the walls until they're defeated by a band of black tiles.

"Do you *mind*?" says Sam.

The stink of old piss is overwhelming. It would make for a good American Apparel shoot.

The security guard is enjoying himself, takes his time grabbing a paper towel, drying off.

I gather my courage, say nothing, and just stride past the guard toward Sam instead, grabbing the pocket by his ass for the suspicious bulge there.

"Fucking A," he says. "What do you think you're—"

While he's occupied with his shake-off, tuck, and zip, I yank the waist belt out from his pocket, give it an accusatory snap. He turns, and for a moment we both stare hard at each other, equally stunned but for entirely different reasons.

It takes a second for him to register the contraband. Sam

puts up his hands, *no más*, and takes a step backward. "I have no *idea* how that got there."

This is real. I feel a vein throbbing somewhere near my temple, a gathering aneurysm probably. I saw him put the waist belt in his pocket; I heard him say he was going to the bathroom. This is real. All of it is real.

The guard's hand drifts to the walkie-talkie in his belt.

"I'm telling you," says Sam, trying out a smile, dipping into a boyish charm that must have worked once, with Liza. "I don't have any idea—"

"Just . . ." I say, the words coming out as a whisper, which surprises me. My tongue feels thick, foreign, metallic. "Just get out of here."

Relief drops over Sam's face, confusion over the guard's.

"Whew," says Sam. "For a moment there I—"

"I said *get out!*" They both seem shocked; neither moves fast enough, so I scream, "*Get the fuck out of here! Now!*"

And they do, quickly.

This is real.

This is not a hallucination, this is not a lucid dream, I am really standing in the men's bathroom on the fifth floor of Sumpter, Inc., with my feet half in and out of my Keds, and the room smells like piss, and I'm holding the waist belt, which I really saw Sam put in his jeans pocket because I was really there, in the fishbowl, standing just behind Tracy.

It can't be real.

Because if the invisibility is real . . .

Then it means Scratch is real . . .

Which means the word FAVOR and the blank space after is real too.

Right . . . ?

Can't be though.

Right?!

My reflection. Cracked in a cracked mirror, which would be a cliché in a movie. My skin doesn't look right in it, either. Nothing does. I don't know if anything will look or be right again, because I just might have a soul that I just might have sold to the devil himself. In which case, I also owe him a favor.

Which part is worse, I don't know.

Yet.

I hold up my phone, frantically click the screen, enter my passcode and find—no missed calls.

I'm completely, and utterly alone in this too.

I have never felt the entire world to be so massive, cold, and unforgiving as it does in this moment, not at age nine when I covered for my comatose parents in the bedroom as the social worker came to visit—*they're at work, no, everything is fine*—not when they kicked me out of the house at seventeen, pushing two hundred dollars into my hand before shutting the door so they could rent out my room to their drug buddy— *we're doing this for* you; *you're too sensitive; you need to grow up, get a thick skin*—not when I looked up at the Lowell Greyhound timetable at 1:00 a.m., bleary-eyed, trying to see how far away I could get.

But the sense of being damned? Now that's familiar.

I pull the card out of my pocket, head for one of the stalls at the back, pick one, open the door, drop the card in the toilet, and flush. Water fills the bowl, swirls, and then sucks it down, into the bowels of the sewer where all the dark, stained things go.

CHAPTER FOUR

WHEN I LEAVE THE BUILDING I see the five-dollar bill is gone. It feels like I dropped it years ago, in a different lifetime, another era. Rain now falls in earnest, so I pause under the portico, try to gather myself.

Get a grip, Fiona. There has to be another explanation.

Astral projection, remote viewing, things I'd always been mercilessly snide about whenever I crossed paths with some holistic New Ager, maybe it's time to reconsider. Or Scratch could be some kind of bar-trolling illusionist/hypnotist, with lock-picking skills and a misogynist streak. I could also be suffering a psychotic break—it's possible I saw Sam palm the waist belt in the fishbowl before I crashed and burned during my presentation, and my mind just tucked it into a hallucination.

Not great hypotheses, but still in the realm of the reality I know. I pull out my cell phone, hoping to see at least a text from Justin, but no, nothing. A small part of my heart shrivels and dies.

The sensible thing would be to go to the hospital and tell them everything, let them sort out what's wrong with me. There's something appealing about the idea of handing it all over to someone else to figure out, letting go. Of course, I just flushed away my only piece of evidence.

"Great move, Fiona. Brilliant." *I'm talking to myself.* That *doesn't seem crazy.*

Then, as if to confirm I *am* crazy, when I look up from my phone, I find Scratch leaning against the hood of my car in the rain, although I could've sworn he wasn't there just a second ago. He wears the same clothes from the night before—black leather jacket, dark jeans, knockoff watch—and his hands are tucked into his front pockets; so casual, easy, and relaxed, like it's a sunny, warm day, not a cold downpour. I struggle to make out his face, but again, it's a mystery.

My stomach twists. *Why can't I see his face?*

"Do you know," he says lightly, like we're picking up our conversation from the night before and nothing has happened since, "that Native Hawaiians consider rain a blessing?"

I call mutiny and say nothing.

"You should feel very blessed today Fiona. Do you?"

A sedan passes by, the driver splashing water on a homeless man slumped by a trash can across the street. He doesn't move. Doesn't stir. Not much of a witness if something else bad happens.

I grip my purse a little tighter. "I'd feel a little more blessed if I wasn't naked when I woke up this morning."

"Oh, that," he says, and I can feel a smile even if I can't see it. "What do you take me for? You were hammered. I'm not going to lie and say I wasn't tempted; you were pathetic yet attractive in a drowned Ophelia kind of way."

A compliment or an insult? I'm not sure. "So we didn't . . ."

"Have sex? No."

A small relief—we were at a bar, he made a pass, nothing happened. I'm still a few steps above Justin on the moral high ground.

"So how did I get back into my apartment?"

Scratch holds out an arm, beckons me closer. I reluctantly take a few steps but stop right at the edge of the portico's eave.

He takes a moment, looking me over. "It suits you."

"What?"

"There's no word in your language. It's a way we identify each other, not through our eyes, but with our souls. Our tribe's unique mark. And I'll answer your other question with one of my own—how did it feel being in the fishbowl just now? Did people see you?"

My throat swells, choking any possible reply.

No, it can't be.

"Was it like you were invisible?" he adds softly. "A ghost-twin?"

How does he know?!

"Was it like the very thing you wished for has come true?" He stands then, takes a step toward me but doesn't cross the boundary of the portico's eave. The rain hits his shoulders, cascades down his sleeves, and this close I see his skin too, with the same dark tinge I saw in my own reflection. Something magnetic about it, a strong gravitational pull.

He lifts his arms slightly, lets the rain hit his palms for a moment. I notice there are no lines on them. "But at what cost?"

He snaps his fingers.

The rain stops. Instantaneous. I can hear other sounds now

that had been drowned out by the rain, the thrum of traffic on the freeway, the rumble of a nearby garbage truck.

"No." I take a step back. "What you're saying . . . it's not real . . . it can't be real."

"Perhaps there are more things in heaven and earth, Fiona, than are dreamt of in your philosophy."

It's impossible to breathe. Impossible to speak.

"Like devils," he says softly. "And souls. And hell. What some call damnation, but I call liberation."

Maybe it's the impossible that's possible.

He snaps his fingers again, and the deluge resumes.

"Get the fuck out of here!" I take two more shaky steps back. "Get the . . . I don't know what the hell your *game* is, but—"

Suddenly I hear the door open behind me and turn just as the security guard steps out.

"Hey, you okay?" he says. "You've been standing out here for a while."

The glass door seems to swing shut in slow motion behind him—in the reflection I see the back of his head where he's starting to go bald, the tag from his shirt poking up behind the collar—and when I turn back to the car, no one's there.

Scratch is gone. Vanished. Not a sound as he left.

I DRIVE, AND DRIVE, AND DRIVE. Eighth to Broadway, Broadway to Nineteenth, Nineteenth to Telegraph. I don't have a destination in mind, but then I don't feel like I have much of a mind at the moment. Instead, I concentrate on the present. The here and now. Dark sheets of rain fall that the windshield wipers can't keep up with; they just blur the taillights in front of me, turning everything into a Monet wash. I click on the radio. Anything for a distraction.

"*. . . residents of Monterrey, Mexico, were shocked to discover the bodies of four children, ten women, and five men in the main lodge of the eight-million-dollar ranch, founded by cult leader and proclaimed incarnation of Jesus, Alexi Maximus. Maximus, a Russian defector and former janitor, began teaching his brand of 'enlightened' apocalyptic scripture in San Francisco, where he developed a following of wealthy patrons . . .*"

Wonderful. I feel numb, anesthetized. I feel like I'm wearing a Halloween mask over a new, truer face. I drive slowly, huddled over the steering wheel, my foot pressing the brake for each sudden stop prompted by the nervous SUV in front of me—a soccer mom probably, lugging kids and worried about hydroplaning.

I could have hallucinated Scratch just now too. It's a half-hearted thought though, no real muscle behind it.

"*. . . all suicides, except for the children, who were given brownies poisoned with a fatal dose of barbiturates . . .*"

I click to another station. "*The armed robber shot six people in the bank before turning the gun on himself after a ten-hour standoff with police . . .*"

Click. I need to find some jazz. That's always good for a rainy day, but it's spot-on the half hour so it's all news or ads. "*Bad credit? No credit? No problem! Our financial experts . . .*"

Movement catches my eye, and I see a driver in the opposite lane slow down to avoid a clump in the road—clothes, trash, hard to say—but there's something strange about the driver, I note a faint, shadowy aura around him, feel a magnetic pull. He must notice me looking, because he meets my eye, gives a grim nod before continuing past me.

What the . . .

After that, I'm grateful for the sudden starts and stops of the SUV in front of me, because it gives me a chance to closely examine the passengers and drivers in cars, people darting through the rain for this or that business, either bothering with umbrellas or not, diners in well-lit cafés enjoying lattes with their afternoon lunch.

Not often at all, but every once in a while, I'm drawn to someone and find they have that shadow, a dark pallor. A woman standing under the wide eave of a Laundromat, smoking—she sees me but pretends she doesn't, shifts her weight into her other hip, scrunches her eyes into a squint, and stares hard into the gutter. A car double-parks and a man gets out of the passenger side, clutching a folded newspaper over his head. He makes a dash for the 7-Eleven, turns, and watches me pass, strangely intent. A bus passes, glowing with fluorescent light, and an elderly woman at the back sees me and presses her palm against the glass, like a greeting or a warning, I don't know.

It's a way we identify each other, not through our eyes, but with our souls.

Of course, I could just be responding to this thought he's planted in my head, interpreting reality through his lens. In which case, he's a better marketer than I gave him credit for.

I'm so fucking exhausted all of a sudden. But somehow home doesn't seem like the place to go—home is where I found the card, or where the card found me, and what if *he* is lurking nearby, watching, waiting to fuck with me again?

So I drive by the Grand Lake Theatre, past the street I usually turn right on. Maybe I shouldn't ever go home. Drive as far as my tank of gas will take me and live off of my savings—all $15,675 of it—until I can pick up a job somewhere, maybe waiting tables, something low-key, inconspicuous. Disappear.

Leaving is something I do well; it's almost become second nature. Never held a job more than three years, never a boyfriend more than two. I've lived in Los Angeles, New York, Austin, Portland, Denver, Miami. Nothing ever feels quite as good as shaking off a whole life, turning the page on everything, leaving all mistakes, judgments, failures behind. Nobody gets in, not for long. I always tell them it's a career move. What happens to those I leave behind is only an occasional thought, easily drowned out in a cacophony of new experiences. I am now protected by the thickest of thick skins—my parents would be proud. My therapist warned that I've never really unpacked. But unpacking is hard, staying is hard, trusting people is hard.

I trusted Justin, and now look what's happened.

A small part of me blames him for everything.

I almost rear-end the SUV in front of me when it stops hard at a light. But the rain is starting to lift, or at least it's not raining as hard in Piedmont. To my right, I see the cement pillars of the Mountain View Cemetery, its gates open.

The one place where everyone has to finally unpack, stay.

I think of all the lives the people under the ground must have lived, how important it must have seemed to them at the time. And then after, not so much.

Christ, I don't even believe in souls, or hell, or heaven. How can something you don't believe in try to ruin you so completely?

There's a sudden flash of light, bright like a bursting star, coming from a knoll near a pyramid-shaped tomb. I see a tall, thin man standing next to a tripod, a sharp silhouette against the retreating, ominous clouds. Either he's impervious to the rain or just doesn't give a shit—even from three or four hundred yards away, there is something relaxed and confident about him, like a rancher surveying his land. I feel that magnetic pull again, so strong that my car drifts into the right-hand lane, almost of its own accord.

And even though he's so far away, I can tell he sees me. Locks on to my car like it's a lost sheep, newly found.

And waves me over.

This is how I meet Alejandro.

I DRIVE UP THE SERPENTINE ROAD, wheels crunching on gravel, past small rounded tombstones, taller ones adorned with Celtic crosses, rectangular granite monoliths. A weary angel rests his head on his hand. I pass mausoleums that look like small Parthenons or domed miniature churches. A small medieval city planted on a hill with stunning views the dead will never enjoy, and of course I think about the grass, how green it is, and why.

When I reach the pyramid I pull over; a fluttery, nervous feeling builds in my stomach. The tall, thin man is leaning into his tripod, eyes fixed in the viewfinder of a non-digital camera, some kind of antique, boxy monstrosity that must weigh a good fifteen or twenty pounds. Brown, curly hair streaked with gray radiates out from his head like a halo, and he wears distressed black jeans, red cowboy boots, a trim, close-fitting rain jacket.

I get out of the car.

"Stop!" Faintest hint of an accent, Portuguese, Italian, hard to say. And I don't know why, but I do what he says. He turns the camera, points it at me. Behind the lens is a black accordion-like extension that meets a metal rectangle, some kind of large film format, four-by-five maybe.

For a moment I just stand there, frozen, waiting. Rain starts to clump my hair—it drips down my cheeks, beads off my eyelashes. It feels good, the cold water. Why does this stranger look so familiar?

He then holds up the most ridiculous-looking flashbulb. "Perfect. Beautiful. Beautiful. Don't move."

And just like that I'm bound. *Snap.* The light blinds me and I blink furiously, trying to see through the glowing orbs that linger. But some kind of magic spell is broken and now I can move again, which I do, cautiously approaching him.

It's when he smiles that I realize where I've seen him before—for years, Sumpter courted the notable portrait photographer Alejandro Xavier for an ad campaign, but he had always been a few hundred thousand dollars out of our price range, and these days exists on a different planet altogether. There was a profile of him recently in the *San Francisco Chronicle*, an art show and auction where he netted a million dollars for one portrait alone, *Girl in Shadow, Girl in Light*, and a documentary about his life—his spectacular rise from Rio de Janeiro street orphan to central California strawberry picker to world-renowned photographer—won a major award in Cannes.

"Welcome," he says, extending a hand. *Welcome*, not *hello*, not an introduction. Maybe he realizes none is needed.

I take his hand. His fingers are slender, elegant, like a pianist's, and his palm is cool and dry. Behind him is the city, the gray waters of the bay, and beyond that San Francisco cloaked in fog.

The rain lightens. In Lowell, we'd look out at rain like this, say *it's spitting*. Maybe that's what's happening now. *God is spitting on me.* If I believed in such a thing as God.

"Welcome to what?" I ask.

He grins, lets go of my hand, raises his arms to the sky in a way that's manic, ecstatic, and turns like everything in his purview is his to share.

"To the damned my dear. To the tribe of dead souls."

Damned. Souls. Tribe. It's a cold, brutal shock, hearing Scratch's words regurgitated through another person, and a celebrity at that. I take a step back. "I'm sorry . . . what?"

"Your darkness," he says. He seems absurdly happy, in a Zen-like way. "We all share it." Now he looks at me quizzically, curious. "Do you even know what I'm talking about?"

My heart races. Deep down, even though I'm fighting this, I do know.

But I don't want to.

His light, burnished skin—a strange shade, and even now that a sliver of sun peeks out from the clouds, it isn't getting lighter. The whites of his eyes slightly tinged with gray. The grass is sparkling with raindrops, the pale marble of the pyramid mausoleum glistens, begins to shine, but he's still slightly in silhouette, in shadow.

I hold out my own arm, roll up the sleeve of my coat. Yes, that same dark tinge clings to me.

I swallow hard, fight back tears. *Damned?* He said *damned.*

No. It just can't be.

I want to sink onto the ground. I want the earth to swallow me, cover me over with a soft layer of fine grass.

"He was just a guy in a bar," I say, my voice breaking. "He was just a guy I met in a bar." If I say it often enough, maybe it'll be true. "I was drunk. I didn't know what I was doing, saying. It's not fair."

"Oh, my dear girl," says Alejandro, and he steps forward, folds me into an embrace. "You know the world we're working with. When has fair ever come into play?" he says softly, like he's trying to soothe a child.

My arms are stiff at my sides. He smells like cigarettes and strong coffee. My shoulders shake.

He leans in and whispers in my ear. "It's not as bad as all that. Or . . . well it is . . . but you don't have to think about it, not every day. And there's wonder in it too. Magic. You'll see."

My cell phone finally rings, and I know who it is, even without looking.

Some days fate just fucks you over completely.

Justin.

I PRESS *ANSWER*. Is it really still Saturday? Did I really just leave the bar sometime in the early hours of the morning? Everything has gone several stages past surreal, and I am now in some new realm where it wouldn't surprise me to see a hailstorm of frogs drop from the sky, or the blue waters of the bay turn bloodred, or see the dead pry themselves up out of the softened ground, heeding the call of some apocalyptic horn.

"Hi there," I say. My bones ache; I am so tired. So very, very tired.

"Hey," says Justin. "Did you try calling me earlier?"

Did I? Oh, right, the bathroom stall. A decade ago. "You didn't pick up."

It's strange, this talking. How easy it is to put on a mask, make believe. *Let's make believe we're doctors; let's make believe we're movie actresses; let's make believe we live on the moon.* Childhood, the most forgiving state of consciousness. *Let's make believe I didn't sell my soul last night.*

"Your voice sounds strange."

"Does it?"

Alejandro sets up his tripod just out of earshot, giving me some privacy. He pulls out a thermos, pours something hot and steaming into it.

"Where are you?" asks Justin.

I laugh before I stop myself.

"Why, what's so funny?"

"Nothing, just . . ." Just I'm standing in a cemetery, just you're in a strange city having an affair with a strange woman, just I might be condemned to hell. "I'm not feeling like myself today."

Intake of his breath on the line. *I shouldn't have said that.* The last time I said that, I was in a low moment. I hadn't even realized I'd scraped my thigh with a fork prong, but he'd brought up the m-word, *marriage.* It wasn't a deep wound—just the slightest beading of blood, really more of a scratch, ha-ha—but Justin got scared, threatened to call the therapist I'd said I'd been seeing but had bailed out on months before. He still writes me pity scripts though. Ambien 10 mg, once daily as needed, which is daily. A side of Xanax as needed, which is also daily. Probably charges my insurance company for our nonexistent visits, which suits me just fine.

"How are you?" I ask, to change the subject.

An odd pause. "We need to talk."

I almost have to cover my mouth; everything is so giddy, so funny, but not. "We are talking."

"In person."

So, this is where he dumps me. A restaurant? Should I suggest Make Westing and perfect the circle of disaster? I feel gypped, preempted—if he's made up his mind to leave me for Pink Coat, there's not much point to my invisible ghost-twin plan. Which means I sold my soul for nothing and made a motherfucker of a bad deal.

It disturbs me, the things I'm starting to think.

"I'm on a flight this afternoon," he says. "I could be at your place by six."

Anything could happen by six. The world could explode, shatter into a hundred thousand million pieces, or there could be a nuclear strike, or we could get forty days and forty nights of rain. For the first time, a flood makes sense to me. I can see where a god would want to wash us all away.

"Sure," I say. I never say *sure*.

"Okay." Justin sounds relieved, like he was planning on this being harder somehow. "Are you okay? Did you sleep?"

Alejandro holds his hand over his eyes. The sun now casts long, dark shadows. Down the hill, I see New Agey woman get out of a beat-up Volkswagen, carrying a pad of paper and some kind of rolled cloth.

"Never better." That could be a tongue twister, or a curse, *never better, never better, never better*.

"Okay. I'll see you soon." There's a foreign ache in Justin's voice, like he's as weary as I am. "I love you."

Words. More hollow, empty words. Apparently we're to see the farce until the end, until he breaks it to me gently: *It's not you, it's me.*

"I love you too."

"'Bye." *Click* goes the phone. It feels heavy in my hand, a dead thing. I watch the woman down the hill wipe one of the tombstones dry with the sleeve of her coat, then she pulls a sheet of paper from her pad, presses it against the etching, and starts to rub something across it. Charcoal. Apparently the cemetery is a draw for all kinds of artists.

"What did you say your name was?" Alejandro takes a long sip from his thermos mug.

"I didn't." *Don't talk to strangers.* Four words that just might have saved me, but now there's nothing left to save. "Fiona. Fiona Dunn."

"Come here," he says, beckoning toward the viewfinder. "Come and see Fiona Dunn."

IT'S COMFORTING to see the world framed in, limited to a box. Contained. The clouds cast stark shadows across some of the tombstones, mottling the wet, hilly landscape with light and dark. But the white of the stones glow, sparkle in the afternoon sun. It all feels cleaned, purified, reborn. A strange counterpoint to the day's events so far.

"Sublime, no?" Alejandro asks.

Sublime, yes.

"Take the picture."

I have no idea where the button is. I use my phone as a camera, everyone does these days, so I can't imagine the purpose of lugging something this boxy and weighty around. Like scuba diving in one of those old suits with astronaut helmets.

"Here," he says, pointing to a thin cable. "There's a button at the end. It will open the shutter, let the light in."

I take the cable in my hand, press the stainless-steel button—it feels like I'm working an IV. There's an actual, soft click.

"Aren't you worried about the rain ruining your camera?"

"This? This is a Linhof Technika. It's a brick shit house. Virtually indestructible."

I look at him. "And it takes good pictures?"

Alejandro laughs. "The camera is irrelevant. I could use an old Polaroid and still capture images that would make Ansel Adams weep. But I am old-fashioned. Sometimes I like to see how far I can perfect perfection. What you just took, it will be like his *Moonrise*. But you will not get the credit, of course."

This actually teases a small smile out of me. "Of course."

He looks at me, somewhat more seriously now. "This is what I traded for. My career. My success."

I know what he wants to ask next, but I don't take the bait. *What did you trade for?* I showed you mine, you show me yours.

He motions me to step away, then he opens something on the back of the camera and nods toward a dark blue duffel bag on the ground about a foot away. "Bring me that film-changing bag, will you? And that smaller leather one?"

I do. He takes a square, flat film plate from the camera, hands it to me without another word, squats down to the wet ground, and unzips one side of the duffel bag. Then he slips his arms into two attached sleeves. The part of me that never turns off immediately starts making associations for a new Sumpter, Inc. bag, the Technika, expandable from a simple twelve-foot duffel to five feet long, depending on how many compartments you unzip. And it has to be waterproof, like this one seems to be.

"Inside the leather one, you'll find a yellow Kodak box."

"Kodak still makes film?"

"For us large-format purists, yes. And I'll take the film plate back."

I hand him the box of film and then, with remarkable dexterity, he zips the bag shut, changes the film inside it.

"It took me a good month to get the hang of this," he says. "I was so disappointed the first time I saw my results in the darkroom. All overexposed, parts of the image completely blackened. I would have thrown the negatives in the trash, but then I wanted to see what would happen. If *he* would honor his part of the deal. You know? Make even my failures grand successes."

I remember then, a bit of the *Chronicle* article. Alejandro's first show, which astonished the art world. *Overexposed.*

"You got what you wanted then."

"No, I would not go that far." He pauses for a moment. I can almost hear the woman down the hill rubbing charcoal on her paper. It's a soothing, white-noise sound.

"I got what I asked for," Alejandro continues. "Exactly that, and nothing more. What I wanted, in my heart, was revenge. Revenge takes you on a twisted journey, until the end has no meaning anymore, until everything tastes like ash. The truth is . . . I hate photography. Absolutely hate it. I mean, everything about it—the people who are drawn to it, like flies to shit, the stink of chemicals, the flattening of the world into a sheet of paper. But the materialism . . . well, I have to admit I enjoy those benefits. Once you're poor, and then you're rich, you'd rather die than be poor again."

There had been a photo in the *Chronicle* too, of his lovely restored five-bedroom Victorian in Noe Valley. I remember because we clipped the picture and added it to our vision board for the Istanbul's demographic.

"But why ask to be good at something you hate?"

"Because that was part of the retribution. I have never felt so righteous as when I was planning my revenge. I miss being that naive."

He unzips the bag, pulls out the film plate, inserts it back into the camera. "When I was sleeping on the streets, a man came, a Western man."

"Scratch?" I ask tentatively.

He chuckles softly. "He hasn't used that name in a long time."

"Why, you don't call him that?"

"Oh he has many names. Lucifer, Iblis, the Son of the Morning, Satan, Melek Taus, Mara, Kölski, Angra Mainyu, der Leibhaftige, Diabolus," he says, adjusting the tripod. "And he takes many forms. Whatever he thinks will work best— woman, man, child. Stranger, friend, lover."

An unnerving thought strikes me. "So he can look like anyone. Even you."

Alejandro smiles. "Do you see my face?"

Of course I can, even the fine lines edging his gray-blue eyes. But Scratch? No.

As if he can see the realization hit, Alejandro adds, "No one sees the face of the devil. We would go mad, apparently. But a good way to know if the person you are speaking to is him."

He looks off into the horizon line, something weary in his expression, and I sense there is more, much more to this story. But he continues with the other.

"It was another kind of devil that came to me as a child," he says. "A man with a camera. For a few days, he took photos of all of us—how we lived, how we stole, how we sold cocaine in the favelas. He was an artist, he said. It was for a famous American magazine, he said. He gave us ice cream, Belém cakes, *sonhos*. And then he showed me an American hundred-dollar bill. I followed him back to the hotel room where he was staying . . . and there he took different kinds of pictures."

There is no reason to ask what kind. It's in his face, a small death there.

"Before she died, my grandmother, who was full Mayan, warned me of photographs. How they could steal your soul, trap them in celluloid. Mine was long gone before I ever met our mutual friend."

Oddly there is not even the slightest trace of bitterness as he says this, or a twinge of pain. It's like he's telling me a story about someone else, about something that has nothing to do with him directly. There was once a woman at work like this;

she'd been diagnosed with lung cancer, given three to six months to live. She was ashen-faced at first, hostile, a broken glass you were afraid to speak to. But then, toward the end, she came back for one last visit, and she was preternaturally calm, kind almost. Like we were the ones suffering, not her.

"I met the devil in Monterey. There was a library in town with a computer, and after months of searching I'd found the American man with the American hundred-dollar bill. Toby Whitfield. A photojournalist in the seventies. He tried and failed to become a fine-art photographer and moved into real estate photography instead. So when I made my trade, I knew what I wanted. The poor orphan would achieve the heights Whitfield aspired to, and then I would reveal myself to him, degrade him, taunt him with my success. *Ruin* him, if there was anything left to ruin. I thought there would be some satisfaction in that. I had damning evidence that I was planning to confront him with before calling the authorities. Then I hired him to come shoot my impeccable house, so he could see the life that would never be his, make his failure visceral. But when the moment came, when he arrived in his beat-up van, with his battered camera, I found no satisfaction. I saw he was a small man, an old man, a broken man. His demons had already claimed him long ago. I didn't even tell him who I was."

There is no bitterness when he says this either.

"So it was all for nothing," I say.

"Not for nothing, no." Alejandro aims his camera at the valley below us, the city. "I have an amazing life, and who knows . . . perhaps I would have committed some sin, an atrocity that would have damned me anyway. As you can imagine, I parted ways with the church long ago. When the favor finally gets called in, yes, I will have a hard moment, and I am not looking forward to death or where I'm going after . . . but why think of that now when there are so many other more pleasant things to occupy me?"

"Compartmentalize," I say quietly. Justin has accused me of doing this too well on more than one occasion, but right now it's all that's keeping me from running from the cemetery, screaming.

"Exactly. I have found that this is what the rich do—enjoy themselves without thinking about what, or whom, it costs."

The cemetery smells of sweet, wet earth, the vaporous release of something intangible. Alejandro looks through the viewfinder, then makes another adjustment to the camera. "Just so you know, there is a small group of us, dead souls. We meet once a month at the New Parish. It helps to not feel so alone."

"That's the bar converted from the old church?"

"Yes. It is written in the book that Scratch abhors churches, even if they've been desanctified. Too painful, like visiting the house of an ex."

"What book?"

"The book of dead souls. Really more of a collection of notes, gathered from those who have gone before us. I will let you borrow my copy until you make your own. It may help."

I notice that small word, *may*. Woefully inadequate. And then, that turn of phrase, *those who have gone before us*.

How many? I wonder.

"Did he give you a card?"

Alejandro nods. "He gives us all one." He thinks a moment, as if he's wondering how much more I can take, the state of me. Then he makes his decision, pulls his wallet out from his back pocket. It's slim, black, leather. And hands me the card.

That same rich, strange texture. The same pyrography.

DATE: *Sunday, November 13*
SOUL: *Alejandro Xavier*
TIME: *12:15 p.m.*
FAVOR:

My hands feel deadened, numb. "Favor is blank, too."

"Oh yes. It's better if it is. It is said that when he calls in the favor, the words there will appear. And then . . . you really have no choice."

The deadened feeling rises from my hands, through my arms, to my throat. So. This is it then. What I've really indentured myself to. "What kinds of favors?"

Alejandro quietly pockets the card back in his wallet. "Why, the worst kinds, of course."

"But I flushed my card down the toilet."

A kindly smile, a shade on the side of patronizing. "It is not that easy to rid yourself of it. It will find you again," he says. "It has been nearly two decades since I got my card and I have never been able to lose or destroy it. Do you want to take another?"

At first I don't know what he means, but then he holds out the camera cable to me, like an adult offering candy to a child after some particularly bad news. Still, I take him up on it, look through the viewfinder. Taking pictures is as good a diversion as any.

I gather the woman with her tombstone rubbings into the frame. It's strange how, through the viewfinder of a camera, you can look at someone as long as you want, and they'll never know it, or suspect. It makes me feel oddly powerful, to be able to invade someone else's private space this way, like peeping through a window. And in the background, the city. Beautiful. The fog has lifted, and the Transamerica Pyramid rises dead center.

A gust of wind curls around my feet.

"Think, Fiona," Alejandro whispers. "Think of all the souls we are stealing."

CHAPTER FIVE

I **HOLD ALEJANDRO'S BOOK OF DEAD SOULS** open in one hand as I ride the small elevator back up to my apartment, in a nervy kind of mood. Shaky, giddy with fear, but also struck with the odd excitement that I used to get in my broke days, when I'd shoplift a can of tuna for dinner, a box of crackers, slide them under my thick coat.

I'm already obsessed with what's here. The whole Justin thing seems smaller, far away. Alejandro was right—it's not a book so much as a thick collection of notes, photocopied and then bound with a plastic spiral. Some of the typeset is inkjet printer, some dot matrix; there are five pages that look to be the same typewriter (the *j* always hits half a line above the other letters); there're even copies of medieval pages and scraps of what looks like cloth or papyrus. Different people have made notes in the margins, a wide variety of hands. Loopy script, compressed, tight handwriting, slanted cursive, and brief, almost stenographic bursts. Here and there sentences are underlined or highlighted, words circled. *Cannot commit suicide until after the favor has been completed—4/18/88. —A.W.* Dates, tons of dates, *11/1/53, 6/18/74, 2/6/1902, 12/19/45.*

Drinking blessed water is no protection—7/3/88. What about free will?—12/6/76 —S.B. S.B. had a lot to say; those initials are scattered everywhere.

It's a catalog of insight that should not be viewed as fact, Alejandro had said. It's simply a collection of unverified thoughts, opinions, opinions on top of thoughts. *Nothing,* he'd told me, *is ever thrown away or reordered.*

Which makes it read like an elevator full of people with Tourette's syndrome, no thread or cohesion. Debates scattered across time, parts crossed out, especially the first few that lists crimes believed to have been favors called in. A conspiracy theorist's dream come true.

Holocaust/Hitler
Khmer Rouge
Charles Manson
228 Incident
~~Jeffrey Dahmer~~ (classic psychopath), S.B.
Spanish Inquisition. Torquemada??? S.B.
Hiroshima
Columbine
The Holodomor

Then there's the list of contributors at the end. *The ones who have gone before*, as Alejandro said. The known debtors, the favors called in, of which there is no doubt.

You should give yourself some time before you look at this.
But I can't resist.
Adele Cameron, sold 7/18/67. Buried her three children alive, then poured concrete and made a patio over their bodies.

Died of natural causes, 2007. Bodies discovered when new owners installed a pool.

James and Frank Aindrea, identical twins, sold 8/14/85. Made a killing in the stock market. Dropped bowling balls from the balcony of their Chicago Gold Coast penthouse in 1994 onto the people and traffic passing by, then got into a fist-fight that ended with James throwing Frank over the railing. Five people, including a four-year-old child, died. James spent the rest of his life in prison, and what was left of Frank was mostly washed away with a fire hose.

The elevator clicks past the second floor, the third. There's always that questionable jolt when it reaches the fourth, like something's wrong with the gears, worn past comfort.

Volodya Uros, sold 6/3/72. Defected from Russia, lived an unobtrusive, modest life in Missouri until one Halloween, in 2001, when he locked the exit doors of the Fuze Box nightclub and detonated a bomb, having earlier soaked the basement in gasoline. One hundred and twelve people died. Uros was caught trying to escape over the Mexican border and was eventually executed in his home state. And he had a son, noted as Alexi Uros, who sold his own soul in 2002. I wonder if there's some kind of genetic disposition for selling one's soul, or if Scratch locks in on our loved ones to further torment us.

I skim through the rest of the book, looking to see if Volodya Uros added pages and find one in badly written English, initialed V.U. *I have sold my soul to devil, but give my heart to God. I go to St. Ignacio two times each day, I make rosary three times, I give one third my salary to Sisters of Charity. There will be forgiveness, this I know. John 5:29—And shall come forth; they that have done good, unto the resurrection of life; and they that have done evil, unto the resurrection of dam-nation. 10/25/01*

Apparently there is no salvation from the usual places, not for the likes of us.

But then, I've never been a fan of the usual places. For a brief period in middle school I became enamored with faith, incentivized by a new addition to class, a girl with neat, brown-bag lunches and pressed cotton shirts. A Catholic from some-where in the Midwest with a forgettable name, she was never without a gold cross on a chain—it popped up and out of her shirt when we jumped rope. I lifted a near identical one from Sacred Heart Collectibles, the contradiction lost on me, but I was thinking maybe the whole problem with my life was my atheistic parents. Her life was so much simpler. Better.

For weeks I wore the cross, not even taking it off in the shower, but like the trainable sea monkeys that came in a box for $1.25, it offered nothing for me but disappointment. My clothes still smelled like lighter fluid, as my parents never re-membered to empty their pockets before dumping clothes into the washing machine. Also mildew, as they never remembered to put wet clothes in the dryer. No magical paper-bag lunches appeared. I was still stuck with whatever I could scavenge from the kitchen—the heel of a loaf of Wonder Bread smeared with ketchup, the crumbled dust of Cheerios from the bottom of the box mixed with peanut butter. Even the gold in the cross wasn't real, just a burnished bronze that left a green circle on my neck. Disgusted, I finally threw it in the trash. That alone was blas-phemy, sure.

But one good thing came out of it—an interest in market-ing. Because it struck me that there were two distinct kinds of people—those who were Oz the Great and Powerful behind the curtain, creating a better illusion of life, a world where you could conjure sea people with tap water, where a purported savior was actually loving and watching over you every day. And then there were the dupes who believed Oz really was a wizard and forked their money over for brine shrimp eggs and religious trinkets.

What does that make *me* though? Getting drunk and selling my soul. *Am I the dupe, then?*

For the first time, the horror of the entire situation is tinged with something else, a certain pissy edge that Justin calls my Yankee intuition, a sixth sense that itches when I think I paid two dollars more for a coffee grinder than it would have cost at another store, or the tip is already slyly calculated in the restaurant tab. The itch is telling me that while the first rule of marketing is desire, the second is misdirection, and nothing deceives people so easily as presenting an absolute. *Offer ends Thursday!* just means you'll be paying retail until the next sale comes up in a month.

What if this book of dead souls is just a log of what happened to people who didn't know any better? Maybe it's not a question of getting out of the contract, but renegotiation. Scratch said he was in sales, a trader, and I *know* those people, the oily film of them. The only thing they love better than a score is a bigger one, and the possibility of five birds in the bush versus the one in the hand is a no-brainer.

What if I just offer Scratch a sweeter deal than my soul? Contracts are adjusted every day—I do it myself.

There's another jolt when the elevator reaches the fifth floor, accompanied by a waning *ding* that also sounds like it's on its last legs. I have to unlatch the inner accordion gate before I can undo the bolt of the wooden door, which opens out into the hall. Taped on the wall in front of me is a paper sign. *DON'T FORGET TO SHUT THE GATE.* The elevator seemed charming when I was looking at the place, but if someone forgets to shut the gate, the thing doesn't work at all, which means taking five flights of stairs until the super finds which floor it's open on.

I tuck the book under my arm, walk down the hallway, searching for keys in my purse. I want to call Alejandro—so many questions burn. But Alejandro specifically said, *Taking in too much at once is never a good thing.* Although just because Alejandro knows more than I do doesn't mean I should trust him in all things.

No, at the moment there is no one, and nothing, I can trust. Not an unfamiliar place, at least for me.

I put the antique key in the antique lock—as usual it takes a good minute to catch. My plan is to pop a quarter Ambien, catch a good nap before I have to face Justin and our "talk." Maybe add a half Xanax too and a glass of wine . . . or make that half a glass. Don't want to inadvertently pull a Monroe, although if the book of dead souls is right, I couldn't kill myself anyway.

But when I step into my apartment, there he is, gaunt, weary, and hauntingly lovely, sitting on my couch. Justin.

And next to him, Pink Coat. They're locked in a tight, and very emotional, embrace.

THE APARTMENT should be on fire—there's no way I should feel this thunderous, murderous rage and it *not* be on fire, bolts of lightning sparking from my eyes before I plunge daggers into their faithless, corrupt hearts, but instead a blend of shock and that other Yankee trait, terminal politeness, takes over. They break apart. Justin awkwardly stands.

You goddamn cheating son of a bitch rises in the back of my throat, but I choke it back down, where it rustles menacingly in my stomach. I quietly shut the door behind me, taking my time to put my keys back in my purse, hands trembling, almost dropping them.

They exchange an intimate look. Two against one.

"I let us in," Justin says. When he's really nervous, he always states the obvious, a habitual tic that makes me ache.

Gone. It's always the strange things you miss when you lose someone you love—the way they used a knife left-handed; their favorite brand of toothpaste, which you eventually got used to; the freckles on their back that they're not aware of, shaped like a constellation. Justin is standing in the middle of my living room, but the Justin I knew, or thought I knew, is gone, and already I miss him.

Pink Coat rudely interrupts and stands too. The hairs at the back of my neck bristle. And then, and *then* she actually has the gall to take a few steps toward me and extend a hand, like I'm holding some kind of work soirée and they inadvertently dropped in early.

"Hi. I'm Sarah," she says.

"Sarah," I repeat, like there are dead things in my mouth. Pink Coat now has a name, and I immediately hate it. I take her hand though, reluctantly, and she gives it a clammy squeeze.

Justin swallows hard. Apparently things aren't going well here.

"God, I've heard *so* much about you," continues Sarah blithely, dropping my hand, looking dangerously like a hug might be next.

How could he dump me for someone so pedestrian? Professionally whitened, even teeth, a slight roll of muffin top over her low-rise jeans, pink turtleneck sweater, and a strand of white pearls that match the teeth. Thick mascara. Pink lip gloss.

"I hope you don't mind me 'tagging' along with Justin," she continues, "but he could really use the extra support right now."

Goddamn, the woman just actually made quote marks with her fingers. And then she gives Justin a prompting, *Let's move this along,* look. History, and lots of it, between them. I see she's left an umbrella by the door, a foreign invader leaving watermarks on the floor. I get a quick visual of stabbing her through the eye with it.

"I know I should have told you earlier," says Justin. "But . . . I didn't know how you'd take it. The news." His arms dangle uselessly by his sides, and he looks so lost, so forlorn that a part of me—

"That's my brother for you. He's *never* been good at asking for help," adds Sarah softly.

The words drop like marbles on the floor. My stomach flips.

My.

Brother.

"So we made a deal when he was eight . . ."

My brother my brother my brother my brother my brother . . .

". . . if he ever ran into trouble, real trouble, I'd drop everything and come running."

Oh dear sweet Jesus, Pink Coat is his sister. I want to cry, I want to scream, I want to claw my eyes out.

"So I'm just going to come right to the point and say it for him," continues Sarah. "Justin has pancreatic cancer. It's spread to his liver. Fiona, it's . . . it's not good."

My brother. The embrace. A *sisterly*, tight embrace; a supportive, sisterly visit . . . *Oh my God oh my God oh my God* . . .

The light touch on his arm before he got into the cab . . .

Brother, her brother . . . he'd mentioned her, sure, but not blond, I hadn't pictured her blond, in fact the photo of their family—*God*, I hadn't really looked, I vaguely remember him pointing to the pictures, names instantly forgotten. I have that tendency with other people's normal families, I blur the particulars to preclude a series of emotions I am tired of: anger, jealousy, longing, more anger, self-pity. A great, dark vacuum of what should have been.

The tinny sound to his voice, the hair, oh dear God, *the hair* . . .

"Your hair," I whisper.

Justin runs a hand almost sheepishly over his scalp. "Wanted to get a head start. Or used to it. Before . . ." His eyes fall to the floor, then up at me, then back to the floor again. Guilty, *he* feels guilty, but not, of course, for the reasons I thought.

I still haven't said anything adequate to the situation, but I can't feel my mouth or my head or my body. My will to do anything has turned to vapor. Sarah—helpful, Pink-Coat Sarah—gently takes me by the elbow, leads me to the couch, where I sink onto the cushion.

Despair doesn't quite touch what I'm feeling right now. *Wretched* is closer.

Sarah sits next to me, grips my arm, all mother hen. "He thought you might react like this. I hope you don't mind, but he told me a bit about you. Your parents."

Oh God, she's still trying to help me. I suppress a very inappropriate burst of laughter, but there is no help for me. I'm beyond help, beyond reach.

I close my eyes for a moment. Rewind the hours, to the bit just after I stepped out into the rain, the glass entry door of the apartment building clicking shut behind me. No, the whole thing needs a rewrite—there's no emotional payoff here. If I were in the editing bay for a Sumpter, Inc. commercial, we'd re-cast too, unless the ending had some kind of romantic/comedic punch line, because no one wants to identify with a neurotic, self-centered, and jealous protagonist. If I were going to shoot this thing, the main character, WOMAN OF TODAY, wouldn't be the suspicious girlfriend stereotype; she would be empowered, confident, able to navigate challenges. Instead of walking barefoot in the rain, she'd have flagged a cab, talked the endearing, supportive minority EXTRA into giving her a free ride.

I'm locked out of my apartment and someone I love is in trouble.

A meta piece of cornball that, but because it's self-aware, it hits as postmodern irony while still stirring the emotional tropes. The cabbie would drop her off, wave away her attempt to pay, and instead of darting to the entry of the apartment building across the street to spy, huddled and shivering—what was that word Scratch used? *Pathetic.* No, instead, she'd have walked over to Justin, taken him firmly by both hands.

What's wrong?

Of course what's wrong couldn't be pancreatic cancer, too depressing for thirty seconds; no it'd have to be something travel-related, with an exotic destination.

There's a malaria outbreak in Niger.

Yes, Justin's a member of Doctors Without Borders, and Pink Coat will be in pink scrubs, cast as an accompanying nurse.

I'm coming with you.

You can't. You're not even packed.

Give me five minutes, I will be.

And then she pulls a small, round Sumpter Omni disc out of her purse, unzips it so that it transforms into a full-size duffel bag. *I'll pick up what I need at the airport.*

SUMPTER. Ready for anything. An American original.

END SCENE.

For a beautiful, intangible few seconds, I am so good at my craft that I almost believe it.

A cool hand picks up one of mine. Thin, piano fingers. Justin's. "Are you okay?"

Am I? No. I open my eyes. Justin sits on the coffee table, hand gripping mine. There are dark circles under his eyes—he hasn't been sleeping either. And it really, truly, breaks my heart that in this moment, he is taking care of me instead of the other way around.

"I just didn't want to tell you until I knew for sure," he says. "Sarah insisted I get a second opinion."

A memory floats down, the early days, when Justin and I were still getting to know each other. Cutting lettuce for salad in the kitchen.

What's your dad do?

Oh, he's an oncologist. Carrot shavings on the floor, a bottle of cabernet sauvignon on the porcelain-tiled counter, breathing. I was happy, happier than I'll ever be again, and didn't know it.

Where does he live?

Seattle.

Finally Sarah cracks—tears bead her eyes. "Bathroom?" she asks.

I nod behind me. "Through the bedroom."

She leaves. Justin and I just sit there, frozen. The floorboard heater crackles and snaps.

"So what's . . ." I begin, then stop. Trying to form the next few words is impossible, I feel submerged somehow, drowning, and the surface of the water is so very, very far away.

Justin holds my hand a bit tighter. "There's nothing *to* do. When the tumor grows, I'll probably get the surgery, do a little chemo, which will help . . . prolong things, a bit. Not much."

"How long?"

"A year . . . maybe."

I collapse into myself then with deep, shaking sobs—I can't help it. Justin moves next to me on the couch, wraps his arms around me, and I press my face into his chest. Sometimes in my dreams, I crawl into his heart like some kind of magic sprite—a sign, my therapist said, of my inherent distrust and aversion to the world. *You can escape everything but yourself,* he'd said.

"It'll all be okay, I promise," says Justin. He strokes my hair, the way it always soothes me. Used to soothe me.

"It's *not.*"

"I've thought things through. I've made you the beneficiary of my life insurance policy . . ."

I sit up. "*Stop*. Just stop it, Justin, you're not—"

"It's half a million dollars. And my father was going to leave me his condo in San Francisco in his will, but he said you can have it."

"Justin, we are not having this discussion, I don't—"

"I need to do this Fiona." Now his eyes bead with tears. "I need to feel like you're going to have . . . something after I'm gone. No one's ever given you anything. Frankly, you've had a pretty shitty life. Let me do this for you." He caresses my cheek. "Let me do this for the girl I love."

It burns, that word *love*. If I'd just trusted him I never would have ended up in the bar, would've never met Scratch, wouldn't have been so emotionally vulnerable, desperate. Easy pickings for any predator. No, this circle of hell I'm in was partly my creation. I opened the door. I let Scratch in. And then the worst moment of my life strikes, a thought that shatters me to my very core, almost makes me crack into a hundred thousand pieces. *I could have saved Justin. If I'd known, I could have sold my soul and saved his life.*

But the world doesn't go up in flames. I hear the rumble of traffic outside—people on their mysterious, self-absorbed, private journeys, no idea what's in store for them. Hoping it gets better, whatever *it* is.

And now I know what hell really is. The realization that no matter what personal tragedy befalls you, the mechanism that winds the clock of reality just ticks along, barely marking your time here and certainly not caring. All of it, *all of it*, completely, and utterly, pointless.

There's a polite cough. Justin and I sit up straighter, wipe our eyes with the back of our hands almost simultaneously. Sarah, helpful sister Sarah, enters the room, tentative as a cat.

"Um . . . Fiona?"

I turn to her and what I see in her hand is the second worst moment of my life.

She holds a business card between her thumb and middle finger, as far away from her as possible, like it's contaminated, like it's a used tissue that could bear typhoid. Water drips from the card onto the floor.

"I found this uh . . . floating in your toilet."

She takes a step closer to offer it to me, restore it to its rightful owner. Ever so helpful, that Sarah, ever so considerate. But I know what it is, can tell by the grain of the card, and that telltale waft of sulfur.

It's what's in store for me.

1 YEAR, 2 MONTHS LATER

CHAPTER SIX

THERE'S A NICE SNAP to the December air, twilight softening the edges of the city. It's good to be walking; it's good to get out of the apartment, the smells of the apartment, to take a break from Justin's day-to-day erasure. He likes his caregiver Opal— no one can't like Opal—always friendly but in an unobtrusive way, a wisp of a woman in her late thirties, who, it's easy to tell, holds an unknown sorrow. She's expensive too, but now there's money, plenty of it. It's remarkable what one can learn while invisible. Passwords to my coworkers' e-mail accounts, gossip splayed out in front of me, *about* me, the closed-door meetings where the real power moves, so that I'm always three steps ahead, maybe five. *It's uncanny*, they say, *she did it again*, they say. Invisibility has pushed my five-figure salary to six.

Your talent, Alejandro once said, *is extremely rare*. I got a twofer, meaning I can be invisible and corporeal, or invisible and non-corporeal, a ghost passing through walls or instantly transporting to a different location, although clothes don't come with me in either instance. A major nuisance. It's been hardly worth bothering with at all since the end of summer, just too damn cold, and by now the novelty has worn off—I don't throw up as much but still occasionally get nauseous—and have come to realize ignorance to a certain extent *is* bliss. You're better off thinking your subordinates appreciate the employment opportunity you gave them, that your coworkers aren't gaming to make you look bad, that your name has never made a layoff list.

That the man you love has an engagement ring, which he takes out occasionally from its resting place in a sock at the back of his underwear drawer, turning it over in his hands, rueful and sad.

Tonight our hospice godsend is making Justin pancakes for dinner, one of the few things he can still stomach, although just the act of eating wears him out for the night. He'll probably go to sleep while she reads out loud to him. They're on a murder/mystery kick, halfway through John Grisham's *The Firm*, surprising because Justin never read when he was well, had no time for it, no patience. One of the strange gifts that cancer brings—time. I don't read to him though, because I can't help but wonder whether he'll live long enough to reach the end.

Everything has become that hourglass, an unanswerable question. Like the bags of ice I buy because it's easier on his stomach, sucking cubes instead of drinking a whole glass of water. Will there be a morning, after he's gone, when I'm pouring the rest of the cubes into the sink to let them melt, disappear? When I carry a bowl of chicken broth, letting the crackers get good and soggy so they're easier to digest, I wonder: *Will this be the last time I make it for him?*

His last his last his last. Anything and everything could be his last. He might not even be alive by the time I get back. My stomach clenches at the thought. Although I'm told I should be thankful—the doctors are amazed he's lasted this long. Surgery proved useless, maybe even incited the cancer to be more aggressive, and now the tumor has pushed out his stomach so that he looks eight months pregnant. They eye it with something that makes me uneasy, trying to hold back how eager they are to cut into him, take it out, write it up in a journal somewhere. Maybe there's a prize among doctors, like fishermen who catch the biggest tuna, get their photos taken with its massive bulk. Will there be a Facebook posting with Dr. Anderson, holding a growth the size of a newborn in his bloody hands, a smile plastered on his face, *8 lbs.!*

Nothing would surprise me, not now.

I pass an Italian goods store, Antonini's. Their storefront window is adorned with pine boughs, small glowing lights, different sizes of Panettone on display, an espresso machine—a La Pavoni by the looks of it. But why the pine boughs?

Oh right, Christmas. In years past, I'd ditch the city, hole up in a cabin deep in the heart of Mendocino until it was over and the garbage trucks picked up the Christmas trees left at the curb with the recycling. I'd joke I was having a "me-cation." I fooled everyone but Justin. He never pressed me.

I pass by Launderland, where Opal takes the soiled comforters because the laundry machines in the basement of the apartment complex are too small. *Single-women washers*, Justin used to say. He hadn't wanted to move in with me, tried for as long as he could to hold out on his own—*I'm not going to be a burden*—but when he passed out and didn't tell anyone for a day, Sarah became immediately useful. She threatened to make him a ward of the state, at which point he caved. It was an unspoken known that when he arrived in my apartment, boxes brought by movers like they were the offerings of the Three Wise Men, that he would never live anywhere else again, except, maybe, the hospital.

"Spare a quarter?"

I look down, and there's a homeless man with a cardboard sign, *PLEAse help, God BLEss*. Older than anyone should be on the streets, with a white grizzled beard and knees poking out of threadbare pants.

I stop, reach into my purse for one of my folded fives, and don't find any. Can't remember the last time I gave one away. When did I stop keeping them? It gives me a prickle of unease, bad juju, like I might somehow hasten Justin's bad end, although I should be beyond superstition at this point. I dig for a quarter, find two, and drop them into the man's waiting hand.

His last his last his last.

And the fact that I could have saved him from all this, if only I'd known.

I keep walking. Fold my arms over my chest, watching my breath trail behind me in the cold air.

But maybe . . .

Maybe is all I'm hanging on to these days.

Because there's a paper in my back pocket, burning like a brand, and a question that I'm going to put to Alejandro, who's been evading my calls and texts of late.

Fuck though, I need a drink first.

EVEN FOR A LAPSED ATHEIST, it feels sacrilegious to drink in a church, but it is the one place I feel relatively safe, where I'm not constantly looking over my shoulder, painstakingly aware of every passing stranger. Wondering if Scratch is hidden in some shadow, about to claim his favor. Alejandro says we're all suffering to some extent from post-traumatic stress disorder, and that God himself wouldn't deny us this small respite, even if we are dead souls, by sharing a drink in a former choir loft.

Besides, Alejandro had said the first time I joined his little group, *we are already damned. There is no such thing as being* more *damned*.

And tonight, as I climb the spiral staircase, I do note a sense of it all falling from my shoulders, the heavy, dark weight of it. Maybe this is how Christians feel, why they come and kneel every Sunday.

Alejandro has a standing reservation for the entire choir loft every Saturday so we can talk freely, although rarely is there a large enough group of dead souls to fill it. It's usually us regulars, with drifters who edge nervously in and out, either still so green they're in denial or old-timers approaching a decade without hearing from Scratch, trying to fly far under his radar, hoping maybe he's forgotten all about them.

Tonight it's just the regulars. Jeb/Dan, Alejandro of course, Ellen, Renata, Jasmine, Mike, and Clarissa. Someone's missing . . . but then I remember, Gary's approaching the ten-year mark. *Probably doesn't want to rub elbows, risk getting contaminated with our bad juju.* His tech company, VUEWORKS, just went public and he's now worth more than a hundred million. Hopefully he'll get a chance to enjoy it.

"Oh, Fiona, you *came*," says Alejandro with his characteristic warmth, his standard welcome. But I can't meet his eyes this time, and he notes this.

"*Fiona!*" Jeb stands to give me a hug . . . or is it Dan? I can never tell the two apart. They're both "frosh" at Holy Names University, an institution I'd never heard of, they both always look like they just rolled out of bed, they're both majoring in cybersecurity, plus they both sport the same übershort blond hair and stubbly goatees. Dan traded his soul to be irresistible to women, and Jeb, who's more of a comic book geek, traded his so he could fly, a trick he also manages to use to score dates by pretending he's a magician and levitating a few inches off the ground.

"Hey . . . *you*," I reply, returning the embrace. He smells like weed.

"Jeb," he says.

"I knew that."

"Yeah, right," says Dan, who's tilted back in his chair, grinning.

Everyone looks at me—*no one* buys it—but I'm late, they're all probably three drinks in, and the vibe is good-natured, collegial. I make a note of Jeb's red T-shirt so I don't make that mistake again, take off my jacket and drape it over the back of the chair, put my bag on the floor, then take my usual seat at the round table. *Like Camelot*, Clarissa is fond of saying.

Only we're no knights.

Streetlight floods through the stained glass window, a copy of the north transept rose of Chartres Cathedral with the Virgin Mary, the Queen of Heaven, surrounded by medieval kings and prophets. Alejandro had named them all once, but I never remember stuff like that. The choir smells of beer, candle wax, old incense, and Murphy Oil Soap.

"The usual?" Renata asks, leaning her elbow on the balcony

rail. Tonight her long, curly red hair catches the glow of the hanging chandeliers made with recycled wine bottles.

I nod, and she signals a waitress below. An associate professor of queer studies at Mills College, Renata always sits closest to the balcony so she can keep an eye on the crowd, watching for *him*. She still has trouble with the idea of Scratch and the patriarchal duality of a good and evil supernatural system, but isn't in a hurry to see him again either. Like me, she didn't believe she was talking to the actual devil, who'd chosen the form of a white middle-aged man to play off her entitlement issues. So she tossed out an ask that was an attempt at sarcasm, not a real wish, and is now struggling with its repercussions.

Oh, yeah? If you really have the power of a deity, make me straight, she'd told Scratch. And he did. A deep blow to her career, and her ten-year relationship. She can't even manage bisexual.

"Gary's ditching us again?" My fingers tap the table, a nervous tic that always sinks me in poker. "I was hoping he'd be buying."

"His daughter has a recital," says Clarissa. "How's Justin?"

"The same. And worse," I say. Clarissa is stunningly beautiful—her ask was that simple—but what's strange is that she hasn't shed the mousy girl inside her. Even though you should be able to imagine her walking down a runway, you can't. Alejandro has tried, many times, to take her picture, and he says that she always blinks or turns her head at exactly the wrong moment. *Anti-photogenic*, is what he calls her. Still, even those photos sell well. *A postmodern attempt at deconstructing beauty*, raved a reviewer.

Clarissa covers my hand with hers for a moment. It's like a shy bird has lit there. "I'm truly sorry."

She's so sweet, so pure, that this chokes me up for a second. Whatever hell turns out to be, I can't imagine her lasting a minute. Once again she's wearing a long-sleeved sweater, mostly to cover the long, thin scars that start at her wrists and extend all the way to her elbows. Her attempt at getting out of her favor. Smart girl, not taking the knife horizontal. Most of us have tried at least once to kill ourselves—I took my entire bottle of Ambien, and all I got was two days of blissful sleep. The makeshift book of dead souls, and Alejandro, confirm it's impossible. *Suicide would cheat him out of his favor, and he is not the kind to be cheated easily.* So we're stuck with immortality, at least until the devil gets his due.

Mike is on his cell, deeply engrossed in conversation—I overhear terms like *financing entity* and *gap analysis*—while Mike's wife, Ellen, eight months pregnant and utterly exhausted, nurses a ginger ale. Mike had been a low-paid accountant on the bottom rung of county government, jealous of his younger brother, who'd made a fortune selling off a startup before the Silicon Valley bubble burst. So he asked Scratch for insider-trading tips and now owns a five-million-dollar house plus a new Corvette, which he never dares to park in Oakland. Ellen, on the other hand, got her heart's desire, which was to bear children—she'd suffered through four miscarriages and years of unsuccessful in-vitro fertilization. But I'm sure she regrets not putting some kind of cap on that wish, because she's on pregnancy number five. Three times she's had twins.

"You look tired," Alejandro says to me. He's tense. Probing.

"I *am* tired." The words come out harsher than I intended.

"You need to align your chakras," says Jasmine—a yoga instructor—without irony.

"I highly doubt aligning my chakras will solve my problems. Or yours."

Where people sit is a source of endless fascination for me, the things people gravitate to without awareness. Jasmine—black, Portuguese, and Japanese, in that order—always, *always* sits directly opposite Renata, a strange friction hovering constantly between them, although even Alejandro doesn't know why.

"It's not about solving your problems," says Jasmine. "It's about accepting them as wisdom."

Did Renata just snort?

"Here she comes, here she comes," says Jeb. And then up comes the waitress, carefully taking the spiral staircase in heels, a foaming glass of dark Guinness balanced on a small tray, along with a coaster, and, praise Jesus, someone's ordered fresh, hot pretzels.

Jeb and Dan settle their faces into a poor attempt to seem disinterested, which immediately the waitress catches wind of. She neatly avoids them altogether and places my drink in front of me.

The next part is always extraordinarily fascinating.

Not everyone chooses an ability, or so Alejandro says. Probably half choose wealth; the next quarter is an even divide between fame, revenge, and good looks; with the rest of us creating a hodgepodge of miscellaneous talents. The first time I met doppelgänger Dan, his had quite the effect—there was a celebrity air about him, like a young and more irascible Johnny Depp—and I started to have thoughts, impure ones, although the desire waned quickly that first night at the New Parish and never came back. Apparently our tainted dead souls develop immunity to the talents of others.

"You . . . work here?" asks Dan (his eyes are blue, I should make a mental note of that), and the waitress, startled, almost blows him off—"No, I'm volunteering"—but then it descends over her like an invisible wave, every physical tell radiating her newfound interest. She relaxes into her hip, slides the tray under her arm, and it caresses her left breast. Even starts to play with her hair.

"Have we met?" she asks, not even realizing she's just dropped a pickup line she'd normally laugh at.

It really isn't fair. It's like watching a farm animal make its way through the paddock to the slaughterhouse.

"I'd have remembered that," says Dan, leaning back in his chair, a king. Jeb's sneakered foot *tap, tap, taps* in anticipation next to him. "But I'd like to get to know you. You got a pen so I can write down your number?"

At this, her face considerably brightens.

"*Gentlemen*," says Alejandro.

Dan sighs but turns his attention back to Jeb, and just like that the spell is broken. The waitress blinks a few times, unsure, and then leaves, casting a wary glance over her shoulder, obviously spooked.

It's not clear why, but through some silent election process, we have nominated and voted Alejandro as leader of our little tribe. Maybe because he found us, was the first person to give us some context of what happened and a place of refuge. He never misses a Saturday at the New Parish, and sometimes I wonder if that's so we don't compare notes. He's the only one who seems completely and utterly comfortable with his decision to sell his soul, isn't particularly concerned about when Scratch might make a reappearance, takes great joy in his present life, and shares its spoils generously with all of us. In his perfected Victorian, a large portrait of Édith Piaf hangs in his living room, splashed with the phrase *Non, je ne regrette rien.*

No, I regret nothing. A thought that itches.

"On the way out," says Jeb quietly to Dan, but Dan just shakes his head, looking into his beer like it might have an answer.

There is always this moment after you've used your unfair advantage, a feeling of triste. There's no way for Dan to tell anymore whether a girl genuinely likes him; every interaction is shaded by this, his dark gift. Ultimately everyone wants to be seen, known, and loved for who they are, and the extent to which that can't happen makes for a rather lonely experience.

Except for Alejandro. Alejandro feels no triste.

I raise my glass, sip my Guinness, and take a long look at the Jesus entombed in stained glass above the space where the altar's been replaced by the bar. He's hanging on the cross, arms outstretched, blood trickling from the wounds in his hands, watching over us, triste. Two thousand years is an impressive campaign by anyone's standards. Talk about viral marketing. *Jesus wept.* Whoever wrote that, was fucking brilliant.

I feel someone looking hard at me, turn to find Alejandro staring—he can sense it, my doubt. He drops his gaze to the table, reaches out a long arm, picks up one of the soft pretzels. His every motion shows restraint, a carefully thought-through refinement. *Why?*

"—and the teacher, I *knew* him in high school," says Jasmine.

"Dead soul?" asks Ellen.

I tune into the discussion, a school shooting in Novato, five dead. I'd wondered the same thing myself.

"I don't know," says Jasmine. "We didn't keep in touch. He was . . . strange. His locker was always stuffed with newspapers."

"So it doesn't mean anything," says Renata.

"It *could*," says Jasmine, and there it is again, their taut frisson.

"*Could* isn't definitive. Anyone see him on TV?"

No one has—just a photo, the usual kind, school yearbook portraiture, and video is hit or miss for seeing the telltale dead-soul darkness. Sometimes shadows are just shadows. But thinking that we can somehow decipher the truth from a bar in Oakland is what draws us here, makes us believe we have some control over the future, which we don't.

Unless.

God, the damned pull of it—hope. It's like the vortex at the bottom of a whirlpool, sucking you down, no escape. Because the real reason I'm tired—beyond tired really, walking the fine line between utter exhaustion and near-dementia—is that the more I read and reread my copy of the book of dead souls, the more one set of initials stands out, *S.B.*, who seems, if not to have discovered a way out of the deal, the trail of one who may have. *Prior of the Dominican Convent of Santa Cruz, Segovia, 1477–1498. Double deal???—6/24/96. —S.B.*

I've combed through the book several times—no mention of S.B. in the list of debtors—which would make him the oldest of recorded old-timers, at least thirty years without Scratch collecting his favor. Alejandro denies knowing anything more about him. *Before my time*, he'd written in a text. Something I have a hard time believing.

"So," says Jeb (brown eyes, definitely Jeb). He pulls a quarter out of his pocket. "Who's up for a game of Paranoia?"

For the first time since I've met him, Alejandro looks unsettled. Games are another form of chance, putting what happens next in the hands of that bitch called fate. But how can he prevent us, the ultimate gamblers, who put all our chips on black?

Yes. Oh yes, I'll play.

CHAPTER SEVEN

"**E**VERYONE KNOW THE RULES?"

Ellen raises a hand, cradling her large belly with the other. "I don't."

Mike winces.

"What?" she says. "You know I went to a Catholic all-girls school."

"Yes, so you keep reminding me." Mike casts a glance at his cell phone, checking the international stock markets. Ever since Gary launched his IPO, Mike's been consumed by jealousy, hell-bent on increasing his net worth so he can have the biggest castle again. Nothing gets his full attention anymore; part of his mind is always on his portfolio.

"Why do you have to *be* like that?" she says.

"Like what?" Something he sees causes his eyebrows to furrow.

She turns to us, exasperated. "It's not just me. Right? You see this?"

This makes him look up. "You can't drink anyway. Just watch and sip your ginger ale."

"I'm pregnant, not dead." She gives Mike a look he ignores,

but he says nothing else. Ellen goes for a pretzel, her fifth. Apparently she now gets pregnant at the drop of a hat, even *on* birth control, and there's a school of thought that poor Mike is going to soon be in the abstinence doghouse, if he isn't already. Half feel sorry for him; half don't. He's not an easy guy to warm up to.

"All right." Jeb claps his hands. "For those who don't know, here's how it works. You whisper a question to the person next to you. Like *Who's probably going to share something embarrassing?* That person names one of us out loud."

"Jeb!" says Dan with a smirk.

"We're not playing yet."

"You *will* share something embarrassing though. Like the time you hacked a Defense Department server and did a file search for *penis size presidents*."

"I was *obviously* leaving a big trail so they would plug the gap."

"Sure thing."

"That's a really homophobic kind of implication," says Renata. "I mean, seriously?"

Clarissa sighs. "Can we please just play?"

"Yes, back to the rules." Jeb reaches into his back pocket, pulls out a quarter. The right side of his face is tinged red from the light streaming in through the stained glass window. "Whoever you name gets a choice. They can find out what the question is and take a drink, or choose *paranoia*, not drink, and forever wonder what the question was."

Renata's eyes lock on to Jasmine. "Sounds fun. Are we starting right or left?"

Oh, this is definitely going to be a lively night.

"Heads right, tails left." Jeb flips the coin. It lands heads. "Okay, I'll start." He leans over and whispers something into Dan's ear, and Dan grins, shakes his head.

"No choice, brah," says Jeb.

Dan, still grinning, coughs into his hand. It's amazing how we're expectantly hanging on to what he says next, how a game has smoothly returned us all to fifth or sixth grade. Next we'll be passing notes—*Do u like me? Y/N/maybe.*

"Jasmine."

Our eruption of claps, catcalls, and whoops causes more than a few in the crowd below to look our way, but fuck it.

Jasmine, playing the moment for all it's worth, slowly reaches for her drink, a cosmopolitan. It strikes me that I don't know what she asked Scratch for. Damn, I should know that.

She gives her drink a swirl with a languid wrist. "All right," she says. "What's the question?"

Dan coughs into his hand again, a blush starting along his cheeks. "Who'd you like to . . . sleep with, tonight?"

"*Really*," says Jasmine with a Cheshire grin. "You sold your soul to score women, but a lesbian, I'm the one you want?" She takes a sip of her cosmo. "That's so, so sad."

Out of the corner of my eye I see Renata, burning.

"I didn't say it made any sense," says Dan.

"Wanting what you can't have makes every kind of sense," says Clarissa quietly.

I'm the only one who notices her eyes flit to Alejandro. All kinds of plots thickening. Now it's Dan's turn to whisper into Renata's ear, which he does—Renata with her arms folded over her chest, like nothing about this is interesting.

"Fiona," she says.

But I need to keep my wits about me, at least until I get to whisper my question.

"I choose paranoia." No drink for me.

"Really?" asks Dan. "You sure?"

"Sure as shit." Something about hanging around Jeb and Dan brings out phrases from my college days—never flattering at an age when crow lines are starting to form. Some words, ideas, people, are best left behind to those in their twenties. They'll find out soon enough.

Renata, not wanting to play but not wanting to be the only spoilsport, leans over to my ear.

"Fuck this bullshit," she whispers. "Just say *Jasmine*."

"Jasmine," I say out loud, and what Jasmine would call prana prickles. No way to politely mask the tension now; it's thick as smoke, and for a few, long moments, Jasmine and Renata engage in some kind of end-of-worlds staring contest, until finally Jasmine places an elegant hand over the rim of her glass.

"I choose paranoia," she says.

Always did, mutters Renata under her breath, although I don't think anyone hears.

So now, here we are. My turn. Why do I get the strong feeling that Alejandro is expecting it, knows what I'm about to say? Maybe because a shade of something like triste finally flits across his face.

I whisper my question into Clarissa's ear. There's a roar of sudden laughter from below, the clinking of glasses—I can feel a draft of cold air skirt along the floor from someone either walking in or out the door. Clarissa leans in farther, unsure, puzzled. I note the soft fuzz of her earlobe, like a peach. Repeat the question.

She looks at me, at Alejandro, me again. "Alejandro?" A tentative lilt.

Alejandro meets my eyes, dead soul to dead soul, shade to shade. He raises his shot glass—bourbon, dark as molasses—and toasts me.

"So," he says slowly, gathering us all in. "I will break a rule and guess my question." He swirls his bourbon once, twice, then drains it in a gulp. Places the empty glass on the round table, rim down.

"Who," he says, "is S.B.?"

ANOTHER CLINK OF GLASSES from the bar below, a shriek of laughter from a drunk girl. I cast an uneasy glance down, half expecting to see Scratch himself chatting her up, for him to raise a glass in my direction, a toast. But I don't.

"S.B.? Who's S.B.?" asks Ellen.

"That's what he just said, honey," says Mike. Dark circles under both their eyes, obviously sleep-deprived.

"I know. You think I don't know that? Christ, I have to pee," she says. "I hate how I always have to pee."

Clarissa fidgets with a strand of yarn unraveling from her sweater, turns to me. "Is that someone you know?"

"No. Those are the initials of someone in the book of dead souls."

"He was a man with a false hope, a myth, a poison," says Alejandro so quietly we all have to lean in to hear. "The kind of idea that can drive someone from just losing their soul to losing their mind as well. As he did."

"Is that why his favor hasn't been called in after more than

thirty years? 'Cause he's crazy?" There, now it's out, an accusa-
tion that's been building in me for months. So why does it feels
like a dagger pointed inward?

Click, click, click, just like that I can see the thought light in
everyone's mind, *Why didn't Alejandro mention him before? And
what else isn't he telling us?* How quickly a mood, and a group
can turn, incite true paranoia. The marketer in me notes this.

"Saul," I say. "His name was Saul Baptiste."

"Is," says Alejandro.

There's a hush at that small word, *is*.

"His initials first appear in 1976 in the book of dead souls,
referencing Torquemada," I continue. "So I did a search for ar-
ticles written about Torquemada in the seventies, and one au-
thor came up consistently."

I had planned to confront Alejandro later and in private,
but the moment is here, now. I pull out the paper from my
back jeans pocket, flatten it, place it on the round table. An
edge touches the water left by Clarissa's snowball, pink with a
line of shredded coconut along the ring. She only drinks things
that look like they were poured by fairies.

Clarissa picks up the paper and her plucked eyebrows furrow. Alejandro, meanwhile, watches me with a frozen intensity.

"The Spanish Inquisition?" says Clarissa.

"Yes," I say. "Torquemada was—"

"The grand inquisitor," finishes Alejandro. Something
about the way he says it feels like a dare to me. A double dare.

"Oh my God," says Clarissa.

"Let me see that," says Renata—an order, not a request.

Clarissa ignores her, holds up a hand—the international
call sign for *hell no*—and reads part of it out loud. "'*Nothing*

in all the universe is ever permanent. How could heaven and hell, God and the Devil, be an exception?' Strange words to come from the deathbed journal of Spain's most effective, and ambitious inquisitor, which leads one to wonder about the true nature of those interrogations, and whether some other agenda was at play."

"Saul's initials are all over the book of dead souls, but nothing else," I add. "Not a copy of this article. No record of his trade." Stab, stab, stab goes the knife.

Alejandro is as still as a marble statue. "Saul had certain . . . beliefs he couldn't be swayed from."

I'm not letting him off so easily. "So what happened to his record?"

For a moment he doesn't say anything, just looks at his empty bourbon glass with a strange intensity. Finally he says, "I removed it. I removed all his notes, which would have been enough to make a separate book. I would have erased him entirely if I could have."

Everyone present is collectively stunned. Removed a record from the book of dead souls? But I thought nothing is ever thrown away or reordered.

Mike stares hard at Alejandro. "So Saul's favor still hasn't been called in?

"As far as I know," says Alejandro slowly, reluctantly. "No."

Electric, the entire group. Alejandro's stock as leader is viscerally plummeting. *Only the cold survive*, Alejandro had counseled me, back in the early days when I trusted him implicitly. *You must prepare yourself.*

And I have. He looks at me with what seems like a mixture of disappointment and pride.

Jasmine eagerly turns to me. "So you think Saul made a double deal."

I say nothing.

Mini-conversations start to take place, heated exchanges, like excited small children in the midst of a sugar rush. Our small group indelibly fractured.

"But that's not—"

"Let me see—"

"When did—"

The paper is grabbed, shared, pulled in different directions, strains from being wet.

I'm apparently not the first to wonder whether our contracts with Scratch can be renegotiated, and there's even a term for it, *the double deal*, which is the Holy Grail for dead souls—equally mythical and unattainable, an urban legend that will not die. It's nothing short of a soul-trading second mortgage, the idea being that you get out of your favor by offering Scratch something better than your soul alone, like, say, the souls of others. Many, many others. The trick is how to get that buy-in from the people you're betraying. It's the conspiracy theory to end all conspiracy theories, and many a night at the New Parish has gone long, exploring the possibilities. Ellen thinks Hitler had all his SS officers agree to sell their souls, which is why he could finally kill himself. Renata is fond of pointing to the Salem witch trials— *Why were they forced to sign their confessions?*—which would also explain how a small group of Puritans with bad footwear were able to take over a populated continent. Mike thinks that the subprime mortgage crisis was a neat way to sell souls, because the original mortgage, bought by other nefarious companies, could be adjusted without the signer's knowledge. *Think of all the mad money that traded hands in 2008, who* else *could be behind it?* he'd said.

All empty speculation, but what's igniting *this* fire is the year: 1976. Nearly four decades. All those years without a favor being called in, who knew what ability or wealth was achieved, walking scot-free through the world, untouched, unscathed. A life, a *real* life, unencumbered by the consequences of hanging your children in the closet or poisoning the water cooler at work. Selling the souls of others could almost be palatable if the consequences were distant, removed. Like the executives who decide it's cheaper for the plant five thousand miles away to keep dumping PCBs into the watershed, even if they get sued, even if people get cancer and die. Death by spreadsheet hardly feels like a crime.

And here regret kicks in, a blatant, two-year-old selfishness that wishes I'd kept this to myself. *Mine, double deal is mine.*

"Where is he now, this Saul Baptiste?" asks Renata.

"He was incarcerated at San Quentin. Solitary confinement," says Alejandro, voice now as soft as a ghost. "Nearly twenty long years ago."

THE LOFT, and the bar, seem to disappear around us. Here I thought I was inciting a revolution and Alejandro's turned it back around, holding us in the palm of his hand, all of us greedy for each and every word that comes next. Acolytes at the feet of Jesus. I note he seems to relish his part.

"It was Saul who came to me as I have come to you, although then we would gather in the basement of this church, on Saturdays," he begins. "Saul had convinced the pastor that we were a group of alcoholics, a branch of AA. *It is a comfort to the wretched to have companions in misery*, he would say to the new ones. This was not long after I had made my deal."

I can see that this is news to some in the group. But maybe that's why Alejandro seems so complacent about his fate—the prospect of Scratch coming to collect growing more distant with every year.

Unless Alejandro's made a double deal himself.

"Saul was brilliant . . . but then, that is what his trade was for. Before, he had been an adjunct professor at a small college, with a few papers published in obscure and easily forgotten journals. His field of study was medieval history, with a passion for alchemy. What little money he had left over from his meager salary was invested in first-edition texts. One such text was *The Alchemy of Souls*, which includes the deathbed confession of Torquemada."

"He started the list. He thought Torquemada might be a dead soul," I add eagerly, a sad attempt to stay relevant, center.

"Very true," says Alejandro. "But what he did not know was that Torquemada was the first to have successfully made a double deal. If you can call what happened to him success. But I will get to that."

Everyone leans in, spellbound. Me included.

"When I met Saul, his career was blossoming. He had gotten tenure at Stanford, was happily married, had a young son. He had gone from having nothing to lose to having a lot to lose, which is when he started taking the idea of a double deal seriously. He felt there had to be a historical precedent, if only he could find it. He began looking at those who rose to great power quickly, and unexpectedly."

"But if you can do a double deal, then anyone could get out of their favor," says Clarissa.

"Really?" asks Alejandro, looking bemused. "And what exactly could you offer besides yourself? It is not as easy as it sounds, getting hundreds of thousands of people to sign away their own souls unwittingly. And how would you structure the double deal to make sure that you yourself were not getting played again? I bet Ellen wishes she had phrased her request a little more carefully."

Ellen bites her lower lip.

"It's a risky proposition," says Alejandro.

He looks at us then, and I can see him gauging how many of us are falling back in line.

Me, I'm going to be the hard sell. "But Saul thought Torquemada made a double deal."

Alejandro says nothing for a moment, staring hard at the table, deep in thought. "Yes, he believed so. Torquemada lists two thousand dead through the Inquisition, another forty thousand confessions, all of them dead souls, or *mortuorum animas*, as they were called then. All it required was the slightest change in word tense in the forced confession, from past to future. Instead of *Have you sold your soul to the devil?* to *Will you sell your soul to the devil?* The people could not read Latin, they had no idea what they were signing. And imagine that, all those new favors at Scratch's disposal. Is it any surprise that violence erupted across the world, from the War of the Roses in England to the genocide of Native Americans at the hands of Columbus? A bloodlust that spanned continents. Torquemada, however, lived to be an old man and died peacefully. At least that is what the official histories tell us. *The Alchemy of Souls* has a different ending, a postscript written by the monk who'd taken his confession. There had long been suspicion of an unnatural pact with Satan, and once the monastery learned the truth, they bricked him up alive in the catacombs, giving him only a candle, a quill, one jug of water, and a loaf of bread."

"Why would he confess when he was so close to death anyway?" Mike asks.

Alejandro shrugs. "Maybe he was a coward, confessing before death claimed him, or maybe he was tired, carrying the burden of his evil deeds. Maybe the murder and damnation of so many innocents drove him mad in the end."

It strikes us then, the cost of the double deal. Our own safety and security in exchange for the souls, and lives, of countless others. Could I be *that* cold? Could any of us? We glance at each other nervously, and for a moment, no one dares to speak.

It's Renata who finally does. "So? *Did* Saul make a double deal?"

"I doubt it," replies Alejandro somberly. "I don't think he was capable. He had become ragged around the edges of his mind by this time. He would arrange a place for us to meet, then cancel abruptly, accuse me of spying for the devil. Sometimes he would call late at night, sobbing. *Where we are is hell, and where hell is, there must we ever be.* His marriage fell apart; his wife took the child away to live with her relatives. I saw him once, in passing, walking in the rain, muttering under his breath, but he did not recognize me, or if he did, he pretended not to. Then I heard he was in prison."

"What did he do?" asks Mike.

"I don't know that either. He has not replied to any letters, and there was nothing remarkable in the news." Alejandro now looks up, meets us eye to eye. "Saul became consumed with the idea of a way out, an escape. This led to his despair, and so I decided that I would not follow him there. I would accept my destiny, such as it is. I would take pleasure where I could, and not perseverate on what is to come. Every man, woman, and child will die—they know it but do not think on it. Being damned is not so different from that essential agony. The only sanity is turning our eyes from the unbearable."

A soft quietude falls then, on us at least—in the bar below there is the murmur of dozens of conversations, the occasional burst of laughter, a familiar hum that transcends language even. In one hundred, two hundred years, they'll all be six feet below-ground. The cemeteries are packed with the long forgotten, and we delude ourselves to think we'll be the exception. Above us the Virgin in the stained glass passively gazes on, arms slack, palms up, her dying son under her calm purview. A monument to acceptance.

We are at that point in the night when the giddy, alcoholic buzz has worn off, when suddenly we're aware of time, our coats, the ride home, and the day ahead, all the thousand, mundane realities. The Guinness in my glass is now tepid, the pretzels are cold, and I feel empty, spent.

Except.

Except I now have a name, a place to look, and possibly, just possibly, a one-way ticket out of hell and a chance to save Justin's life if I play my cards right. An ember that glows, warmly.

CHAPTER EIGHT

IT'S LIKE PANDORA'S BOX, it's like the small clear bottle that says *Drink Me*, it's like the one door in the castle that the Beast says not to open, this thought, this double deal.

Thinking about it doesn't mean I'll do it. Thinking about it can't harm anyone.

It consumes me the entire drive home, a Möbius strip of thought I can't shake even when I let myself into the apartment building, step into the elevator. The weight of the world seems to shift beneath me as I close the accordion gate.

Could it really be possible?

When it was just conjecture, when it was just a myth, talking about the double deal was like speaking of winning an $800 million lottery—something that could happen to somebody, sure, but not me.

If I could save Justin though. Get Scratch to reverse his cancer . . . could I live with myself if I didn't try?

The *how* of it though, and the *what* of it.

Hypothetically, *purely* hypothetically, it's not like one can start their own inquisition now. There are laws against that, constitutional rights. The impediments of modernity.

Still, I can't turn off the part of my mind that rolls by a bank and wonders how I'd rob it.

Warranty cards? Sumpter sends one out with every bag and pack, a warranty card that promises a full replacement within the year if a purchase has some manufacturing deficiency, although really we're just collecting data for future marketing campaigns and product development. And no one really fills them out anyway, except the occasional elderly retiree. They're the same demographic that licks and stamps the Publishers Clearing House sweepstakes envelopes, although I doubt they'd be attractive prospects for Scratch when they've already got one foot in death's door. They wouldn't be able to do much in way of favors.

Although there was that old man who plowed into a farmers' market with his car.

That's horrible. *I'm a horrible person for thinking that.*

But then I get a visual—Justin healthy again, Justin himself again, the two of us walking hand in hand down Shattuck on a day when no one's occupying anything. The weather clear, and brisk. It's a thought that constricts my throat. I'm surprised at how thick my want is.

The elevator grinds to the fifth floor, and my cell phone buzzes in my pocket. I pull it out. Missed a few from Justin, but it's Renata's that makes my heart skip a beat.

Hve u seen the news?

Renata? *Why on earth would Renata be texting me?*

What news? I text back.

She sends an *Oakland Tribune* link, and as I walk down the hall, I click on it.

"Oakland Executive Shoots Thirty, Attempts Suicide
at Christmas Recital Rampage." By D. Peters.

My stomach flips.

Today six children and five adults are dead, with ten
more in critical condition following a shooting rampage
during a Piedmont elementary school Christmas recital
held at the school district's Alan Harvey Theater. Police
confirmed that they have arrested and will charge VUE-
WORKS CEO Gary Fulton in the mass shooting, the
worst the East Bay has seen since the Oikos University
rampage in 2012.

With one hand, I dig through my purse for the key, heart
beating so loudly I wonder why no one opens their doors to in-
vestigate.

Sources at the scene report that in the middle of the
performance Fulton, who had been seated in the upper
balcony, stood, brandished an Mk47, and started randomly firing on the crowd. Among the casualties was his
own daughter, six-year-old Beth Fulton. Sources also say
his ex-wife, Carol, who had been volunteering behind the
scenes, was seriously injured as the panicked audience
rushed for exits.

This is why Gary had missed our meeting. Time to pay the
devil's due.

Holy shit fuck Scratch is in town.

I read on.

Fulton apparently then tried to commit suicide by leaping off the balcony. He has been hospitalized at Highland Hospital with minor injuries.

The Piedmont community is in shock, noting that Fulton had been a devoted father and was a big supporter of local charities. Last year *Esquire* named him one of 40 Sexiest Single Millionaires, with an estimated net worth near $150 million.

Then there's an embedded video captioned:

WARNING GRAPHIC CONTENT: Shocking cell phone footage captures recital massacre.

In a daze, I pause at the door, hand just above the antique doorknob. Press *Play* on the video. A tableau of children on a stage dressed as elves, singing off-key while paper snowflakes drift down from the lights above. *"Dashing through the snow"* (they pretend to hold reins in their hands), *"on a one horse open sleigh, o'er the fields we go"* (they pretend to crack a whip), *"laughing all the way, HA HA—"*

—An eruption of shots, so fast it sounds like fireworks but then several elves fall—a man rushes the stage—*the shooter?*—no, he swoops down to pick up a boy—*his son?* —and starts to run but is hit, a bullet splitting his head open like a ripe melon. The cell phone drops to the floor as people scream, shout, more artillery fire, and I can hear him above the fray, Gary, his voice is hoarse, agonized: *"I don't want to do this; I don't want to do this! FOR THE LOVE OF GOD, someone stop me!"*

The cell is grabbed from the floor and pointed at Gary. A man from behind tries to throttle him but Gary uses the butt of the gun to punch him in the stomach, the head, and then he points the automatic rifle at the crowd, pulls the trigger, bursts of light from the gun's nozzle followed by more screams (*how are there not more fatalities?*). The frantic cell phone holder swoops in to the stage again, where teachers and parents are dragging/carrying the children off the stage. I see a girl cradled by a frantic, middle-aged woman, the girl's arms and legs gone lifeless and limp—

Someone close to the cell phone holder says, "*We've got to go. We've got to go* now."

—then another shocked rush of screams and the cell phone turns to Gary, teetering on the edge of the balcony. He drops the rifle over its edge, holds his arms out like a diver contemplating a pool, and just lets himself fall forward. Ready to leave his life, and what he's done, behind.

Fuck. Oh fuck.

End scene. Cut to a reporter, camera A. I hit *Stop*.

Shaken is not the right word, I feel like all the bits and pieces of me inside have come loose, that they're in danger of scattering out into all directions, an atomic explosion.

Then I notice streaks of black just on the doorknob that make my racing heart stand very, very still.

They look like scorch marks.

But I don't have to touch them, *wouldn't* have time to, because at that moment Justin opens the door, jaw clenched and eyes ablaze with what can only be described as an unholy fury.

"WHERE HAVE YOU *BEEN*?"

I don't understand the question at first, my mind still on that Piedmont elementary school recital. I can almost smell it, blood and cordite in the air.

"Didn't you get my texts?"

Husky—Justin's voice has dropped an octave in the past month or so, raspy from coughing, a case of acute bronchitis that will never get better. Always gaunt, he's now skeletal, except for his belly, which is engorged with the tumor, a dead thing that pulls and twists his energy into a corrupted mass of cells. Not unlike my immortal soul.

"Your texts?" I repeat stupidly. Impossible to hear the cell buzzing in the bar, of course, but I should've been checking it periodically, or at the very least read them before I came in through the door. As if to spite me, my cell buzzes in my hand. More about Gary I'm sure.

"*That* you'll probably read, since it's not from me," he says curtly. "You smell like a bar, by the way."

He's right, so I say nothing, trying to think of a reasonable cover story, and for a moment I almost think he's not going to let me in to my own apartment, but then there's a polite cough from behind him. He steps aside, glowering, petulant.

Opal, perfect Opal, gathers her purse from the couch, already mentally through and out the door. I do the thing that annoys him the most, which is to ignore him.

"Everything go all right?" I ask Opal.

"Fine," she says with a false note of cheer.

They exchange a look, hard to define.

"Fine," she adds more firmly.

I step past Justin into the apartment. He's completely redecorated it over the past year, and it's now perfectly organized. It gives him something to do and I have the cash, so where my cheap IKEA shelves used to be is an Italian modular bookshelf made with translucent plastic, the couch is now vintage mid-century, the coffee table an iron checkerboard Florence Knoll. We don't have furniture anymore; we have pieces.

Were those really scorch marks on my doorknob?

The video was a shock—I'm probably gestalting a worst-case scenario. Opal slips her purse strap over her shoulder. "He got a pancake down, no syrup. I put the extras in the freezer—nuke them for five seconds and they'll be perfect."

No sign of Scratch, no shadow lurking in the corner, no faceless man sitting by the window, nursing a drink. Maybe it was oil on the doorknob. I'd complained to the super weeks ago that the lock was getting hard to turn. The apartment smells mildly like piss and all the other smells that are supposed to take that one out—bleach, Comet, Pine-Sol. Justin's stomach is too big for adult diapers, and the pressure of the tumor causes accidents.

"Thank you, Opal."

She nods, puts a light hand on Justin's shoulder, and then brushes past me, leaving behind the rich trail of a perfume I wouldn't think she'd choose for herself. Maybe she's tired of smelling like Pine-Sol and bleach.

I want to touch the doorknob, see if it *is* an oily residue just to be sure, but I don't want to attract Justin's attention. *Later, after he's asleep.* Plus his face is darkening in the way a frustrated two-year-old's might. It's horrific how easy it is to infantilize the sick, but hard not to. There are bodily fluids that must be addressed, quick changes in temper, the occasional mental vacuity. The truth is sometimes I feel like Justin's dead already, that I'm just clinging to the husk of the man I used to know.

"Good night," I call after her, shutting the door.

Justin glares. His eyes are lighter, the cancer having spread to both irises. I didn't expect that, looking into eyes that are both familiar, and strange.

"It was just one drink with some coworkers." I take off my jacket, place it over the back of the couch. Drop my bag onto the cushion. "No big deal."

"No big deal," Justin spits. "*Fine*. No big deal."

Now it's his turn to ignore me, which he does by settling on the couch, picking up the remote and flipping on the TV. *Click.*

News, of course. An officer standing next to a squad car, more officers just behind him, a show of force, a projection. *We've got this handled, ladies and gentlemen, move along, move along.*

But if the super came, Opal would've mentioned it. Her copy of the key has the hardest time, since it's new.

The officer in front, older, weary, and worn, says, "*We believe this to be the act of a single, disturbed mind. There is no evidence to suggest that this is an act of terrorism—*"

"Right, because only Muslims are capable of terrorism!" says Justin. He does this now, talks to the people on TV.

I reach into my pocket, where I keep Scratch's card in a silver metal case. Take a peek. Nope, nothing after the word FAVOR.

"*It appears to be the lone act of a lone gunman, and the community is no longer in danger . . .*"

Lone gunman, my ass. No firm data on how many dead

souls in Oakland; it's not like there's a census, but if Scratch is collecting, we could be in for months of horrible violence. I try not to think that maybe I'll be responsible for the next gruesome scene. My photo posted on the Internet, interviews with neighbors. *She was so quiet,* they'll say. *Kept to herself.* But my wonderful assistant, Tracy, will be only too happy to throw me under the bus. She tried to launch another smear campaign last month, something about my intermittent hours, lack of focus. *Yeah, her life is tragic, but I'm the one who has to clean up her shit,* she'd written to some of the other assistants. *We're a fucking business, not a charity.* The League of Overly Ambitious Underlings. She couldn't understand how she was thwarted so quickly—*Guess who knows all the underlings e-mail passwords? Too bad one of them accidentally forwarded it to HR,* oops!—but the thing is, she's right. My performance and judgment *are* off. Like the call from the *Washington Post* reporter who wanted to do a feature on the Istanbul, but I lost the Post-it note I'd written her number down on, forgot all about it. Only I blamed Tracy and sent a note to HR—a nice addition to a growing list of infractions and complaints about her.

"Anyone who knows anything should contact police or call the anonymous tip line . . ."

I know something, all right. Was it a message? A warning? Or maybe just a promise of things to come.

I GINGERLY SIT DOWN on the couch next to Justin, leaving him his own cushion. Sometimes being too close physically sets his frayed nerves even further on edge. *Everything prickles,* he says. He notes this small kindness, but pretends not to.

I slip my phone out of my bag under the pretext of reading his messages when really I need to catch up on the chatter. Someone's made us our own text group.

Everyone checked their cards?—Mike

Mine's clean—Jasmine

Clean—Renata

Is he still alive?—Jeb

Life support—Renata.

VUEWORKS stock dropped ten points before closing bell—Dan

Not a good sign. Supposedly there's always a fluctuation in whatever you got from Scratch right before he collects, or so Alejandro said. Like a power surge that can either suck away your ability or increase it substantially. *Call me immediately if you have a hard time becoming invisible, or turn invisible without planning to.* A tremor before the quake.

So do you think he knew? Is that why he didn't come?—Clarissa

NASDAQ dropped five. Statistically not relevant.—Mike

Justin turns up the volume. *"We ask the community to re-main vigilant and report any suspicious behavior . . ."*

A passive-aggressive move, I haven't mentioned his texts yet. So I click over to Justin's contact, find five from him, un-read.

Can you pick up some Pepto-Bismol on your way home? XOXOXO—7:20 p.m.

Feeling awful. Christ, I hate this. Need that Bismol. XOXO—
8:15 p.m.

On your way home? Situation desperate.—9:36 PM

Two missed calls. 9:47 and 10:12 p.m. No voice mail messages.

Having that much fun, huh? Shitting up a storm over here.—
10:28 PM

You know what, don't bother. See you when I see you. All
shat out and buying new sheets on eBay. Thanks for your love and
support.—10:42 PM

A moment passes. Two.

"You know I hate this," he says suddenly.

I run my hand through my hair, utterly exhausted. *I hate
this too.* "Anybody would. And I'm not much use. I'm sorry."

"Don't . . ." He stops himself, struggles to find the words,
and looks me in the eyes. A glimmer of old Justin there. "Don't
just talk *at* me," he continues. "Talk *to* me. What is going on
with you? Really?"

It would be so lovely to tell him, all of it, every dark and
twisted detail. You never know, he might even believe me, or
not hate me for missing the one chance to save him. But to
voice it here, in front of him, in the place we call home feels
dangerous, like it might bleed out into unexpected places.

He reaches out, cups my chin in his hand, just like the old
days. "Forgive me."

"Forgive *you*—"

"It's not easy for you either. Sometimes I forget that. Or I
don't forget, but I don't care the way I should."

Oh Christ, I don't want these feelings right now, they won't help, nothing will help. Tears start. So I try to push him away instead.

"Yeah, you've been a real possessive, neurotic, pain in the ass lately. Sure, it sucks that you have cancer, but that's no excuse to take it out on me. You might not have noticed, but someone I love is suffering."

I slipped—it's not often I use the four-letter l-word. It costs me dearly every time.

He laughs, lets his hand drop to take mine—so thin, *damn* so thin. "There you are, the Fiona I used to know."

I entwine my fingers in his. "There you are, the Justin I used to know."

A commercial for fabric softener plays on the TV, *"for clothes that smell as fresh as the great outdoors."* He rubs the back of my hand with his thumb. It's the nicest moment we've had in months, and I realize my part in that. I've been so obsessed with finding a way to save us both that I haven't been present for him in the here and now. But what good is a double deal to cure Justin's cancer and save my soul if our relationship falls apart in the meantime?

"I really fucked everything up royally, didn't I?" he asks softly.

"*You* fucked up everything. Getting cancer wasn't your fault."

A thin, bitter smile. "Technically I know that, but it still feels like it though. And I hate needing people just for the basics. I don't mean to take it out on you."

"Justin, *I'm* the one who's been distant."

"And I'm jealous, you know."

"*Jealous*."

He hesitates a moment too long. Tries for an awkward recovery. "That you can go out. I'd love to ditch this place and hit a bar, forget things for a while."

I lean my head against the back of the couch. He was going to say something else instead, something truer, but I don't want to press. "We can go out. There's no law stopping us."

"The looks though. That double take."

The double takes *are* horrible. The last time we went to the store together and he looked four instead of eight months pregnant, people would look, and then look again, *hard*, trying to figure out what it could possibly mean, this man with a protruding belly. Was he a man or a woman? Was he on some gender-changing testosterone regimen? And the small children, they would take a step back, obviously afraid, reaching for adult hands or hiding behind adult legs as we passed.

Justin stares at the coffee table. Something indecipherably sad and resigned flits across his face. "I'm jealous that one day you'll move on. Be with someone else. Even though that's selfish of me."

Here's what he didn't want to say. "Justin, it's a little early to be talking about—"

"There," he says quietly, firmly. "In the envelope."

I look to the coffee table and see it—a manila envelope, torn open. My heart stops momentarily. Justin releases my hand and I try, and fail, to keep that hand steady as I reach over, pick it up.

It's addressed to me, or the nickname Justin gave me, which I shared with only one other person on earth.

Scratch.

For the Invisible Girl. We will meet again.
Soon.

I CAN FEEL THEM, a series of psychic fractures that start in my heart and then cascade out through my limbs, a crackling fear that trips along the floor, rises up the walls, slips through cracks and corners into and out of the building, down the street, radiating like the aftershock of an atomic blast. Fear, the word *fear* doesn't cover it. Fear is for things like walking down the street alone at night, for the moment you're about to be pulled into the womb of an MRI, fear is looking under the bed as a child, ready to find a monster. Fear is just an aperitif to sheer terror.

He *was* here. He was here, in my apartment complex, a door the only thing standing between him and Justin. My heart pounds wildly, like it's about to fly up and out of my throat. I wonder if this is how the children felt after the first eruption of gunfire, as they saw their classmates crumple to the stage. But at least they could run away. A possibility of escape.

I have to find Saul Baptiste.

Justin watches me closely. "You're not even going to look?"

The envelope—right. Whatever's inside, Scratch has touched, and now Justin has touched, witnessed. *Soon.* I reach my hand in, expecting the worst, a missive that will connect and consume us all. My fingers touch smooth photographic paper. I pull out a series of eight-by-ten photos, black-and-white, all pictures of me, Alejandro's work. He's been intent on trying to capture the unique shade of dead souls, invisible to the eyes of regular people but visible to the camera if the aperture is set right. Something about ray bundles and whether the soul can be quantified.

They're not bad—I've never seen them before, and for a moment, narcissism trumps fear and I'm absorbed by my own images. The first is the picture taken at the cemetery a little more than a year ago. I look startled, eyes wide, caught midturn, creating a blur that makes me look like a ghost. Another photo, this one of me standing by a tall window at Alejandro's Victorian, looking pensively out at the street, wearing one of his shirts, my hair askew. It looks more intimate than it is. A few too many drinks at the New Parish and I'd inadvertently ghosted myself, vanishing and then reappearing in his living room because he'd been describing a new mixed media piece he picked up. Of course, that meant I'd left my clothes behind, so I'd done the practical thing and crashed in his guest bedroom, curling up under a cashmere blanket. Didn't wake up until later in the morning, the smell of strong black coffee percolating. He asked if he could shoot me, and I was flattered—who wouldn't want to be part of a master artist's body of work?

I can see why Justin would think . . .

And then I get to the next photo. Must have been taken earlier when I was still asleep, the blanket either fallen or pulled slightly to reveal everything from the waist up. It's artful of course—I look like a classic reclining nude, porcelain skin, light nipples—but it's creepy too, slightly pervy. I'd always assumed Alejandro was gay. We all did. He caught it though in this one, the slight shading that extends around my body, a dark aura.

But how did Scratch get a hold of them, and why would he . . . ?

Justin sits next to me with a fixed intensity.

I know it then.

Something about my favor will involve Justin.

No. No, no, no, no.

"That night you didn't come back," he says.

I want to confess, I want to tell him everything, but it would all sound like a lie now, a confabulated story so outrageous that it would have to be covering a more mundane, disgusting truth. I should have told him before, and now it's too late. So I say nothing. Guilt by silence. *Devil takes all.*

Magnanimous, Justin takes my hand again. Something achingly wise, near Buddhist, in the gesture. "I'm glad you have someone. I am. And I don't think I have much longer left. I just . . . if you could just hold off for now . . ."

On the TV there are helicopter shots hovering over the managed chaos surrounding the theater. White triage tents, ambulances still pulling up, people already starting to gather around the periphery of yellow police tape.

The thrust of all I want to say is hard to swallow, so instead, I lean into his shoulder, feel the push of his tumorous belly against my rib cage. My mind races down all the paths it has raced down before. *I could stay invisible forever . . . If Scratch can't see me, he can't find me, right? And the card, it doesn't come with me when I'm invisible, so maybe if I don't have it he can't call in his favor . . . Or I could vanish somewhere if I do see him, let him try to catch me.*

Alejandro has warned us that our talents won't work with Scratch, the way they won't work with other dead souls. Those who have tried to get out of their favor, thinking they're clever, end up setting off a series of circumstances that lead directly to

Scratch anyway. *Selling your soul is spiritual slavery. And the first casualty of that isn't the promise of hell but free will*, he'd said.

But then how do we know he's telling us the truth? That nude photo was an unnerving violation, doesn't fit the person I thought he was.

Saul Baptiste might have the answer. If I can find him.

CHAPTER NINE

IT TAKES THE WHOLE NEXT MORNING and part of the afternoon before Opal shows up—an accident on the bridge—but I managed to do a little Internet research while Justin napped. Alejandro was right. No mention of Saul in any of the news archives, although I found a PDF on the site of a student lawyer–led defense club, which noted the strangely long duration of one "Saul Baptiste's confinement in solitary"—called "the Adjustment Center" at San Quentin. The initial charge was something that didn't necessarily warrant solitary—bank robbery gone bad, he had passed a note to a bank teller telling her to give him ten thousand dollars, and when a pastor tried to stop him, he shot and killed the man—but later infractions in prison itself, like knifing an inmate in the foot, throwing feces at a guard's face, led to his being moved there. *Is that the whole story?* asks the student article. *Or is he a political prisoner?* There was an old photo of Saul taken shortly before his arrest too, leading a march in a pro-Communist takeover of the Golden Gate Bridge. Square-jawed with a beard and thinning hair, he looks like a doppelgänger for Philip K. Dick. I try to see his dark shadow, but it's not picked up by the lens.

I have to go. Opal doesn't buy my work-emergency excuse—she had to stop herself from rolling her eyes—but I whispered to Justin that I have to meet *him* in person, explain why I won't be seeing him for a while. Justin nodded quietly, a gift.

I hate this, having to lie. Two lies already before I'm even out the door. And it does unnerve me—*oh, what a tangled web we weave, when first we practice to deceive* and all that. But the end also justifies the means, and if I can save Justin's life as a result, I'm sure he'll forgive these small trespasses. Plus I just may be the only person on earth who could even get close to Saul. Invisibility has its uses.

So I grab my coat, my keys, ignore my cell, which is blowing up with more dead soul chatter about Gary—Emergency mtg., 7:00 p.m.—and strike off for Marin.

———— ∿ ————

UP CLOSE, the prison doesn't look the way I expected, certainly not the San Quentin I always pictured across the bay. From the bridge, it always seemed like a fortress—impenetrable, formidable—an impression cemented by the stories my parents swapped with their druggie friends, tall tales about barbed wires for miles, dungeons, secret booby traps to prevent escape, guards with assault rifles surveying it all from a tower equipped with heat-seeking bullets.

The reality is more like Disneyland took a wrong turn into Soviet bloc architecture. The original Gothic structure looks like a fort or a monastery, but there are other buildings too—a brick one that could pass for a nineteenth-century factory, along with flat-topped, monolithic cement structures of unknown purpose.

And surprisingly there's only one public gate into the prison, manned by a solitary, slightly pudgy guard. I pause at the stop sign, put the car in park, roll down the window. My plan is to pretend I'm lost and ask for directions while I get a good view of the front entrance so I can park somewhere out of sight and then ghost in.

"Hello," he says with a smile. "Visitor parking is there." He cheerfully points to a nearby part of the lot. Then he hands me a logbook, which I wasn't expecting. All it takes is a beat of my hesitation for him to take a look at me more closely. Not a regular, obviously.

I see what other people wrote and note several entries for "Museum" under "purpose." *There's a museum at San Quentin?* Sounds good enough, so I do that too. I pass the clipboard back to him, and he looks at it for a good minute.

"Tourist?"

"Sort of," I say. "I live in Oakland. But I've never been over here."

He nods at this, his suspicions somewhat eased. "Saw the show, huh?"

"Yes," I say, no idea what he's talking about.

"That week it came out, we had to expand the hours. Bus in folks from San Rafael. Thank God it's died down. ID?"

I show him my license, and he notes it, then he waves me through. "Brown building to your right. No photos or using your cell phone on prison property. Enjoy."

I slowly roll into the lot, feeling a minor thrill of victory, but then it strikes me—the prison's sheer enormity. It'd be easy to wander the hallways all day, and I don't have the time. Not surprisingly, interior blueprints weren't available online, although I do have a photo printed on my inkjet of the exterior doors to the Adjustment Center, or so the Web tag said. I've never tried ghosting somewhere unfamiliar, based only on a photo. Essentially I'll be winging it, surrounded by more than four thousand inmates and armed guards. *Great.*

I feel security's gaze on me, clocking time. I can't imagine that disappearing in my car while he's watching would be a good idea.

Well, nothing for it.

I get out of the car, see the sign for the SAN QUENTIN STATE MU-SEUM, right next to the SAN QUENTIN HANDICRAFT GIFT SHOP. *God bless America.* If there's a bathroom with a lock, I might just be able to pull this off.

I walk by another sign, USE IT AND LOSE IT, over an icon of a cell phone, and enter the door to the museum.

The air is tepid, and a small, useless fan whirs on the floor. Cinder-block walls painted beige, the floor lined with yellow and white checkerboard linoleum tiles, well worn. There's a desk with a sign-in log, a half-filled mug of coffee with powdered creamer floating on the top, and a scratched old wooden chair, empty for the moment, and a bell, the kind you see in hotels.

I have the place to myself, for now. In case there's a camera, I pretend to be interested in the small labyrinth of displays, keeping an eye out for a bathroom sign.

There's a bit of rope from the last prisoner who was hung, a model of the death chamber that was, according to the descriptive card, built by the inmates it would later kill, an assortment of confiscated shivs. Headline news clippings from across the century blown up serve as wallpaper, detailing the most horrific executions, the wildest murders. If the museum was anywhere except the grounds of San Quentin, it'd seem like a cheap carny sideshow, but because of the proximity to actual death-row inmates, it offers a shiver cemeteries can't touch. I wonder how many of them were dead souls. How many had a choice.

"That was for 'Bloody Babs,'" says a voice out of nowhere.

I turn to find a sixties-ish man in a worn, CASH, SAN QUENTIN T-shirt, a slightly gleeful twinkle in his eye. He points to the glass case I've landed in front of. There's a blindfold wrapped around the head of a foam dummy, and next to it a black-and-white photo of a woman who could pass for a 1950s film star.

"She wanted a blindfold before they gassed her, said she didn't want to have to look at the people watching. Under-standable, I guess."

I'm expected to reply, so I say, "Interesting."

"Susan Hayward played her in the movie."

Just then a family of six enter, a macabre Sunday outing for the kids. Real tourists judging by the tucked-in T-shirts, brand-new sneakers, and identical cargo shorts. The littlest, wearing a striped prison hat, rings the bell twice before her mother shushes her.

"Duty calls," he says. I guess he must be the curator and the inhabitant of the empty chair.

"Is there a bathroom?" I ask.

He nods, points me to the back of the building. There's a sign hanging from the ceiling: RESTROOMS—DAMES & GANGSTERS.

Strange how a few decades can turn horrific crimes into quaint spook stories, give murderers the shine of celebrity. The victims aren't represented in the memorabilia; they're part of the story, but not the focus. Never are. I pass by rusted manacles, a straightjacket yellowed by time, brown wooden tombstones with numbers only, 41876, 26213. It's not inconceivable that if Gary survives, he'll be incarcerated here too.

A problem I intend to avoid altogether.

I reach the nook with the restrooms, find a repurposed cell door painted bright pink with DAMES in block print. Inside, there's a stainless-steel toilet, plain mirror, stainless-steel sink— leftovers from the last prison refurb maybe.

I click the lock and take a look at my watch. The sign on the museum said it closes at four thirty, and it's three thirty now. Plus I bet one of the little girls in the family will need to hit the bathroom soon—they always do.

I quickly pull the photo of "solitary" from my back pocket. It shows a long hallway with what looks like thick, steel freezer doors painted white, each with a narrow, rectangular opening for food trays and handcuffing. Cement floors, not painted, burnished to a high shine. The floors, I've learned from the Internet, need to be easy to clean because most solitary inmates try to kill themselves at some point, hoping the time it takes for the guards to suit up is longer than it takes to bleed out.

It's a very, *very* long hallway.

I hope the bathroom lock holds. I can imagine the stir that'd be created at finding a pile of clothes with no person attached to them, the mere seconds it'd take to review the video footage, connect my name to the log. Start a manhunt.

Fuck.

I close my eyes, picture the hallway in my mind. The quiet hum of the bathroom fluorescent light slowly, slowly, starts to fade away.

IT'S COLD IN SAN QUENTIN. That's the first thing I notice, followed by the stink of unwashed bodies, the echoing reverb of shouts muffled through steel, hands pounding against narrow slits of windows. I shiver, look down. Naked. Check. Invisible. Check. Desperate. Check.

Something white hits my foot—a crumpled, flattened piece of paper folded into a triangle, attached to a clear fishing line. Just as quick, it's yanked back and slips under one of the metal cell doors. Shoots out again but this time I step out of the way, watch as it slides into the cell directly opposite, where the note is obviously plucked because when the fishing line is yanked back, the note is gone.

Next, a folded newspaper glides from another cell down the hall under the door of another. Fascinating. It's like watching frogs snag flies—a lot of activity for what's supposed to be solitary confinement. But then, what else do you do when you have nothing but time on your hands?

Now my problem is finding out which cell holds Saul. There are so many.

An idea strikes the next time a note shoots out from a door. This time I grab it, tug at it three times. Follow the line of string to the small, narrow window.

Just as I expected, an inmate presses his face against the pane of glass to see what happened. Young—too young to be Saul—white and thin as a rail, with tattoos that wrap around his neck and up the scalp of his shaved head. From his point of view, it must be quite the show, because all he sees is a note floating in midair, drifting back to him airborne like it's held by a ghost, which in a way it is.

I open the meal-tray latch. Drop the note inside. Slowly . . . slowly, the inmate edges forward. Reaches out a tentative hand.

"Where is Saul Baptiste?" I whisper through the slot.

He jumps back like an electric shock passes through him, and his hand starts a junkie tremble. And while yes, it's the disembodied voice that startles him, I think there's another part reacting to Saul's name. He looks the way we look when we talk about Scratch.

"Wha?? Wha??" His eyes dart around his cell, expecting a prank maybe, a bored guard's attempt at breaking up the monotony.

A voice behind me, muffled through glass. "Who wants to know?"

I turn and see another inmate, thick-necked with a dark goatee, peering at me, or right where I'm standing. He licks his dry lips. First I feel the telltale magnetic pull, and then I see it, the dead soul shadow, immune to the bright fluorescent lights.

Christ, he does see me.

My heart starts to race, but then I remember, the cell doors are thick, and this is the most secure part of the most secure prison in California. I leave the skinny junkie and approach.

He meets my eyes directly. Then lets his drop and linger over my breasts. Yes, he sees me. I fold my arms protectively over my chest.

"You gotta watch out," he says. "One of the guards is a dead soul, too."

Damn. Hadn't considered that.

The inmate takes the rest of me in, eyes roaming appreciatively over my body. It's disgusting, a violation, a pornographic act, and a part of me—a huge part of me—wants to spirit away back to the museum bathroom. But I've come this far. I've got too much skin in the game, and he knows it.

He leans his forehead against the glass. "What do you want with Saul?"

"I want to ask him a question."

He laughs. "Good luck with that, little sister. Just don't get too close. He just got another five years for biting the ear off a doctor."

Not the kind of news I was hoping for. Maybe he really is crazy, like Alejandro said. "A doctor. What kind of doctor? Is he ill?"

"*Loco.* Swallowed a spoon. Too dangerous for the psych wards, so they stick him here. Illegal as shit." He spits on the cement floor. "And you, you got nice ears, little sister. I'd hate to see anything happen to them."

This does get my attention. But I can always disappear entirely. At least that's what I tell myself.

"What cell is he in?"

"Come in here and I'll whisper it in your ear. Might be the last thing you hear." He exhales softly, leaving a cloud of fog on the glass, then licks a small circle with the tip of his tongue.

For half a second, I actually think about it; that's how bad I want a double deal. Corruption is like a credit card: once you start spending, small acts of treachery don't seem like a big deal, not when you're over your limit anyway.

But then I realize I have some bargaining collateral of my own.

I smile. Press my finger against my side of the glass. "Can you guess why I'm here? Maybe I just hang out in prisons for fun . . . or maybe my favor's been called in."

. Ah, that gets *his* attention.

"So," I continue. "If you want to explain to *him* why you got in the way, that's really up to you. I'm sure he'll understand. He seems like the forgiving type."

This has the intended effect. He now appraises me differently. "I don't believe you." But he sounds like he's trying to convince himself.

I lean in, whisper, "You heard about the Christmas recital massacre?"

He whistles and claps his hands, almost in appreciation. "Seriously? That was one of us? Sick. That was totally, *totally* sick."

It makes my stomach churn, but this is wasting my time.

"Now," I continue. "Which cell?"

HE'S EXTRAORDINARILY THIN, hunched over on his singular bed, which is fastened into the wall, floating. Face shadowed even under the stark fluorescent light, bald at the top of his head, with white straggly hair that reaches his shoulders. His orange jumpsuit hangs on him, bags around his waist—more of a scarecrow than a man anymore. I wonder if it's some kind of hunger strike, or if he suffers from anorexia. Or maybe, if he's completed his favor, he's trying to kill himself the only way left.

There is nothing else in the bleak cell except for a toilet, a sink, and a thin gray mattress with a thin gray blanket. Not a single personal item—not a book or a photo or a scrap of paper.

He rocks back and forth, humming softly, like he hears a symphony no one else can, fingers tapping along to the inaudible melody. Maybe the guards won't let him have anything in his cell. What *else* has he eaten? I hesitate a moment outside the door. If he's aware of me, he doesn't register it.

"Saul," I try quietly.

Nothing. No response. I remember how scared the skinny junkie was at the mention of Saul's name, and I realize how completely, utterly stupid my next act will be. The man has traded his soul, bitten off the ear of his last visitor, and lost everything he cares about, possibly his mind too. He's locked in a cell behind thick cement walls, isolated from the general population because he's determined to be that dangerous. But I have to know. There's no choice really.

I decide it's easier to walk through the cell door than to try to close my eyes and ghost myself inside. It's a tight space—I never can tell exactly where I'll end up with the ghost thing, and I want to stay close to the exit. Walking through walls is a trick I've been working on for the past two months, something that takes a lot of concentration and a certain verve, because I can feel it, the wall, each wire pressing as it passes through my flesh. I taste the insulation, and the drywall, and if there's a telephone cable, I even pick up bits of conversation.

I let my mind relax, then take the first step into the door. My foot passes through, then I reach in an arm, and then the rest of me goes through easier. Once I'm in, I'm left with the aftertaste of something acrid in my mouth, lead paint maybe.

Still, Saul doesn't look up.

What if it isn't Saul?

But then he does look, a twitchy, sideways glance. His pale eyes are rheumy, cold, mercilessly intelligent, and completely insane. I recognize a desiccated version of Saul's protest picture. Older, yes, but also like something is consuming him from the inside out.

"There's no point, point, point," he says, to himself or me, it's not clear. "Not the first, not the last, not the last, not the first."

He jumps to his feet quicker than I would have thought possible, and instantly he's a mere inch or two away from my face, staring with a near feral intensity. "*Abandon all hope, ye who enter here.*" I feel something charged between us, a kind of static electricity.

My heart pounds and I take a step back, but I didn't come all this way to leave empty-handed. "That's from a play, right?" My voice is shaky, but it's offering, an attempt to direct him. Gauge how mad he is.

He leans in a little closer. "*Dante,*" he whispers furtively, like someone else might be listening in. "I can feel it when a new one's here, I can always feel it." He taps his index finger on his temple. "Here, I feel it in my head. It won't stop; it never stops. The words, the words, the words. Sometimes I paint them on the wall. They wash it off. The bastards wash it off."

A wave of goose bumps ripple across my skin. But it's something like a conversation. "Where do you get paint?"

He smiles then, or makes a grimace. "Alejandro says he'll bring me paint, but he lies. He never does. He never does."

Alejandro. Either he's not as out of touch with Saul as he claims, or this is just another reveal of Saul's madness. Hard to say.

"So I paint with what I have," Saul continues. "Blood or shit. Shit or blood."

The words seem to strike him then, a flicker of lucidity, because he deflates, turns away, stares hard at the unforgiving, cement wall. I notice a spot on his thin mattress has a slight indentation from all the years he's spent sitting there. And there are scars on his neck, repeated cuts across his jugular vein—one still looks raw, not entirely healed. I wonder what he uses to cut himself.

He seems to read my thought. "I have friends," he says quickly. "Real friends, not like Alejandro. They slip me things, under the door. I always think maybe this time, maybe this time. Maybe this time it will work. I'll be blessed. Death is a blessing for the damned." He traces a finger across his throat, slitting it. I swallow hard, judging the distance of his teeth to my ears. Maybe a foot and a half.

My reaction amuses him.

"Look, look at my fingernails." He holds them out for inspection, and I see they are cut down as far as humanly possible, not a single millimeter of nail left.

He giggles. "You know what that is?"

I shake my head.

"That's perseverance. That's what hope does to you. Makes you think you can escape, makes you think you can dig, dig, dig out your jugular vein with your fingernails."

He must not have completed his favor. He's condemned to this life until he does.

"At least I got some paint out of it," he adds with a giggle, writing in the air with his finger. "Took two buckets for them to wash away the cantos."

Hope does desert me then. *Here we are, ladies and gentlemen, the longest surviving dead soul. The expert on double deals. See how wonderful his life is.*

Saul inhales, deeply. Gathers himself. "But I'm forgetting my manners."

He pulls the gray blanket from the bed, flicks it out like a matador's cape. "Behold, the handmaid of the Lord. To think I have been blessed with Saint Theophilus's angel of absolution. Here, take this my lady. It is cold. And predators abound."

I wonder what this would look like to a passing guard, a blanket held aloft midair, taking the shape of shoulders. But it *is* cold, and I'm naked, so I take it, wrap it around me, and it does feel better. Steadying. Next he pulls up the mattress, places it in front of the window.

"The bastards," he says. "They're always looking. Always looking, never seeing." With the mattress up, he seems to settle a bit himself. "There," he whispers. "There." He turns to me. "Now you can let me see you properly. We can pretend to be civilized for a moment." He waves at his now barren, steel bed platform. "Two people, meeting on a park bench. Light conversation."

It's more of a command than an invitation. "Aren't there cameras?"

"Oh yes, oh yes, but you see . . ." he points to the upper right corner, where a camera is embedded in the wall. The lens obscured by brown mud.

Then I realize it's not mud.

"Like I said, I could feel you here. I was prepared, just in case." He bites his lower lip, expectant as a young child, and I think about my ears, how I'd like them to stay on my head. But at this point it's an unavoidable risk.

I relax my mind, and let the invisibility ebb away, starting with my feet, continuing up my knees, my thighs, my belly. I'm glad for the blanket now, a small modicum of modesty. It's when my neck becomes visible that that the nausea hits, worse than it's been in a long time, and I have to make a run for the toilet. I kneel before it, vomit the sandwich I'd eaten for lunch, along with pasty white bits of what I assume is paint from the door. Christ, I never knew that shit stayed inside me.

Saul doesn't seem fazed in the least. "Take your time, my angel of absolution. They're going to assume I'm trying to kill myself again, but it will take them ten or more minutes to suit up." He settles on the bed platform. "Ten minutes is an eternity here."

CHAPTER TEN

THUMP, THUMP, THUMP on the door outside. "Saul? What you doin' in there Saul?!"

I quickly spit the last of what's in my stomach, wipe my mouth, look for whatever it is that flushes the toilet. A button in the wall, apparently.

"*I'm thinking about what to eat!*" shouts Saul. He grins, holding his knees and rocking back and forth on the bed platform quickly. A child filled with glee at his prank.

"Dammit, Saul, I'm five minutes from clocking out today," says the guard. "Can you cut me some slack?"

Oh God, my stomach. Something else rises, but I take a deep breath, calm myself.

Saul has to cover his mouth with his hand again to suppress a giggle. "*How is Doctor Slovenko?*"

Water gurgles as the toilet flushes. I feel sick, feverish, like this place has given me sepsis. Wonder if I've recently walked through any walls that contain asbestos—what a sick joke that would be if I got cancer after Scratch collects his favor.

"Don't look so worried," Saul says softly to me, patting the space on the platform next to him. "He can't break in without his comrades and a face shield. Worker's comp wouldn't cover it. Come. Sit."

Thump, thump, thump. "*Saul!* You're ruining my whole weekend, Saul!"

Christ, what I wouldn't give right now to be home. The feeling is so strong that I feel the room start to shimmer . . . but no, I can't go home. My clothes would be found in the museum toilet, my car in the parking lot, there would be questions, attention. I can't afford any of it. So whether I like it or not, I have to see this fucker through.

I gather the blanket around me, pad over to the space next to Saul. Not that there's much of it—the entire cell is smaller than my tiny walk-in closet. Like a coffin with headroom.

He looks happy as I settle next to him. Practically beams. "This your first time in the Q?"

I nod.

Thump, thump, thump on the door.

"*That's it, Saul!*" hollers the guard. "I'm gonna count to five and if you don't remove the mattress, I'm going to have to go get the team. You know that'll add another year, right?"

"It's not so bad here," he says. "I never went in much for people anyway. Don't miss much, except . . ."

"*Five!*"

His face falls, and I wonder if he's thinking of his lost wife, his lost son.

". . . the rain," he adds, putting an effort into a smile, covering. "They never let you out in the rain, never out, always in."

"*Four!*"

"Sometimes, when I'm in the shower, I turn the water cold, close my eyes. Like *this*." He closes his eyes, raises his head up slightly, and I wonder if he can feel it, the rain on his face, or if just believing he can is enough.

"*Three!*"

"Saul," I say quietly, so the guard can't hear. "I came here to ask you something."

"I know," he says, eyes still closed, his mind and spirit somewhere else.

"What do you know about the double deal?"

"*Oh for Christ's sake Saul, you're really pissing me off!*"

The question obviously pains him. His eyes slowly open. "No, no, no, no, no."

"But in the book of dead souls," I persist. "You wrote notes about it. Torquemada."

"*Two!*"

"Torquemada," Saul repeats. "*Torquemada.*" Something catches then, I sense different neurons firing. His eyes widen, just a bit.

"Snare trap."

"What? What's a snare trap?"

"*One!* Thanks, Saul, don't you be fucking asking me for extra pudding this week, you goddamn son of a bitch!"

Thump, thump, thump, then the sound of boots clomping down the hallway, a buzz and a click as a gate is opened and closed. The prospect of a forced entry has set off all the inmates in solitary. I can hear them kicking their doors, screaming, yelling. Shouts of "*You go Saul!*" "*Whatcha gonna eat next, Saul?*"

Saul looks at me, more cogent now. "They don't understand. Here, the world is safe from me. Relatively. But I have to keep convincing them. Everything I touched, I corrupted. Worlds, they cannot cross. *They cannot cross*. It bleeds that way. Makes its way through and on."

His gaze drops to the floor, and I can sense I'm losing him again. "*Saul*," I say. "What's a snare trap?"

"Everything you think," he says bitterly. "Everything you do. Your little, small, inadequate hopes about double deals, escape, regaining what's lost. All of it, all of it . . ."

Suddenly he grabs my neck, presses his fingers into my esophagus, and squeezes, squeezes hard. Pulls me to him.

"A snare trap," he whispers lightly in my ear.

A PART OF ME IS TERRIFIED, not that he'll kill me, which he can't, but that I'll have to ghost out without learning what I came here for.

"Saul!" I manage to gasp. I try to pry his hands off my neck, but he has a remarkable, wiry strength, like a gymnast's.

He squeezes tighter. "The more you struggle, the worse it gets. *Snare trap.* He's always five steps ahead. You think you've figured a way out, because hope, that dirty bastard, tells you so, but he's *five steps ahead.* He's always five, five, five steps ahead. You just dig yourself deeper. And deeper. And deeper. Abandon hope all ye who enter here."

I start to feel dizzy, light-headed. "*All right!* All right, I abandon hope, okay? Fuck, okay?"

He leans in. I can count the inches between his teeth and my ears. "No. You don't. I can tell. I can *smell* hope on you. A *disease.* A contagion."

Just as suddenly he lets go, shoulders sagging, spent. I take in deep, wonderful breaths. My neck aches. I'm sure there will be bruises. Something else to lie to Justin about.

"Saul, *please*," I say, rubbing my neck. "Someone I love . . . I could help him."

Saul closes his eyes. I can almost hear him think *Foolish girl, stupid girl.* "Your love is beyond help. Not the first, not the last, not the last, not the first. It's done. It's already done, but you won't believe it."

A feeling rises, that familiar sense of being utterly over-whelmed, utterly defeated. *It's impossible.* All of it. I feel like the girl I used to be, trying to hold the lock firm while my father pounded the door, used a screwdriver to force it open. The hor-rid anticipation of the blows to come.

Think, Fiona, think.

My mind races through the little I know about him, seek-ing a crack, what could move him, and then my eyes light on scratches made in the cell's painted walls. His initials, S.B. Dug with his fingernails probably.

Recognition. He sold his soul to achieve recognition. *Ah, there it is.*

"I had to see you," I say, hoping he believes me. "I had to see you in person, because Alejandro removed things about you from the book."

Saul's eyes fly open. Bingo. "He altered the book?"

I nod. "He said you'd tried but failed to make a double deal. That it drove you mad."

Success. He jumps to his feet, starts to pace two steps north, two steps south, two steps north, running a hand through what's left of his ragged hair. A caged animal.

"*I* failed . . . *I* failed," he sputters. "Everything Alejandro knows, *I* taught him."

I blow on the embers. "Not according to him. Said he hadn't even talked to you in nearly twenty years. Wasn't sure what became of you."

At this, I think I've overstepped because the look Saul gives me is one of pure, intense, and vicious hatred. This is followed by a very bizarre and bitter laugh. "Well, he said *that*, did he?"

I don't reply, let him fill in the gaps with his own paranoia. Try not to think about how long before the guards come, force their way in. But his hate makes him clear, at least for the moment.

"We were supposed to come here *together*. A pact," he says. "I shot him, you know."

"Alejandro?"

"No. The man who had abused him as a boy."

I wonder if he's mixing up his facts, or his insanity is mixing them for him. "But you shot a pastor. Alejandro told me it was a photographer who'd hurt him."

"Alejandro says many things. He was supposed to come in with me, finish him, but he couldn't, drove off. So I took the blame, alone. And he deserted me, except for letters. A few. Too few." He presses his fists on both sides of his temple. "He says he will buy me *paint*, but he never does. He never does."

Here I tread carefully. "Saul . . . is it really possible, the double deal?"

A pause. He looks at me, a condemned and haunted man. "Alejandro asked me the very same thing, and I will tell you what I told him. I would not recommend it. Let it go, go, go."

But I'm not ready yet. Letting go would mean putting Justin in a casket in a few months. Or maybe days.

"No point, no point, no *point*," continues Saul emphatically. "*Thinking* you can make a double deal and win, *that's the snare.*"

Just then something slides under the door—a note, folded and attached to clear fishing line. Saul grimaces, bends over, and retrieves it. Opens the paper, a torn page from a Bible.

"Catfish. Catfish hears the guards coming," he says. "Five."

I press on. "Did you tell Alejandro it's pointless?"

He smiles. He's missing a couple of teeth. I wonder if they came out when he bit the doctor. "I tell everyone it's pointless. But human beings do as they do—it's our best and worst quality. Alejandro though, he lies. Lies. He wants it all for himself. Only so many souls, you know. A limited supply. Can't sell the same one twice. And it takes many, many souls for a double deal. Tens of thousands, at least. Would you want them on your conscience?"

But if I don't, then I have Justin's death on my conscience.

Thud of more boots down the hall, unknown gear being locked and loaded. *Thump, thump, thump.* "*Saul! We're coming in, Saul!*"

Saul looks wan, and a little older than when I entered. "You'd better leave."

I stand. It's bad news, but good too. I've confirmed that Alejandro is a liar, that the double deal is possible. Now all I have to do is figure out something choice enough for Scratch to consider, in an iron-clad offer that doesn't backfire. Something that only condemns the guilty, not the innocent. Maybe an offer that targets convicted murderers, pedophiles, corrupt government officials. Flush the world of all the evil people. A niche campaign. That would be a good, not a bad thing, right?

Saul reads my determination and it seems to depress him

further. I hand him the blanket and begin to set my mind to that place where me, and reality, blurs.

"Wait," Saul whispers.

BANG, bang, bang on the door outside.

He stands, takes a step toward me, holds a hand out to my left breast, hesitates.

"May I?"

Although this wasn't part of any deal, I do feel indebted in a certain way, and such a look of longing, desperate loneliness passes over his face that it would feel immoral to deny him. Strange how that barometer of morality can shift.

I nod.

Gently, he reaches out and tentatively cups my breast, like he's holding a captive bird. Closes his eyes. "Thank you."

I do not realize at the time that this will be my last act of mercy on this earth.

IT TAKES LONGER than it should for me to reappear in the museum bathroom. Usually ghosting is near instantaneous, closing my eyes in one place and opening them in the other, but I sense more time has gone by. I even have the faintest memory of the distance traveled, the route my talent chose—a large open room where guards stood watch behind bulletproof glass, then through a hallway behind a kitchen, the smell of bacon burning.

I look down to make sure I'm all here, and I am, so then I look in the mirror. Horrible—pale, with dark circles under my eyes, and my hair looks thinned out, like I lost some along the way.

Call me immediately if you have a hard time becoming invisible.

God, I want to, I really want to call Alejandro, but now I know he's already planning his own double deal. He is my competition, a thought that burns. Probably shot the photos to drive a wedge between me and Justin . . . but the handwritten note, that was definitely from Scratch. Am I next on his list? *Are they in cahoots?* One of my father's favorite phrases, directed at friends he suspected were police snitches, or delivered Baggies of white powder that felt light. The standard drug-induced paranoia.

Knock, knock, knock. "Everything okay in there?" The curator's voice.

Right. Museum, prison—I must get dressed, present a mask of normalcy. It helps, having something concrete to do. I hastily throw my shirt back on, ignoring the throb of my mutinous stomach, pull up my jeans. It's hard though, my hands are actually trembling with rage.

Goddamn son-of-a-bitch. All that "I would accept my destiny, such as it is," don't "perseverate on what is to come," Zen bullshit. Tearing out the pages specific to Saul, *denying* he knew what happened, obscuring, deflecting, concealing. The only thing worse than being an expert liar is getting duped by a better one. *Fuck me.*

Knock, knock, knock. Why does everyone knock in threes?

"I'm almost done," I call out, running a feverish hand through my hair. Christ, I look guiltier than hell. What will they *think* I was doing in here?

"I'm going to have to call—"

I flush the toilet, throw open the door. The curator stands in front of me, perplexed, and the little girl from the family holds his hand, legs crossed in that pained, "I have to pee *now*" pose.

"I'm so sorry," I say as brightly as possible. "I thought I was over the worst of the stomach flu."

He pauses.

"It's been going around," he finally says, scanning me closely, looking for what, I don't know. A telltale white powder beneath my nose perhaps. Something explosive. A cake with a shiv inside.

The girl yanks desperately on the bottom of his T-shirt.

"Well, we're just about closing up." He peers behind me, still unsure. "Not a journalist, are you?"

"No. Why, *should* I be?" My attempt at lightening things up plummets to the floor and dies there.

"I have to *goooooo*," says the girl.

I give a smile that never works on children, grab my purse, and make a hasty exit. Feel the lingering gaze of the curator on my back.

I'm behind. How many souls could be traded anyway in the Bay Area? How would Alejandro go about collecting their acquiescence? The technical aspects present themselves—limits of time and access to people, moving them. The hardest thing in marketing is to actually get people to do something they weren't thinking of doing. Imprint them with an idea, stick an unforgettable jingle in their head, sure, a half-million-dollar ad buy can get you that, but to actually change behavior? Get a stranger to make a call, click a URL, switch auto insurance? That takes creativity and the will of a pirate.

But Alejandro has thrown down a glove, and as of now, as of today, I accept.

If rage were flammable, mine would light up the city.

CHAPTER ELEVEN

THE TRAFFIC ACROSS the Golden Gate Bridge hadn't been bad for a Sunday, and the streets are relatively clear—too cold for the natives, so mostly tourists out and about, determined to have their vacation, weather be damned. I'm making good time. Will Alejandro be home? Probably not, with the emergency meeting. No, Alejandro will want to calm everyone's nerves, settle them back into resignation. More souls for him. I wish I could get Tracy on a SWOT analysis—she's brilliant at evaluating threats and weaknesses, exploiting opportunities.

It doesn't help that at every corner, in every car, at every intersection, I imagine I see Scratch. *Tick, tick, tick.* There he is, hunkered down in an alleyway—there he is, standing in the shadow side of the streetlight—there he is, crossing the road with the collar of his jacket up, head down against the wind. Close but not close. There's something sublime about the anticipation, a darker version of foreplay.

My card is stashed in the organizer under the stereo, and at each stoplight I open the case to check it.

FAVOR

Still blank.

Reassuring but also oddly disappointing. I'm not first on his list, which feels like a slight of some kind. I'm that competitive. But no, I need time, as much as I can get, because I have a strong, black foreboding that whatever Scratch is planning will involve Justin. There is that thread through all the collected favors of dead souls. I wonder if I can still make a double deal even after my favor's been called in. *Damn, something else I should have asked Saul.* Not that I would have gotten a straight answer, just the two had been bloody hell. My neck still aches from where he gripped it, won't be surprised if it's already bruising.

I pass by Alejandro's Victorian—dark as sin, not a single light on—and pull into a parking space under a lonely Japanese maple. The sun set an hour ago, and there's no foot traffic. Dogs have been walked, dinners are being prepared, children are doing homework. The thrum of what used to be middle-class and is now enjoyed only by the dot-com emperors—no one to notice the woman in the parked car under the maple tree who simply vanishes. Strange things like that don't happen in this kind of neighborhood, this tranquil oasis. They have no idea they live so close to a monster.

Is he though?

It's hard to reconcile this new version of Alejandro with the man I've implicitly trusted from that first photo shoot in the cemetery. Always immediately available to any of us, he's taken more than a few of my late-night calls, when Justin is asleep and I feel the weight of it, my damnation, a crushing depression that makes me feel like an invisible demon sits on my chest. Just his soft laugh would ease it somewhat. Or he'd say something strange, something that wouldn't seem comforting but was. *Everything you think is unbearable is actually bearable, because if it wasn't, you'd be dead.* Sometimes he'd stay with me on the phone until the first rays of dawn hit the sky, when the pulse of life would kick in, shadows banished.

Maybe Alejandro isn't planning a double deal. It strikes me right then that I am, after all, naturally paranoid—this whole mess started because I thought Justin was cheating on me—and that I'm taking the word of a deranged murderer with a penchant for earlobes. Which one is laying the snare trap?

But Alejandro was the one who took the photo, a crack now in my relationship with Justin. No doubt about that. It helps, somewhat, with the lingering guilt surrounding my planned trespass.

Non, je ne regrette rien.

I set my mind on the Édith Piaf canvas, mounted on the nine-foot-high wall in Alejandro's living room. Édith has a nice view of the marble fireplace—imported from Italy—and Edwardian bay window. I visualize the Victorian couch, reupholstered with a modern, teal-orange geometric design, the Karl Springer parchment coffee table, brass Koch and Lowy floor lamp, vintage orange crates repurposed as end tables. Alejandro may be a lying bastard, but I have to give props to him for style.

I listen to the soft rustle of leaves. A few drop, land on the windshield before they're blown off into the sidewalk, the gutter. I close my eyes—

—and feel cold hardwood under my bare ass.

Open my eyes.

To an empty house.

INCROYABLE. And it truly is, because there had been so much stuff before, the clutter of an artist constantly at work. Where are the rumpled magazines thumbed through to the point of disintegration? Where are the books—stacks and stacks of books lining the walls in delicately balanced columns, tottering from smallest to largest—the lenses, and lens caps, the strategically placed coasters to discourage placement of glasses directly on the antiques? Where are the stacks of unopened mail, odd bits of machinery from cameras in the midst of rehabilitation? And the *dust.* Where's the dust? Because while Alejandro had excellent taste, he hated the idea of a regular soul entering his apartment, floating around and disturbing his organized disorganization, or worse still, throwing out a favorite cheese that could be mistaken as rancid.

The spot where Édith used to hang is slightly darker, a testament to Alejandro's westward facing windows and slope of a lot that always caught the end of a sunset.

I stand, the darkness enveloping me. Just for kicks I pad over to a light switch, try it. But no, the electricity has been turned off too.

That bastard. No mention, not a single one of a move, not in all the recent dead-soul meetings, not in any of the calls he *did* take, although now I see why he hadn't been picking up the landline.

Who is *Alejandro?* I decide to see if there's anything left that can tell me.

Kitchen—bare, not a single crumb, cabinets cleaned—if a regular soul has been allowed in, he's definitely been moved out for some time, a week at least. I note that the candy-apple vintage GE fridge is still there, with matching 1960s stove—a small mint, he paid, to have them delivered from Minnesota and refurbished to working condition.

They're so perfect here, he'd said, the first time I'd come. *Ghosts from the past, materialized in the present. Resurrected.*

The foyer is barren of anything except a crumpled bit of packing newspaper, remnants of foam peanuts, a pencil. The dining room is empty too, although here he's removed the twenty-six-thousand-dollar crystal chandelier, lonesome wires hanging from the ceiling above. During the tour he pointed out each feature, with the price tag, the only one of us un-abashed by his wealth, where it came from. I didn't wonder why at the time. I do now. Up the curling stairs, the banister so newly polished it still smells like Murphy Oil Soap, through the five bedrooms, each with its own marble fireplace and tall window views. Empty.

Tellingly, no rolls of toilet paper in the bathrooms.

I drift back down the stairs, a ghost in a ghost house. It feels bigger but smaller too, without all of Alejandro's stuff. Everything I own could fit in his living room alone. So many possibilities. I cross back to the arched entry, decorated with crown molding and painted a soft white. Lean against one of the Grecian columns. Picture me and Justin living here. We would need more furniture, but casual, Californian, like a Sloane leather sofa, some kind of Swedish coffee table in an earth tone, a thick shag area rug. Maybe paint one red wall, for pop. Of course, even with my steadily advancing career and advancing paychecks, the mortgage would be out of reach. I could easily rob a bank, but toting the loot would be problematic.

Pop, pop, pop. I can almost hear Justin popping corn in the kitchen, which means we would need a flat-screen TV, right over the fireplace. One of those new ones, that's curved. Five bed-rooms though, what the hell would we do with five bedrooms? Even if we each had one as an office, that would leave two.

The c-word makes a surprising appearance. Sticky hands, tiny feet. The c-word usually follows the m-word, but neither has ever been in my lexicon. I was happy enough just to have the same person to sleep with from one Saturday to the next; I never really thought that the things that happen to other peo-ple could *actually* happen, and happen to me. Hypothetically, I could ask Scratch for anything with a double deal. Why not ask for everything?

Good God, am I seriously considering the American dream?

It makes me momentarily breathless.

I wonder if you can have "ands" with the double deal if you offer enough souls in exchange. Or maybe it's just the syntax—I need a pithy, concise but unmistakably pointed ask that encom-passes a range of wants. Something that has the precision of a slo-gan, a tagline. Something that won't leave me like Ellen, with too much of a good thing, or like Renata, who got so little. *Sumpter, Inc., An American Original.* Legend says it took a five-person marketing team six hundred hours to come up with that one.

But the bigger challenge is getting enough people to agree to sell their soul. How to slip it in?

Forms. If there's one thing people don't bother with, it's reading forms—take subprime mortgages, or credit card agree-ments, or student loans, which are hardly ever repaid and are costing the nation trillions.

Holy shit, I think I got this.

It's that moment I always think will never come, when after hours and hours of meetings and bleary-eyed research, looking at colors until you can't tell them apart anymore and the words from your product descriptions start to blur, after focus groups and surveys and ad hoc polls among staff, split-tests for messaging and long calls with creative, the moment when you're standing in a shower, or picking up an avocado in the store, or putting the key to your car in the ignition and it hits you. The perfect campaign message. Less than a sentence usually. Sometimes just a dangling participle. I don't have what I would call a complete plan yet, but if there's a contest of double deals among dead souls, I could be—no, I *am*—the front-runner.

I just need to convince an inordinate number of people to buy into a bad deal that ends well for me and horribly for them. It's not like there isn't a precedent. Tobacco companies have been doing that for decades.

A small sense of guilt tugs. But no, not just *anyone*, not innocent people. I'll hone in on a perfect niche group of people who would probably end up in hell anyway. I'll be doing humanity a favor, ensuring they don't miss that final destination.

It feels right to be naked in this moment, newly born.

I'm just starting to think about heading back to my car when I hear a creak, followed by the soft *shush* of a screen door closing. There's only one in the house, from the kitchen to the small back deck that leads out to the teeny rectangular lot Alejandro had turned Southern Gothic, complete with crumbling columns and a turret folly. He shot his *One Foot in the Grave* series there. It wouldn't be like Alejandro though to leave a door unlocked; he was meticulous that way.

The lights flick on, then off.

And the faintest draft wraps around my ankles, rises, bringing with it the telltale whiff of sulfur.

THERE HE IS, standing in the darkest part of the dark entry, and *goddamn*, as hard as I try to I can't see his bloody face, even though I'm looking right at him, less than a yard away. It's like there's a weird synaptic interruption—sometimes his face looks fuzzy, other times staticky, and I get the feeling that I *do* see him, but the memory, thought, image, is erased instantaneously. It's infuriating, and petrifying. A shadow that can never be illuminated.

"You look stressed," he says. "Like you could use a little rest."

I feel the hard throb of my heart against my rib cage. I'm standing on the edge of a diving board, about to jump into unknown water. *How many people will he tell me to kill? What will he make me do to Justin?* I desperately want to cover my breasts with my arms, but suspect this might seem weak, so I don't.

"Is this small talk?"

"All talk is small talk," he says. "It's the saddest form of communication ever invented. Completely inadequate."

He walks past me into the empty living room, *creak, creak, creak* of the parquet floors. Stands in front of the Edwardian window, takes in the view of the Victorian on the opposite side of the street, exterior clapboard painted yellow with white trim, windows glowing warmly, obnoxiously, like a Thomas Kinkade painting. Beyond that, there's a grand descent of rooftops sloping down to the dark singularity of a major road, and in the distance the beacon of the Golden Gate lights rise through a thin layer of fog, then the black ocean that merges into the black night sky.

I press my question into the back of my throat, try to quell the urge to run, disappear. He would just find me. Like the card, he will always find me. I watch him watching the house across the street. It casts enough light so I can see what he's wearing—dark denim jeans, an old thermal long-sleeved shirt, ragged denim vest with the sleeves cut off, boots of some kind. So innocuous on the one hand—from the back I could practically cast him in the Istanbul commercial as a bike messenger— so dangerous on the other. I remember Gary holding out his arms on either side like Jesus on the cross before letting himself fall from the balcony railing.

"Guess you don't have the card on you," Scratch says wryly. Casually sticks his hands in his pockets.

Throb, throb, throb goes my heart. "Why?"

He shrugs. "I've been trying to catch up on my writing, but there's so much of it these days. I lose track."

"You lose *track*?"

"You don't have to get all huffy about it, love. Not like I can program an app. Wish I could. Be a lot easier."

The lights flick on, flick off. "Have you written *me*?"

"That's just the thing," he says. "Damn if I can remember. Oh no, right, I did. Been out drinking too much, I suspect. Speaking of which, anything left in the fridge?"

I'm stunned, and while I try to find words, while my mind tries to compute them, he walks past me again—closer this time—almost brushing my waist with the cuff of his sleeve. Heads for the kitchen. Lights flicker, but falter again.

I suppress the strange feeling that we are repeating something begun eons ago, that my smartest move would be to ghost out, or at the very least, run.

But instead, I follow.

"AH, THERE IT IS," says Scratch, holding the door of the red fridge open. Only when he says *there* it sounds like *ter*, that strange, foreign lilt again. He reaches into the belly of the fridge and pulls out a six-pack of Guinness, the cans beaded with condensation, and cradles them like a newborn.

I remember something I can't believe I'd forgotten over the course of the year. I never drank Guinness until that first time, with Scratch.

"Not as good as tap, but 'tis what it is." He plops the six-pack on the kitchen island with the Koa countertop—illegally imported from one of the last groves in Kauai, *endangered*, Alejandro had said proudly—ignores the small stack of coasters purposely left behind, and pulls a can off the plastic ring. Pushes it in my direction.

Did Scratch bring the beer here, or plant them earlier? If the electric is off, the fridge wouldn't be working. It strikes me how little I know about the devil, what the limits of his power might, or might not be. How vulnerable I truly am.

I don't touch the beer, although my mouth does water at the sight of it.

The lights flicker again.

"Damn electricity," says Scratch, popping another can open. "Doesn't seem to like me very much." He holds his up. "Cheers."

"Thanks, but no thanks." I remember what happened the last time I went drinking with Scratch. It's not much ground to hold, but I hold it.

At this, he clutches at his heart theatrically. "Oh, now that really hurts my feelings. Making me drink alone. Holding a grudge." He shrugs again and raises his can to where his lips should be, takes a long, slow sip. And I realize this is theater, a performance of a human being, not an actual one I'm standing across from. It's a thing with the limbic, emotional range of a shark.

"You don't have to . . . you know," he twirls his finger. "Stay invisible. Takes more effort these days, I'd imagine, and I can see you perfectly well anyway."

"I'm fine," I say tersely.

"Ah," he says. "I see. Like the house?" I recognize the attempt to change the subject, draw me out, reveal something. I would do the very same thing with an ornery focus group participant.

I run a hand along the edge of the wainscoting to give it something to do. "It's a house."

"It's a good house for a family. Don't have to try to wedge a pram in an elevator."

My hand stops. *Can he read my mind too?* Would I kill to live in this house; would I sell the souls of the entire world, times two, to have a life, a real life with Justin? Maybe. But demonstrating interest is death in any trade. And what I need to buy right now is time.

I wrinkle my nose. "Smell that?"

"What?"

"Mildew. Probably some kind of black mold in the walls."

"Ha!" He takes another sip, and I sense he's eyeing me in a different way. Like there's more to me than he thought. "You're a right funny one. What does black mold do again?"

"Asthma. Pulmonary hemorrhage."

"*Really*," he says with genuine interest. "I had no idea it was so dangerous. Something to remember." Now he leans against the back of the island, holding his drink like we're at a party, that same, feline ease. "You haven't asked."

"Asked what?"

"What's on your card," he says, pronouncing it *cerd*. "What your favor is."

This does cause my blood to chill. But I'm not about to give him the pleasure of knowing. "Maybe I don't care."

He slaps his thigh, utterly delighted. "Damn, but don't you remind me of Lizzie."

I don't take the bait.

He takes another sip, and again makes another appraisal. "Borden. Lizzie. Haven't you heard of her?"

"Sure, Borden makes great cream cheese."

"Oh now," he says, wagging an index finger. "Now you're just feckin' with me."

I offer him a sly smile. It takes every ounce of nerve times infinity to slowly approach the kitchen island, right next to him. I grip the edge, lift myself up so I'm sitting on it, bare feet dangling. The smell of sulfur so intense now it feels like it's kindling the passages of my nose. I'm very aware of the curve of my stomach, the soft indent of my belly button, and maybe he is too because his breath becomes ever so slightly ragged. Then slowly, slowly, I reach down for the can of Guinness, pop it open. Feel the mist of carbonation on my fingers. Take a sip. Yes, it's not as good in a can, but it'll do.

He leans in. I feel his breath against the bare skin of my invisible shoulder. "What exactly are you up to, Fiona Dunn?"

The first rule of marketing is desire. There is no part of this world, or any other, where that isn't true.

CHAPTER TWELVE

HE DOES KEEP HIS WORD, I'll give him that. Afterward, when I'm back in the car and I pull the card out of its case, I note that the inside is scorched, a small pile of ash covering the space after FAVOR. My heart starts to pound. But when I brush the ash away, I see there's nothing new written. Still blank. I flick the overhead car light on for just a brief second to confirm, but no, not a single word marks it. I even try to hold it sideways to see if the indentation from the writing might still be visible—I can see something, but it's not legible. The ash stains my fingertips black.

Ash. I remember that first day I met Alejandro, the woman in the cemetery working away at her gravestone rubbings. It gives me an idea. I dig around in the car until I find a thin piece of paper—tucked in the folds of the backseat is a folded *Street Spirit* a homeless man gave me over a year ago. It's yellowed, but it might work. I tear off an article—"Stop the Anti-Poor Laws"—and press it over the card. Then I scoop what's left of the ash from the organizer under the stereo, rub it over the paper with my index finger.

It works, a little. I see a name, *Justin.*

My hand starts to tremble. *I was next. He was going to tell me to do something to Justin.* A real and true panic starts to build, the kind that makes me want to find something sharp, something to dig into my skin until I can catch my breath again.

I bought some time. I hold on to that thought, time, anchor myself in it. The cost I can't think about. Not now. Maybe never.

I flick the light in the car off. I hunt for my shirt, find it cold and crumpled on the car mat. Put it on. Christ, all I want to do is go home, shower for the next half hour, wash him off of me.

Hands gripping mine, pressing them to the flat surface of the Koa wood.

I hope it's enough. Oh dear God, I hope it's *enough* time.

Tracing his finger along my upper thigh.

"Just save me for last," I'd asked, at the moment before, the moment when a woman can almost get anything. He buried his faceless face in my hair.

"Lovely as you are," he said, "that's a little much."

We worked out an alternative. We made a trade.

And if I fail? The memory of Gary shooting his daughter on the stage hits, even though I thought I'd safely bricked it away.

My stomach surges and my hand reaches for the door latch, pushes it open. A passing car presses its horn, swerves to avoid a crash, but I don't care, I lean over the asphalt, the Guinness making a return journey, not as pleasant as before. When it's out, I sit up, press the back of my hand on my clammy forehead, close the door again.

This wasn't supposed to happen. I feel violated, cheap, and guilty. Here I am, committing the very act I'd mentally tried and convicted Justin for just before I'd made my first trade with Scratch. A bitter irony. *But it's* for *Justin*, I tell myself. *This is all for him.* Still, I sense a hollow spot in the wall where that thought lives. A whisper of an idea in my father's voice, *You sure you're not doing this to save your own ass? 'Cause you'd run if you could. Only this time you can't, kiddo.*

"Fuck you Dad," I mutter. I brick that thought into its own compartment, seal it tight.

Pants. I remember the jeans I'm sitting on—I don't think they'll let me in the New Parish without them. As I push the seat back, pull them on, I wonder if the dead-soul regulars are there now. Scratch dropped a hint, the only one of the night. *Spending a lot of time at Fourth and Bellway, aren't we?*

My cell tucked in the center console buzzes with a new message. I grab it, find I've missed several because, just like my clothes, tech doesn't come with me when I ghost.

Three from Opal—Justin has a fever, slight but concerning. Can I pick up some Tylenol on the way home? Couldn't find any in the apartment so gave him some Advil. And what time will I be back? She has plans with her cousin who's in town. A movie, about eight thirty, but if it's a prob, no prob. Also we're out of butter.

One from Justin—selfie on the couch, holding an ice cream sandwich.

Last one was saving for u but . . .

It wrenches my heart and makes me feel hollow, distant, like an astronaut on another planet receiving messages sent from a dead Earth decades ago. I don't know who I am anymore, or what it is exactly that I'm becoming.

Messages from Renata, Jasmine, Clarissa.

Where r u?—Renata

Here. NP. Coming?—Jasmine

Yes.—Renata

Anyone heard from Alejandro?—Clarissa

MIA.—Jasmine

OMG. I'm scared. I'm really scared u guys.—Clarissa

Where's Fiona?—Clarissa

Don't panic. Heading for New Parish.—Renata

I'm leaving, I gotta get out of the city—Jasmine

Don't. I'm coming—Renata

I couldn't get last, Scratch said being the last one wasn't possible—there's already a huge backlog of favors to collect and new dead souls trading daily. *I'm thinking of outsourcing*, he said wryly. *Or cloning myself.* One of the reasons he likes to collect in a batch. After that neither one of us spoke, because we were occupied with other things. Strange that I couldn't see his lips but could feel them.

So I got fourth, as in he moved my name down to fourth on his list, as in he'll collect the favors of three dead souls before my card is inscribed again. Whether he means our weekly New Parish group, he wouldn't confirm or deny. But what really set my heart alight was that I was able to renegotiate even a small part of the deal, and if one thing can be changed, then really anything's possible if I can get his buy-in. I just need to craft the double deal carefully, not leave any part of it to chance.

Unless this is just another twist in the snare trap. Fuck what Saul said, he's in solitary with no one to love anymore.

Buzz. A new text from Justin.

Home soon?

Stopping off at store for some Tylenol, then home, I text back. Not a realistic time-frame given I'm actually headed for the New Parish—maybe there will be an accident on the freeway, or I'll hit a dog. Duplicity is becoming disturbingly second nature.

Ok. miss u. XOXOXO

I'm doing this for him, I tell myself. I'm a good person. I have to do a bad thing, maybe several bad things, but I'm doing bad things for a good reason. *That's morally cogent, right?*

The thing is, I'm not sure if even I believe me.

I click back over to the group text.

OMG!—Clarissa, and then she posts a link. I'm so scared I'm crying right now.

A URL, standard blue font, underlined. So simple, so innocuous. I don't want to click it, I want to roll down the car window, throw my phone out onto the street, and watch it get run over by a passing car, smashed to pieces, but I know that's no protection. So instead I press the URL and land on a small image of a video screen, which I enlarge with my index finger. Another news story, with the thick bottom rolling ticker that appeared on 9/11 and never went away.

He kissed my finger, after licking my palm.

"Get a grip Fiona," I tell myself out loud. Never a good sign, talking to myself. Always a last resort for when the world starts getting shifty.

And I press *Play*.

A WOMAN IN A TRENCH COAT holds a microphone in front of an unassuming white bungalow that, in San Jose, easily costs more than a million. She's bathed in a secondary bright light that blanches her face to mime-white. Local news. Asian, she works too hard at making her voice deep, falls into the familiar cadence of Tom Brokaw.

Authorities are seeking any information about the whereabouts of Ellen and Michael Alibozek, who were not found in the house with the bodies of their seven children. The grisly discovery was made earlier this afternoon after a family member received a disturbing e-mail Christmas card from Ellen's Yahoo! account and notified police."

Ticker below: *DOW PLUNGES 14 POINTS FROM GREEK DEFICIT WOES.*

My heart starts to beat faster. I turn up the volume.

What we are about to report next may be unsuitable for some viewers, and discretion is advised. But police have confirmed that the children were murdered, dismembered [said with dramatic emphasis, a sick kind of relish, knowing this will air to millions online], *and that two one-way tickets to Paraguay were purchased using the Alibozeks' credit card after the expected time of death. We do not have a copy of that Christmas e-card; however, it was allegedly posted on the father's Facebook account, and a KTRW viewer sent us screenshots taken before the account was disabled at the request of authorities. Again, what you are about to see is extremely disturbing. Parts of the image have been blurred."*

MIAMI METRO OFFICER INDICTED IN DRUG STING

Cut to Ellen and Mike, both wearing Santa hats, arms wrapped around each other's waists, standing in front of the Christmas tree, smiles frozen on their faces, *Happy Holidays from the Alibozek Family* plastered just beneath them in some

cheesy font, Brush Script probably. The petrified look in their
puffy eyes is what grabs you first, sheer terror flattened into a
JPEG, so at first you don't notice the tree, but that's okay because the editor at KRTW helps us out on that front, slowly
zooming over Mike's left shoulder so you can see the ornaments. Pixelated but still discernible, a little hand hangs from a
pine branch next to blue ornaments, shiny tinsel. Just below, a
little foot.

"We're just getting word . . . yes . . ." The reporter's voice cuts
in, excited. *"We're just getting word that police will be making an
official statement in the next few minutes . . ."*

The zoom drifts down to the grandly wrapped presents at
the tree's base—small bodies among them, something that
looks like an arm poking out between two legs, attached or not
attached, hard to say, since the more graphic parts are blurred
but that's no help, no help, and just as *those* images are fixing to
my brain, never to be removed, the camera pans up to the top
of the tree where the star should be but is adorned instead with
a tiny head, blinking lights pushed through empty eye sockets.

And then—*God help me*—I open a new tab, click over to
Google, scanning the stories for the time, the *time*. I don't
think I breathe for the next few seconds. When I find it, I
praise all the deities that have ever been worshipped, because
the bodies were discovered four hours ago. Before I made my
trade with Scratch.

A surge of relief hits—there're still three he'll collect before
me—but that relief is quickly followed by the start of tears—oh
good God, *Ellen*, Mike—but I don't have time to dwell, to feel.
For all I know, Scratch is collecting his next favor now, and
there's still so much to do, figure out.

This Google article has a hi-res version of the screenshot—nothing the authorities can do, it's gone viral—and with my index finger and thumb I enlarge the field just over Ellen's shoulder, at the window behind her. Barely visible in the reflection is a figure, almost destroyed by the flash of the bulb. Someone took this picture. Scratch?

Or Alejandro.

As if he can sense the very thought of his name, suddenly, he calls.

IT FEELS WRONG. It feels all levels of wrong, all levels of stupid, answering that call, but I do.

"Tell me he has not called in your favor," says Alejandro quickly before I can even speak.

I don't know what to say, so I don't say anything. Instead, I look in the rearview mirror. No one on the streets, all lights off in Alejandro's house. A streetlight pops on, and then they all do, small bursts of light.

"Tell me, are you *okay*?"

I keep my eyes on the mirror. For all I know Alejandro is hidden somewhere, watching. "Why did you take a naked picture of me?"

I can hear him exhale softly on his end, wherever that is. "I would like to tell you a pretty lie, but the truth is I am an artist, a thief . . . an opportunist. You looked so beautiful in the morning light. Like Manet's *Olympia*. I can resist many things, but true beauty, never. Perhaps, if souls can be trapped in photos, some part of yours will be preserved in that moment, forever at peace."

I start to laugh. Then I start to cry. And then I can't stop either.

"My dear girl, you must stay calm," says Alejandro, "and gather yourself. I am afraid the days for weeping are over. You must be clear now. Present."

A gust of wind pushes through the limbs of a barren tree behind me. Without its leaves, the branches look like veins, arteries.

"*Present*," I say bitterly. "As if I could be anywhere else. As if I could be in the *future*. I have no future."

"We all have futures," says Alejandro softly. "That is entirely the problem. But I am so glad to have this moment in time with you, before yours unfolds. When you are still you."

Here he is, the midnight Alejandro I remember, the calm voice in the storm that I used to trust. A part of me wants to lean in to it again. But I see the real man now—pretending to fill a paternal void when really it was a strategic act to manipulate me down the line. The thing about a lie is that for the lie to stick, your mark has to want to believe it.

Never again. But will I pretend to trust him so I can fish for information?

Hell yeah.

"You're right . . . as usual," I say, adding a soft sigh for effect. "Did you hear about Ellen and Mike? It's so horrible . . . I can't even . . ."

Now it's his turn to say nothing.

I keep digging. "There was a photo. And the thing is . . . I know this is crazy . . . but the others are saying they saw someone reflected in a window. The person who took the picture. And that person . . . it looked like you."

He doesn't deny it, an answer in and of itself. *Saul was right.*

Time to close in. "Some are even saying . . . well they think you might be *working* with him. I told them that was crazy. That you would *never* . . . and they're only looking at it on their cell phones so the image isn't great. When I get home, I'm going to bring it up in HD—I'll be able to get a clear enough close-up to show them they're wrong."

It's quiet on the line, and I can feel him weighing his answer. If the others have turned on him, then I'm his only ally. He could lie some more, in which case I'll be completely alienated when I see the HD image, or tell the truth and try to keep me on his side as long as he can.

It's cold outside, and the car is starting to fog with condensation. I draw a fishing line with a big, fat hook.

And he bites. "Yes . . . I am working with him," he says quietly. "For a long time I saw it more as a partnership, one that benefited us both. Now, I am not so sure. But you knew that, I suspect. A tenacious intellect. I can see why he has taken a genuine shine to you, which is rare. Whether that will turn out to be a good or bad thing, I cannot say."

Headlights appear in the rearview mirror, an approaching car momentarily illuminating me, my bruised lips, my disheveled hair. *Yes, he has taken a shine to me.* A bad thing. A very, very bad thing.

I close my eyes, listen to the car roll by. Open them only after its damning light has passed.

"You know, I once read a story called *That Hell-Bound Train.* It was about a man who sold his soul in exchange for a watch that could stop time," says Alejandro. "The man thought he was very clever, because he could stop the watch at his happiest moment, and live in that moment forever. But the problem was that he could never decide which was his happiest moment. There was always something to look forward to, something better just ahead. Only he never found that time, and died, never having used his wish. The train for hell came to collect him, and as he was riding it, he decided that the train was better than hell, *anything* had to be better than hell, so that is when he stopped his watch."

"So he escaped."

"No, you do not understand. It is the idea of escape that binds you tighter. Cleverness didn't cease his suffering. It perpetuated it. Our choices have consequences. You have made your choices, as I have made mine. We have to eat the fruit of the trees we planted, no matter how bitter it tastes. But I can, at least, help ease others into the inevitable. Like Opal is easing Justin into the inevitable."

A bitter laugh escapes me. "So this is *compassion* on your part."

"Of a kind, yes. Think of me as a minister of the damned. Art and ministry are not so different, in the end. Different venues to ease the minds of those suffering. Both equally futile, but all that matters is maintaining the illusion. For most, the illusion is enough. But you . . . you *think* you want to see beyond it."

"The Oz behind the curtain."

Alejandro laughs. "Yes, the Oz who is no Oz, just a man like any other."

"You *already* made a double deal." A statement, not a question.

A long pause. "Very prescient. But I do not think the truth will make you feel any better. Let's just say I do not recommend it. Anything can become hell. Life especially."

"So just give in? Like Mike and Ellen? You think that's preferable?"

"I think it is what it is," says Alejandro. "Delaying the inevitable only causes more pain. For yourself, and others. Eventually it leads to madness. You see what happened to Saul's mind."

I grip the phone tighter. "How do you know about that?"

"Go home, Fiona. Spend what time you have left with Justin." I can hear raw emotion in his voice, true triste. "One day you will look back on even these hard times as happiness, compared to what comes next. But in a way, I envy you. Knowing it will all end, eventually. Take some comfort in that. Enjoy what is good in you, your humanity, as long as you can. Once it is gone, you can never truly find it again."

With that he hangs up on me.

I drop my phone, slam my hand on the dashboard, hard. "Fuck!" Slam it three more times, "Fuck, fuck, fuck!"

Then I grab the steering wheel, holding on for dear life because I want to punch my fist through the windshield, I want to feel the scrape of broken glass against skin, I want pain, and the release that comes with it.

It's been a decade since I've felt so abandoned, so alone, and so completely, utterly screwed.

Think, Fiona. Breathe. I lean back in my seat, look down for the card. Still on the console where I left it. Still blank after the word FAVOR. *There's time*. I pick it up, put it on the dashboard, wondering at its stark whiteness. It almost glows, as if it has a soul of its own. I can taste my dried tears on my lips, and when I think about what I'm about to do next, whether it's right, or wrong, I can't tell. Right and wrong are ghosts, long gone. So I focus on the last noble thought I had, which is to save Justin's life, or at least try. The only compass I have left.

CHAPTER THIRTEEN

WHEN I FINALLY GET TO THE CHOIR LOFT, it feels like the after-party of the damned. Just Renata, Clarissa, and Jasmine. Empty chairs where Jeb and Dan would usually sit, a gaping space marking Mike's, Ellen's, and Alejandro's absences. Even the Virgin pressed in stained glass appears wan, bereft, forlorn.

I pull up a chair, note the noise it makes scraping across the floor. Surprisingly not too many patrons of the New Parish present on a Sunday evening, so it's a noticeable sound. Random heads below glance up momentarily, then look away.

My purpose is dark, and I wonder how well I'll be able to hide my true intentions. Renata in particular is a sharp one. But before any major deal, the first order of business is a competitive analysis—I need to know if anyone else is planning a double deal, and what their offer might be so I can trump it. *Only so many souls,* as Saul said. A limited quantity. And Alejandro already has a jump on all of us.

"Nothing from Alejandro?" Clarissa tremulously asks.

I shake my head, trying to emote the same despondence when really just the mention of his name makes me seethe.

"Not even a text?" Clarissa appears on the verge of tears. She bravely blinks them back. I remember that look she gave Alejandro, wonder how far their relationship went.

"It's really real, isn't it?" says Jasmine. She rolls a straw on the table with her finger. "It just didn't seem real until now."

True. The thought of Scratch calling in our favors was always comfortingly abstract. We could focus on our conspiracy theories, swap stories about our daily lives, enjoy the fruit of our gifts. The book of dead souls was a record of what happened to people we didn't know, more like a history book than a predictive model for our own future, and we read it like it was just a collection of horror stories told at a campfire by counselors, holding their flashlights under their chin. How could such insanity possibly seem real in the twenty-first century? There are rovers on Mars, for Christ's sake. Nanobot viruses. Selling your soul is just such a medieval idea, like contracting bubonic plague or being tortured in an iron maiden.

"Do we have a choice?" asks Clarissa tentatively. "About doing the favor?"

"Do you think Ellen and Mike would have done *that* if they had a choice?" Renata's tone is caustic.

Jasmine takes her finger off the straw. "So what, he just calls in the favor and we're robots? What about free will? I thought the Bible was big on that."

A waitress approaches, and we all immediately fall into a guilty silence. At first I order a Guinness, but then I quickly change it to a whiskey.

"We *had* free will," says Clarissa, once the waitress is out of earshot. "We could have said no, at the beginning."

"You don't have to be such a fucking martyr, Clarissa," says Renata. "It's not like we were presented with the fine print. At least, *I* wasn't."

Clarissa looks into her glass, eyes welling with tears again. "I just wanted to be pretty."

Renata snorts.

"What?" says Jasmine. "What *exactly* is wrong with that? Please, enlighten us."

"Well let's start with how we value women's bodies . . ."

Three. There's three of them left. I could be sitting next to tomorrow's evening news. I should leave, I shouldn't be so visible in their company and they seem more interested in bickering than a double deal—but no wait, there's Jeb and Dan too. No one's heard from them. *Would* Scratch be here just to collect our small group? Why did he drop the location of New Parish's address? Either someone told him about it, or our theory about the devil abhorring churches is complete garbage and he's been here, watching us all this time.

Now a tear does roll down Clarissa's cheek. "I just wanted to be *noticed.*"

His hand at the small of my back.

Christ, *not now, not now.* I have to maintain the facade that I don't know any more than they do. I feel eyes flick toward me, Jasmine's. She suspects something.

We're all quiet again as the waitress returns with my whiskey. *She* also suspects something—we're far too still, tense. "Um, anything else I can get you girls?"

Renata bursts out with an inappropriate laugh.

"We're good, thanks," says Jasmine, shooting daggers in Renata's direction.

The waitress clocks us and walks away. Looks back once over her shoulder, long enough to get a good description of us. I make a mental note to pay in cash.

"It's just *pathetic*, that's all." Renata's wild hair is wilder, like she hasn't even bothered with a comb today. "Selling your soul to attain some bullshit patriarchal idea of beauty."

I raise the glass, take a sip. My mouth is instantly on fire, but the burning feels good at the moment. I'll need more of it before the night is through. And God, trying not to think about what happened at Alejandro's house only triggers more thoughts—I feel like my pores exude sulfur. I look up to the Virgin pressed in glass, her gaze cemented downwards, something judgmental in her aspect tonight. *Where were* you? I ask her silently. *Where are your angels, your saints?*

No reply. But then there never is, not from that side of the house.

"Like *you* did so well," says Jasmine. "Really, *bravo*." Maybe this is what she asked Scratch for—the ability to piss Renata off, not that it's hard.

"What *is* it with you anyways?" says Renata. "You've always had it in for me—"

My cell buzzes and everyone stops, stares.

I pull it out, look. "It's just Justin."

They still look, not believing me. Our tribe is disintegrating into something out of *Lord of the Flies*. I hold the screen out to them, proof.

Must be a lot of Tylenol. Either that or you got into a car accident and are in a hospital in which case I forgive you.

I'm grateful for the excuse to exit. "He's getting sick. I

should go." I knock back the rest of the whiskey, which makes my eyes water.

"He's been sick for a year," says Renata. "Why the rush tonight?"

She's suspicious. Is she planning a double deal too? But then she's Renata, of course she is. Maybe they all are, maybe they're *in cahoots.*

"We should check," says Clarissa.

I'm confused, as both Renata and Jasmine appear to be.

"We should check our cards," says Clarissa, firmly, decisively. "And each other's."

It's a splash of cold water, instantly sobering, although damn, there's that part of me that notes the visual cliché of the moment, laying our cards on the table. But to avoid it would seem suspicious, so I reach into my purse and pull out my silver business card holder. I open it, take out my card, lay it down. Completely and utterly pristine. No one would ever guess something had been written there earlier.

They all lean in. A mixture of complicated emotions brew—if not me, then who?

Clarissa's next, she places her birdlike purse on the table (vintage, round), and pulls out an eyeglass case. Gingerly cracks it open like she's opening a ring case, anticipating a proposal. A smile teases.

She plucks the card out of her case, lays it on the table. FAVOR: blank.

Two down, two to go.

Renata stares at Jasmine, Jasmine stares at Renata, but Jasmine must want to move things along because she reaches into her back pocket for her wallet, opens it to the slots for credit cards, pulls out hers and places it gracefully on the table. FAVOR: blank.

This leaves Renata in the unenviable position of being last, and it does feel like we're drawing straws and the odds are accruing against her. She seems nervous, unusually so. Sweat beads her forehead. Her foot *tap, tap, taps* the floor of the choir loft.

"This is bullshit," she says, crossing her arms over her chest. "I'm not playing."

Jasmine focuses on her with a laser-like intensity. "Where is it?"

"I don't have to tell—"

Something lights across Jasmine's face, a *knowing*, and she leans forward aggressively, yanks Renata's shirt—Renata tries to push her away, but fails—and sticks her other hand down the front of Renata's shirt, feeling for her left breast.

"Hey, get the fuck off—"

And before she can finish her sentence Jasmine pulls out Renata's card, triumphant. Slaps it down on the table, like we're playing blackjack and she's got a king and an ace.

The card is thick with writing.

MY FIRST THOUGHT is *Damn, only two more left before me*. I pick up my whiskey glass, realizing too late it's empty.

Maybe the favor was inscribed before I made my trade with Scratch.

"When did it happen?" The words tumble out before I really think about them, too late to realize that this is not the most appropriate or sensitive first question. And I haven't even read what's there.

Renata tries to scramble for the card but Clarissa is quicker, snatching it and scanning it quickly. Her lips purse.

"But it only tells you to steal an ambulance," she says. "That's not so bad." She looks at us all, her face beaming at the thought we all might get off so easily too. "That's not so bad at all. Right?"

"It's just the beginning," says Renata thickly. "Not the whole favor."

"And how exactly do you know that?" asks Jasmine.

Renata stares hard at the table, having a hard time focusing. For the first time I notice there are six empty shot glasses in front of her. I'm not the only one seeking liquid courage.

Without looking up, she says, "Mike texted me when he found something written on his card. All it said was to go pick up a Christmas tree. After that, I didn't hear from him again."

A revelation. Everyone, including me, assumed that the favor would be inscribed in its entirety. The idea that we might be stepped along through the horrific process is chilling to say the least.

"You could have mentioned that before. Let me see it."

Clarissa hands the card to Jasmine, obviously stunned, and Jasmine reads it. Renata slumps a bit in her chair, runs her hand along the balcony rail. I want to ask again about what time the card was inscribed, but that would raise a red flag, and I can't afford any red flags.

"How long have you known?" asks Jasmine, pointed and angry.

Praise Jesus.

"An hour ago. I thought something electrical was burning in my car."

I surreptitiously check my cell phone for the time. Goddamn, *after*. Her card was inscribed *after* I made my new trade.
Does that leave two more before me, or does Renata only count
after she's completed? Technicalities I should have thought of.
The devil is truly in the details. I'm starting to see why Saul pre-
fers solitary confinement to a double deal; there are already layers to just my simple contract adjustment, layers I'm sure
Scratch was well aware of. I have to craft the language for my
double deal so that it's unassailable, perfect, with all conditions
thought through. It has to appear fair but lean toward protect-
ing my own interest, like the credit card agreements you never
read until your rate jumps from 3 percent to 33 because you
paid a day after the bill was due.

"Has anyone heard from Jeb and Dan?" I ask. *What if their
favors are being called in too?*

"No," says Clarissa. "Not even a text back."

I have to go see them then—*fuck*, I thought I was buying a
decent chunk of time to figure out next steps. My cell vibrates
on the table again. We all look at it.

Fine. Whatever. Just go to hell.—Justin

Renata laughs, and Jasmine slaps her arm.

"What?" says Renata. "That's so meta."

But I'm not offended, I'm relieved, because I can viscerally
feel the *tick, tick, tick* of each and every second. There's nothing
else I can glean here.

"I'll walk you down," says Jasmine.

Clarissa looks alarmed. *You're leaving me with* her? obvious
on her face.

I would rather make a clean break by myself, but there's no

way to gracefully deflect Jasmine's offer. So I just murmur a "sure," grab my coat, throw some bills on the table and sling my purse over my arm. Realize that I missed a button putting my clothes on in the car, and there's a peeking gap in my shirt at breast level. I slide the coat on to cover it.

Together Jasmine and I cross the choir loft to the spiral staircase—*are the floors always this squeaky?*—and I take one last look over my shoulder at a crumbling Renata and a dazed Clarissa sitting under the stained glass window, night rendering Mary a dark virgin.

I wonder when, or if, I'll see them again.

CLANG, CLANG, CLANG as we go down the precarious spiral staircase.

There's a somber energy on the first floor of the bar—day before Monday blues—but something else too, like the bones of the church, its original purpose, are seeping through. For the first time I notice the raised stations of the cross carved between the arched pillars, advertising for a populace that couldn't read, the foundations of a marketing campaign that began two thousand years ago and twisted into strange places. The first slave ship called *The Good Ship Jesus* for example. Or the Inquisition. The Crusades. Proof positive that any message can be corrupted. We're so capable in that respect.

Jasmine opens the thick, mahogany door for me—a soft exhale as cold air meets warm—and I step past the marble font that used to hold holy water and now collects business cards in a large glass jar—*Win Half-Off Happy Hours, Every Week a New*

Winner!—and into the cold, cold street. Barren trees reach toward a clear, obsidian sky.

We're barely out the door when Jasmine edges a little too close into my physical space.

"What's *he* like?"

She knows. How does she know? I feign ignorance. "Who? Justin?"

She slips her arm in mine. "Come on. *Him.*"

"I don't know what you mean," I try, although it's not my best effort.

Jasmine pulls me tighter. "Knock it off, I know what you're thinking."

"How would you know what I'm thinking?"

I hear Jasmine's voice reply in my head. *Clairvoyance.*

I think I must be imagining things, so I focus on a number.

"Seven," she says with a small, proud smile.

I feel naked in a way that walking around invisibly nude never came close to. "Did I miss that somewhere?"

"No. I can manipulate thoughts a tiny bit too. Actually, more like misdirect them. Whenever you wondered, I'd just tease out one of your brilliant marketing ideas to distract you."

"I thought we were immune to each others' abilities."

"Not so much after a few drinks. Why do you think Alejandro had us meet in a bar and always paid the tab?"

I take a moment to absorb this. The sound of our footsteps on the sidewalk echo in the still, night air. "So what's Alejandro been thinking?"

She shrugs. "I don't know. He never drank."

"What do you mean? He always had—"

"Water. The waitress brought him water with a bit of flat coke to make it look like bourbon. I talked to her tonight. She said he'd told her he was an alcoholic but didn't want us to know, and could she please play along. Tips were generous. Now . . . what's *he* like?"

We're only a few yards from my car. What does it matter anyway? "He's a right sick bastard."

"But you were able to . . ." Lets the words trail away.

I appreciate her tact. "I don't think sex would qualify for a double deal though. No offense."

"None taken."

We're at my car. I pull out my key, and she stuffs her hands in her jacket pockets, one of those puffy ones designed for skiing, but it never snows in Oakland, or anywhere close.

I open my car door, but she doesn't follow the visual cue.

"I'm not even thinking . . ." she says. "Well . . . let's just say there's just some people I'd like to close up with." I can see her breath hang like smoke, illuminated by the pale streetlight. "If I had the time. Like my ex."

She says it in a heavy, loaded way that implies she's expecting me to ask. Reluctantly, I do. "Your ex?"

"She cheated on me with Renata, back when Renata was gay. I didn't even know it until I met Renata for the first time. She sure knew who *I* was, because boy did I get some graphic imagery. Then I went home and said stuff I wish I hadn't."

Too much information, and I don't have the time. *Tick, tick, tick.*

She must hear, because her smile turns rueful. "I'll let you go."

It's one of those awkward moments I'm no good at, when

something wise and supportive should be said and all I have is the keen desire to pass into the next moment, and the one after that, alone if possible.

She nods, hearing that trail too, and starts to turn around but stops. "You're going for it, aren't you? The double deal?"

Am I?

I am.

"Maybe we all should," she says, and then suddenly I think of the Guinness sweating on Alejandro's Koa countertop right before I picked it up, opened the tab, took a sip.

What exactly are you up to, Fiona Dunn?

Jasmine gives a slight smile, a slighter wave, and then walks away.

I'm left with that feeling I get when Tracy picks up one of my cast-off ideas and then runs with it as her own, and I wonder if instead of gauging my competition, I just created it.

CHAPTER FOURTEEN

I **AM NOT DOING** what I should be doing. If I were smart, I would go to the store, pick up the Tylenol, endure Justin's wrath, and try to squeeze in a power nap afterward. I don't know if it's a good idea to try to find Jeb and Dan; I'm in that exhausted state where reality feels distant, where bad decisions get made. There are microlapses in my consciousness. I reach Birch Street and I don't remember any of the four miles leading up to it.

And Justin is royally pissed. I texted *On my way* and he didn't respond, I called three times, no answer. In the olden days, the pre-cancer days, if I was working too late or I missed another one of his "bring your date/partner" work functions, I would make amends with a package of white frosted mini-doughnuts and a box of Jujyfruits.

But then I've done something far, far worse than just miss a function. Many worse things actually.

At the next stoplight my eyes drift closed, the rumble of the engine like a lullaby, so it's a shock when the car behind me honks in protest—for a good few seconds I have no idea where, or when, I am. I see the light is green. The car passes around my left, an angry swerve with another fierce honk, and when I put my foot on the gas, I press too hard and almost hit it. The driver flips me off.

Easy. Take it easy. I'm more careful with the gas this time. I really put my mind to it, the pressure, but it feels strange. It's like being suddenly aware of your heart, that you must clench it, release it, that your lungs need to expand, contract, expand—one of the reasons I always hated meditation, the knowledge of all the gears that must turn for you to live another moment.

I should go home. I'm going home.

The car seems to make a different decision though, and it skips the left turn toward home, like we've switched places—it's the driver, I'm the vehicle—and heads for the highway ramp instead.

I wonder if maybe I'm losing my mind.

There was a famous PR stunt in the late sixties where a radio DJ went two hundred hours without sleep to raise money for a cause, crippled children or children with cancer, something like that. All the scientists got excited at this opportunity for a risky, live human experiment, and after a hundred and twenty hours awake, he started to have hallucinations—opened a drawer and saw flames shoot out, forgot the alphabet, and thought one of the scientists was an undertaker come to bury him. I wish that everything I've seen and done in the last day could be attributed to a hallucination. Make that the last year. Saul chose madness, and at the moment madness seems very attractive, a respite, a place to shelter, either temporarily or forever. But how do you go about losing your mind on purpose?

I bet there's a wikiHow on that.

The car continues its journey toward Holy Names University, and I just hold the wheel, let it take me.

Not much traffic on a Sunday night, so when it weaves across the line occasionally, we don't hit anything—I note the pronoun *we*: I've personified the car. I'm regressing. We pass the blur of the neon sign from Justin's old workplace, Fealtee, a "word that doesn't mean anything" word that sounds close enough to a real one, and hell, the domain was available. Ostensibly the company's purpose is to safeguard people's personal info—a "gold lock" account will send you a text if someone applies for a credit card in your name—but Justin shared that the other, bigger side of the pie is selling the metadata to the NSA. After you sign up, a bit of spyware is installed, tracking every click, Google search or Pandora play, even the content of e-mails. *No one ever reads the privacy statement*, Justin once said.

Damn though, Fealtee's benefits have been amazing.

I check my cell. I think there's a law against this now, driving and checking your phone, but I'm not sure. No text messages from Justin. A small part of me is relieved. I hope he's asleep by the time I get home. It will all work out in the end though. It'll all come out in the wash. He'll see.

Next is a billboard for the college—HOLY NAMES UNIVERSITY, BUILDING THE PEOPLE WHO BUILD THE WORLD—and the car takes the exit. I look in the rearview mirror. No one behind me for a mile. Then I catch my own reflection. It stops my breath.

Part of me is missing. A good chunk from my chin to my neck is completely opaque—I can see the backseat headrest through my throat. This has never happened before, partial invisibility. I reach my hand to my neck, feel the warmth of my skin, the pulse of my jugular vein, but in the mirror it looks like I'm holding air.

Halfway down the off-ramp, I quickly flip on the car's interior light—again something you shouldn't do while driving, especially in Oakland—and I get the faintest sense of something vanishing, or more like *escaping*, but with the light on I'm returned to normal, fully visible.

Did I just imagine that? Or is it a sign that Scratch has already called in the other three favors, and I'm next? The only person I could ask is Alejandro, and he's dead to me. I flick the car light back off. The world, already unbearably harsh, seems like an even harsher, colder place without him. A gust of wind picks up a lonely plastic grocery bag, lands it in the gutter. A homeless man pushes a rusted grocery cart down the sidewalk, a ratty umbrella propped over his sleeping bag, tins of food. No, there is no one to lean in to, to trust, not now.

But then there's something else to think about because as we approach the campus, I wonder what's going on. Students gather on the sidewalk, huddled around their cell phones, chatting. The traffic that passes the campus slows from the rubberneckers trying to get a good look. I put my blinker on for a left-hand turn, and as I pass through the entrance, I catch a millennial couple in the gleam of my headlights, which blanches them, renders them into pale ghosts. Throngs of other students mill about on the pavement, on the lawns, their faces lit with some kind of heightened thrill.

Then I see strobing lights ahead, bright flashes caught in a hovering mist, blue and white. Then I hear sirens. Like every ambulance in the whole city is hurtling toward us, announcing their imminent arrival like the horsemen of the apocalypse.

UP AHEAD, police blockade the road that loops through the oak-studded campus. An officer with an orange glow stick waves me to turn around—*Go back*, he mouths. *Go back*—but an ambulance has just come up behind me so I slowly pull my car over to the soft shoulder where another couple of cars have been ditched too.

I can feel my heart flutter in my throat. This isn't good. There's no way this can be good.

I pull out my cell, scanning for news, but this is so new I don't see a thing under *Holy Names*, or *Holy Names* + *Jeb* or + *Dan*. Which means there's only one thing for it—talk to an actual person. I kill the engine, turn off the lights, and slide over to the passenger side to ease out of the car as two more ambulances drive by. *Goddamn*. Really, *goddamn*.

The grass is packed with a spectrum of people, older professorial types and a mix of students from an assortment of races, some weeping, some murmuring, all straining to see over one another's heads to whatever *it* is. A couple of more boisterous lads have climbed onto the branches of the oak trees for a better look.

I sidle toward an unassuming group standing under the eave of an ugly, three-story squat building. Goth girls huddled together, wearing dark vintage clothing, thick eyeglasses, and obviously new combat boots. One twists her blond hair nervously, another bites the end of her black fingernails. I fold my arms over my chest, wrap my jacket a little tighter and catch Hair Twister's eye. I know that as a person older than twenty-two, I am ancient, suspect.

"What happened?" I ask her.

Conflicting emotions—the politeness her middle-class parents raised her with competes against not wanting to seem like a pushover to her friends. So I get a middle-of-the-road, ambiguous shrug.

It's Nail Biter who answers. "Total massacre." Her voice is scratchy in an assumed kind of way, like she's practiced it in the mirror. "Sorority sister party. I don't think any of them survived." I note that her vintage clothes look like actual thrift-store finds, a size too big. Poor girl on a full-ride. A kindred spirit.

"No one knows *anything*," says the tallest girl, with jet-black hair and a tongue piercing, obviously the alpha.

"I heard Darren talking to police." Nail Biter has some spunk. "He *saw* it."

"But he can't know if they're all dead. No one can know that." The other girls shift their stance slightly, leaning in Tall Girl's direction, getting into pack formation. It's the hardest age to conduct focus groups with because they tend to coalesce around the biggest personality and then just repeat the same things.

"Do they know who did it?" I ask.

It's the tall girl who answers, obviously unable to contain herself. "Santa Claus."

I'm expecting the others to laugh at this lame joke, but none do.

"*Santa* Claus?"

Tall Girl cuts her eyes at the others. "I guess we know which bitches have been naughty this year, right?" Now the smirks appear. Nail Biter looks like she wants to add something but doesn't.

More sirens, more police cars. The officer who flagged me to turn around joins two others, and they immediately close off the exit.

"Shit," whispers Tall Girl. "Are we on lockdown? Should we lock ourselves in a classroom or something?"

We all pull out our cell phones, each of us thumbing searches to find more info.

"I got a text," says Nail Biter. "We're supposed to proceed to the gym in an orderly manner. Keep the road clear for emergency responders, stay with a group. Report anyone in a Santa suit."

"Fuck," says Tall Girl. Not as funny now that it's confirmed.

Santa Claus. Given recent events, definitely sounds like a dead-soul favor being called in, but was it just one of them or were Jeb and Dan working together? If it's both, then I am truly, and royally screwed—that would put my name next on Scratch's list. I wonder if we're all going to be given a macabre Christmas theme, what the purpose of that could possibly be. So many brutal murder sprees in such a short time will set off national debates—liberals blaming socioeconomic policies, conservatives the plummeting values of the left, and religious nuts Oakland's close proximity to San Francisco.

I almost want to ask the girls if any of them know Jeb or Dan, but then that would link me, and unlike Saul, I'm not interested in a sustained prison term at the moment.

Should I go and see?

Dicey. Lots of eyes around, plenty of opportunities for a misstep, and after what happened in the car, invisibility feels like a risk. But it could be hours before the real news leaks or photos make it online.

No, I need to confirm, know where I am on the list.

There's a rustle of activity on a grassy knoll to the left, some kind of school administrator standing on a folding chair with a megaphone, while a professorial type helpfully holds up a flashlight to illuminate his torso, which makes it look like the administrator's body has been cut in half.

"Everyone, we're experiencing technical difficulties with the loudspeaker system. Please proceed to the gym in an orderly manner, and keep to the left of the road to allow emergency vehicles to pass. Police will take down your contact information and ask you a few questions, then once the campus is cleared, you can return to your dorms. The police chief will give an update on the situation in fifteen minutes."

I drift away from the girls—everyone is so focused on the administrator that no one notices me step into the shadow behind a looming shrub. I'm grateful I chose a black jacket and dark denim jeans, because even without my talent it doesn't take long for me to almost completely disappear from view.

I find a lonesome spot near a Dumpster where the foliage is particularly thick. But really, even if someone saw what happens next, who would believe them?

NO PROBLEM WITH THE INVISIBILITY, a relief, and the next hardest part is moving through the crowd—people are packed so tightly together on the left side of the road that I have to slip through the in-between spaces, trying not to bump or brush against anyone in the process. But once I'm through, I have the right side all to myself. It's cold, I always forget about cold—the air, the grass, even the paved road beneath my bare feet is freezing—but it always feels primal, this walking among people, naked and invisible. Empowering in a strange way, to see but not be seen.

Soon the road diverges, and while the crowd moves left toward the gym, I turn right, where I see strobing police car lights up ahead. A soft wind blows through the barren trees. Eventually the rooftop of a white colonial house comes into view, and then a Southern Gothic porch, with a sign perched on a small, rounded second-floor balcony, the Greek letters ΦΚΨ painted in gold.

This is where the ambulances are thick.

I duck under the yellow police tape. The tension is fraught, palpable, a barely ordered chaos of first responders and technicians. I step past paramedics working on the body of a young blond woman, stabbed or shot is hard to say but there's so much blood it looks like she took a bath in it. She's wearing footed pajamas. They push at her heart, but her glow is gone, I sense nothing there anymore.

Not the way she probably expected her life would end, although at that age the very idea of an end would seem unfathomable.

Where will she go? I wonder. Is there another side of the equation, a heaven? If so, I can't imagine why it's so underrepresented here on earth, why the devils and the damned have the run of the place.

It's not until I get closer that I see what happened to her face, or what's left of it. A blurry, runny red mess, like someone used the smudge tool in Photoshop. I've seen this before, in a documentary I dragged Justin to about the untouchables in India and how throwing acid in women's faces was considered justifiable in certain circumstances. Turning down sexual propositions, for example. The top of her pajamas have melted into her skin.

The complete and utter brutality is definitely Scratch's signature. If there was any doubt that this was a dead-soul event, it's gone now.

Good God, what will he make me *do to Justin?*

Better not to think about that. It would be like climbing a ladder and looking down, paralyzing me, and my window of opportunity will close, and then Justin will die, and then I will be damned *and* alone.

I take a quiet, steadying breath. Head for the porch. A police officer almost steps into me, but I manage to dodge at the last second. Too close. I feel painted wood beneath my feet, make my way up the creaking steps, get the sense that I'm walking in slow motion—shouts inside, *"We found another one!"*—and turn my shoulders to avoid another paramedic carrying a girl. Her arms flop listlessly, her face burned beyond comprehension, and a viscous liquid fills her eye cavities.

Don't think about it.

I put my hand on the rail to steady myself.

Maybe Scratch *knows* we talked about the double deal at the New Parish—he seems to know almost everything else. But then he is the devil—he would know everything, right? Be able to do anything? That wouldn't leave any room for free will though, in which case, how could anyone be saved or damned if they never had a choice in the first place?

It's another Möbius strip of an existential puzzle. *Don't think about it.*

I reach the top of the porch. The front door is open, an inviting Christmas pine wreath nailed to it. Music, *music* from inside, high and tinny, like it's playing through a bad speaker.

Bing Crosby, it sounds like, crooning "Jingle Bells," the song the little girls in the pageant were performing just before they were cut down. A cosmic joke or a spooky coincidence?

I step through the doorway. Pass by a detective. He looks grim, and I soon discover why.

The living room. Blood spatters the white walls—*God, so much of it*—and what must be ten or twelve girls strewn about, no one working on them but technicians with latex gloves, cataloging, gathering evidence. The sorority sisters all wear similar pajamas, with duckies, and puppies, and unicorns, like they were auditioning for Cindy Lou Who. There are remnants of some kind of Christmas festivity—pine needle garlands draped along the stair rails and pinned in loops to the wall, a folding table with platters of sugar cookies, frosted brownies, a keg, bottles of peach schnapps and red plastic cups. A coffee table is turned over, broken, and a floor lamp knocked to the floor flickers wanly.

Feelings. It's hard to feel anything because it's so shocking it looks fake, like this is just a film set or at any moment the girls are going to jump up and yell *You got punked!* A viral horror Christmas flash mob.

Murder as spectacle? Some kind of Bernays stunt?

There's a germ of an idea that tugs at me. I step over to a window adorned with paper snowflakes. Someone pulled the shade half off, leaving streaks of bloody handprints. I can see what's happening behind me reflected in the glass—an officer looks down at the face of a girl, his own reads heartbroken— and I can see what's happening on the other side of the window, the flashing ambulance lights, officers talking into their radios. The only thing I don't see is myself, which is as it should be.

So why do I feel like I'm being watched?

Something catches at the corner of my eyes, a shadow flitting through the trees, the movement too big to be anything but human. Then it's up in the tree—I see the shimmer of branches trembling—and a few leaves drift down, fall to the grass. Then it's gone.

Scratch?

But I can't think about it because just then my foot registers something wet, and cold. I look down to find I've stepped in a pool of blood. Beyond the blood is the curled body of a girl lying on her side, her face thankfully turned away from me.

Fuck. This presents problems. Serious problems. Another step and I'll leave a footprint for sure, evidence that could definitely be traced to me. I'm going to have to ghost myself out.

That feels risky. And to where? If I ghost home, I'll be leaving my clothes behind, the car. I click through how long it will take before they run the license plate, discover that not only is it registered to Fiona Dunn, but said Fiona Dunn visited San Quentin earlier. And then what would they make of my clothes left in a heap tucked away in the shrubbery, with my purse, wallet, and cell phone? The panicked trail of text messages. Did someone mention Jeb and Dan? Christ, I think they did. Ghosting back to the shrub is also risky—a couple of feet off and I'll be a very visible naked woman out in the open, something I'm sure the officers will take note of.

Another pair of technicians wrestle a gurney through the door, and a third heads straight for me.

There was that three-story building, with a long, flat roof. I can ghost there, sort out the rest after. No one ever looks up. My best worst option.

Just as I'm about to close my eyes, a gust of wind blows through, rustles the fliers on a bulletin board festooned with craft paper holly leaves and red tissue paper bunched to form the berries. *Calculus Tutoring just $20/hour*, *Toys 4 Tots Car Wash!*, *Start the New Year with Piedmont Pilates*—and another that catches my eye.

Data Mining Interns Needed for High-Tech Company. Followed by the Fealtee logo.

Good God, standing in the pool of some unknown girl's blood it comes to me. An offer for a double deal that the devil himself couldn't possibly turn down.

The technician spots the girl by my feet, and his skin blanches.

"Ashley," he says, his voice bereft.

Oh fuck, he knows her.

He takes another step toward me, so I close my eyes, let the world fade—

CHAPTER FIFTEEN

—**A**ND OPEN THEM to a world of ash. Everything around me is gray or in the state of becoming gray, a shadowy version of reality with no sound, no color, the boundaries of forms blurry, smudged. Things are tree-ish, building-ish, people-ish, but otherwise indistinct, unreachable. I sense I'm pulled through space and objects, fast and slow at the same time, like I'm speeding up or the world is slowing down around me. *Vortex*, a word from my college physics days; *purgatory* a word from the girl with the perfect lunches. I taste wood, cold air, metal, car exhaust, paint, flesh, bark, paper, blood, water, tar, all the things I pass through, creating a new taste, indescribable. But then I realize all sensation is movement, a current of raw experience, not separated or isolated by increments of time, identity, the things that bind.

It's beautiful. It's terrifying. It's sublime. *Ashley, Jennifer, Hannah, Alice, Sarah, Rachel, Kara, Cindy, Delilah, Grace, Tina, Marnie, Beth.* I know their names, they're here somehow, but they're losing their form too, becoming absorbed, consumed. *Ashes to ashes, dust to dust.*

This strikes me as funny, so I laugh, or I think I laugh but my jaw feels like its being pulled away from me, my body stretched out into all directions.

Ghosting. I ghost, you ghost, he/she/it ghosts. We ghost, you ghost, they ghost. *Is this what getting high is like?* I can see the appeal now, discarding the weight of self.

Then I get a sense of up, pulled up to the sky while the ground falls away, and the vortex begins to collapse, the world hardening again, becoming bits and pieces of this or that.

Is this the train from the story Alejandro spoke of? If I had a watch, would I stop it here? There's something nice about everything all mixed and smudged together. Simpler. Once again I'm a ghost in a ghost world, and I wonder if I let it go, all my boundaries, what it would feel like to not be anymore.

A man's soft, bitter voice. *Apple never falls far from the tree.* My father. He's here, in this gray hinterland. And then I think I see him, a tall, lanky shadow with the telltale right-hand quiver. Or is that just me, my memories floating out into the ether, echoing back before they dissipate, disappear?

Still. There's a surprising bit of emotion, seeing him again.

CHAPTER SIXTEEN

COLD CONCRETE under my feet. The wind blows through my hair, tickles my naked shoulders. I hear voices, sirens, traffic. I'm back. A part of me doesn't want to open my eyes, a part of me wants to ghost again, see if I can get lost forever in that gray hinterland. *Can Scratch collect if I don't exist anymore?*

But that thing called self, it sticks, my ferocious will to be.

So I open my eyes and the world looks new, achingly beautiful. I'm on the roof and, godlike, I can see the rooftops of all the campus buildings, the tops of trees, bent and twisted, the police spreading out on the grounds below, their flashlight beams penetrating the darkness like shooting stars. A good crowd has formed outside the perimeter wall, a mix of what looks like concerned friends and family, and police are now trying to create a detour so more don't join them. News vans have taken the prime spaces along the sidewalks, and while crews fix lights, reporters check their hair. Traffic snakes slowly through the intersection, and I can see the jam extends at least two miles, maybe more.

Even if I can retrieve my clothes, there's no way to get my car out. No good explanation as to why it would be on the campus. I imagine all the hours that will be wasted, time spent trying to come up with a reasonable lie, time spent sitting in a police station while they take my statement. If they run the plates, will they find out I visited San Quentin earlier? Is their database that good?

I'm running out of time on all fronts. I'm either losing my ability or it's becoming hard to control, a sure sign I'm moving up on Scratch's collection list. *Should I wait?*

But I'm so damn *close*. The Fealtee flier. I need to get home, boot up Justin's laptop, see if what I'm thinking about offering Scratch for a double deal is even possible. If it is, I can solve all my problems with one carefully worded trade.

And the big shadow in the trees that I saw earlier. Whatever that was, it can't be good.

A plan starts to materialize—not the best one—that involves me climbing down the drainpipe, then—

I hear a cough directly behind me.

I TURN, STARTLED, to find Jeb and Dan behind me, no trouble telling them apart tonight. Jeb's wearing jeans and a T-shirt I've seen him in many times before—it reads FE, IRONY—and blood clumps his hair, stains his shirt. His right arm is horribly burned, looks like the charred top of an overdone pizza. With the other arm he holds an incoherent Dan around the waist, like he's propping up a drunk buddy, a listing ship. Dan is in full Santa gear with a red velvet suit and a white fake beard pulled halfway down his chin, blood smeared across his face and white gloves.

What's the fastest way I can ditch them? is my immediate, horrible thought.

"I didn't," whispers Dan to a vacant spot just over my shoulder. "I didn't. I didn't. I didn't."

Tears have left streaks in the blood on his face. His right eye twitches. He will never be the same again.

"What did you *do*?" I ask Jeb. Short, terse, interrogatory words. Not the right ones, not *Oh my God, what happened?* or *Are you hurt?* Not the faintest hint, or breath of compassion. It frightens me how unnatural empathy seems at the moment.

Jeb, looking equal parts terrified and stunned, says, "I didn't do anything. Dan . . . he . . . I tried to stop them."

"What do you mean, *them*?"

"I knew about the party." His voice is hoarse, ragged. "I was going to swing by the sorority later, but I didn't know Scratch had called in his favor. Which is weird, totally weird, because we *promised* each other, you know, blood-brother promise that if Scratch called in the favor . . . we'd tell each other. I mean that's fucked-up, right? That he didn't tell me?"

"Jeb, what do you mean *them*?"

"They just did what Dan told them to. Like his power . . . it was *amplified*. No one would do that to themselves. I can't . . . I can't even . . ."

"Was Alejandro there taking pictures?"

He shakes his head. "A girl. She was shooting the whole thing on Dan's cell. The lights were going on and off, like when *he's* around. And then I think . . . no I know I saw . . . oh God, he was there. The devil, he was . . . oh God. Oh Jesus fucking Christ."

Something catches in my throat, a fluttery feeling I don't think a word exists for, a strange mix of fear, excitement, desire, and despair. "Are you *sure*?"

A teardrop of sweat trickles down Jeb's forehead. "He was outside under that big tree, smoking. I felt him before I saw him—turned and there he was, exactly the way I remember, white blond hair, wearing a hoodie. No face. Half the girls were dead by the time I got there. And he was just . . . looking at the sky. Like nothing was happening. Like it didn't even matter. Watched me run into the house, didn't try to stop me. All I could do though was get Dan out. Too late for anything else. And then we saw you through the window."

The movement in the tree. "That was you?"

He nods. "After what happened, that's as far as I could get us."

"I *didn't!*" says Dan, louder and more emphatically this time, and we both quickly shush him. Dan's knees buckle and Jeb struggles to hold him upright, looks at me, pleading. Will the adult please take charge?

Dammit, I have things to do. *Tick, tick, tick.* And now there will be bloody footprints, Jeb and Dan's on the rooftop, little bits of DNA evidence forming connection points, linking us all together. What will they find of me, I wonder? A fallen hair? Flake of skin? Plus my car, my clothes, my wallet, my cell phone. Too many variables to keep track of, layers and layers of complication when all I wanted was time. Why didn't I just ask Scratch for more time?

"Fiona?" Jeb's voice is tentative, wan.

In the distance, I hear the drone of helicopters approaching. The rooftop is suddenly less appealing.

I press the back of my hand against my forehead, try to find the best way out considering the clusterfuck material I'm surrounded with. I may have to leave them behind, let them take the fall.

As if sensing my mutinous line of thought, Jeb says, "I can't fly well anymore . . . not since this morning."

I look at him intently. "Your card?"

"Nothing," he says.

"Show me."

His face goes pale, shocked that I'd even ask, but the helicopters are getting closer. He reaches into his back pocket with his good arm, pulls it out. His fingers tremble as he hands it to me.

Cautiously, I take it from him.

FAVOR: *blank.*

The damned wellspring of hope rises again. I'm not next, there's one left before me.

"It means I'm close though, right? That's what Alejandro said, that our powers wouldn't work so well . . . when we're close?"

He's hoping I'll correct him, tell him he's wrong, but instead, I look away, calculating. Dan's completed, Renata's on her way, but Jeb . . . he could be useful. He *is* close, which means he's probably third on Scratch's list, and until his favor's called in, I know I have some breathing room. My own canary in a coal mine. Plus he's a cybersecurity major. That could be very, *very* useful.

Whir of chopper blades, closer. Not long now until we're spotted.

"I didn't," whispers Dan. He rubs a bloody hand over his

bloody mouth, chokes back a sob. "I didn't. I *didn't*. Jeb knows. Jeb sees." He quickly reaches into Jeb's pocket and pulls out a cell smeared with even more blood. "You can see, too."

My eyes meet Jeb's. "That's the phone that filmed it?"

He nods. "I grabbed it from the girl. Thought it'd buy us some time."

Wind wraps around my ankles, a soft caress. The pale glint of the moon emerges from behind a cloud.

So. This is how bad I'm fucked.

A favor. Scratch called it a *favor*. Favors are picking up an extra half gallon of milk at the store, running down to the meter to add another quarter, favors are rides to the airport and liking a friend's new page on Facebook. *Favor* was not the right word, not at all, it can't even begin to encompass everything happening right now. But there is no time, not for regrets, or emotions. I must get out of here. I must get out of my favor, *somehow*. I must succeed.

Here are my materials—a boy who can fly, a boy who's incoherent, and a Santa suit.

Possibly. Yes, possibly, yes.

"Get him out of the suit. Hurry."

JEB HAS DROPPED ME OFF in the narrow space between the eave of the building and a Dumpster. It was more like falling than flying and I scraped my hands on the landing, but better than the alternative, ghosting. The Santa suit is too big, the pants are cold and wet with blood, and there are small, scorched holes from where drops of acid fell. I don't know the whole story, and

I'm not sure if I ever want to. But the black leather belt cinches the waist enough, and so I grab the suit jacket, slide it over my shoulders, push out the beard, mustache, and hat, which Jeb wisely tucked into the sleeve before dropping it so a gust of wind couldn't carry them off somewhere else.

I slip the beard over my face, tightening the elastic to hold it on tightly. Grab the hat, place it firmly on my head—my hand registers a clump of dried blood—and try not to think too much about the next part. I can't be killed, but that doesn't mean I want to get shot.

A helicopter flies directly overhead, pressing a large beam of light through the trees like fingers. When it passes, I look up to where Jeb's head peers over the edge of the rooftop, a dark silhouette.

I wave. He waves back, then his head disappears. A few seconds pass, and then I see him—it looks like he's jumping from the building, the barely discernible form of Dan hanging from his neck, their trajectory the tree just above the shrub where I stashed my clothes. In spite of everything, it's weird, spooky, and wonderful to see them in flight. They land in the tree's serpentine branches, perfect timing because moments later another helicopter swoops in, directs its beam to the rooftop where we all were just standing.

I watch Jeb carefully fix Dan's arms so he's gripping the tree's trunk, and then Jeb softly drops to the ground. Darts behind the shrub. Its branches rustle and then Jeb emerges, holding a bundle of my clothes under his arm. He pauses, and then flicks my father's brass Winston lighter on. A small flame dances on its tip. What a bitter moment that was in my childhood, slipping it out of my father's pants pocket when he was too high to notice, and to think I carried it with me all those years, a souvenir of hard times. More than a decade for its purpose to reveal itself.

Jeb flicks the lighter off.

My turn.

I run.

Bolting out of the shadow of the Dumpster, I brush past officers who turn to look, startled—*Hey, is that . . . ? Did you see . . . ?*—and make a mad dash straight for the police cars blocking the entrance, arms pumping hard, trying to make the most of the moment between their sight, thought, and realization. Men and women in navy fatigues drop their hands to their gun holsters—shouts of *stop! stop!*—but I can't, I won't, because I have to train all their eyes on me.

I make it past the entrance, jump over the intersection of two squad cars, sliding over the hoods just like they do in the movies, but the landing isn't as graceful—I fall on my face, feel the scrape of asphalt against my hands again—

Click, click of guns locking.

—and stand to the screeching of brakes, traffic that has to swerve to miss me. There's a huge mass of people held back behind police tape on the sidewalk. I feel their collective gaze land on me—

"Hands on your head, hands on your head!"

Click, click, click. Static of police walkie-talkies. *"Stop, right now! Hands on your head!"*

So I do, I stop. Hold out my arms to each side, raise my hands, open palms. Then slowly turn so everyone, *everyone* sees me. Or at least they think they see me—what they see is a suit, so recognizable that it fills in features, not from sight, but memory. Gestalt in action. They'll notice I'm slight, but their minds will jump to the most obvious conclusion. Male.

Although they'll also figure out there was an accomplice, because at that moment my car detonates.

Amazing how simple it is, when gasoline meets fire. Every car a bomb under the right circumstances.

Screams, shouts, the panicked horde run en masse, pouring past the police tape, the chaos and fear epic, unstoppable. As expected. And although officers aim at me, we're all soon absorbed by the crush of crowd, and there's no possible way to shoot me without taking some innocent lives.

As the tide of humans overtakes us, I join them, running for a yard or two before pulling off my hat, pulling off my jacket, and disappearing entirely. Leaving only the suit, and a false impression, behind.

CHAPTER SEVENTEEN

IT TAKES TIME TO GET HOME; every lost moment is viscerally painful. I managed to slip on a bus for part of the way, settling next to a crazy old woman who talked to her hands for four miles—"They won't come clean, they never comes clean"—while I sat naked and invisible on a grimy vinyl seat, cold, shaken, worrying that at any moment there would be another fluctuation in my invisibility, that I'd suddenly be revealed in the harsh fluorescent light. Caught.

My time, I know, is rapidly approaching. I told Jeb to meet me at my apartment, but there's no way to know whether he'll keep his word, bring my things, or if he'll take off with Dan, try to run away, or in his case, fly.

I would.

The bus is slow, stopping too often, taking too long to let passengers off and on. *Tick, tick, tick.* Ten minutes alone spent on a vet in a wheelchair—getting him on, finding the straps to secure the wheels, lifting the front seats—so I'm a wreck by the time I get off two blocks from my apartment. A light rain starts, and I wonder if this is *his* doing, some kind of ironic replay of our first meeting. Maybe Scratch is out here hidden in shadow, watching me panic, enjoying the show. Or filming it. Not a particularly comforting thought walking down the nearly deserted streets, but then it strikes me—this is the one common thread among all the recent horrors. They've been filmed. They've been viewed widely. Is this what Alejandro offered? Reach?

Rain beads my hair, my breath forms soft clouds of mist in the cold air. This is all someone driving by might see, small puffs of vapor, appearing and disappearing for no reason. I wrap my arms around my chest, trying to stay warm. Focused.

Alejandro once said that all evil is simply an inversion of good, that it's not possible for one to exist without the other. Trying to make the world one thing or the other is an exercise in futility, a misunderstanding of the nature of reality. Of course, he said that from the comfort of a double deal. A part of me still can't believe he's been selling us out all this time, but a part of me can. Look at all I've been capable of.

I reach my apartment and encounter the same problem the night I sold my soul—locked out. Again, irony. I could try to ghost in, but that might leave me in the gray space, or I could wait and follow someone in, but that would still leave me locked out of my own apartment. A veritable quandary.

But then the hairs on the back of my neck prickle. The sense of being watched again. Jeb? I turn around quickly, scanning the street, the rooftops, hoping I'll see him, that he's brought my things.

Nothing, and no one that I can see.

And then the electricity goes out, building by building, window by window, streetlight by streetlight, until the whole block is dark. I hear a click in the entry door. Reach out a tentative hand for the door handle, find it pulls open easily. No electricity, no magnetic lock.

As soon as the door's open, all the lights on the block come back on instantaneously.

A coincidence, I tell myself as I step into the foyer. *Rolling blackouts*. But even I don't believe me.

I PRESS MY EAR against my apartment door and hear the monotonous drone of the television, interrupted by canned laughter and applause. No idea what time it is, but the hallway is empty.

I could reappear, knock. I'm late, but not completely unthinkable, not I-fucked-someone kind of late.

Although I did.

Christ, I did.

But that was ages ago. And I did it to buy time, so I could save Jason.

No, Justin.

Fuck.

My heart starts a panicky roll, the kind that arrives after a fifth double-shot cappuccino, when I'm far over my stress limit and pressed against a hard print deadline. I feel unmoored, untethered, a balloon drifting into the upper atmosphere where the air is thin. For a moment, I don't know if I'm entering the gray in-between space again, or if this is some other kind of fluctuation I haven't experienced yet.

I put my hand on the doorknob, firmly. Grasping. Landing. This helps somewhat. The smooth, cool metal is familiar in my palm, worn away from the hundreds of tenants before me, the marks left by Scratch gone, no match for Opal's industrious cleaning. I take a breath. I need to move myself into the next moment of time, and then the one after that, until I have my double deal, warnings be damned.

I could try walking through the door. Not the same as ghosting, a lower-risk proposition. Without much of a choice, I decide to try it.

The first thing to do is relax—not easy. I imagine my right foot as porous, empty, and tentatively press my toes against the door. They pass through. It's harder than it was earlier in San Quentin though—I can feel the grain of the wood, sense the striations—and it takes more effort to push the whole foot in, but it works. Eventually I feel the hardwood of my apartment floor with the tips of my toes.

Almost there.

I push my hip against the door, feel it start to move through but then it stops. The wood seems to be hardening around me, and for a heart-pounding moment I'm stuck.

Relax. If worst comes to worst, you can ghost in.

I take a longer, deeper breath. Focus on my body becoming like particulate matter, empty, without flesh. My hip rushes through, so I step into the door with my shoulder, chest, and head.

Almost there.

I taste paint, and wood, and something wriggling, moving—*termites? powder-post beetles?*—and while my left eye captures the empty hallway, my right one sees Opal and Justin slumped over opposite ends of the couch like wilted flowers. Some inane sitcom plays on the TV, a rerun better forgotten.

Are they okay? I've seen dead bodies today, too many of them, and they are so very, very still.

With a final heave, I get the rest of my body through, stumble a few steps, and almost knock over a Tiffany lamp on the entryway mid-century table. It wobbles, but I catch it before it crashes to the floor.

Breathe, I tell myself, righting the lamp. Then I turn toward the couch.

Tiny Opal looks even tinier curled up on the cushion, like a child just barely entering adolescence. *The Firm* has landed on the floor, facedown. Justin's head lolls back on a pillow Sarah had insisted on planting here—it's shaped like a baseball and worn through, so stuffing pokes out of its edges, a holdout from his childhood. I lock in on his chest, and to my relief it rises, falls, rises.

This smallest of movements brings me back to something like feeling, but feelings right now will serve no one. I'm a wreck, and I need to somehow make myself presentable, reenter the facade of who I used to be.

Which is becoming harder and harder to remember.

WHILE THE SHOWER RUNS, I brush my teeth to get the taste of wood and bug out of my mouth. Spit in the sink, watch the water swirl with the foaming toothpaste. Then I turn on the hot water faucet—separate from the cold, again something that seemed charming at the time—and take a look at the state of my hands. Raw, not bleeding much, which is good, but there's grit and dirt embedded in the skin. I grab the soap and run it over my palms, ignoring the sting.

No car, no purse, no cell phone. Late. A robbery of some kind. That's the only plausible excuse. But does it make sense?

I rinse off my hands, reach for a face towel, let it sit under the faucet that's running hot now, steaming.

My car was stolen. I could even report that to the police, make the narrative complete. Left my cell in my purse, which explains why I didn't respond to Justin's texts. All I had when I went in for the Tylenol was my wallet and keys.

I pause, catch a glimpse of my reflection in the fogging mirror of the medicine cabinet. My hair is straggly, purple bruises blooming around my neck from where Saul strangled me, there's a smudge of blood on my cheek from the bloody Santa beard. But what's more disturbing is that my dark shadow seems a tinge darker.

I turn off the hot water and hold up my hand. The shadowy aura seems to float out from it like a mist.

The word *contagion* comes to mind. Then something Saul said. *Everything I touched, I corrupted.*

I quickly pop open the medicine cabinet, grab my bottle of Xanax. Shake three pills into my palm. Then I turn on the cold faucet, cup my hand underneath, swallow the pills, and chase them down with water that tastes like rusty pipes.

My cell was in the car, Officer, so I decided to just walk home. Call when I got in.

I could even report that I'd given Dan a ride once—he'd mentioned how he'd hot-wired cars for joy rides when he was a teenager. Lead them in his direction.

I step into the shower, let the water run over my body, face and hands. Doesn't take long for the Xanax to kick in, especially on an empty stomach.

I've never felt less like myself in my entire life. It's like my soul, the who-I-am, is disappearing, becoming invisible, and something else entirely, the not-me-of-me, is shining through.

I don't know why that seems to make sense, but it does.

Don't think about it.

My mantra for the day.

I PUT ON MY COSTUME, which at the moment is a terry-cloth robe. Grab a small towel to rub my wet hair with. My story is straight. It's time to start my narrative.

They're both still asleep when I walk into the living room, turn off the TV. I walk over to Opal, give her shoulder a gentle shake.

Her eyes slowly blink open, like a cat.

"What?" she says, trying to sit up, still groggy. Blinks some more, trying to focus on my face. "Oh, you're home."

Now to unroll the lies. "I got here a few minutes ago, but you looked so . . . peaceful."

"You took a shower." A statement, not a question, the barest hint of suspicion in her voice. "Where were you?"

I start to rub my hair with the towel. A good liar doesn't forget about body language, it conveys messaging so much better than words.

"I walked back. The car was stolen." *Which reminds me, I still need to report that.*

"Why didn't you call?"

I don't like the tone she's taking, it's borderline aggressive.

"Cell was in the car."

But Miss Opal, she misses nothing. She crosses her arms over her chest. "You could have borrowed someone's."

"*Thank* you. Next time my car is stolen, I'll remember that."

She opens her mouth, about to say something else, but thinks better of it. "Did you at least *get* the Tylenol?"

No missing *that* inflection. "Like I said, my car was stolen." She clenches her jaw.

"Thanks for staying late," I say in a tone that adds, *and now, you can go*.

"I can run to the store."

"That's okay, I'm sure we'll survive. Really, thanks for all you've done." I wrap my hair in my towel, daring her to say one more word.

Opal definitely radiates something other than her typical helpfulness. Jealousy? Possessiveness? Contempt? A female passive-aggressive vibe, but she doesn't have a choice really—she *is* the hired help, so she retrieves *The Firm* from the floor and places a bookmark in the last quarter of it with a marmish, proprietary gesture. Picks up her purse, then her jacket.

I have been weighed, and judged, and found sorely lacking. I wonder though at the intensity of her fervor. Something to probe Justin about later.

She stands, gives me a curt smile, glances down at Justin, her brow furrowing, then she casts a final, suspicious glance in my direction before walking to the door.

She pauses there. "You sure you don't want me to go to the store?"

"Quite."

She stands for another moment. Hoping Justin will wake up perhaps? What *is* going on between them?

"Again," I say. "Thanks so much for staying late."

She doesn't reply, just opens the door and closes it behind her with an accusatory click.

Maybe it's time to call in a new hospice worker, change things up a bit. The last thing I need is someone looking closely at anything in my life, and me in particular.

And then I see them. The photos in the manila envelope, only they're not where I left them, tucked under a coffee table book, *Designing Brand Identity: An Essential Guide for the Whole Branding Team*. The envelope is out, facedown, the tab open. She's seen the photos. *Christ, why did I leave them out?*

But what's really disturbing is that a part of me doesn't care at all, or I care but only from a purely logistical point of view—what kind of disruption this will cause for Justin, how that disruption might affect my next steps. I feel no shame, no regret. No triste. *Maybe it's just the Xanax evening out my ragged edges. Maybe I shouldn't have taken three.*

Too late now. At least Justin's asleep and I can have some time on his laptop. I'm about to head back to the bedroom when I notice that sweat beads his forehead, and his cheeks are flushed. I gently place my hand on his forehead—warm, not hot, a good sign—but my touch wakes him because he opens his eyes, fixes them on me. They're strange, distant.

"How did he take the bad news?"

At first I don't know what he's talking about, and it's that instant, that lapse, that confirms it for him.

He pushes my hand off his forehead, turns his face away, staring up at the ceiling. "So it's like that, huh."

I'm too tired, too utterly exhausted, to respond.

"Well," he says. "Maybe we should just stop pretending. Maybe we should break up."

THE MOST DEVASTATING WORDS of my life, they truly and righteously sting, but at least I'm feeling something. I am grateful for that.

"No," I say. "Don't be stupid." I settle into kneeling, pressing my hands under my knees, an old schoolgirl nervous tic.

"Well, let's rewind. The car was stolen." Flat, not believing.

"You were listening to me talk to Opal?"

"I woke up when you came into the room."

"You didn't seem awake."

"Nothing is what it seems anymore."

Oh Jesus Christ fuck, we're going to get into a domestic fight, *now*? The day has been like a Quentin Tarantino movie shot in a single take. Have I even had a single moment to myself? Taken a single breath?

"*You* didn't seem too upset." He continues to stare at the ceiling. "You love that car."

"It's just a car." My shoulders stiffen. Everything I've been trying to hide is somehow tangible, present, like there's a third person in the room neither one of us want to acknowledge.

"It's the first car you bought with your own money."

I ache for something stronger than a few Xanax, the caliber of drug that my parents kept on hand. There was that relaxed ecstasy that always washed over my parents' faces just after they'd shot up, abandoning me, yes, but escaping too. At the moment I can see how the only way out sometimes might be through a needle.

"You want something to drink?" I ask.

"Sure, honey, I'd love something to drink."

A bad sign, him calling me *honey*, a retro-misogynistic hausfrau dig. But it gives me something to do, so I stand, head for the kitchen to get him a glass, open the fridge for the ginger ale. Grab a can. Unfortunately we're fresh out of Guinness—a Guinness would be wonderful right now, and I thought we had a six-pack unless I drank it all and don't remember.

This strikes an off note somewhere deep in my subconscious.

I pop open the ginger ale, feel the carbonation tickle my fingers. *His hand, brushing my thigh.*

Stop, Fiona. Just stop and get off that bus right now.

"So the car," he says, picking the line back up on our fight. "Not important?'

"Maybe," I say, my voice hollow, "some things don't seem as important anymore."

"That word again, *seem*."

"Maybe I've just lost my appetite for materialism, Justin. Maybe I don't care about anything but you."

It's the first true thing I've said all night, and it makes him quiet for a moment. I open the cabinet door, toss the can in the recycling bin, reach for his glass, and notice my bottle of Ambien in the spice rack. I always take half before going to bed, half when I wake up in the middle of the night to pee. Light sleeper or no, an Ambien would knock Justin out for the night, definitely, and I need some alone time with his laptop. See if what I'm even thinking about for a double deal is remotely possible.

I glance over my shoulder. Justin's turned his face to the TV. A child's tinny voice, "*You're in big trouble bucko,*" followed by a rush of applause and canned laughter.

"What *is* this crap? And why are they all wearing acid-washed jeans?"

"It's nostalgia TV," I say, reaching for the bottle, keeping an eye on him. "People long for the eighties, for simpler times."

"AIDS, the Cold War, and Reagan?"

"They don't remember those parts. Or they choose not to remember."

It's a little bit of legerdemain on my part, popping open the bottle and slipping a large, white pill in Justin's glass. Am I really about to drug my cancer-stricken boyfriend?

I am.

"Can people choose what they remember?"

Bubble, bubble, bubble. The pill disintegrates in the ginger ale, creates a long white spiral. "Absolutely." I pick up the glass, give it a swish. "Memory is shaped by desire. Rose-colored glasses, all that."

"Maybe one day you won't remember me," he says.

"That's not true. You know that's not true."

I carry his drink back to the couch, where he struggles to sit up. The doctor had warned that the tumor would eventually start pushing on his lungs, his heart, that it'd be better to have another palliative surgery, but Justin's recovery from the last one was long, and painful. *No more*, he'd said one night when I was rubbing his back while he vomited. *Never again.*

I hand him his drink, which he takes without looking at me, and I sit in the spot recently vacated by Opal. We're an infinity away from anything resembling the people we used to be—he's thickly padded behind the wall of cancer, an experience I can't even begin to fathom, and me, well I'm trapped behind a maze of lies and damnation. The only difference is I chose my snare trap, while he got a bad roll of the genetic dice, or there was DDT in the water, or carcinogens in the air.

Would that be better, to suffer and not be able to trace the cause to any one thing in particular? I'm not sure.

"I know it might not feel like it at the moment," I say. "But I'm loving you the best way that I can."

Not much of an offering, granted, but still I'm surprised at his laugh, quick and bitter. One thing Justin has never been is bitter.

"Well, I won't be a burden for much longer," he says. "Dad is coming out to visit. And Sarah."

At first I don't understand, but then I do, and it's worse. They're coming out because they've gotten the call. The *you probably don't have much more than a few weeks to live* call.

He keeps his eyes fixed on the TV. "Dr. Edwards thought the news might be easier coming from Dad."

"Oh Jesus," I say, my heart in my throat. "I should have been . . ."

Here. I should have been here.

Justin stares hard at his drink, and for a panicky moment I think he knows, can see the remains of the pill fizzing away. But he just takes a long sip.

Christ though, is it safe? Giving him an Ambien?

He looks up at me with raw, naked emotion in his eyes, and I get a glimpse of him, the Justin who used to be inside the Justin who is now, a Russian doll nesting inside another. It causes a singular ache.

"I wrote my obituary today." He tries an ironic grin, but can't pull it off. "I just couldn't picture you, or Dad, or Sarah doing it. But there wasn't enough. I think I got one paragraph, three hundred and twenty words, total." He looks down into the glass again, as if the answer lies there. "I mean, what have I done really, with my life? Got a degree from Stanford, worked in a cube."

I reach out, grab his hand. It's pale, and cold, and half-dead already. "I know you think it's over, but it's not. I'm not giving up hope."

"I'm not *giving* up either," he says. The dark circles under his eyes are deeper than I remember, like skin is sinking into bone. "It's all being *taken* from me. Minute by minute. Second by second. And I see you already, without me. Sometimes I watch you in the kitchen, putting the water on for coffee, and I think how you'll be doing that a year from now, that the light will hit your face just . . . there . . ."

He lets go of my hand, reaches out and traces his index finger along my jaw.

"But I won't be here to see it. Something will be on the news, a war, or a new movie, a scandal, and I won't be here to know. Although that's strangely comforting too. That it will all rage on anyway."

"I don't want to *be* there, in that moment you've imagined."

He smiles now, a genuine one. "What, you're going to throw yourself on my funeral pyre? I thought they only did that in India."

"I was going to, but they banned suttee."

"And how would they prosecute for that anyways?"

"Karma police?"

There, *there* it is, the soft twinkle in his eye, the way he looked the first time he approached me—I was reading something pretentious, *War and Peace* I think, to keep anyone from asking me for spare change. My car was in the shop and I was waiting for the bus, trying to shut out the cold, and the rain, and the fact that I'd just been laid off from a struggling dot-com.

I didn't even notice him, just registered someone tall and reedy step under the protection of the bus stop roof. He asked me a question that I found intrusive until I looked up and saw him, and *once* I saw him, the high cheekbones, the dark, wet hair and voluminous eyes, I wondered *Why is he talking to me?* In my experience people like him didn't talk to people like me. He seemed too . . . normal. Together. A whole human being. I'd worked with many of them, and had even on a few occasions made a friend, but in time they'd pull away, sensing my dark side, the broken, never-to-be-fixed parts.

Only Justin seemed to find them interesting. Only Justin didn't turn away.

He reaches out for my hand, which I give him, and he pulls me to him. He is it, my last tether to the person I want to be, to the life I want to live. I scoot forward and lie next to him, curling myself around his body, and rest my head against his still-beating heart. He strokes my hair, wraps his other arm around my waist. This is the only place I am ever real, where I don't feel the negative tug of all my angst-filled ramblings. I cannot—will not—let him go. If I have to sell all the souls in the world to keep him with me, so be it. Because aside from Justin, what has the rest of the world ever given Fiona Dunn, daughter of addicts?

Nothing. Absolute, and utter, fucking nothing.

CHAPTER EIGHTEEN

TAP, TAP, TAP. The sound tugs at me, pulls me away from something else, something important, the edge of a dream that has something to do with Alejandro's massive camera, the flash that looks like lightning but feels radioactive, contaminating my entire body until I glow with it, his disease.

Tap, tap, tap.

No, that's an actual sound, like something's knocking on glass. My heart gets a jolt of adrenaline—*intruder?*—*Scratch?* *What time is it?*

12:45 a.m. Shit, I must have fallen asleep on the couch. One too many Xanax. I raise my head and find Justin asleep too, head resting on my right arm, which is now completely numb.

A firmer, harder *TAP!*

I turn and there's Jeb staring at me through the window like a ghost, with the dark form of Dan slumped against the rail of the fire escape. He waves for me to come over. Holds up my purse.

He brought it. He was true to his word. It's a miracle of sorts, an honorable dead soul. And while getting my stuff back throws a bit of a wrench in my narrative, although I don't much like the idea of letting the boys in because it's a further intrusion of all *that* into my personal space, a hacker or two could be very useful for my double deal.

Worlds, they cannot cross, Saul said. *It bleeds that way.*

Fuck Saul.

I hold my finger to my lips. Jeb gives a curt, impatient nod. They must be freezing.

I begin the delicate process of arm extraction, but moving it slightly causes Justin's eyelids to twitch. He *is* a light sleeper—he's often said that just the act of me turning over in the bed wakes him several times a night, and I don't know how much I can rely on the Ambien. But I was able to walk through the door. Surely I should be able to just pull my arm through and out?

I look at my arm, willing it to slowly, *slowly* disappear, dissipate, and to my relief, it does. First the fingers, then the wrist, then the forearm, dissolving like ice in the sun—so gradual that Justin's head just naturally sinks down to the baseball pillow. A soft sigh escapes his lips, and I wait a moment, to be sure. He's out.

Instinctively I reach my hand to push myself up—but there's no hand, just a stump of what used to be my arm with a gradient blur where visible flesh disappears. I get the strange feeling that there *is* an arm but it isn't mine, like I'm staring at a thing through the glass of a museum case, a casual observer.

It's unsettling.

So I do the next reasonable thing and imagine my hand and wrist returning, starting with the forearm . . . but no, it stays invisible.

You're just exhausted, I tell myself.

Worlds of possibility open up, bad ones. What if my arm is lost in the gray space? What if it never comes back?

With a mounting panic, I start with the fingers this time, imagine the tips of them with my inexpertly polished nails, and for a moment they flicker into visibility—*success!*—before they flicker out again, like a TV with bad reception. Worse still, the invisibility that ended with my forearm now starts to creep along my upper arm, reaching out and up to my shoulder and then collarbone. Now my heart starts to thud in earnest, but even though I will it to stop, the fractal spread continues until I start to look like someone has taken an ice-cream scoop and just carved away a good chunk of my body. More of me disappears, evaporating down the side of my body to my left leg and up my neck until I feel the glimmer of it, an icy shiver, along the ridge of my jawbone.

I can't control it. *Holy shit*, for the first time, I can't control it.

I shut my eyes and try ghosting to the window, an all-or-nothing gambit, and for a moment I'm in that numb, in-between gray space, not feeling the press of my body on the couch or the floor beneath my feet, no sound, no *thing*, just a strange, opaque emptiness.

But then I hear a sound, a tentative *tap*, and when I open my eyes I'm by the windowsill, Jeb staring at me intently through the glass. *It worked*. I feel like I narrowly missed getting hit by a car.

I turn to see if any of this has disturbed Justin and almost gasp out loud. Because while I am standing by the window I am also looking at my body, or the half of it remaining, still curled up next to Justin on the couch, still wearing my robe. It—my body—is practically split down the middle. I see half my brain, half my lungs, half my heart, half my face. The curved half ridge of my spine.

What the fuck?

For a few, horrific moments I think this is how Justin will finally discover my secret, waking to half a girlfriend, but then who is *in* that half? As if it's reading my mind, it turns to me, that half head, stares at me with a discerning right eye.

Blinks.

My knees give out and I slide to the floor.

Tap, tap, tap. I look up at Jeb, still trapped on the other side of the window. He meets my eyes, raises a tentative hand.

He sees me. I hold up my arms, and they're both there. I dare to look back at the couch and now there's only Justin, the terry-cloth robe draped over the couch and onto the floor.

"WHAT THE HELL HAPPENED?" Jeb whispers after I slide open the window. "What *was* that?"

I'm so shaken all I can manage is, "I don't know." It reminds me of a recurring nightmare I used to have as a girl, where I went to a funeral only to find out, when I approached the casket, that it was *my* body being mourned.

That eye. That eye staring at me from half my head, that moment, that *moment* of me, looking at me.

But which one was *me?*

A gust of cold air blows through.

Don't think about it.

I reach out for Jeb's hand, but he pulls it back. His hand is horribly swollen now, the burned edges of skin starting to pucker. God, it must hurt like hell. Instead, he quietly steps through the window into the living room, striving for balance without touching a single thing. I can see he's on the last of his last nerves, and honestly I'm not far from crumpling into a heap myself.

Next, I draw a nearly comatose Dan through the window. He's wearing a black garbage bag that reeks from trash, and my jacket over it.

"Best I could do," mumbles Jeb. "Had to walk halfway here—flying is just out now."

Blood's still caked across Dan's mouth, chin, hands, and he moves like someone's performed a lobotomy, as floppy and listless as the straw man, eyes wide, open, dilated. Shock has taken hold. I wonder what's on the other side of it.

I slide the window shut. A soft *thwump*.

Still Justin doesn't stir. *Good.*

I beckon for Jeb to follow me, and he loops one of Dan's arms around his own neck, half-leading, half-carrying him to the bedroom. Once we're inside, I give a final glance at the couch—Justin, still asleep, *praise the pharmaceutical industry*—and then gently close the door. Flip on the overhead light.

Wish I hadn't.

In a desperate move for shelter between evictions, my parents once brought me with them to a real crack house, someone's home long abandoned, exterior the color of faded mildew. The whole structure listed slightly to the side, as if it had given up decades before. It took a half hour of threats and a close-fisted punch to get me inside. As soon I stepped through the door, I knew I'd made a mistake. Walls hacked away, pipes sto-

len for salvage, mattresses on the floor and people on the mattresses, or what used to be people. Ghosts where people used to
be. Later when I saw photos of refugees, victims of war hunkered down along the side of some desert or jungle road, I rec-
ognized that same thousand-yard stare, which I now see
reflected in Jeb's and Dan's eyes.

Boys no longer.

Suddenly self-conscious, I grab a pair of yoga pants and a
small T-shirt Opal's laid out on the bed. Thoughtful, thoughtful Opal. Hope they're not doused in mercury.

"You were like . . . split in half on the couch," whispers Jeb.

"I know."

"How'd that . . . how'd that happen?"

"I don't know." I look at his injured arm—shit, what to do
about his arm? He can't die until his favor's called in, but it
could get infected. He could lose it.

First, fix the things you can. I go to the closet, pull out one
of Justin's old shirts and a pair of his pants that are going to be
too tall for Dan, but will have to do.

"Let's get him dressed."

Jeb makes a move to try, but his fingers are too raw, so I approach Dan. He's as obedient and passive as a young child
while I take off the jacket, tear off the bag, leaving him naked
except for his underwear, which he's pissed in. I find a clean
pair of Justin's underwear in the bureau, ones he hasn't worn in
a while, pre-tumor.

Don't think about it.

Then I head for the bathroom, grab the wet facecloth. Dan
will clean up, but Jeb, what to do about Jeb? I open the medicine cabinet, grab Justin's bottle of oxycodone. A morphine

substitute should help the pain some. When I come back, I find Jeb is sitting on my bed, slumped and vacant.

I ignore him, start to clean off Dan as best I can, hope the warm water will have some wakening effect.

It doesn't.

Right. I pull Dan's underwear down, lift his feet, one after the other to get him to step out of the underwear, pull the clean pair up and over his groin, his waist. I pick up Justin's shirt from the floor—

"Oh . . . oh Christ," Jeb says. It's the broken, lost way he says this that instantly chills me. I turn and find he looks utterly terrified.

And then I smell it, that faint waft of burning sulfur.

A TENDRIL OF SMOKE rises up from behind Jeb. It loops into a curly *S* before dissipating.

"*Shit!*" Jeb jumps to his feet and I see he's left bloodstains on my duvet—*great, something else to hide from Eyes-Everywhere Opal*—but there's a scorch mark on the cover too, still smoldering. It doesn't make sense, until it does.

His favor's been called in.

Jeb frantically turns around. There's a hole burned right through his back jeans pocket.

"Your card," I whisper.

He tries to get it with his swollen hand but his fingers are too thick, too clumsy. "Shit, shit, *shit!*" He reaches into his pocket with his good hand, pulls out a cell phone and his card.

Black ash falls to the floor.

Jeb gives me a pleading look. He wants a way out—*want*

isn't the right word; he's *desperate* for a way out. I might be able to use that. Everything around me comes into a sharp, laser-like focus—the acrid smell of piss from Dan's underwear lying in a heap on the floor, the lingering scent of smoke, the cell phone, Justin's laptop closed on the pouf chair in front of the window, its white power light on, winking. Justin hasn't used it much because it's hard now for his fingers to type, some nerves pressed by the tumor, the doctor explained. So it's quite possible his login and password to the Fealtee site are still cached, if not saved.

This is my palette. These are my instruments. *Yes. Possibly yes.* Jeb reads his card, pale as a stunned rabbit.

"It doesn't matter," I say.

"It says Transamerica building, seven a.m." His lower lip starts to tremble. "Does that mean all I have to do is go there?"

"Let me see." I reach my hand out, and reluctantly, he hands it over. I trace my finger along the writing, still warm. But is Scratch anticipating what I'm going to do next? Is he giving me these pieces, knowing I'm just pulling my own snare trap tighter? Because something about this feels like a piece has been moved on a board. *Your turn, love.*

I turn the card over, find the back white, pristine. How does he *do* that?

"Renata thinks . . ." I start to say. "Well, *we* think maybe it's not written all at once. That it comes in stages. Otherwise, you wouldn't go. Right?"

He struggles with that for a moment.

It's 1:00 a.m. We have six hours until Jeb has to be at the Transamerica building. Six hours to focus, to at least get a decent proposal for a double deal. It's better news than I thought. But I need Jeb clear. Unobstructed. Confident.

"Jeb," I say softly. "Jeb, I think I know a way to get us out of this."

"The double deal?" His voice is choked.

I nod.

"But Alejandro, he said—"

"Alejandro made a double deal himself—that's why he's never been worried."

"No," he says. "No, he . . . how do you . . ."

"This isn't a conspiracy theory. This isn't paranoia. I talked to him and he flat out admitted it."

For a moment, I think this is too much for him—his whole body trembles, his eyes dilate, and I think his mind might snap. So I take everything very slowly, very calmly. I have to conduct him through the next steps, none of which he's going to like.

I CROSS OVER to Justin's side of the bed, grab a half-full bottle of VOSS and pull the oxycodone from my pocket. I shake four oblong blue pills out into my palm.

"Take these," I say.

He stares at them like they're toxic, poisonous. Even without Jasmine's clairvoyance, I can tell what he's thinking—is this some kind of self-serving gambit, should he trust me?

Looks like we're all playing paranoia now.

"All right, just take two. But you need to relax and it will help with the pain. If we're going to get through this, it's together. We need each other."

Something settles on Jeb's face, a weary resignation that

ages him. He takes the water from me, uncaps the bottle, holds out his hand for the four pills, swallows two of them, thinks about it, then takes one more.

Justin hates those pills, only takes a quarter tab if the pain is so bad he can't think. *If I don't have much time left, I want to be present for it.* It occurs to me that maybe I should have kept a few oxycodone back for myself—I don't know if, for the next few days, I want to be present either.

Tears bead at the corner of Jeb's eyes, but he checks them. *Good soldier.*

Are you crying? My father's voice. *You want something to cry about? I'll give you something to cry about.*

For a moment it feels like there are several versions of me standing in the room—a toddler, a young girl, a teenager, a whorish twenty-year-old wearing leggings and an oversize man's shirt. What is it that comes through time, anyway? Because when I see Jeb's face, I see him as a five-year-old, a pubescent boy, and the older man he might still become. And in his face I see my own, that lost look when I got to the Greyhound bus stop and looked up at the destinations, just words on a sign, no meaning.

"And we've got to do something about Dan," I say. "He can't stay here, not now."

"What? Where is he going to go, how can we—"

"I wasn't planning to stay." Dan's voice from behind us, deep and scratchy.

We both turn, surprised, to see Dan suddenly cogent, reaching for Justin's gray knit utility shirt, which I'd left on the floor.

Jeb's shoulders relax, just a bit—Dan's about six months

older and was always the alpha in their friendship. "Dude, you're back."

Dan quickly slides the shirt over his head and looks furtively at the window, like he's purposely cutting us out of even the periphery of his vision. I recognize the emotional distance. My usual heart *d'jour*.

Jeb takes a tentative step toward him. "Dan?"

Again, Dan doesn't answer and reaches for the jeans instead. Pulls them on—too long in the legs, so he rolls them.

"I'm cutting out," he says.

Jeb stops, looks like he's been slapped, and slapped hard. "What do you mean you're—"

"I mean I'm *going*." Dan stands upright, also looking older than he did just a day before. "I've done my . . . I've done it. And now I don't know, maybe I can . . . I don't know. Go somewhere and forget about it."

"But I *saved* you, man. I got you *out* of there . . ."

There's not even a hint of an internal struggle as Dan crosses the bedroom over to the window with its view of the fire escape and the solid brick wall of the neighboring apartment complex. Twists the window's lock. And to my surprise, it slides open for him easily. It hasn't budged since I moved in three years ago.

"What about your phone?"

Dan ignores us. We're the past, ancient history tinged with bad juju. He's probably thinking about what's next—hitching a ride maybe, trying to get out of Oakland before the police connect the dots and his face gets plastered on the evening news too. Cutting off the wounds that are still open, bleeding.

"It'll just lead them to me. You know that."

Jeb reaches his burned hand out. "Dan . . ."

For just the slightest fraction of a second, Dan pauses, and I worry that he's changing his mind. But then without a word, a glance, he slips out the window and onto the fire escape, another second or two before he quickly drops down the ladder and out of sight.

Sound of traffic outside, the steady pulse that never ends in a city.

And I'm left with the heartbroken shell of a boy. An asset, ripe for exploitation.

CHAPTER **NINETEEN**

MY IMMEDIATE PROBLEMS LINE UP, a series of dominoes. While I'm hoping the Ambien keeps Justin asleep, there's no telling how it will affect him, the boy in my room is in no physical or mental state to leave, and there's the small matter of finding out if my double deal is even possible. Plus, only six hours left.

And I can't shake the sense that I'm not driving this, that I'm being led, missing something obvious. The window opening, it bothers me. It's never been that easy to open before. The sudden electric outage. If I learned anything from Bernays, it was how to uncover the hidden layers of psychology behind every damn thing made by man in the world, the subtext no one's supposed to see. How a coalition of the seemingly unrelated can lead to an impression, to a view, to perceived reality. *All of us, rats in a maze, thinking we're actually going somewhere.*

I approach the window, slowly push it closed. It slides in the grooves easily, like it's brand-new. *Scratch was here.* He didn't just deliver the manila envelope, slide it under the door—he came inside and saw this room, my things. The six-pack of Guinness in Alejandro's red refrigerator. The six-pack of Guinness missing from mine.

But how on earth would he know I'd go to Alejandro's? I didn't tell anyone, I didn't even know myself I would go there until after I'd talked to Saul.

Jasmine can read thoughts. Could she read mine from that far away? Can she read them now?

"Jeb . . ." I say, looking out in the alley below, watching the shadows carefully. "We need to clean you up."

No answer. I turn and find Jeb trembling—his breath is rapid, shallow, his skin looks cold and clammy. He won't be very useful if I let him fall apart. "Jeb," I say, taking an authoritative, parental tone. "Take a shower."

Jeb looks at me, incredulous. Holds out his burned arm.

"A bath then, you'll feel better. You can't be walking around covered in blood."

This seems to be a thought that requires extra processing, so I leave him to it, walk to the bathroom, turn on the light, and pull back the shower curtain, half expecting Scratch to be behind it. But no, it's just the same old porcelain tub, dull and scratched, with a long rust stain by the drain that looks like blood. I start the water running, warm but not hot.

When I return to the bedroom, Jeb is trying to peel off his shirt, but his hand, it's obvious it hurts too much, even with the drugs. So I reach under the mattress and take out a pair of scissors. An old habit I've never been able to shake off, keeping something sharp and pointy close by.

The aching look he gives me, like I'm planning to stab him with it. Like he's wishing I *could* somehow. End it, his misery.

I ignore him and start with the back of his T-shirt, slicing it cleanly up the middle, and then continue cutting along the top of his right sleeve. That side slides off with a sigh. Next the left sleeve, and then the fabric falls and puddles on the floor. Jeb reaches for the top button of his jeans, but no, his fingers are too swollen, so I do this too. When I've pulled them down to his ankles, he steps out of his pants, wordlessly heads for the bathroom, and I follow him to make sure he doesn't slip, settles in okay in the bathwater. While he steps in the tub, testing the water's temperature with his foot, I grab a clean facecloth with the vague idea of cleaning his wounds. But when I turn back around, Jeb is sitting in the water, facing his reflection like it's an enemy, clenching his jaws tightly. Holding so much in.

"I don't know what to do," I say, placing the facecloth gently along the side of the tub. "I'm going to go look it up . . . what's best for chemical burns."

Smallest of nods.

I remember once, at the New Parish, Jeb said he wished he could fly away, up through the atmosphere into orbit, pass out from the lack of oxygen, and then become a cold satellite himself, alive but not alive. It reminds me of Alejandro's watch story.

He slowly edges his back down into the tub until the water covers his chest, neck, and most of his face. Blood, not his, clouds the water, blossoming into an opaque pink.

A QUICK PEEK through the door—Justin is, thankfully, still asleep on the couch, although the thought nags that I'd assumed he was asleep before when he was just pretending. But that 10 mg of Ambien is no joke.

So instead I close the door between the bedroom and living room, quietly flick the lock, just to be on the safe side and an easy enough thing to explain away—*I didn't want to wake you, didn't realize the door was locked . . .*

It's astonishing how much easier they're coming to me, these lies. Almost every single thought I have now comes with a twin, a way to direct perception away from the truth.

Dan's cell rests on the bed, just next to the scorch mark left by Jeb's card. There's a video on it that I don't want to see, but need to. The double deal is important, but so is a narrative that will keep me out of prison after. Dan was right—the police will use the phone's GPS to track him, and I have to explain why it's here.

So I reach down, pick it up. Find the icon for photos, then a still of a white Santa beard stamped 8:45 p.m.

I take a deep breath.

A slow zoom out reveals Dan sitting in the center of the plaid couch, Santa cap jauntily askew, fake white beard and mustache giving the video a pornish feel. Soft music in the background, more fifties Christmas hokum, *"Toyland, toyland, little girl and boy land. While you dwell within it, you are ever happy there."* And inside the getup, like the suit is wearing *him*, is poor Dan looking utterly terrified, hands gripping his britches.

The camera continues to zoom out and now another layer is added, a true David Lynch touch, because there are about twenty girls, all wearing footed pajamas, Santa caps perched on their heads. They sit on Dan's right, his left, at his feet. All captured, captivated, enthralled.

His dark talent grown stronger.

The camera continues to zoom, revealing the coffee table and an array of glass beer mugs, each almost filled to the top with some kind of clear liquid. I have a bad feeling I know what it is.

One of Dan's hands releases his suit pants, and, struggling, like he's trying to force it back down, his hand beckons a girl at his feet to come closer.

A blonde scoots forward, hair flat as a Barbie's. Her face is alight, obviously thrilled to have been chosen for this special treatment, and there's a tangible ripple of envy among the others.

Dan reaches out with his hand, unsteadily cups her chin. Watching a dead soul in the act of completion causes a sublime shiver, like I'm standing on my future grave, looking at my name chiseled in my future tombstone.

His arm, emboldened, like it's operating under a separate consciousness of its own, helps raise the girl up and settles her on his lap. His right leg starts to quiver. The girl though, she doesn't notice his discomfort, and instead, looks inordinately pleased. Drapes a long, lovely arm around his shoulders.

"Have you been a good girl this year?" Dan's voice, the words forced. He glances nervously at the camera, at whoever is standing there for confirmation that this is right, this is what he's supposed to say.

Someone else is in the room, prompting him. Alejandro? Scratch?

The girl crosses her feet and arches her back slightly, provocatively. "No, Santa. I've been a very, very, *very* bad girl."

Again he glances at the camera. Appears to be listening to something said, although we can't hear it on the camera mic.

He swallows. "Santa punishes those who have been naughty. Sneaky little children."

A murmur offscreen.

Dan tries for a smile, fails miserably, and then leans into the girl, kisses her on her berry-red lips, a kiss she returns, hungrily. Entranced, she reaches down to rub his thigh. Even with the poor-quality cell video, I can see his shadow begin to darken, but what's truly disturbing is that it spreads to the blond girl on his lap, across the couch, wraps around the legs of the coffee table, then up, around and through the other girls gathered around him, until the whole room is thick, *pregnant* with his shadow. It's like one of those sped-up videos of mold spores spreading and eating decaying matter.

Everything I touched, I corrupted.

Dan reaches down and picks up a mug. He hands it to her, raw despair visible. She takes it, smiling.

Another inaudible murmur off-camera. The lights flick off, then on.

He tucks a strand of her blond hair behind her tiny, perfect ear. But it's impossible to understand *why*, because the Dan I know isn't capable of what's coming next. Is he acting of his own free will? If he wanted to stop, to bolt out of the house, could he? Or are we somehow puppets when Scratch comes to collect, no way to refuse?

The true gravity of my double deal hits then—if I give him access to the millions of souls I think I could trick, what in God's name will he ask *them* to do? What could it trigger? It's not hard to imagine the magnitude—everyone is just waiting for an acceptable reason to cleanse the world of everyone who doesn't think like them, a calamity we're long overdue for. How much would it take to launch a new dark age, twenty-first-century style?

Or has it already begun? Guantánamo Bay instead of the Tower of London, chemical warfare instead of Greek fire, anthrax instead of bubonic plague, cops shooting unarmed children, and young people running through the streets of Iraq holding severed heads as trophies in the same age we've identified the Higgs boson particle. All of it captured, recorded, and shared piecemeal on cell phones. Horrific images pressed into our brains willingly or unwillingly, every terrorist group or sadist trying to top the one before to light up the twenty-four-hour news cycle. Christ, think about how much worse the Inquisition would have been with Twitter around.

Dan leans in closer, whispers something in the poor girl's ear. The damned lens zooms in, capturing a soft glaze of her eyes, like she's in a deep trance, sleepwalking.

Without warning, she holds the mug to her lips, drinks, and then she starts to scream horribly, at least until her lower jaw melts away. Then there is just a gurgling, choking sound as her voice box dissolves, the acid eating through her skin from the inside out, and *still* she keeps drinking until her mug is empty, acid pouring down her neck, burning flesh. The mic does pick up the sizzle as the acid eats through her stomach, staining her pajamas with a yellowish, bloody smear.

Dan is visibly shaking, pale. The dying girl on his lap slumps into herself. Her body begins to seize.

Another murmur off-camera.

He squints his eyes tightly, presses his hands against his ears. "No, no, no, no, no, no."

Again, something inaudible. Is it the words themselves, do

they somehow have power over us? Because he opens his eyes, nods at one of the other girls, her long brown hair tied back from her face in a tight ponytail, and she reaches for a mug. *Oh God, is she going to drink too?*

Scratch uses us to wreck the very things we cherish most, rendering the rest of our lives unlivable. Gary shot up his daughter and her classmates publicly, destroying the cherished bubble of his perfect 1 percent life; Mike and Ellen butchered their children. But there's a subtheme here too, something to do with Christmas, or God at least, like a mad revenge grindhouse flick.

Dan gently pushes the dying girl off his lap, stands, and settles her into his spot on the couch—something strangely tender, almost chivalrous in the gesture. I imagine when the public sees this, everyone will blame some kind of drug use, because the reality of what comes next is impossible to comprehend.

Dan steps out of frame—more whispered instruction—and then the ponytail girl, holding the mug unsteadily—a splash hits the carpet, which, off-camera, sizzles—without closing her eyes, without any thought or hesitation at all—throws the cup of acid in her own face. Her skin smokes and melts like butter.

The video ends with her screams.

AND THE MONSTER WAS HERE, in my apartment. Police will trace the car to my address. His cell signal to my apartment. There's blood evidence everywhere, and plenty of witnesses at the New Parish to link me to him as a drinking buddy. How to explain it?

Dan stole my car.

My parents were expert stage-setters—when things got hot, when they were tipped off that the police were about to make an arrest—they would take an immediate break from the drugs until they were sober enough to implicate one of their friends. Stashing rolls of cash in pockets, planting crack pipes in passed-out hands, making sure to leave several bags of weed so that it looked like their friends were the dealers. My job was to wipe down the hard surfaces of fingerprints.

So the first thing I do is call the police on the nonemergency number, report my vehicle stolen, my purse and cell were in it, and I walked all the way home, etc. They'll be in no hurry to do anything, not until they match the VIN to the car that just exploded on the Holy Names campus.

Now for the rest of the evidence. Dan, the psychotic killer, acting alone, got my address from the registration, decided it would make as good a place as any to lie low. I came home, took care of Justin, and then went to my bedroom to relax. Only I found Dan there. He'd broken in through the bedroom window, which I never checked because it was always too hard for me to open. His fingerprints are all over both sets of windows. *That's good.* But did I fight back? Why not?

He held a pair of scissors to my throat.

I take the scissors off the floor, press one of the sharp tips against a vein near my jugular. Push it slightly, hard enough for the blood to bead. Then I wipe my prints from the handles with my shirt, toss them back to the floor.

The bloodstained duvet is good enough as is—evidence to the crime scene, check. But not much evidence of an altercation. Carefully, so I don't alarm the neighbors above or below, I place the lamp on the floor, punch a hole in the shade. Next I pull out drawers, throwing clothes around to look like the room was ransacked, open the doors of the armoire, yank out papers, scattering them randomly. It doesn't look half bad.

Valuables. Dan would definitively have taken valuables. I grab an old glasses case from Justin's sock drawer where we keep a few hundreds in case we need a cab late at night for a ride to the hospital. I then take the Istanbul out from my closet, unzip the waist belt, stash the bills in it. I have a small jewelry box where I keep Justin's recent purchases that I never wear—diamond stud earrings from Tiffany, a ridiculous Rolex watch that makes my skin break out in hives, a vintage emerald brooch shaped like a row of peas. Giving me things he knows I'll keep, that will remind me of him in the long-distant future when he's gone. I shove them all into the waist belt too.

And the ring. The engagement ring I'd seen Justin stow away in a sock in his sock drawer. I dig around for that.

There's a soft splash of water in the tub. He's still so trusting, that Jeb, in spite of the world demonstrating firmly that he shouldn't. His DNA will be harder to fit into the narrative, unless he was an accomplice.

He was with Dan. They came together, but Jeb was injured badly. I used that to divide them after Dan threatened to kill me. With Jeb in the bathroom, I was able to convince Dan that he should leave Jeb behind, that Jeb would just hold him back. So Dan took what he could, left me to be Jeb's problem. But no, he wouldn't have just left me—I could have called the police. So he tied me up instead, with what was left of Jeb's T-shirt.

I grab a strip of it, wrap it around my wrist and pull it tight, twist my arm so hard that it leaves marks on my skin.

Then I do the same thing with the other. For good measure, I take a longer strip of the T-shirt, wrap it around my throat and yank hard. It'll look convincing with the small bruises starting to form from where Saul choked me.

The ring, where's the ring?

I go through all the socks again, feeling the toes but no, it's not there. Did Opal take it? *And she had the nerve to judge* me.

Next I grab Justin's laptop. I'll have to destroy it afterward, maybe toss it out the window so no one can recover the browser history.

But what about Justin? How long before he wakes up?

Among all the ransacked items on the floor is a roll of black duct tape, something I bring with me to all photo or video shoots because it's the go-to item for when shit goes wrong—you need a skirt hemmed fast; you need to mark an actor's spot on the floor; the cable from one of the ancillary lights is frayed and might electrocute the production assistant.

It'll all work out in the end. It'll all come out in the wash.

I'm doing this for him. I'm doing all this for love.

Am I?

A lingering doubt makes an appearance again, one I thought I'd safely bricked away, *You sure you're not doing this to save your own ass?* The truth is I don't know anymore, it's all I can do to hang on to the frayed end of a burning rope. The rest, well the rest will have to be sorted out later.

"WHAT THE HELL DID YOU GIVE HIM?" Jeb slips back through the door to the bedroom, black duct tape in hand. I couldn't do it myself. I couldn't risk his waking up, *seeing* me do it.

"Is he okay?"

"Define okay. If you mean breathing, yes. But he didn't move at all. Not when I taped up his wrists, his mouth—"

"So he's okay." I adjust the pillow behind my back.

Jeb gives a noncommittal shrug. But we're close now, we're almost through the hardest part. I finally have some time to think. It's still dark—my favorite time for thinking, when most of the world is asleep. I swipe a finger along Justin's trackpad to wake it up. The laptop is warm on my lap.

Jeb crosses over to Justin's side of the bed and flops down on it. He works at the edge of the tape, sticking and unsticking it. "I didn't realize a tumor could get so big. That must suck."

"You got the video ready?"

Jeb pulls at a bit of the tape. "I still don't see why we have to post it."

Christ, we've been through this ten times. I carefully modulate my voice though, to make it calm, authoritative. "Because, Jeb, we need to implicate Dan. Or do you want to get a double deal and then spend the rest of your life in prison?"

He says nothing, digging at the edge of the roll with his fingernail.

"Dan left you behind, remember? He's not your friend, not anymore."

"And you are?"

"I'm you're partner. We're partners in this." *He forced me to get the laptop, Officers. I don't know why, I thought maybe he wanted me to transfer money into his account.*

A background appears on Justin's laptop, a selfie taken years ago, Justin holding an outstretched arm to capture us leaning

our heads together, the Tetons in the background, gray, threatening storm clouds gathering just above them. It'd rained the
whole time. We hadn't minded.

An ache, a physical pang.

Jeb sighs but grabs Dan's cell phone, clicks over to the
video. "YouTube?"

I nod.

"Whose account?"

"Just make a new one."

He sighs again. Early twenties—the worst years ever to be
alive.

Justin's login and password appear on the screen. Not surprising, this was a work loaner and I can't imagine Fealtee al-
lowing their employees to wander around with an unencrypted
data portal. Login has been saved, *Just!n5!0*, so I try the passwords I know first, ones he's handed over to his bank accounts,
credit cards, so I can pay the bills online for him. F!0N@5!0,
!WHODUNN!T, NOT@P@SSWRD5!0.

None of them work.

"The video is uploading." Jeb drops the cell on the bed,
peers over my shoulder. "Is that the Rockies?"

"No," I say tersely.

"You look happy."

And I do. Here I am, staring at my picture, myself looking
back at me, a creepy déjà vu. The funny thing is I don't remember being happy. I remember being worried about ticks, or that
Tracy was taking advantage of my radio silence to erode my
credibility at work, or that I'd left the front burner of the stove
on. What would I tell the girl in the photo, if I could? Beware
the man who offers a drink in Make Westing? No, she was too

sure of her world, that one, thought she knew every inch of the bottom of the rabbit hole, the darkest bits, and had escaped it.

"That time you asked Alejandro about the double deal," says Jeb. "Dan and I were up all night talking about it. Dan said . . ." His voice cracks, but he rallies. "Dan said we should create a game app. *Mr. Evil Deeds*. You know, people could sell their souls, do bad shit, and unlock levels. Kill a nun and you get a gold hamster. That kind of stuff."

"It's not a bad idea," I say. Christ, I wish, at the very least, I hadn't balked at the m-word, that I'd done the normal thing, cry with happiness or something. Justin deserved that.

"Coding would be a bitch though."

Think, Fiona, think.

Justin always substitutes an exclamation point for *i*, an @ for an *a*, a zero for *o*. Something occurs to me, a disturbing possibility. I try it.

0P@L5!0

The laptop hums as the desktop appears. Password accepted. I feel a tight ball of icy jealousy somewhere in the lower quadrant of my stomach, something I haven't felt since I saw Justin get into the cab with Sarah in the pink coat.

"All right!" says Jeb. The phone vibrates on the bed, and he reaches for it. "Video's uploaded too. I'm going to create a Twitter account and post it with hashtag sorority sister massacre."

There has to be an innocent reason, although I seriously can't think of one, but there *has* to be. The last time I thought Justin was cheating on me, well, that was the door Scratch came through, and if I suspect him now . . .

"Great," I say thinly.

Wouldn't there be some relief too? An absolution of my

own sins? But I just can't picture it, the two of them together. Our own sex life came to a soft, unattended close when the pressure of the tumor on his intestines started causing unexpected accidents. No, what I *can* picture is Justin offering her the use of his laptop—maybe to look for a good movie on Netflix—and her changing the password since he wasn't using it anymore. Staking her claim about as subtly as a cat spraying its territory with urine.

I open the Firefox browser, click to Recent History. Good, it hasn't been deleted. There are more than a few Google searches of my name—"Fiona Dunn Promoted to Global Communications Manager," an article in the *San Francisco Chronicle*, then there's my Facebook page, obligatory when you're in marketing but not something I actually use—why hand over your personal data to the biggest unpaid survey in the history of time?—my Twitter account that I haven't updated in a year.

What exactly are you up to, Ms. Opal?

"That's not the Fealtee site."

I turn, startled, to find Jeb watching me intently. "I know," I say. "I was just . . ."

Right.

Next I scroll through Justin's bookmarks, and there it is, the Fealtee backend Joomla! URL. I click it and a simple white screen appears with another prompt for a login and password. For this one I'm quietly pleased that F!0N@5!0 still works—*not so easy to change that, huh, Ms. Opal?*—and click *Yes* at the prompt *Save this password*. Of course, this is just the company intranet, but Jeb's assured me he can easily hop into the main content of the website. We just have to change something minor to demonstrate proof of concept to Scratch, a sentence in the terms and conditions section, a forty-page volume of text. Justin says only 0.001 percent of users read the first few pages before they click *I accept all the terms and conditions*.

Not exactly the signed confessions of the Inquisition, but it just might do.

CHAPTER TWENTY

WHILE JEB DOES HIS HACKING THING, I grab my own laptop to start working out the language of the double deal, my exact conditions. Still no sound from the living room, which hopefully means Justin's asleep. It will probably do him some good, a decent night's sleep, although I worry that Jeb might have bound his wrists too tightly with the duct tape. He has enough circulatory issues as it is. I almost want to check, but the important thing is to close this deal.

Jeb's arm is getting worse. It's swollen and pus drips down from where the acid hit his skin. His face glistens with light sweat, a fever.

So, what do I want from this double deal, and what will I give in exchange? The single biggest question ever faced in the life of Fiona Dunn. Best start with the basics.

I, Fiona Dunn, am hereto released from the contract made Friday, October 12 with . . . (what is his name? He told me once, but I couldn't understand) *. . . with the person or entity known as "Scratch." Said entity also promises to restore one Justin Goodman to health, and endow Goodman and Dunn to an estate valued at $10 million.*

Where could the catches be? "Health"—health could have different interpretations. Cancer-free is more like it but then what if *I* get cancer? One in three people will. Or what if Justin takes after his grandfather, who died of a heart attack before he was fifty? If I'm going through with this, I want a nice, regular-lifetime to enjoy with him.

Another thought tingles. *What if he leaves you?* Odds aren't good with the whole institution of marriage, I know because I've researched the demographic. Women in marriages can afford the Bauhaus, ultra-modern and at $359, an affordable alternative to a Louis Vuitton, while we offer women post-divorce a sixty-five dollar version, the Horizon, in canvas without the removable sternum straps and ports for electronics. There are two divorces every second, which means we've sold about three times as many of the Horizon and plan to expand the line with baby bag options for single mothers.

What is Opal's intent? How much longer before she turns the hairline fracture into a real crack?

Don't get ahead of yourself, Fiona. First things first.

Said entity also promises to restore one Justin Goodman to good health, ensure that both Goodman and Dunn remain in good health for the duration of a typical human lifespan (seventy-eight years), and endow Goodman and Dunn to an estate that would currently be valued at $20 million.

Because $10 million won't be much if and when we reach our seventies, the way inflation's going.

Jeb sighs again. Sighing seems to be his thing.

"What?"

"It's just you would think they wouldn't leave the endpoints so vulnerable. Seriously." He bites his lower lip.

"Can you access the terms-and-conditions page?"

He just mutters under his breath, so I leave him alone and read through my offer again, think of about another fifteen or twenty things I could add. But I know the more complex it gets, the more opportunities there might be for some twisted interpretation. Money and stellar health should be good enough for the daughter of crack addicts.

What if I'm settling though?

Because if he *were* to leave me, it's conceivable he could get all the money. I don't want to have excellent health into my seventies and watch Opal, or some other woman, waltz away with the prize while I burn with my evil deeds.

Said entity also promises to restore one Justin Goodman to good health, ensure that both Goodman and Dunn remain in good health for the duration of a typical human lifespan (seventy-eight years), and endow Goodman and Dunn to an estate currently valued at $20 million, unless Goodman should end relationship with said Dunn, in which case all funds would go direct to Dunn, and Goodman would lose health entitlements.

No, that seems a little over the top, vindictive. I can afford to give him his health. I strike *and Goodman would lose health entitlements.*

Now that I've made this magnanimous concession, I almost feel virtuous.

"*Ha!*" says Jeb. "*Ha*, double ha!" He turns the laptop to me proudly, and there it is, the simple word-processing screen with the entire terms-and-conditions text readily accessible, alterable. Eight-point-two million users who just checked the box and moved on. Who has time to read anymore? Funny thing is though that once you click that checkbox, you're legally bound to every six-point-font word. Once, I asked Justin how many people sign up daily, and he said it was around twenty thousand, double when they really hit the mobile advertising.

Numbers that will definitely get Scratch's attention.

But it makes me sad, the next part. There can be no further complications, and right now, Jeb is a complication.

"Jeb, you know you've got a fever going there. I have some Advil in the bathroom."

He wipes his forehead with the back of his good hand. "Shit, you're right."

"It's not fatal," I say with a forced smile. "And it's all going to be over soon. But you're not much use passed out."

I stand, grab the water bottle, head to the bathroom. *I played on our friendship, Officer, he didn't even notice me slip the Xanax into his drink. But he was threatening to kill me. I didn't have a choice.*

"What should I write?" he calls from the bed.

"Something jokey." It's awkward, but I manage to fit the bottle under the faucet, start to fill it. The air is filled with vapor from his bath, clouds the mirror. The bath towel is wet under my feet. "Not the actual thing. Just proof that we can do it."

I hear the buzz-hum of the cell on the bed again. *What's that about?* I pull the water bottle from the sink, look into the medicine cabinet mirror, but all that's reflected behind me is the window and the indigo sky, which is now tinged with the slightest gossamer of pink. What time is it? Shit, I need to remember to call in sick. A bad back this time; I've already supposedly had the flu.

Then Jeb steps into view, holding the roll of black duct tape.

"That was Jasmine," he says, his face wan. "I'm so sorry, Fiona."

He raises his arm, the good one, and lands a solid punch on the back of my head. I fall—*She read my mind, why didn't I choose clairvoyance? So much more useful*—and feel my skull hit the back of the porcelain bathtub.

And then nothing.

MY HEAD FEELS THICK, impossibly heavy. There's a high, tinny ringing in my left ear. Something warm and wet trickles down the back of my neck. My mouth—I can't open it. I taste blood, and glue—the duct tape I gave Jeb, ha-ha—and my tongue finds a tooth is loose, barely hanging on.

Somewhere close by, I hear something *tick*.

I open my eyes. It's a struggle. They would much rather stay closed, they would much rather that I go back to sleep, or back to wherever it was that was black, silent, and still.

I'm in some kind of a van.

Tick.

My sight is blurry at first. An amber light from outside shines in through the back of the van window, casts eerie shadows on the floor. It's cold. My cheek feels numb. I'm lying on a bench, hard metal—*a police van?*—but no, there's all kinds of cubbies with emergency gear, a gurney, a defibrillator, an oxygen tank.

An ambulance.

Tick.

Renata's favor. Steal an ambulance.

Tick.

Ambulances. I hate them. Only been in one once, after my mother OD'd and I'd made the frantic call to 911. The technician kept asking me questions I didn't know answers to—*What did she take? Did she use a needle?*—during the long ride to the hospital, and when it became apparent I wasn't going to be much use, he ignored me for the rest of the way. She was so pale, so stiff, I was sure she'd died. I was all of nine.

Tick.

I try to move my hand, sit up, but of course I'm bound, taped to something unseen behind me. My shoulders ache from being pulled back so hard, so no telling how much time has gone by, or how close I am to Scratch calling in my favor.

Tick.

Is that a sound in my head, or real? I look over to where it seems to be coming from, and see black duffel bags, the army/navy kind, cheap, easy to get anywhere, and far more durable than anything Sumpter, Inc. makes. They're packed tight, the zippers straining from whatever's inside. I see a wire sticking out of one of them.

Tick.

Why do I get the feeling that I'm in the underground garage of the Transamerica building? That Alejandro is out there somewhere nearby filming?

I start to laugh, but can't because my mouth is taped shut. It's suddenly grotesquely funny that all my ambitious planning has landed me here, in the belly of a new disaster with unknowable repercussions. Since I'm immortal, what will happen when the bombs go off? Will all the bits and pieces of my tissue, scattered among debris, still quiver with life? I imagine a crow pecking at a choice morsel, my flesh making it through its stomach, out the other end, still horrifically sentient. Or will all my broken parts try to find one another, reassemble into some strange new Frankenstein form? I picture my hand, cut off at the wrist and crawling through the rubble, looking for my missing stump of an arm.

No. Stop. That's not helping.

I've been laughing so hard, tears have formed.

Tick.

I could ghost out. Maybe it wouldn't be so bad, stuck in the gray space where all the colors blend into one.

Face it—Jeb and Jasmine have probably already made the pitch. You're done for anyway. It's a defeatist idea, and like all defeatist ideas, easy for me to believe. There's a part of me that's always known my life would end badly—maybe not *this* badly, even my paranoid imagination wasn't that creative—but I've always felt a certainty during the good times that they wouldn't last forever. That happiness was a mirage, bringing with it a foreboding sense of impermanence. Suffering is much easier for me. Familiar and comfortable as an old sweater.

And Justin, what about him? I picture him waking up in the living room, bound, scared, alone. Opal won't get there until eight, and when she does? When he sees the ransacked bedroom, the blood on the scissors?

Tick.

Imagine living with that for the rest of his short life.

Tick.

No, I can't.

I try my feet, and while they're bound to each other they're not tied to anything in particular. If I'm right and I am in the Transamerica parking garage, then there are people parking

their cars, starting their day at work. Praise Jesus it's not a weekend. I kick the side of the ambulance, righteously loud thumps
that would wake the dead if there were any in the vicinity.

Tick.

THUMP, THUMP, THUMP.

Like the guard pounding Saul's prison door, like my neighbor knocking to give me my wet clothes, like my heart when
Justin said the m-word.

Tick.

THUMP, THUMP, THUMP.

I kick the wall of the ambulance until my bare feet feel
numb, the shock of it creeping up my legs. I kick it with force, I
kick it with glee, I kick it until the metal gives slightly, dents. It
feels real, cathartic, this return to ordinary violence. My screams
are muffled, but they're loud, and I pull at the duct tape binding
my wrists, I go all in for the fight until finally I see someone
peer through the ambulance window, a security guard.

He tries the handle, and it's unlocked. He opens the door,
flashes a light in my eyes, and his own widen when he sees the
duct tape.

"Holy shit," he says. "Are you okay?"

Sweat drips from my forehead, my chest heaves, and I try
to scream *Bomb!* but it comes out as "Ommm." He frees my
feet first—*Christ, why doesn't he free my mouth first?*—then my
hands, and then finally, finally, grabs the edge of the tape on
my mouth, says, "This is going to hurt," and quickly rips it off.

"Bomb!" I shout.

He turns, sees the duffel bags.

Tick.

We run.

I RUN FAST, faster than the guard who pauses along the way, screaming at people to "*Get out, get out now!*" I hear the crackle of his walkie-talkie as I run up the stairs, the elevator that dings as the doors open to a small family, the mother carrying a newborn in a Björn and pushing a toddler in a stroller. The father of the brood clocks me, bloody, disheveled mess that I am, probably not sure whether he should be concerned on my behalf or if I'm the one who's dangerous. *Yes and yes.*

"Everyone out!" shouts the guard. "Everyone out now!"

Up the stairs, my legs and lungs burn but I push through it, the pain in my head is fierce, but I propel myself up, steadied by the handrail—Level 4, Level 3, Level 2. Tags here and there, a foreign, spray-painted language of one gang to another. Level 1.

Cold, bright air—I want to stop, take deep breaths, but there's no time, no time, so I run, my knees wobbly, my calves aching. Gold and orange streak across the dawning sky, which is marred only by a scattering of small clouds, like tossed pebbles. A security camera tracks me.

No time, no time.

So instead, I jump over the yellow rail that separates the parking structure from the sidewalk, keep running, and I get lots of looks now, everyone's head turns to watch the pale woman in yoga pants and a T-shirt, blood clumped in her hair, running barefoot. They give me space as I run by, as if I'm going to stop along the way and light into one of them.

If they knew what I knew, they'd be running too.

I sail past store windows, catching my panicked reflection.

It's so strange to be so damn visible, the center of everyone's attention. By now someone's probably made a call to the police—I run past an ATM machine and that camera will be recording me too. A digital trail. The pain at the base of my skull throbs like a metronome, and I find my strides start to sync with it, right left, right left, *throb throb*, *throb throb*.

I smile. I don't know why I do that. Maybe it's that famous runner's high, a false rush of endorphins landing around the fifth mile of a marathon, but there is a sense of relief, almost a sense of joy, because here I am, at the end of it. What will or won't happen will or won't happen. Not a light at the end of the tunnel perhaps, but the closest thing to closure I will ever get.

And the light, the light is so impossibly beautiful. It refracts across the glass of office buildings, imbues everything with an angelic touch. Christmas lights wrapped through the limbs of small, impeccably pruned trees still glow, storefronts sport Santa decals, intricately cut paper snowflakes. Montgomery Street smells like cold concrete, car exhaust, and pine needles. Someone's soaped *Have Yourself a Merry Little Christmas* across the window for a children's clothing store.

Why is everything so beautiful just before it's gone forever?

"Hey! Hey you!" I look back over my shoulder and see a cop holding a large walkie-talkie to his ear. *"Hey, stop!"*

Oh, fuck it. With so little left to lose, I decide to abandon the rest, so I pull my T-shirt up and over my head—shock on the face of a little girl holding her mother's hand at the crosswalk—feel the icy creep as I turn invisible—brief stop to yank off my yoga pants—and then I am truly, gloriously free. Free of self, free of image, free of notice, or judgment. Free of the small, nagging demands of desire. I want nothing except to run.

And then there, standing on the corner of Commercial Street in front of the East West Bank is a tall, familiar figure next to a Linhof Technika that I would recognize anywhere, anytime.

I should be angry, furious, I should feel rage and hate but the damn truth of it is that I'm glad to see Alejandro.

A small crowd is gathered, watching the artiste at work. Alejandro, celebrity photographer with his iconic, radiant hair, wearing couture jeans that look sculptural, a red leather jacket. He chats up a large Midwestern tourist in drawstring shorts and a T-shirt, I LEFT MY ♥ IN SAN FRANCISCO. I slow down from a dead run to a jog, then to a brisk walk, breathing hard, each breath wonderfully, gloriously painful. Pain is a tool for clarity; I see that now. Suffering the only compass you'll ever need.

Of course Alejandro spots me and grins. *Beams*, is more like it. Like a proud papa.

"Fiona Dunn, stop where you are, that is just so, so . . . perfect."

His crowd looks puzzled—*who is he talking to?*—but I stop. Not because I have to, but because if there's such a thing as karma, then we are karmicly connected. God how I've missed the sound of his voice.

There's a flash and I wonder if part of my soul has been pressed into his film, shadow and all, or if there truly is nothing there to be photographed at all anymore.

Then I hear the explosion behind me.

CHAPTER TWENTY-ONE

TASTE OF BLOOD and gravel in my mouth, an ache like every bone in my body has been fractured, and when I open my eyes, I think a fog has set in but it's dust and smoke hanging in the air. I can't hear a thing. Hard to move—my body warns me not to—but I'm not in a mood for listening to my body, so I turn onto my side, ignoring the black dizziness that threatens. Push myself up onto my knees. A little girl's shoe is half buried in rubble—pink with a My Little Pony leather appliqué, *Darlene* written on the sole in blue Sharpie.

Sirens are the first real sound I hear. Thin and distant.

I struggle to get up on my feet, and when I look down, I see my body covered with white, fine dust, and I can't tell whether I'm still invisible underneath. Curious, I hold up my right arm, brush off some of the dust. I can see straight through. I guess it makes sense, the fine particles acting like a kind of body paint, rendering my invisibility useless. I feel vulnerable and exposed—truly naked.

There are others in the haze of smoke, people standing bleary-eyed on the pavement, trying to absorb the last few moments. Everything is coated in the same dust. Everything is camouflaged.

I feel something hard rolling around in my mouth, and I spit it out—the bloody tooth that came loose when I got clocked against the tub. This starts a coughing fit. I grab a bike rack to hold myself upright until it passes.

I don't think Alejandro even flinched.

I turn to look behind me. A blazing plume of fire and black smoke consumes the Transamerica parking entrance, and a mushroom cloud of white smoke curls up toward the sky. Something beautiful and captivating about it, like a flower blossoming.

Why did I just think that? It's not the right analogy; I should be feeling other things, thinking other things. Even the sight of a man's bloody face draped over a parking meter doesn't move me.

Am I dead? Is this hell?

I turn to look back to where Alejandro was standing and through the crowd of stunned, frozen zombies, I see another familiar form. Wavy, jet-black hair that reaches his shoulders, black denim, and cowboy boots. Clothes that are pristine, dust-free. Scratch. He walks like he's in another space or time that doesn't have much to do with the present situation, fast, but not in a hurry. A crying toddler makes the mistake of reaching out for him as he passes, and it's not that he ignores her; it's that she's so unimportant he doesn't see her in the first place.

I note the path he's on, look down the street and see Alejandro, also coated with dust, waiting farther down on a corner with his camera propped over his shoulder.

I cross the street to follow them.

DO THEY OR DON'T THEY see me? There's no acknowledgement, but they don't seem to be in any particular hurry either, a strange bubble of calm in the midst of chaos. Two friends taking a casual morning stroll. I follow about a block and a half behind them. Shouts and cries as strangers guide strangers to a bench, to the curb—*Are you hurt? Did you see what happened?*—trying to staunch bleeding, wrapping jackets around the ones in shock, comforting each other. So many good Samaritans, people with pure hearts. Maybe I don't have one of those anymore, maybe the dark shadow has retreated inward and rotted it out. Even Justin, my love for him, feels remote, like a radio signal slowly losing its cohesion as it drifts off into space.

A fire engine screams by me, kicking up more dust in its trail. I wonder about the dust. If it's toxic. Probably is.

Up ahead, Scratch and Alejandro turn left on Columbus Avenue and then my heart does feel something—fear that I might lose them. So I walk faster.

I pass Mr. Bing's Cocktail Lounge and a wizened Asian man opens the door, peeks out, sees me, quickly closes the door. What do I look like, anyhow? I pause in front of the restaurant window that's merely cracked, not shattered, and catch my broken reflection. Nearly scare myself to death. Because that's what I look like—death warmed over, or so the saying goes. My naked form covered in dust looks feral, alien, but there's something else unobservable but strange. I step in, look closer.

My eyes are gone.

Just hollow, gray sockets where they should be. But of

course, my eyes are blinking, washing away the dust. Still it feels like my soul, who I am, is disappearing, and something else entirely is being born, taking its place.

When I look back up the street, I see Scratch and Alejandro have turned left again—all I get is a glimpse of Alejandro's camera before it disappears, so I cross the street and pick up the pace, past the Tosca Cafe, the Underground (*Rock 'n' Roll Posters, T-shirts, Jewelry & More!*), to where Columbus splits with Broadway, bits of paper and ash floating through the air like snow.

And I don't even know why I'm following them. Anyone with the smallest hint of sense would just give up at this point, go home and take a nice warm shower, spend their last sane minutes with their loved ones before their favor is collected. The laptop is gone, my access to the Fealtee site is gone, and for the life of me I can't think of anything else to offer. But my legs keep moving, my lungs keep working, my heart keeps beating. The present keeps evaporating into the past, and the future comes as it will, displacing everything.

———— ⌯ ————

ST. PATRICK CHURCH is closed for renovations, or so the sign says. Imposing metal scaffolding is propped against the front brick, Gothic-style facade, making it seem even shabbier compared to the glass and cement monolith of the Metreon across the street. A door to the left, below ground level, swings shut, catching my eye. The softest *click*. None of the people milling about Mission Street notice—they're too busy swapping stories, glued to their cell phones for more information. Some are coated with dust, others just brushed with it.

No one ever thinks the worst is yet to come. Always our greatest failing.

A young woman in nurse scrubs starts toward me, concern clouding her face, but once she sees me, the hollows where my eyes should be, she stops, suddenly afraid. Takes a nervous step back. Her companion of the moment, a skinny redheaded jogger in shorts and an old hoodie, pulls at her sleeve, points to her cell. The jogger wears sneakers with bright orange soles that look like NASA designed them. I'd call the color anitra.

No sign of Alejandro or Scratch as far as I can see up the hilly road ahead, which means the most likely scenario is that they went into the church, through the swinging door. Of course, this shoots down our favorite dead-soul theory, that Scratch hates churches. Maybe all this time Renata was right to scan the New Parish for him—maybe he was in the shadows all those Saturdays, knocking back Guinnesses and getting some other stooges drunk enough to sell their souls.

What else were we wrong about?

Everything, probably.

I remember Alejandro holding the door open for me at the New Parish the first time I went to a meeting. I was nervous, imagine, *nervous* about going. I still thought I was in the throes of the worst time of my life.

I paused before crossing the threshold. That Yankee intuition prickling.

"Don't *worry* so much, Fiona," Alejandro said, with a characteristically warm, broad smile lighting his face. "In here, we are surrounded by the very things the devil cannot stand, bitter reminders of a loss he cannot bear. Here he will not come. Here we are safe from his interference."

It still didn't feel right, but he just laughed. "Look . . . look above you."

I did. It was the first time I saw the glow of the Virgin, radiating the light, laughter, and warmth from inside. It eased me somewhat.

Alejandro could tell. He placed a soft hand on my shoulder. "Would I lie to you under the Virgin herself?"

Maybe. I thought it then, but I know it now. *Yes.*

Hopefully I'll have better luck under the gaze of Saint Patrick. I hear he's the one who can banish snakes.

I STEP PAST THE THRESHOLD and into a small storeroom, dimly lit by long tubes of fluorescent bulbs—faintest smell of mildew. The lights flicker, on, then off, then on again. *Yes, Scratch is here.* The linoleum floors are nicely smooth under my feet compared to the debris-filled sidewalks outside, and even though the air isn't fresh, it's not filled with dust. I take a moment to breathe deeply. Shelves line the walls of the room, stacks and stacks of accordion files, old suitcases, dusty plastic containers, a leather bowling ball bag. In the corner sits a small statue of Mary, the kind you see in backyards, her nose and hands broken off, paint weathered away. Boxes labeled *Cavanagh Altar Bread* stacked on a pallet, fifty pounds each. Jesus pressed into small wafers—or not the body of Jesus yet, at this point he's just wheat and flour. The priest says words and then it turns into the body of Christ, and then people eat him.

I've always been curious, so I approach one that's open, pull out a small wafer marked with the cross, or an *X*, depending on how you hold it. It's lighter than I thought it would be, like it could just float above my palm. I open my mouth, place it on my tongue. It tastes like paper, with the consistency of foam, and after a few strange moments it dissolves into a mush. I don't know what else to do, so I swallow. For luck, I guess.

Suddenly above me I hear the muffled sound of a whimper, followed by the scrape of something heavy being dragged across the floor. I get a rush of adrenaline—fight or flight, the oldest of instincts—but I'm so exhausted, so spent that I would rather know than wonder. I just want whatever is going to happen to happen.

For what I know might be the last time, I close my eyes, imagine my corporeal body reappearing. There is that icy creep again, but I'm blessed with an easy transition. When I open my eyes, I look down to my arm where I'd brushed the dust away, and I see my flesh again. Bloody, bruising, but there.

It's the only real home we ever know, our bodies. It feels good to be home again. But it's cold in the storeroom, and I start to shiver, so I grab an old priest's robe that's hanging from a hook on the back of the door, put it on. Too big, but it's warmer.

The lights flick off, then on again.

I've made mistakes—I realize that now. My own paranoia that first took me out of my apartment in the rain, made me doubt Justin, talk to a stranger in a bar. Trusting Alejandro just because he knew more than I did. Fucking Scratch to buy more time. And before that, being too scared of what might happen to seriously think about a future with Justin, or a real life. Trying to stay small, invisible, safe, all that worrying and fretting for nothing. Lying to everyone, including myself, framing it all within the context of saving Justin, my supposed deep and abiding love for him, when really I was just lonely, and scared, and desperate to save my own skin.

I wonder if I ever really left that purple room in Lowell, if the girl I used to be is still there, pressing her headphones hard against her ears. Choosing to stay compartmentalized because it's safer than venturing outside, risking real love, and the pain that comes with it.

At the back of the storeroom is a thick, plain wooden door. Beyond it is my reckoning, where the faceless Oz waits for me.

CHAPTER TWENTY-TWO

THE DOOR CREAKS as it opens, and I step into a dim hallway, not sure what to expect. I find cement block walls painted yellow, the continuation of linoleum floors, and a couple of new but cheap light fixtures overhead. Empty. Quiet. It's interesting, the back part of the church no one sees, plain and unadorned, like the wings of a stage. A quiet despair that reminds me of San Quentin.

I head down the hall to a waiting staircase, dark railings worn smooth by many hands, rubber treads on the gray marble so no one slips.

Another sound from above, the hard click of Alejandro's flash. Some unintelligible murmuring.

They're here.

It terrifies me completely, but there is only one way, and that is forward. I reach out for the railing, grab hold of it tightly. Anchor myself. Pull myself forward, take a step up. Then another. The sixth step nearly does me in because my ankle twists and I almost fall backward, but I manage to hold onto the rail until I can recover my balance. I look down and find there's a gash just above my heel, blood smeared down all along my foot. Behind me, I see a trail of my bloody footprints leading to the storeroom.

What a perfect, unassailable bit of evidence, linking me to whatever scene is playing out above. Part of Scratch's plan for me, no doubt. But how did he know? What if I hadn't followed him, what if I'd gone home, what if I'd let a stranger guide me to a bench until an ambulance came?

Because I'm not a person, I'm a demographic, predictable. I predict behavior every day—my industry depends on it. And I'm in the presence of a master marketer, the source code of envy, desire, narcissism, all the ingredients for a successful campaign. We're in the same line of work, after all, a thought that triggers a bitter smile. And if Saul is right, everything I do to escape just tightens the snare trap. Maybe the trick is to stop struggling. Unless that's what my demographic would do too.

I take the next step.

There are portraits on the walls, photos housed in dusty black frames, all priests, apparently, who've been pastors at St. Patrick. Their names and the dates of their tenure are written in soft pencil on the yellowing mats. I try to focus on them instead of the muffled, whimpering sound that echoes down the stairwell. Take the next step. Father Ashton, 1919–1938, bald and old with thin, mean lips; Father Fitzpatrick, 1938–1941, young and slim, looking into the camera like a soldier with a thousand-year stare. Take the next step. Father O'Brian, 1941–1951, stout as Santa with a jolly smile to boot. The next frame holds a newspaper clipping with Father O'Brian bowling: "St. Patrick's Charity Bowl a Smash Hit for Troubled Tykes."

I reach the landing. Wipe my mouth with my hand, which

leaves a blood smear there too. *Not that it matters now.* A small window, round like a ship's portal, lets in some light, but there's no seeing through it, not with the dust and ash. I hear the keen of more ambulances, the whir of helicopter blades. A lament that feels like a homecoming of sorts.

I grab the railing, take the next step.

Father Graham, 1951–1958, skinny as a blade of grass with crooked teeth; Father Dempsey, 1958–1976, his round, bald head reflecting some of the light from an overhead fixture. He has the kindest eyes of the lot. The next frame contains an article: "City Mourns Pastor Murdered During Bank Robbery. Professor Held for Questioning."

I hear the loud click of Alejandro's camera again, his brick shit house. More murmuring. My heart beats faster, but I take the next step, reach the final set of stairs.

It's the next portrait that causes me to stop, that takes my breath away. Father Torquemada, 1976–1980. An accompanying article: "New Parish Priest Named Pastor of St. Patrick."

The name. The *name.* It can't *possibly* be a coincidence.

When I look closer, I notice the photo is askew in the mat, probably rattled free with the explosion. I lift the frame from the wall—heavier than I expected, the glass is thick—and turn it over, leaving bloody fingerprints, but I don't care. I pry up the small metal tabs, remove the back of the frame.

I pick out the photo, slowly turn it over.

And the face grinning back at me? Sans triste, with his curly locks clipped short?

None other than Alejandro's.

IT'S NOT POSSIBLE.

"It's not possible," I whisper out loud. As if these are the magic words that will somehow make it true, revert the evidence in my hands to something that makes more sense. Any kind of sense.

A photo taken thirty-seven years ago, but Alejandro doesn't look like he's aged a day—a *day*—the same crow lines gathering near his eyes, the same patches of gray in his hair, he stares into the lens looking bemused. An expression I've seen flit across his face thousands of times at our dead-soul meetings when we're swapping theories about the latest crimes, deep in discussion about double deals, when we all got a little too drunk, a little too loud, a little too despairing. With us, but never *of* us. We all clung to his calm, his acceptance, as proof that no matter how bad it got we could have the same presence of mind. That we wouldn't go insane. The story about growing up in Rio de Janeiro, the man who came to take photos. Lies. *All of it*, lies. The long sessions at the New Parish, playing us like we were rubes, like he was the P. T. Barnum of the dead-soul circus and we were the dancing bears. Creeping into our interior minds, mucking about with the machinery, keeping us isolated, dependent on him. All those midnight calls when I thought he was easing my pain and instead he was surgically extracting useful information.

And the name, *the name*—Father Alejandro Torquemada. A relation? The beneficiary of some kind of immortality inheritance?

But that's impossible too, friars weren't allowed to procreate—or they could, but not legitimately. No name to pass down. No heir.

Unless.

I start to breathe faster, a panicky roll in my chest.

Unless he is *the* Torquemada.

Alive and causing torment for more than five hundred years. *Non, je ne regrette rien.*

Anger hits, or more like a murderous rage. It feels good, this rage, like power, clarity; it makes my fingers tremble but it drives all the pain away. I tear the photo into pieces, let them fall from my fingers. I might not be able to kill him, but I will make him suffer, and suffer greatly.

The lights flicker again. I hear a gasp, like someone's choking.

It's my rage that delivers me up the last few steps, to a door with a small sign nailed in the wood—SACRISTY—then through a carpeted room with high ceilings, bright white paint, past a long row of polished cabinets, to an arched door with another small sign—SANCTUARY—which is already open, just a bit. I step through it.

SOME THINGS should never be seen. Some things should never be spoken of. What I see in the church is one of those things.

IT TAKES A MOMENT for my eyes to adjust to the dim, solemn interior of St. Patrick, and when they do, I sincerely wish they hadn't.

The smell hits me first. Blood and piss and shit and vomit.

Alejandro's Linhof Technika is set up in the center of the aisle facing the altar, empty pews on either side heading all the way to the back. Gorgeous columns fronted by statues of nuns and saints, Gothic arches that direct the eyes upwards to Tiffany-style stained glass windows. A marvel interrupted only by rough, metal scaffolding, drop cloths and sheets of plastic. I don't see Alejandro, not at first. I don't see Scratch.

There are forms in the sanctuary, statues, although a part of me knows they're not statues. I quickly compartmentalize that thought, banish it to the mausoleum where I keep all the real shadows.

I wish I could compartmentalize smell too, because I now detect the faint, trippy notes of rotting flesh and something else I can't identify. But it's harder with smell. Smell knows how to bypass thought; it just jumps right to the limbic system, triggering emotion. A massive advantage the perfume industry has over hard goods.

One of the forms moves. An arm, I think.

I focus on the light. Diffused, it streams in through the stained glass, which has miraculously survived the shock wave, illuminating Saint Patrick in a pointy hat like the pope's. He holds a staff and a cross, stands on the back of a snake, eyes solemn and sad. It's beautiful, and unlike the New Parish, still holds the effect of worship. It would be a nice place to think. To reflect.

Except. I hear something gurgle, a drowning sound.

I take a step farther out into the sanctuary. Although it's not really one anymore.

Dark metal cables stretching out in all directions, like a vast, filigree spiderweb. Trapped in the web are things that look like people, cables attached to their bodies, holding them in place, anchoring them to the columns and interior scaffolding.

There's a click and a sudden blast of light from Alejandro's camera that blinds me, and I'm left with floating red orbs and a memory that wants to surface. Something about that night in Make Westing.

"Oh, Fiona." Alejandro's voice rings out in the empty cavern, tinged with his characteristic warmth. "You *came*." When I turn and see him sitting in one of the pews, hands folded calmly on his lap, I wish I had followed his advice and left it all alone. "Although I should not be so pleased, should I? You just photobombed my picture. And it has taken me so long to compose. Although it is still not complete. Not yet."

It's just that I didn't know him at all. "Should I call you Torquemada?"

He claps his hands. "You see? I told him you were a clever girl."

Oh yes, I'm a very, *very* clever girl. And while I don't know quite how I'm going to destroy him, the first rule of marketing is desire. After five hundred years I'm sure Alejandro—Torquemada—desires something. For now, I have to play along until I see it. So I force my wooden legs to move although they don't want to, they'd prefer to crumple beneath me. Take another step into the sanctuary. Note the poinsettias arranged in front of the altar, and a cradle set on the floor.

Something wet and warm drips onto the tip of my nose. I look up and see feet dangling above me. A body held aloft, hands forced in prayer, ankles bound with barbed wire. But it's not the barbed wire that's causing blood to drip. It's because the body has been flayed. Stripped of all flesh, except the scalp.

Renata's wild red hair catches some of the light.

"Come." Alejandro holds his hand out, beckons me forward. "Come and see, Fiona Dunn."

And I do. Oh Jesus fucking Christ, I do.

HOW TO DESCRIBE IT?

A few years back, there had been a fierce discussion among the creative team at Sumpter when an exhibition rolled through town, the plasticized corpses of human beings and animals flayed alive. Sometimes they were cut in sections; sometimes they were holding their skin, or organs; sometimes they were sliced through so you could see the layers of flesh, fat, and muscle, like the rings of a tree trunk. All of them were posed artistically, whether they were staring at themselves in a mirror, cradling a baby, brushing their nonexistent hair, or riding a flayed horse into war. The eyes, and exposed orbital sockets, gave them all a fiercely determined gaze, and without their skin, they became strangely anonymous, interchangeable except for gender.

Was this art? Was it an abomination? Temperatures ran hot around the water cooler. But to me, without their skin, the bodies just seemed like the medical plastic models used in high schools—remove the exterior rib cage to reveal the plastic lungs, which could then be removed to reveal the plastic heart. I even pitched a campaign that would subtly point to the exhibit, with nude models instead of flayed ones, private parts covered by Sumpter packs, but the team thought we'd risk our staid market share in the Deep South, our bread and butter.

It's different, witnessing that degree of brutality and violence leveled at people you know, even if you don't know them well, even if minutes before you would have sold each and every one out to score your double deal.

Would you have done *this* to them though?

The perceptive part of you answers *Maybe*. The honest part of you answers *Yes*.

Somehow I find my voice. "Is this your favor?" I ask Alejandro. "Is this what Scratch called in?"

But Alejandro doesn't answer.

From somewhere at the back of the church though, Scratch does.

"I would say that what we have here is more of a collaborative effort. Including you, Fiona. You might not realize it, but you've been quite the inspiration."

I catch a movement out of the corner of my eye. Renata's head shifts slightly to the left.

Jesus Christ. They're still alive.

RENATA'S HEART. It's beating.

I stand in the aisle of the church, next to Alejandro's camera. I try not to look, to see her pulpy red heart clenching and unclenching, quivering in the cold, still air. Her flaccid lungs that fill, go limp like a deflated balloon, then fill with air again.

I try not to look but that's not possible, it's mesmerizing and horrifying in equal measure. All the compartments of my compartmentalized mind break apart, shatter in a hundred thousand pieces, and I *see* it, I see it all.

Wings. Renata has wings, a Christmas angel. They radiate out from her back, her skin draped over a lightweight frame, the structure a dark shadow visible through her translucent flesh, which glows from the light behind her. She hangs from metal cables that pierce her wrists, a puppet's strings. How is she still alive? Her eyes twitch, land on me. Her eyes must feel so dry, naked, without lids to blink. Her jaw drops like she's about to speak, but she has no lips anymore, and no tongue. I see these realizations strike her and then watch as her heart starts to beat faster, panicking. Bloody saliva drips down her chin and onto the floor.

A Christmas angel for a Christmas nativity scene.

Beneath her, a straw-tufted wooden box, a manger. To the right stands Mike as Joseph, posed in supplication, the eternal, holy cuckold. His cables are connected to Renata's, so when he drops his arm slightly—ever so slightly—it pulls on the hooks in Renata's wrists, causing her to shudder.

Behind the holy family stand two shepherds, identical height, curved staffs nailed into their hands, Jeb and Dan. Jeb's eyes plead with me, for death probably. Death would be like winning the lottery at the moment. Clarissa, another angel, hangs just above the altar, her eyes and head forcibly raised up toward heaven by a metal hook in her forehead, her skin draped over another winglike structure. Her toes barely touch the altar's surface, caught in the moment before her ascension.

Ellen as Mary kneels next to the cradle, her flayed hands sewn together in prayer. Her body, with a drooping, postpartum belly, is also held upright with a series of cables and hooks. At least two in the muscles behind her shoulders.

Where's her baby? She was pregnant the last time I saw her . . . unless . . .

I take a step forward to see what's in the manger. What I

find almost makes my knees give out. *Oh God . . . Oh dear God . . .*

Click goes Alejandro's camera. I hear him pick up the tripod, adjust it slightly. *Click.*

Aside from the occasional creak of one of the wires, the muffled wails of sirens outside, it feels remarkably peaceful inside the church. Still. The very stillness feels profane. If there are devils, then there must be angels, so where are they? *Where are they?!* I want to scream. Wouldn't this qualify for some kind of angelic intervention?

Maybe there are no more angels. Or maybe they gave up on us. Something that Scratch has taken full advantage of. Saint Patrick, pressed in glass, has no answers.

"Why . . . how are they still alive?" I manage to ask. It's hard work, standing upright. "You said after we completed, we'd be mortal again."

"Fiona, are you implying my good friend Alejandro lied to you?" That familiar lilt. I hear his footsteps on the marble as he approaches, until he's standing just behind me. I can feel his soft breath tickling the back of my neck. "I can't imagine why he'd go and do a thing like that. *Lie.* Did you lie to her, Alejandro?"

Alejandro looks up from behind the viewfinder. "I might have . . . misdirected. Apologies. The truth is that Scratch has some discretion in the matter."

"Oh, that's right," says Scratch, not bothering to mask the pride in his voice. "I am the devil, after all."

"You are," says Alejandro.

To Ellen's left stands Gary, or who I assume is Gary, clutching a decanter of yellow oil. And behind him is Jasmine. Poor

Jasmine holds a box that looks like a treasure chest, a dark cape with a regal cowl draped over her shoulders.

Only it's not made of cloth. It's her skin.

Shit, oh shit, oh shit. I can feel the edges of my mind start to disintegrate. Because even an atheist like me knows there's something missing. *We three kings of Orient are.* I see only two.

Me? Am I the third king?

"So," whispers Scratch. "Do you think we'll break the Internet?"

CHAPTER TWENTY-THREE

YES, TODAY'S EVENTS will definitely break the Internet. I try to imagine it, the rush the reporters must already be experiencing, anchors hustling back to the studio, editors managing the flow of social media and trying to be the first with the whole story online. Careers would be made with just the bomb blast alone. But *this* full-on blasphemy too, on top of everything . . .

Blood pools on the cool flagstones, drips over the edge, forms a trickle that reaches out under the pew benches, like tentacles.

And yet I'm still standing, at least so far. There are two dead souls here, and one slot left in the nativity scene. I need to make sure it's Alejandro, not me, strung up behind Jasmine and holding the frankincense. *Only the cold survive*, he'd said. I'm going to show him just how cold cold can be. First, I take a cue from my ever-unfaithful assistant, Tracy, and begin the process of undermining.

I cock my head to the right. "It's a little . . . gauche, don't you think?"

"*Gauche?*" replies Alejandro hotly. "My work has been

called many things, but never that. I think it is your perspective that is gauche."

Still, Scratch takes a step toward me, stands shoulder to shoulder. "How so?"

"Well . . . you're bludgeoning the message to death. If there is one, which isn't even clear. I mean . . . what's all this supposed to accomplish except some brief notoriety? It will freak people out, but then they'll just move on anyway."

It's so strange—I can't see Scratch looking at me, but I feel it, a quiet, dark probe.

Click. "Do you *mind*, Fiona?" Alejandro says. "You're in the way of my shot."

I step aside—and a bit closer to Scratch. Barely a centimeter between our bodies.

"Well," says Scratch. "We didn't actually sit down and create a marketing plan."

"That's your first mistake. Everyone thinks marketing is easy, that a trained monkey can do it."

Scratch barks out a laugh. "You continue to surprise me, Ms. Dunn. And you should know that it's rare that I'm surprised anymore."

I detect the slightest dig at Alejandro. I add a wedge. "Then you're surrounding yourself with some boring company. So, what is the point to all . . . this?"

Ellen shudders. Something like bile pours out from a gash in her womb. I feel vomit rise at the back of my own throat, but I push it down and keep the tears back, hold very, very still. Reveal nothing.

Scratch sighs. "It's just been so hard to escalate the conflict in the Middle East. Always brewing, never boiling over. Never raging across continents the way it could. But this . . . such a direct affront to Christianity, and right before Christmas. Now *that* could be the spark."

"Huh." It's noncommittal, the kind I trot out in meetings to passive-aggressively discount an idea.

"You don't agree?"

I see Alejandro's shoulders tense.

"It's an idea . . . but you're in the wrong town for that. You should have staged this somewhere in the Bible Belt. *That* would have people *really* losing their minds. And just how are you connecting us all to Islamic terrorism?"

"Oh, the digital trail has been set," says Scratch. "You might be surprised at how much is in your bank account, and where it came from. Although in my narrative, you're just an agent of Saul. Time for that poor bastard to fall too. But . . . you're saying that we haven't chosen the right *place*."

I lay into the hard shilling. "Christians are generally happy when something bad happens in a city they consider Sodom. But I would have assumed you thought that one out."

Scratch lets his hand fall to the back of the pew, starts to rub at the wood grain. Finally he says, "Why didn't you think about that one, Alejandro?" His tone is deadly.

Alejandro turns, unsettled. "It is not so easy to start an inquisition in the twenty-first century. And I delivered everything you asked for."

"Five hundred years ago."

That's the number one problem with launching a successful campaign. The expectation that you can easily do it again. I am now in my element. A bull shark in shallow waters.

———— ⌇ ————

I ALWAYS HAVE TO settle myself, my mind, before I make a pitch, but I've never had to do that before under this kind of duress.

There's a taught frisson now between Scratch and Alejandro. Five hundred years—a long time to build up disappointments, unspoken resentments. Shouldn't take much. I can sense Scratch's keen interest, his flickering curiosity.

It's quiet for some reason in the church. An expectant hush.

Alejandro stands back from his camera, stretches his arms up above him, and yawns. A typically male dismissive gesture—I've seen it hundreds of times during a hard negotiation.

Scratch leans in conspiratorially. "*He* used to be a shepherd. Then he wanted to be a great Christian. Then a great artist. Can never make up his mind, that one."

He wants me to play. And there's no use blurting out a pitch—it always starts with this kind of banter, feigning an interest in things that aren't interesting. Every client likes to be courted. Wooed.

"Times have changed since then," I say.

Alejandro grabs a small duffel bag, the same one I first saw him with in the cemetery, and digs around in it for a second or two. "My dear Fiona, I have a million following my Twitter feed, another five hundred thousand liking my Pinterest boards. I am well aware that times have changed."

And here it is, my moment. I turn to Scratch. "Now that . . . *that* could be potentially interesting."

"What?"

"Adding a celebrity to the tableau. Giving people a hero to

mourn. A face for the epic attack on our American way of life. The immigrant who worked his way up to such great heights, fulfilling the American dream, cut down by terrorists."

Alejandro pauses his search. "Are you *serious*?"

"An unknown assailant who killed Ellen and Mike's children, forced them to pose in front of their dismembered bodies."

Alejandro stands. "A *known* assailant. A woman with a troubled past, enamored with a violent, extreme terrorist group, seeking salvation."

"Oh, please," I say. "That's a tired trope."

"*Tired trope* . . ." says Alejandro in disbelief. He looks to Scratch, but the devil himself doesn't seem to be too interested in backing up his star protégé at the moment. "*Tired trope*?! Do you know you are not the first, fourth, or even fiftieth dead soul to come up with the idea of inserting a line in a website's terms and conditions? *We* even tried it once. It worked for a day, but then someone complained. Barely up twelve hours."

I ignore him and focus on Scratch, who listens with a preternatural stillness. "What you need is a creative mind . . . someone who could access the data and come up with subtle ways to manipulate people, like through their social media streams, the stories that appear in their feeds, gradually ratcheting up their discontent until they take action. There's a reason the Egyptians are calling their children Facebook."

I see a line of worry now flit across Alejandro's brow. "Oh, come on. You are not seriously—"

"*Your* whole issue is about concealment. Not all this, what you've just done here. You're all about manipulating the masses without being seen. Edward Bernays could leverage stunts because there were limited outlets for dissemination. Those days are over. Too much noise."

I hear the creak of a cable, and a guttural moan.

"But this," says Scratch. "*This* will get heard *above* the noise."

He's caught on the line, and I slowly reel him in. "Uh-huh. And before you know it, it'll be old news soon as Miley Cyrus sticks her tongue out and shaves what's left of her hair. People move on to the next outrage, always. Wars are unpopular because every economy is tied together. Sure, random violence is up, spots of terrorism, some targeted military strikes . . . but most of that is done with drones now. So you're forced to go door-to-door, which you do enjoy, the actual one-on-one *trade*, but I'm sure you strike out sometimes, and eventually there will be a tipping point when more souls go to heaven than to you because there's no way you can keep up with a population of nine billion people. Your second biggest problem is scalability."

He raises his hand to his chin, which I can't see. Rubs it. This blurs the tips of his fingers. "I thought you were an atheist."

Now it's time for the hook. "As you said, many are until they meet you."

Here Alejandro's worry turns to real concern. I am enjoying every second of his discomfiture. "But this is *art*, this is—"

"What you want is to target the people with a penchant for evil," I say, ignoring the devil's wingman. "And then subtly encourage them into acts that will damn them to hell. Blow on the embers digitally."

Scratch turns his head ever so slightly in my direction. "How do I target these people?"

"Simple," I say. "The same way every company is manipulating people. Big data and paranoia."

THERE IS A STRANGE MOMENT that follows—it's heavy, pressing, charged, electric. It reminds me of the tropical depressions back East, when there could be no mistaking a storm on the horizon.

Finally Scratch speaks. "You can do this? I thought your specialty was desire."

"Desire and paranoia are sides of the same coin. Fear is always easier to implement."

Scratch nods, apparently thinking.

I say nothing else. Hold my breath.

And Alejandro, the ever calm, mysteriously unshakable Alejandro, is, for the first time I've ever seen, overcome with emotion. His eyes well with tears and they fall, one after the other, which at first causes a thrill of triumph to course through my body—*who's triste now, motherfucker*—but then there's something not quite right about his expression, which is exultant, ecstatic. He lets his hands fall, drops to his knees in supplication to our chosen god Scratch.

Did I misread Scratch? Did I blow it?

Some kind of wordless ask passes between them, the kind of nonverbal communication that happens with long-married couples, which makes me feel cheated in some way, left out. I feel the petulance of a child watching adults conferring about a topic only spoken about behind closed doors. But I don't dare say a word.

"*Please,*" says Alejandro, barely more than a whisper.

Scratch holds out his hands, palms up.

Alejandro gasps and then falls forward, pressing his face in Scratch's palms. He sobs fiercely.

"Oh, thank you, thank you, thank you." His voice breaks with emotion.

Fuck. He's sobbing with joy, with relief, which makes my stomach clench with fear. I know who's going to be the third Wise Man now, and it's me. My skin tingles, anticipating its imminent removal. The vomit rises at the back of my throat again. I wonder how long it takes, being flayed alive. How long Scratch will keep us alive for the display.

Scratch drops his hands and Alejandro lifts his head up, reaches into his back pocket, retrieving his card. Holds his palm out flat, and places the card on top of it.

Scratch lifts his index finger, writes a word in the naked air, a word which then burns into the card.

Completed.

The card then bursts into flame and disappears entirely, leaving only a pile of black ash.

Alejandro stares at his empty palm with something like wonder, and awe. "Thank you."

I mentally prepare myself for an unthinkable degree of pain. Which one will cut into me first?

So I'm not prepared for what happens next.

Alejandro, looking younger, lighter, and happier than I've ever seen him, reaches into his duffel bag and pulls out a bloody, sharp knife, grabs it by the blade, and offers me the handle.

"And now, lovely Fiona, if you could do me this small kindness. We are short, you see, of one king."

I LOOK TO SCRATCH FIRST, wondering if this is some kind of test or a bizarre setup for a new nightmare, but it's impossible to read the expression of someone without a face. I can't believe he'd just let me kill Alejandro—that seems too clean, too simple, too much what I want at the moment. Saul's mad voice whispers in my ear, *It's a snare trap.*

"Come, my dear," says Alejandro, a quiver in his voice that hits a false note. "The first kill is the hardest. After that, butchery becomes like anything else in the world. Just a chore."

"How many have *you* butchered?"

He smiles, but it's not a smile. Not really.

"You lose track over the years. Everything just starts to blur together—faces, time, names. So you learn to live in the moment. You are what you are in the moment. What happens, happens. Afterward, you wash the blood off. And it always washes off. Always. Blood stains little except clothing. And memory." He holds up the knife a little higher. "See for yourself. I can tell you want to."

And I do. How much different would it be, after all, from cutting myself? I just need to sink the knife a little deeper, and this time into someone else's skin.

A cacophony of creaking, guttural groans rises from the sanctuary, a Greek chorus of dead souls. They might not have their tongues, but they edge me on all the same. Not people anymore—just pure want and desperation and pain.

Maybe. Maybe I can do it for them.

Take the knife, a voice whispers in my head. *Kill him and be done with it.*

So I take a step forward, reach out for the weapon. The handle is cool in my hand, made with some kind of bone or ivory, engraved with Spanish words and the sigil of a medieval lion. It feels good, holding it, a natural extension of my rage. All the times I was abandoned, beaten, betrayed, the nicknames at school, the shame of falling-apart shoes, the prick of my first pair of scissors in the fleshy part of my thigh, the release that followed, the shame that followed after that. All this rushes from my heart, through my arm, down my fingers, and into the blade. I press the tip against Alejandro's throat, and a drop-let of blood beads. This also feels good. I'm awash in endorphins, a murderous high that's righteous and powerful.

I'm not a dead soul, or a person, I am a god. It's fury that makes gods. *Vengeance is mine. I will repay, saith the Lord.*

Alejandro's gaze turns inward, expectant, hopeful.

Why does this feel like a trap?

I pause.

Because maybe it is.

It was so easy selling Scratch my soul, a barely noticeable blip on the screen of my life with such stunning, bitter repercussions. I must be careful. I must think this through.

"What about them?" I ask Scratch, nodding toward the nativity scene.

"What *about* them?"

"If I do this, if I kill Alejandro, then you . . . end their suffering. Now."

He doesn't say anything at first, and I think I've overstepped, but then he just laughs. It echoes. "I think you missed your calling, Fiona—you should have gone into sales."

Alejandro though doesn't seem amused. He seems worried.

Scratch leans forward slightly. "I can see you're going to keep me busy. I could force you, you know. Call it in as a favor."

"Then your favor would be called in and you'd have no more power over me."

"Until *you* die." Flint in his tone.

I respond just as coolly, offering nothing. "Until I die."

There is another, longer pause. I'm being reevaluated for sure.

"All right."

"All right?"

This is too simple. Again, I have a feeling I'm playing right into his hands.

"Once they get to hell," Scratch continues, "they might not thank you. So we have an agreement?"

Don't. Don't do it. But there's the tug again. Although they can't speak for themselves, I know that this is what they want. It's what *I* would want.

I nod.

Scratch raises his index finger, and I watch him write cursive in the air, the word illuminated by fire. *Completed.*

Jeb falls limp on his cable.

Completed.

Then Renata.

Completed.

Then Clarissa.

Completed.

Ellen.

Completed.

Mike.

Completed.
Gary.
Completed.
Jasmine.
Completed.
Dan.

I don't know how it's possible, but I feel it, the loss of their souls. Like there's more negative space all of a sudden, more air than there should be. I hope they find some sort of relief, wherever they are now. But I doubt it.

I grip the knife handle tighter.

Alejandro raises his chin slightly, expectant. "I am ready, my dear." Closes his eyes. A hint of a smile teases his mouth, and he's about to speak again—

—when he's cut off by the blast of a shot ringing out, the impact of the bullet causing the front of his skull to explode, spraying blood and bits of brain across my face, the camera, the floor. Alejandro's body crumples, falls to the cold flagstone. For a moment, his right hand twitches, like he's processing an electric current. Then it's still.

The gray cast to his skin, his dark shadow, lightens and then gradually, slowly, disappears. For a moment, he looks at peace. Then his skin crumbles, five hundred years of decay happening in five seconds, leaving behind only a blanched, white skeleton, and a pile of gray ash.

CHAPTER TWENTY-FOUR

MY FIRST EMOTION is anger that someone has cheated me out of my revenge, followed closely by relief that someone has cheated me out of my revenge, which is quickly followed by shock. Because when I turn to see who has done this evil deed, I find Justin standing in the doorway of St. Patrick, both hands gripping a gun, smoke still drifting from the barrel.

Justin. Good God, Justin.

I turn to Scratch, but the devil is nowhere—gone, vanished.

Justin puts the gun in his coat pocket—*Where the hell did he get a gun?*—runs down the aisle—*When's the last time I saw him run?*—clasps me in his arms. "Oh my God, oh my God, are you okay? Are you okay?"

Is this hell? Did I really die and go to hell? Because this isn't right, nothing about this is right.

Justin pushes me away slightly, examining me for injury. "Are you really . . . what the hell are you wearing?"

I start to shiver. It's uncontrollable and my teeth chatter.

He presses a hand against my cheek, like I might be running a fever. "Oh, Fiona," he says, his voice breaking. "My Fiona."

He takes off a dark navy peacoat, which I'd bought for him a year ago and has never been worn. Flings it out like a matador cape and wraps it around my shoulders.

"There," he says, running a loving hand over my matted hair. There is still gum from where the duct tape bound his wrists.

He looks different. His shirt hangs off him. His tumor looks smaller. I feel the weight of the gun in his coat pocket, still warm.

"How did you know where I was?" I ask.

At that, he looks down for just a fraction of a second too long. "I turned on your Find a Friend app. When you were asleep. Opal suggested it. We were worried about you."

We. When did *they* become *we*?

"But I don't have my phone."

This seems to surprise him. "Well . . . who does?"

Oh, the digital trail has been set, Scratch had said.

"Stolen," I lie. "Probably one of . . ." I nod in the direction of the dead-soul web.

Justin wraps an arm around my shoulder, gathering me. "Well. Let's get out of here before the police come."

We are both lying to each other now; I know it. I look at Alejandro's skeleton lying askew in the aisle, and envy him.

A QUIET RIDE HOME. Even with the priest's smock and Justin's wool peacoat, I'm cold. We drive slowly through the streets in Opal's car, an old Volkswagen that is neat, vacuumed, well cared for. Smells like the strawberry air freshener hanging from the rearview mirror. We're cleared through a police checkpoint, and then onto the freeway. The sky is tinted pink, smoke and dust creating a glorious sunrise, and it makes me sad that Alejandro isn't in this world anymore to capture it.

I wonder if Scratch will ever call my favor, if I'll end up in prison, insane and alone like Saul. But I feel like there is some other plan in store for me. Something worse. Something to do with Justin.

He has a jitter about him—he turns on the heat, turns it down, turns it up. I recognize that jitter—guilt.

"Where did you get the gun?" My first words. They sound stark.

"Just . . ." He takes a hand off the steering wheel, runs it over his head. I note the first blossoming of what looks like new hair sprouting. "I bought it online. Just in case I couldn't . . . you know . . . take it."

"You would shoot yourself? Why not just OD?"

His eyes cut sideways. "What the hell kind of question is that?"

But if he was a dead soul, there'd be a shadow. No one I can call now to compare notes with.

I fiddle with a button on his peacoat. "I'm just wondering if I know you."

"That's really funny," he says. "That you're wondering if *you* know *me.*"

We don't say anything after that for a while. We get on the San Francisco–Oakland Bay Bridge, joining a long, thick vein of traffic. Everyone leaving the city in the same, small arteries. Stop and go. Stop and go. Makes me think of the beat of a heart, the pulse of blood through veins. Renata's heart, exposed to the air.

The ocean below is still, dark, and pensive.

"I bought the gun," he finally says. "I put it in my coat

pocket. I decided I'd go to a park early one morning, before anyone got there. Take care of things."

It causes me to wince, because I know it's true. He has always been that considerate.

"I know it'd ruin the life insurance policy, but I didn't want to be in the hospital. My mother was in the hospital. I hate the way they smell."

His mother died when he was eight. He rarely, if ever, speaks of her.

"I'm sorry," I say. "I just feel weird. It's not every day your boyfriend shoots a man you were about to kill. Who doesn't ask any questions about, say, a church filled with flayed bodies." I try to inflect it like a joke, but neither of us smile.

A van in front of us, the bumper adorned with a bumper sticker: COEXIST.

"Look, I woke up, or came to . . . Opal found me, untied me. The place was a mess, you were gone. I don't even remember what happened; the last thing I knew we were talking. I tried calling the police, but they were busy, so Opal gave me her keys and since then . . . fuck, let's just say I'm a little overwhelmed."

The thought occurs to me that maybe I'm being paranoid. Maybe I don't know how to be any other way. He reaches out for my hand, and I give it to him. Raise his hand to my lips, kiss the knuckles.

Only they smell like Opal's perfume.

NOT A HARD TIME getting a parking space, not on a day when people are packing up and leaving the city. At least four spaces right in front of our apartment building.

322 J. LINCOLN FENN

"It was just an explosion," I say, watching a mother pack her minivan across the street. She has two toddlers and four barely closed suitcases.

Justin slides the stick shift into park. "Rumor is that it's a terrorist attack planned by an inmate in San Quentin. Someone leaked a highly classified document."

"Right." Someone like Scratch. I bet my name is in that document.

I find the handle of the door, open it, step out of the car onto the sidewalk. Blue sky now, a small skittering of white clouds. I think about the card in my wallet, in my purse, in my apartment. Whether there are words written on it. I think about Justin's fingers that smell like Opal's perfume. My knees almost give out.

"Here," says Justin. He grabs my elbow and props me up. His shirt seems to hang even looser now. His cheeks are fuller, healthier. Rosy almost.

"I don't know if I can walk."

"Then don't," he says, scooping me up and into his arms. He's only done this once before, carrying me into the cabin at the foot of the Tetons. When he was stronger, when he was cancer-free.

He carries me over to the entry, gently sets me down and reaches into his pocket for his keys. The tumor is definitely smaller, and his jeans hang just below his hip. A click as he unlocks the door.

"Ready?" he asks brightly.

We are playing roles now. I offer a wan smile.

He knows.

He knows I was the one who trashed the apartment, made

Jeb tie him up. How he knows, I'm not sure. I want to speak into the wall I've created, I want to argue my case—I didn't mean for any of this to happen, the only reason it happened is because I love him so much, I was afraid I was going to lose him, so I did something stupid, even for me, and that everything I've done since then is for him, for *us*. All I wanted to do was fix the mess I made.

But I know in my heart it's not true. None of it is. I'm a good liar, but not that good. The truth is I was paranoid, and jealous, and never really trusted him. I always kept a psychic bag packed. Until I sold my soul, nothing terrified me so much as real intimacy, the kind where you risk your heart, actual feelings. The truth is that the most important thing to me is *me*. I wanted a double deal so I wouldn't end up in hell. The truth is that to whatever extent he's now corrupted, it's because I introduced the contagion.

The apple doesn't fall far from the tree.

I remember my father looming in the doorway—Christ, his skin, I remember his skin now, that strange, gray cast. *You think you're a good person, but you're not.* I always thought it was the drugs that made him look that way. I was wrong.

He was a dead soul too.

Justin holds open the door for me while an invisible shock wave ripples through my body. I almost want to laugh, although there's nothing funny, not really.

"Ladies first."

THE ELEVATOR CREAKS, and groans, and I can't help but think of the metal cables spinning around the pulleys that carry our weight, like the web stringing up the dead souls in St. Patrick. Justin holds me up around the waist, and I lean my head on his shoulder, savoring these last moments.

The truth, it hurts. But for the first time in my life, I'd rather see and feel it in every excruciating detail.

The elevator reaches the fifth floor, jolts to a halt. He unclasps the metal gate, pushes it aside like a fan. Opens the door. Gallantly offers his hand, and I take it. We step into the hallway—he slips his arm around me again, warm, protective, an illusion. That woman—Lydia, Gloria, something—pokes her head out the door of her apartment.

"Oh my goodness gracious," she says. "Are you two okay?"

I offer another wan smile. "Looks worse than it is."

She seems doubtful. "You should see a doctor, honey."

"Hospitals are packed," says Justin. "But my hospice nurse is here—she can fix her up."

Of course she's still here. *Everything I touched, I corrupted*, Saul had said. *It bleeds that way.* I feel ribs under Justin's shirt. It's the first time I've felt them in months; they were covered by the tumor.

"I'll be fine," I say. "Everything is going to be fine."

I'm sure she'll be more than happy to tell her story to the news media, once I'm officially pegged as a suspect. *There was that time when I found her clothes in a heap on the stoop. She never was friendly. Kept to herself.*

"Thank you," says Justin, in a tone that implies *now go away.*

She hesitates, uncertain, but then closes her door, leaving me with the man I don't love as much as I do myself. One who has some nefarious plan for me.

Gently he guides me down the hallway to our apartment door, and I lean on him more than I need to. I can almost feel his cancer melting away under my fingers. Strange and miraculous. We get to the door, and pause for a moment.

I think about all the things I'd wished I said to him, long ago, I think about all the time I wasted pursuing work, cultivating fear, being invisible, here but not here. I think I might even have been happy. Isn't that a strange thing to consider, that I was happy but didn't know it? Another thing I lost that I didn't know I had.

I take a deep breath. He smells like old Justin—clean, healthy, just a touch of sweat. I look at his face, and his eyes hold a wall between us. We regard ourselves as these new creatures, capable of unspeakable acts, of treachery.

"I really loved you," I say. "Even when it didn't look like it, I loved you."

"I know," he says. "I've always known."

He opens the door. A waft of Opal's perfume escapes.

"But it is what it is."

I could run; I could try to ghost one last time. But I'm tired of running, and tired of being a living ghost. I can't imagine how Alejandro endured living in this shadow world all that time.

I step into my apartment. He follows.

And shuts the door behind him.

CHAPTER TWENTY-FIVE

OPAL IS STANDING in the kitchen area, cooking something on the stove. Not hiding how at home she is. Something meaty in the oven, a roast maybe. Justin hasn't been able to digest that kind of protein in months.

There's been a shift too in the arrangement of furniture. The couch now faces the window, not the TV, which does create a nice buffer between the door and living space, and draws the eyes to the fire escape and a peek of the lake view. I wish I'd thought of it.

Opal looks up, sees the state of me, and takes the spoon out of a pot—*Beans? He hates beans*—and places it on a spoon rest I didn't know we had.

"Oh my God," she says.

"I found her like this," says Justin. He doesn't mention shooting anyone. "I thought it was better to bring her back here until the hospitals clear up."

It feels practiced, what they're saying. Scripted. And her skin—I'd recognize that dark shadow anywhere. She must see mine too. But Justin doesn't have one. There's some small comfort in that.

My teeth chatter. My body is actually going into shock.

Opal walks toward me with an affectation of concern. "We need to get her into the bathtub. Clean her wounds."

Here they are, talking about me in third person. I'm the child now.

"That's what I thought."

"I'll get the kit."

What kit, I don't know; we never had a kit. Still, I let Justin lead me to the bedroom, which has been restored to order, except for the mangled bedside lamp, which sticks out of my modern trash can, looking like it's trying to eat it. Subtle changes here too. My papers, for instance, are missing. Trashed too or simply stored in the closet?

Justin turns the light on in the bathroom, goes in. I hear him turn on the faucet, the rush of water into the tub. I take off his peacoat jacket, drop it on the bed—the coverlet with the bloodstains is gone, replaced by a simple white sheet over the feather comforter. I think for a moment. *Yes. Just in case.*

I reach into the peacoat, pull out the gun, slide it under the mattress where I kept my scissors. My fingertips leave a slight smudge of dust on the white sheet.

"Do you think you can take it hot?" Justin calls out.

"No, medium warm."

Creak as he turns on the other faucet. I reach down for my purse, placed on the floor next to my bedside table. Grab my wallet, and pull out my card. It doesn't even concern me in some strange way; I feel beyond worry or care at this point. It's more a distant sense of curiosity.

FAVOR: *blank.*

No, Scratch has some other plan for me in mind for sure. I slip the card back in my wallet, the wallet back into my purse. I want to sit on the bed, but my bloody, dusty self would cause more work for Opal for sure. I almost feel like a guest here. Not in my own room.

"I think we're set," says Justin. He comes out of the bathroom to retrieve me. My heart aches for the concern in his eyes to be real.

He smiles gently, pushes the priest's smock off my shoulders—loose anyway it simply falls away into a heap on the floor. I see I'm cut and scraped and bruised in more places. A really nasty gash just below my rib cage that I hadn't even noticed.

"Jesus. Maybe I should've taken you to the hospital." An unscripted thought, which seems to create a wavering confusion.

"Oh, we'll fix her right up," says Opal brightly.

She stands in the doorway with a crowbar in her hand. He sees it, and for just a few seconds I think he's going to charge her, take her down, but then he just takes a step away instead.

"I'm sorry," he says, not looking at me—he can't. Reaches down for the coat on the bed, then into the pocket where the gun was supposed to be.

Opal smiles. Something glitters on her hand, and then I see it—the engagement ring Justin had kept in his sock drawer.

I thought I'd known the worst pain, experienced the worst horrors.

Once again, I was wrong.

EVERYTHING THAT HAPPENS next happens fast, but in slow motion too—I am inside myself, my consciousness, but outside it as well, an observer. There is the surprise in Justin's face when he finds the pocket empty, followed by his shock when I disappear, not entirely from view because my form covered in dust is still visible.

I see Opal lift the crowbar over her head, start running for me—her face is contorted, her dark shadow radiating out like a poisonous gas cloud—but I'm too fast, I slip my hand under the mattress, pull out the gun—Justin is still trying to process what's happening, trying to understand—when I shoot Opal in her right shoulder. Blood spatters and she doubles over with pain, dropping the crowbar. It falls to the floor with a clatter. Justin takes a step back, runs his hand through his hair, now a few centimeters thick.

He makes a sound, but I'm not sure if it's a word exactly. I shoot her again, in the stomach. Smoke drifts lazily from the barrel, smell of burning cordite.

She's not going to die of course. She won't be eligible for that gift until Scratch calls her favor in.

Unless this *is* him calling his favor in.

She crumples to the floor, kneeling, hand reaching out to the floor. Justin rushes to her side.

"Holy shit!" he yells. "Holy shit!"

He's frantic, looks at her the way he used to look at me. How and when did I lose him so completely? But then it's obvious what she traded for—his health to return. Who wouldn't fall in love with someone who'd sell her soul to save your life?

When he turns to me, he's all rage and desperate fury, a side I'd never have thought him capable of. Not *my* Justin, a man who slowed down for pigeons that landed in the street, who kept the fridge stocked with my favorite sodas, who watched TV while I read my focus group reports, my head resting on his lap. Who would stroke my hair gently, idly, loving me even when I was absorbed in other things.

He grabs the crowbar.

I shoot him in the leg. Raise the gun and put his head in my sights.

But no. *No, no, no, no*. Never.

Maybe the apple can fall a little farther from the tree.

EVEN WITH ALL THE POLICE and SWAT and Army Reserves headed deep into the city, I'm sure that three gun blasts reported in a building known for peace and quiet will draw the appropriate law enforcement agencies. Sooner than later, if Scratch's threat of a digital trail is real.

God, I could use a Guinness.

I shut the bedroom door behind me, ignoring the moans. I'm not as worried about Opal tied and gagged on the bed—frankly I don't give a shit if she's suffering—but Justin looked pale, and even though I tied a tourniquet around his leg, he *is* just recovering from cancer. I'm hoping that whatever deal Opal made extends to other conditions.

I still love him. This surprises me. I didn't know I'd loved him so much.

I tie the belt of my terry-cloth robe a little tighter and head for the fridge. The six-pack of Guinness is still missing, but there's some cooking sherry, an oloroso. What the hell. I pull out the bottle, take a few sips from it, and remember why I hate sherry. But the alcoholic buzz, that I like. I tuck it under my arm. My stomach grumbles. Might be eating prison food for a while. So I put the sherry on the table, then go to the sink to wash the blood off my hands—it *does* wash off, something Alejandro was right about—and take the roast out of the oven. Pork, nicely browned. Baked beans in the pot Opal had been stirring, and I also discover some freshly baked corn bread on top of the fridge. I pull out a carving knife, a plate, forks and the butter. I set myself a place at the table, using a real placemat from a set Justin had bought from QVC.

A knock at the door. Not an authoritative, *we've got you sur-rounded!* kind of knock, not a Gloria imperative knock; it's more a question, mildly inquisitive. But of course I know who it is.

I cross over to the door, unlatch the chain lock, open it.

Scratch, my faceless friend, stands in the doorway, fingers hooked through plastic six-pack rings, although I note there're only four cans of Guinness left. But then we'd drank the other two at Alejandro's house. Among other things we did.

"Something smells good," he says. "Mind if I join you?"

And really, at this point, why the hell not?

SCRATCH TAKES OVER the hosting duties, retrieving the roast from the kitchen counter, placing it on a cutting board, which he then places on the table. His movements are neat, direct, like a professional waiter. He gets himself a placemat, plate, even brings the salt and pepper, a loaf of bread from the cabinet. He's good with the carving knife too—perfect slabs of meat fall away—but then given the expert flaying I've recently seen dis-played, it shouldn't seem that remarkable.

A muffled yell from the bedroom—Opal hearing another voice, trying to catch his attention, inviting rescue. But he either doesn't hear or doesn't care.

"Nothing I like better than a home-cooked meal," he says. He pops open the tab to the Guinness, pours as much as he can into a glass. It's nicely cold—instantly, condensation starts to form. He places it in front of me.

I pick up the glass, take a deep, appreciative sip.

He sits in the chair opposite me. "Strange as it might seem, not many like to eat with the devil."

"You could force them to." I pick up a knife to start into the pork on my plate. It smells divine. "Call it in as a favor."

"But then it's not the same, is it? It's not an act of genuine affection."

I take a bite. Wish I hadn't shot Opal before she'd started the gravy. "Is that what you want, genuine affection? Does that even exist?"

"Ha!" he says, pointing his knife at me. "People say so. All the time. *Please, spare my child, take me instead.* Blah, blah, feckin' blah. When it comes time to collect my favor though, you'd be surprised at who people offer instead of themselves. Other considerations kick in."

I reach for a piece of corn bread and slather a good amount of butter on it.

"Take you, for example," he says.

"Me." The corn bread has actual corn in it. A nice touch.

"Yes, *you*. So hot and bothered for a double deal, you fail to see the obvious right in front of you."

"Which is . . ."

"Your very pursuit of it undermined the relationship you

were desperate to preserve. Created an opening for someone else to step through. Ms. Opal. Sold her soul to get Justin to love her instead."

I take a swig of Guinness to wash the corn bread down. "But his tumor. It's gone, or almost all gone now. I thought she'd have traded—"

"No. *He* traded his soul to save his life."

Why am I even having this conversation, breaking bread with him? Where will this ever lead except to unhappy places? But the thought prickles.

"He doesn't have a dark shadow though."

Now it's time for Scratch to become suddenly interested in his slice of pork. For a moment he says nothing.

Sirens. Distant, but on their way.

He stabs a chunk of meat with his fork. "Why do you think that is?"

Why indeed? My mind clicks through all the possibilities: A) Scratch is lying, and isn't he renowned, after all, for being the father of lies? B) Justin found some way to mask his dark shadow, or C) Scratch is telling the truth, in which case Justin has already completed his favor.

The last thought is like a gut punch, which means it's probably true.

"What did you ask him to do?" I whisper.

Scratch smiles. "He took Jeb and me into Fealtee headquarters, where Jeb was able to directly hack into the NSA mainframe and send me the entire database of information in an encrypted file. But with everything else happening in the area these days, I think agencies will be too busy to notice a little blip of unusual activity."

I drop my knife on my plate. Misdirection. Everything he's done has been to misdirect.

"Here's my problem though. What good is dissemination," he says, holding the fork up to his mouth, "without the right messages?"

———————∽———————

IT'S A JOB OFFER. And maybe this is what was planned all along, why he allowed Alejandro to finally, mercifully die. Because he'd found a replacement.

A part of me is immensely flattered. The rest, not so sure.

The sirens now, closer.

"So . . . are you offering *me* a double deal?"

He chews thoughtfully, and swallows. Picks up his glass of Guinness and takes a sip. I let my fork trail through the liquid remains of the beans on my plate, making a kind of rainbow.

"Not so much a double deal as a choice, one which, of course, skews a bit more to my benefit."

"Explain."

He leans in, rests his lower arm on the table. "Your soul. While I never like to turn down a soul, one more in my collection isn't going to make a tremendous difference for me. It's like giving a billionaire a penny."

I start to open my mouth to protest.

"Not that I'm saying there is anything particularly *inferior* about your soul. But why take one when you can take a hundred million? That's the kind of number that feels . . . exciting. Fresh."

If I could see his mouth, I have no doubt there'd be a grin there.

I lean back in my chair. Body language is key in any kind of negotiation. It's important to seem calm, uninterested. "And my role and responsibilities would be . . ."

"Developing the messaging. Launching the campaign. Metrics and all that good stuff. I'm hoping for big conversions, obviously. Like you said. *Scalability*."

I brush some crumbs off my lap. "So this is the plan that's to your benefit. What's in it for me?"

"Oh, I don't know . . ." He twirls his knife in the air. "Not going to hell for starters. I certainly enjoy it, but few others do."

The siren is just outside now; I hear the *chirp, chirp* as the squad car is parked.

"Don't worry," says Scratch. "I left the door to the elevator open. It'll take them some time to climb the stairs."

Always hated high-pressure salesmen.

"Plus, if you're working for me, I won't call in your favor. Which, in this case, you might really want to avoid. It involves someone I suspect you still have feelings for. Maybe the only person other than yourself you care about. Is it just me, or do you think this would be better as a sandwich?" He reaches out for two slices of bread, drops them on his plate, then stabs another piece of pork, lays it out on the bread.

"Why, what did you have in mind for my favor?"

He arranges the pork slices neatly. "You know all the horrors of the world are born of love. Someone loves someone else, they get hurt, they turn their wrath and despair upon the world. Love is a scourge, a disease, a feast for madness. Do you have mustard?"

"Of course we have mustard." *Easy, Fiona. Don't let him see you sweat.*

"Real mustard or just the kind you Americans squirt on hot dogs?"

"What did you have in mind for my favor?"

"I never reveal proprietary information."

"How can I choose if I don't know what I'm choosing between?"

He laughs and stands. Heads for the fridge. "Well," he says. "You know how much I enjoyed that foie gras sandwich. Fond memories of that night."

In desperation, I try one last time to ghost. No such luck.

"Ah, ah, no cheating," Scratch says. "Oh look, Dijon! You're rather civilized, after all."

The pork suddenly doesn't feel so good in my stomach. It rumbles, like it might be slightly off. "So you just want me to make you a sandwich."

"Exactly." Scratch plucks the mustard from the fridge, and returns to the table. "Only I thought it would be interesting to mix it up with the ingredients a bit."

"In what way?" I wonder how long it will take the officers to climb all the stairs. They have to have someone buzz them in first. That should give me a couple more minutes.

He dips the carving knife into the mustard, spreads some on the pale, white bread. "I was just thinking . . . we have everything we need right here. Wouldn't it be fun to make our own foie gras?"

I don't know what he means at first—my mind trips to ducks and geese . . . the lake nearby?

He picks up the sandwich, and I watch as the point where it meets his face blurs slightly. The pork I ate is turning mutinous. I can feel a small rise of vomit at the back of my throat.

"Only question is: what could we use as a gavage? We'd have to measure their throats to get the right diameter. Maybe take a trip to Home Depot. Although it's hard getting me out of Home Depot, so many sharp things there."

Another muffled yell from the bedroom, louder this time.

"And look what they tried to do to you. Really, what do you owe them except contempt?"

Oh dear God. Oh Jesus fucking Christ.

Scratch picks up a napkin, dabs at where I'm estimating his mouth would be. "Just think, we'd be starting a whole new food trend. One even PETA wouldn't question."

I laugh—God help me it's funny and I laugh. I laugh so hard tears stream down my cheeks, I laugh until my ribs and stomach ache, I laugh until I'm at the edge of hysteria, and then I'm past the edge into some new territory that is simply beyond—beyond hope, or love, beyond fear, or anger. An empty void where my heart used to be.

CHAPTER TWENTY-SIX

IN THE END, it is Alejandro who guided me. Saul too, in his strange, mad way. And although the weeks that followed were torturous, soul numbing, and bitter, I hang on tight to whatever small glimmer of humanity I have left.

There is only one way to win when you deal with the devil, which is to never deal with him at all. Every word, thought, action, only leads to a series of interdependent and unknowable consequences, until you don't even know who you are anymore, until you're lost in the gray ambiguities. The middle of a blizzard at night. The gray hinterlands.

So I turn down the offer to be his right-hand woman, even though it would have spared me this favor, my personal immolation. And I do it with no illusions. I'm sure Scratch will easily be able to find a replacement for me—a dead soul willing to sell out millions to save themselves, in which case those millions are doomed anyway. I'm not saving anyone from anything. I know the world I'm in.

But I also know that here is where I stopped running, where I took some responsibility for my own actions. I had choices in the past; I made the wrong ones. So did Justin. And

I'm not going to blow this last opportunity to make a course correction. Just because my hands are bloody doesn't mean I need to immerse myself completely.

I do have more compassion for my parents now. I understand that sometimes you only have bad options.

I get two plates from the cabinet. I set the table.

I tried to be kind, during. I sat on a chair next to the bed, reading aloud from the different mysteries they'd both enjoyed. I felt compassion for them too when I stuck the plastic oil filter into their throats, and poured a special protein shake enhanced with thick, heavy whipping cream. I cleaned their bodies carefully every day. It took two weeks. Scratch, being Scratch, healed them both from their gunshot wounds, although Opal will linger, alive and suffering for years afterward. She wasn't able to complete her favor, which was to kill me, so she still carries the burden of immortality, at least unless he decides otherwise. I picked out a nice mausoleum in the cemetery for her. I might be compassionate, but that doesn't mean I forgive her.

It did nearly drive me insane, truly, watching Justin's belly swell again. I had some hard moments.

I get a loaf of bread from the cabinet. Scratch bought it especially for this day. It's a nice, thick French loaf, with an amber crust. Slices nicely under the serrated knife.

I get the tomato from the fridge, a plump heirloom, along with a head of lettuce and specialty mustard that Scratch swears will convert me forever. Lakeshore Wholegrain Mustard with Irish Stout.

I place the mustard on the table. Go back to the counter to slice the tomato. Wonder what kind of cheese he's going to pick up. Next I pull off the first leaves of lettuce and throw them away—I always think the outside ones have the most pesticide. Wash the next four off and pat them dry.

The police are onto me—they questioned me intensely this morning but had to let me go because their evidence so far is circumstantial, digital. I'm expecting a search warrant, but I might have about a week more of freedom.

I wish though that I'd taken the apartment across the hall a couple of years back when it opened up. Two hundred more in rent, but it had a nice view of the lake. I've come to appreciate nature more now that I know I'm going to permanently be separated from it. A hummingbird flew to the windowsill the other day, peeked at me, hovering, and it was so beautiful, wondrous, I was briefly overcome with pure joy. Small things like this mean more these days.

I place the tomatoes on a white plate. It's smooth, and white, and modern. Another one of Justin's QVC purchases. I place the washed lettuce leaves next to the tomato slices, making a fan.

Then I reach into the fridge for our homemade foie gras. It helps, somewhat, that there's a French word for it. And I hope Justin is finally at peace.

I place the two livers on another, longer plate, with the carving knife next to it. I remember something Scratch had said that rainy night in Make Westing, an eternity ago. *It's the suffering that gives it flavor.* In which case this should be the most delicious meal ever. Still, it's hard to ignore the rotting smell from the bedroom. We'll have to get them both out soon, or the neighbors will get suspicious.

Occasionally, despite my best intentions, my tenacious will to survive and that fiendish thing called hope, pull at me. *It's not too late, you could still take Scratch's offer. You could be rich, you could make anyone love you—why not sell the world when no one in it gives a shit about you?* I try to push these thoughts away. But I worry how well I'll hold up in the end. How much I can really stand.

You can escape everything but yourself.

There's a click in the lock, and I pause, holding the plate in both hands, the good hausfrau. I'm even wearing an apron.

The door opens, and my guest arrives. Time to see this farce to the end.

I put a smile on my face. Press it there. "Bon appétit."

It is monstrous, what I'm about to do; yet it's also strangely my finest, most selfless moment. *Sublime,* as Alejandro would say.

ACKNOWLEDGMENTS

BEFORE YOU PUBLISH your first book you have this concept of the writer alone, churning out magical pages that magically land in a bookstore, but the reality is that a book requires the hard work, input, and support of many.

Thanks to my family I was fed and given the inordinate time needed to write. My husband was my rock during the rough patches, and my son a daily inspiration to keep going no matter how many wolves howled at the door.

My champion of an agent, Jill Marr, saw the potential of fifteen pages I'd sent her, which evolved into a book proposal and then this book. I'm thrilled it landed in the Gallery Books family, and working with the insightful Ed Schlesinger has been a true pleasure.

Finally I'd like to thank my readers, because without you this would just be an object sitting on a shelf in a room. Your imagination brings it to life and inspires me to continue.